P9-DFP-812

1.25 Cone grunlit
on dallor

BERLITZ

WORLD-WIDE PHRASE BOOK

BERLITZ
WORLD-WIDE
PHRASE BOOK

BY THE EDITORIAL STAFF OF
BERLITZ PUBLICATIONS, INC.

GROSSET & DUNLAP • *Publishers* • NEW YORK

COPYRIGHT © 1962

by

BERLITZ PUBLICATIONS, INC.

ISBN: 0-448-01418-1

1972 PRINTING

CONTENTS

The arrangement of the language sections follows in general geographical language grouping and the most probable routes for American travelers. Therefore, more than one of these languages may be of use to you in many places you may visit in your travels.

How to Use This Phrase Book

This book will enable you to make yourself understood anywhere in the world. You will be able, without study, to speak to people in their own language on any continent and in any country. For, although the world languages are many (more than 2,000), over 90 per cent of the people on this planet speak one of the 16 languages included in this truly world-wide phrase book.

It is easy to use. Simply look up the appropriate English expression in any one of the 16 language sections and pronounce it as it is written in italics and capital letters, giving special emphasis to the capitalized syllables.

Here is an example in Spanish:

> **Where is a good hotel?**
> ¿Dónde hay un buen hotel?
> DOHN-*deh eye oon bwehn oh-*TEHL?

The Spanish is written correctly on the second line; the third line shows you how to pronounce it.

The phrases offered represent the essential choice of expressions, tested by many years of Berlitz research, that people need for immediate communication. The choice varies somewhat from language to language. For example, "bull" would have a high frequency in Spanish; "lion" in Swahili; and while "wine" would have a high frequency in French, it would have a low one in Arabic where its use is counter to Islamic custom.

The vocabulary is organized for you in short sentences, easy to repeat and remember. There are no grammatical explanations to worry about, since each phrase stands by itself and will be readily understood by the people with whom you speak. Furthermore, the phrases are of such importance in everyday life that they will be used constantly by the people speaking to *you*. Thus, if you learn them, you will understand what is said to you as well as be understood by others.

As increasing numbers of Americans travel and live in foreign lands on business, government service, or just for the pure joy of traveling, they realize the importance and pleasure of being able to speak to people of other countries, not only abroad but *right here* in the multilingual United States.

Even a slight effort to speak a foreign language is a compliment to one's foreign friends. It will not only facilitate your travels and help you in emergencies, but make your everyday contacts a thousand times more pleasant. It will make you friends, save you money, and make your trip a fascinating adventure. Who knows, it may even keep you out of jail! What is more, the use of this simple book will set you off to a flying start in all the principal languages of the world. The confidence and enjoyment you will derive from actually using them in your travels will be a source of interest and inspiration to you long after your return.

FRENCH

Facts About French

French is spoken as a native language by over 70 million people and as a second language by a vastly greater number. Besides being spoken in France, Belgium, Switzerland, and Luxembourg, it is spoken throughout North Africa and has remained the official language of many new central and western African states including the Congo. In addition, French is a second language throughout the Middle East and is still widely used in Viet-Nam, Laos, and Cambodia. In the Western Hemisphere, French is (along with English) the official language of Canada and is the language of Haiti and the French islands of the Caribbean.

French is a Romance language descended from Latin, and for hundreds of years it was the international language of diplomacy and culture. Today it is one of the five official languages of the United Nations.

Advice on Accent

j is soft, pronounced like the **s** in *pleasure*. We have expressed this as **zh**.

u (written in the phonetics as **ew**) should be said as an **ee** with lips pursed as if for whistling, and holding your nose at the same time.

French nasal sounds can be recognized in the phonetics by the ending **ng**. Practice pronouncing them by holding your nose.

You Already Know Some French

Forty per cent of English words are of French origin, dating from the time that the Normans conquered England. For this reason you will discover countless words you already know. But watch out! They sound quite different when the French say them.

English words that end in -*ent* are the same in French: president, resident, patient, accident.

Almost all English words ending in -*tion* are also the same in French: revolution, constitution, institution, nation, etc.

Most adverbs ending in -*ly* in English end in -*ment* in French: generally *généralement*, rapidly *rapidement*, truly *vraiment*, etc.

English words ending in -*ble* are often the same in French: possible *possible*, honorable *honorable*, capable *capable*, etc.

Many English nouns ending in -*ty* end in -*té* in French: facility *facilité*, quality *qualité*, eternity *éternité*, etc.

French is so widely used on menus that many French words for food are also familiar to us. In addition, we use many French words that are unchanged in English. For example: *rendez-vous* (go there), *c'est la vie* (that is life), *encore* (again), *r.s.v.p.—réponse s'il vous plaît* (an answer, please), *bon voyage* (good trip).

1. FIRST CONTACT

Yes.
Oui.
Wee.

No.
Non.
Nohng.

Good.
Bien.
B'yehng.

Thank you.
Merci.
Mehr-see.

You are welcome.
De rien.
Duh r'yehng.

Excuse me.
Pardon.
Pahr-dohng.

It's all right.
Ce n'est rien.
Suh neh r'yehng.

Please.
S'il vous plaît.
Seel voo pleh.

I would like ...
Je voudrais ...
Zhuh voo-dreh ...

What?
Quoi?
Kwah?

This.
Ça.
Sah.

Where?
Où?
Oo?

Here.
Ici.
Ee-see.

When?
Quand?
Kawng?

Now.
Maintenant.
Mehnt-nawng.

Later.
Plus tard.
Plew tahr.

Who?
Qui?
Kee?

I
Je
zhuh

you
vous
voo

he
il
eel

she
elle
ehl

Your name?
Votre nom?
Voh-truh nohng?

Good morning.
Bonjour.
Bohn-zhoor.

Good evening.
Bonsoir.
Bohn-swahr.

Good night.
Bonne nuit.
Bonn nwee.

Good-by.
Au revoir.
Ohr vwahr.

How are you?
　　Comment allez-vous?
　　Koh-mawng tah-leh-voo?

Very well, thank you, and you?
　　Très bien, merci, et vous?
　　Treh b'yehng, mehr-see, eh voo?

How much?
　　Combien?
　　Kohm-b'yehng?

I do not understand, please repeat.
　　Je ne comprends pas, répétez s'il vous plaît.
　　Zhuhn kohm-prawng pah, reh-peh-teh seel voo pleh.

one	two	three	four	five	six
un	deux	trois	quatre	cinq	six
uhng	*duh*	*trwah*	*kahtr*	*sank*	*sees*

seven	eight	nine	ten	eleven	twelve
sept	huit	neuf	dix	onze	douze
set	*weet*	*nuhf*	*dees*	*ohnz*	*dooz*

2. ACCOMMODATIONS

Where is a good hotel?
　　Où y a-t-il un bon hôtel?
　　Oo yah-teel uhng bonn oh-tell?

I want a room . . .
　　Je voudrais une chambre . . .
　　Zhuh voo-dreh zewn shahmbr . . .

for one person	for two persons
pour une personne	pour deux personnes
poor ewn pehr-sonn	*poor duh pehr-sonn*

with bath
　　avec bain
　　ah-vehk behng

for two days
  pour deux jours
  poor duh zhoor

for a week
  pour une semaine
  poor ewn suh-menn

till Monday
  jusqu'à lundi
  zhews-kah luhn-dee

Tuesday
  mardi
  mahr-dee

Wednesday
  mercredi
  mehr-kruh-dee

Thursday
  jeudi
  zhuh-dee

Friday
  vendredi
  vawn-druh-dee

Saturday
  samedi
  sam-dee

Sunday
  dimanche
  dee-mawnsh

How much is it?
  Combien est-ce?
  Kohm-b'yehn nehs?

Here is my passport.
  Voici mon passeport.
  Vwah-see mohng pass-pohr.

Here are my bags.
  Voici mes valises.
  Vwah-see meh vah-leez.

I like it.
  Cela me convient.
  Suh-lah muh kohn-v'yehng.

I don't like it.
  Cela ne me convient pas.
  Suh-lah nuh muh kohn-v'yehng pah.

Show me another room.
  Montrez-moi une autre chambre.
  Mohn-treh-mwah ewn ohtr shawmbr.

Where is the toilet?
  Où sont les lavabos?
  Oo sohng leh lah-vah-boh?

Where is the men's room?
  Où sont les lavabos pour hommes?
  Oo sohng leh lah-vah-boh poor homm?

Where is the ladies' room?
  Où sont les lavabos pour dames?
  Oo sohng leh lah-vah-boh poor damm?

Hot water	**a towel**	**soap**
de l'eau chaude	une serviette	du savon
duh loh shohd	*ewn sehr-v'yett*	*dew sah-vohng*

Come in!	**Please have this washed.**
Entrez!	Veuillez faire laver.
Awn-treh!	*Vuh-yeh fehr lah-veh.*

pressed.	**cleaned.**
repasser.	nettoyer cela.
ruh-pah-seh.	*neh-twah-yeh suh-lah.*

When will it be ready?
  Quand est-ce que ça sera prêt?
  Kawn tess kuh sah srah preh?

I need it for tonight.
  J'en ai besoin pour ce soir.
  Zhawn neh buh-zwehng poor suh swahr.

for tomorrow.	**Put it there.**
pour demain.	Mettez-le là.
poor duh-mehng.	*Meh-teh-luh lah.*

My key, please.
  Ma clé, s'il vous plaît.
  Mah kleh, seel voo pleh.

Any mail for me?
  Y a-t-il du courrier pour moi?
  Yah-teel dew koo-r'yeh poor mwah?

Any package?
  Un paquet?
  Uhng pah-keh?

I want five airmail stamps for the United States.

Je voudrais cinq timbres avion pour les États-Unis.

Zhuh voo-dreh sank tehmbr ah-v'yohng poor leh zeh tah-zew-nee.

I want to send a telegram.

Je voudrais envoyer un télégramme.

Zhuh voo-dreh zawn-vwah-yeh uhng teh-leh-gramm.

some postcards.

des cartes postales.

deh kahrt pohs-tahl.

Call me at seven in the morning.

Appelez-moi à sept heures du matin.

Ah-pleh-mwah ah seh tuhr dew mah-tehng.

Where is the telephone?   **Hello!**

Où est le téléphone?   Allô!

Oo eh luh teh-leh-fonn?   *Ah-loh!*

Send breakfast to room 702, please.

Faites monter le petit déjeuner à la chambre sept cent deux, s'il vous plaît.

Fett mohn-teh luhp-tee deh-zhuh-neh ah lah shawmbr sett sawng duh, seel voo pleh.

orange juice   **ham and eggs**

jus d'orange   oeufs au jambon

zhew doh-rawnzh   *uh zoh zhawm-bohng*

rolls and coffee

petits pains et café

puh-tee pehng eh kah-feh

I am expecting someone.

J'attends quelqu'un.

Zhah-tawn kell-kuhng.

Tell him (her) to wait for me.

Dites-lui de m'attendre.

Deet-lweed mah-tawndr.

If anyone calls me I'll be back at six.
> Si quelqu'un me demande je serai de retour à six heures.
> *See kell-kuhng muhd-mawnd zhuh sreh duhr toor ah see zuhr.*

Tell me, please, where there is a drug store.
> Dites-moi, s'il vous plaît, où il ya une pharmacie.
> *Deet-mwah, seel voo pleh, oo eel yah ewn fahrmah-see.*

a barber shop	**a beauty parlor**
un coiffeur	un salon de coiffure
uhng kwah-fuhr	*unh sah-lohnd kwah-fewr*

What is the telephone number?
> Quel est le numéro de téléphone?
> *Kell ehl new-meh-rohd teh-leh-fonn?*

What is the address?
> Quelle est l'adresse?
> *Kell eh lah-dress?*

I want to change some money.
> Je voudrais changer de l'argent.
> *Zhuh voo-dreh shawn-zheh duh lahr-zhawng.*

What is the rate to the dollar?
> Quel est le taux pour un dollar?
> *Keh-lehl toh poor uhng doh-lahr?*

ten	**eleven**	**twelve**	**thirteen**
dix	onze	douze	treize
dees	*ohnz*	*dooz*	*trehz*

fourteen	**fifteen**	**sixteen**	**seventeen**
quatorze	quinze	seize	dix-sept
kah-tohrz	*kehnz*	*sehz*	*dees-sett*

eighteen	**nineteen**	**twenty**	**twenty-one**
dix-huit	dix-neuf	vingt	vingt-et-un
deez-weet	*deez-nuhf*	*vehng*	*vehn-teh-uhng*

twenty-two	**twenty-three**	**thirty**
vingt-deux	vingt-trois	trente
vehnt-duh	*vehnt-trwah*	*trawnt*

forty	**fifty**	**sixty**
quarante	cinquante	soixante
kah-rawnt	*sehn-kawnt*	*swah-sawnt*

seventy	**eighty**
soixante-dix	quatre-vingt
swah-sawnt-dees	*kah-truh-vehng*

ninety	**hundred**	**two hundred**
quatre-vingt-dix	cent	deux cents
kah-truh-vehn-dees	*sawng*	*duh sawng*

three hundred	**four hundred**	**five hundred**
trois cents	quatre cents	cinq cents
trwah sawng	*kahtr' sawng*	*sehn sawng*

six hundred	**thousand**	**ten thousand**
six cents	mille	dix mille
see sawng	*meel*	*dee meel*

hundred thousand	**one million**
cent mille	un million
sawn meel	*uhn mee-l'yohng*

My bill, please.
Ma note, s'il vous plaît.
Mah noht, seel voo pleh.

3. EATING

Where is a good restaurant?
Où y a-t-il un bon restaurant?
Oo yah-teel uhn bohng rehs-toh-rawng?

A table for two, please.
Une table pour deux, s'il vous plaît.
Ewn tahbl poor duh, seel voo pleh.

Waiter!
  Garçon!
  Gahr-sohng!

Waitress!
  Mademoiselle!
  Mahd-mwah-zehl!

The menu, please.
  Le menu, s'il vous plaît.
  Luh muh-new, seel voo pleh.

What is good today?
  Qu'est-ce que vous avez de bon aujourd'hui?
  Kehs-kuh voo zah-vehd bohng, oh-zhoor-dwee?

Is it ready?
  Est-ce que c'est prêt?
  Ehs-kuh seh preh?

How long will it take?
  Combien de temps est-ce que ça va prendre?
  Kohm-b'yehn duh tawng ehs-kuh sa vah prawndr?

This, please ...
  Ça, s'il vous plaît ...
  Sah, seel voo pleh ...

and this.
  et ça.
  eh sah.

Bring me some water.
  Donnez-moi de l'eau.
  Doh-neh-mwahd loh.

a glass of beer
  un verre de bière
  uhn vehr duh b'yehr

milk
  du lait
  dew leh

white wine
  du vin blanc
  dew vehng blawng

red wine
  du vin rouge
  dew vehng roozh

a cocktail
  un cocktail
  uhng cocktail

a whisky soda
  un whisky soda
  uhng whisky soda

soup
  de la soupe
  duh lah soop

fish
  du poisson
  dew pwah-sohng

meat
  de la viande
  duh lah v'yawnd

bread and butter
du pain et du beurre
dew pehng eh dew buhr

a sandwich
un sandwich
uhng sawn-dweesh

roasted chicken
du poulet rôti
dew poo-leh roh-tee

veal cutlets
des escalopes de veau
deh zehs-kah-lohp duh voh

pork chops
des côtelettes de porc
deh koht-lett duh pohr

leg of lamb
du gigot d'agneau
dew zhee-goh dah-n'yoh

beef stew
du ragoût de boeuf
dew rah-good buhf

salt and pepper
du sel et du poivre
dew sell eh dew pwahvr

a steak ...
un bifteck ...
uhn beef-teck ...

rare
saignant
seh-n'yawng

medium
à point
ah pwehng

well done
bien cuit
b'yehn kwee

frog legs sautéed
des cuisses de grenouilles sautées
deh kwees duh gruh-nooy soh-teh

a dozen snails
une douzaine d'escargots
ewn doo-zenn dehs-kahr-goh

I don't want any sauce.
Je ne veux pas de sauce.
Zhuhn vuh pahd sohs.

with potatoes ...
avec des pommes de terre ...
ah-vahk deh pohm duh tehr ...

fried
frites
freet

rice
du riz
dew ree

an omelet
une omelette
ewn ohm-lett

And what vegetables?
Et comme légumes?
Eh kohm leh-gewm?

peas
des petits pois
deh ptee pwah

carrots
des carottes
deh kah-roht

beans
des haricots
deh ah-ree-koh

string beans
des haricots verts
deh ah-ree-koh vehr

onions
des oignons
deh zoh-n'yohng

cauliflower
du chou-fleur
dew shoo-fluhr

salads
salades
sah-lahd

lettuce
laitue
leh-tew

tomato
tomate
toh-maht

cucumber
concombre
kohn-kohmbr

Please bring me another fork.
Veuillez me donner une autre fourchette.
Vuh-yeh muh doh-neh ewn oh-truh foor-shett.

knife
couteau
koo-toh

spoon
cuiller
kwee-yehr

a glass
un verre
uhng vehr

a plate
une assiette
ewn ah-s'yeht

What is there for dessert?
Qu'est-ce qu'il y a comme dessert?
Kehs-keel-yah kohm deh-sehr?

caramel custard
crème au caramel
krehm oh kah-rah-mehl

fruit
fruits
frwee

pastry
patisseries
pah-tees-ree

strawberry tart
tartelette aux fraises
tahr-tuh-lett oh frehz

ice cream
glaces
glahs

cheese
fromages
froh-mahzh

Camembert
Camembert
Kah-mawn-behr

Roquefort
Roquefort
Rock-fohr

Swiss cheese
Gruyère
Grew-yehr

Black coffee, please.
Du café noir, s'il vous plaît.
Dew kah-feh nwahr, seel voo pleh.

With or without sugar?
Avec ou sans sucre?
ah-vehk oo sawng sewkr?

a coffee with cream
un café crème
uhng kah-feh krehm

tea with lemon
du thé au citron
dew teh oh see-trohng

mineral water
de l'eau minérale
duh loh mee-neh-rahl

A little more, please.
Un peu plus, s'il vous plaît.
Uhn puh plew, seel voo pleh.

That's enough.
C'est assez.
Seh tah-seh.

The check, please.
L'addition, s'il vous plaît.
Lah-dee-s'yohng, seel voo pleh.

Is the tip included?
Est-ce que le service est compris?
Ehs-kuh luh sehr-vees eh kohm-pree?

It was very good.
C'était très bon.
Seh-teh treh bohng.

4. SHOPPING

I would like to buy this...   **and that.**
   Je voudrais acheter ceci...   et cela.
   Zhuh voo-dreh zahsh-teh suh-see...   *eh suh-lah.*

I am just looking around.
   Je regarde seulement.
   Zhuh ruh-gahrd suhl-mawng.

Where is the department for...
   Où est le rayon des...
   Oo eh luh reh-yohng deh...

    raincoats?
     imperméables?
     ehm-pehr-meh-ahbl?

    men's clothing
     vêtements pour hommes
     veht-mawng poor ohm

    women's clothing   **hats**
     vêtements pour dames   chapeaux
     veht-mawng poor damm   *shah-poh*

    underwear   **shoes**   **gloves**
     sous-vêtements   chaussures   gants
     soo-veht-mawng   *shoh-sewr*   *gawng*

    stockings   **socks**   **shirts**
     bas   chaussettes   chemises
     bah   *shoh-set*   *shuh-meez*

In America my size is...
   En Amérique ma pointure est...
   Awn nah-meh-reek mah pwehn-tewr eh...

    toys   **perfumes**   **watches**
     jouets   parfums   montres
     zhweh   *pahr-fehmg*   *mohntr*

costume jewelry
bijouterie fantaisie
bee-zhoo-tree fawn-teh-zee

toilet articles
articles de toilette
ahr-teekl duh twah-lett

sport articles
articles de sport
ahr-teekl duh spohr

Show me ...
Montrez-moi ...
Mohn-treh-mwah ...

something less expensive
quelque chose de meilleur marché
kehlk shohz duh meh-yuhr mahr-sheh

another one
quelque chose d'autre
kehk shohz dohtr

a better quality
une meilleure qualité
ewn meh-yuhr kah-lee-teh

bigger
plus grand
plew grawng

smaller
plus petit
plewp tee

I don't like the color.
Je n'aime pas la couleur.
Zhuh nehm pah lah koo-luhr.

I want that ...
Je voudrais cela ...
Zhuh voo-dreh suh-lah ...

in green
en vert
awng vehr

in yellow
en jaune
awng zhonn

in blue
en bleu
awng bluh

in red
en rouge
awng roozh

black
noir
nwahr

white
blanc
blawng

gray	brown	pink
gris	marron	rose
gree	*mah-rohng*	*rohz*

lighter	darker
plus clair	plus foncé
plew klehr	*plew fohn-seh*

I'll take it with me.
Je l'emporte.
Zhuh lawm-pohrt.

Please have it delivered.
Veuillez le faire livrer.
Vuh-yay luh fehr lee-vreh.

A receipt, please.
Un reçu, s'il vous plaît.
Uhng ruh-sew, seel voo pleh.

Where is there a book store?   a flower shop?
Où y a-t-il   une librairie?   un fleuriste?
Oo yah-teel   ewn lee-breh-ree?   uhng fluh-rist?

a food store?
un magasin d'alimentation?
*uhng mah-gah-zehng dah-lee-mawn-tah-
    s'yohng?*

Where can I buy . . .
Où est-ce que je peux acheter . . .
Oo ehs kuhzh puh zash-teh . . .

stamps	toothpaste
des timbres	du dentifrice
deh-tehmbr	*dew dawn-tee-frees*

5. TRANSPORTATION

Taxi!
Taxi!
Tack-see!

Take me to the airport.
Conduisez-moi à l'aéroport.
Kohn-dwee-seh-mwah ah lah-eh-roh-pohr.

Turn right ... left.
   Tournez à droite ... à gauche.
   Toor-neh zah-drwaht ... *ah gohsh.*

Straight ahead.
   Tout droit.
   Too drwah.

Not so fast! **Hurry up!**
   Pas si vite! Dépêchez-vous!
   Pah see veet! *Deh-peh-sheh-voo!*

Stop here! **Wait for me.**
   Arrêtez-vous là! Attendez-moi.
   Ah-reh-teh-voo lah! *Ah-tawn-deh-mwah.*

How much is it to ... ? **and back?**
   Combien est-ce pour ... ? et retour?
   Kohm-b'yehn nehs poor ...? *eh ruh-toor?*

How much by the hour? **by the day?**
   Combien à l'heure? à la journée?
   Kohm-b'yehn nah luhr? *ah lah zhoor-neh?*

Show me the sights.
   Montrez-moi ce qu'il y a à voir.
   Mohn-treh-mwah suh keel yah ah vwahr.

What is that building?
   Quel est cet édifice?
   Kehl eh seht eh-dee-fees?

Can it be visited?
   Peut-on le visiter?
   Puh-tohng luh vee-zee-teh?

I want to see the Eiffel Tower.
   Je voudrais voir la Tour Eiffel.
   Zhuh voo-dreh vwahr lah toor eh-fehl.

To the railroad station.
   À la gare.
   Ah lah gahr.

Porter!
Porteur!
Pohr-tuhr!

I have two bags.
J'ai deux valises.
Zheh duh vah-leez.

A ticket to ...
Un billet pour ...
Uhng bee-yeh poor ...

one way
aller simple
ah-leh sehmpl

round trip
aller retour
ah-leh ruh-toor

first class
première classe
pruh-m'yehr class

second class
deuxième classe
duh-z'yehm class

Where is the train to Bordeaux?
Où est le train pour Bordeaux?
Oo eh luh trehng poor Bohr-doh?

When does it leave?
Quand part-il?
Kawng pahr-teel?

Is this the train for Strasbourg?
Est-ce bien le train pour Strasbourg?
Ehs b'yehng luh trehng poor Strahs-boor?

When do we get to Rennes?
Quand arrivons-nous à Rennes?
Kwang tah-ree-vohn-noo zah Renn?

Where is the dining-car?
Où est le wagon-restaurant?
Oo eh luh vah-gohn-rehs-toh-rahng?

Open the window.
Ouvrez la fenêtre.
Oo-vreh lah fuh-nehtr.

Close the window.
Fermez la fenêtre.
Fehr-meh lah fuh-nehtr.

Where is the bus to Versailles?
Où est l'autobus pour Versailles?
Oo eh loh-toh-bews poor Vehr-sigh?

I want to go to Fontainebleau.
Je voudrais aller à Fontainebleau.
Zhuh voo-dreh zah-leh ah Fohn-tehn-bloh.

Please tell me where to get off.
Veuillez me dire où je dois descendre.
Vuh-yeh muh deer oozh dwah deh-sawndr.

Where is a gas station?
Où y a-t-il un poste d'essence?
Oo·yah-teel uhng pohst deh-sawns?

Fill it up.
Faites le plein.
Feht luh plehng.

Check the oil . . .	**water**	**tires**
Vérifiez l'huile . . .	l'eau	les pneus
Veh-ree-f'yeh lweel . . .	*loh*	*leh pnuh*

Something is wrong with the car.
Cette auto ne marche pas bien.
Seht oh-toh nuh marsh pah b'yehng.

Can you fix it?
Pouvez-vous l'arranger?
Poo-veh-voo lah-rawn-zheh?

How long will it take?
Combien de temps faudra-t-il?
Kohm-b'yehng duh tawng foh-drah-teel?

Is this the road to Lascaux?
Est-ce bien la route de Lascaux?
Ehs b'yehng lah root duh Lahs-koh?

Have you a map?
Avez-vous une carte?
Ah-veh-voo zewn kahrt?

Where is the boat to . . . ?
Où est le bateau pour . . . ?
Oo eh luh bah-toh poor . . . ?

When does it leave?
Quand part-il?
Kawn pahr-teel?

6. MAKING FRIENDS

Good day.
  Bonjour.
  Bohn-zhoor.

My name is ...
  Je m'appelle ...
  Zhuh mah-pehl ...

What is your name, Sir?
  Comment vous appelez-vous, Monsieur?
  Koh-mawng voo zahp-leh-voo, muh-s'yuh?

Madam?
  Madame?
  Mah-dahm?

Miss?
  Mademoiselle?
  Mahd-mwah-zehl?

I am delighted to meet you.
  Enchanté de faire votre connaissance.
  Awn-shawn-teh duh fehr votr koh-neh-sawns.

It was a pleasure seeing you.
  J'ai été très heureux de vous voir.
  Zheh eh-teh treh zuh-ruh duh voo vwahr.

Do you speak English?
  Parlez-vous anglais?
  Pahr-leh-voo zawn-gleh?

I speak only a little French.
  Je ne parle qu'un peu français.
  Zhuhn pahrl kuhng puh frawn-seh.

A little.
  Un peu.
  Uhng puh.

Do you understand?
  Comprenez-vous?
  Kohm-pruh-neh-voo?

Please speak slowly.
  Parlez lentement s'il vous plaît.
  Pahr-leh lahnt-mawng seel voo pleh.

I am from New York.
  Je suis de New York.
  Zhuh-sweed New York.

Where are you from?
  D'où êtes-vous?
  Doo eht-voo?

I like your country very much.
J'aime beaucoup votre pays.
Zhehm boh-coo vohtr peh-ee.

your city	**your house**
votre ville	votre maison
vohtr veel	*vohtr meh-zohng*

Have you been in America?
Connaissez-vous l'Amérique?
Koh-neh-seh-voo lah-meh-reek?

This is my first visit here.
C'est la première fois que j'y viens.
Seh lah pruh-m'yehr fwah kuh zhee v'yehng.

May I sit here?
Est-ce que je peux m'asseoir là?
Ehs kuhzh puh mah-swahr lah?

May I take your picture?
Puis-je vous prendre en photo?
Pweezh voo prawndr awng foh-toh?

Come here.
Venez ici.
Vuh-neh zee-see.

This is a picture of my wife.
Voici une photo de ma femme.
Vwah-see ewn foh-toh duh mah fahm.

my husband		**my son**
mon mari		mon fils
mohng mah-ree		*mohng fees*

my daughter	**my mother**	**my father**
ma fille	ma mère	mon père
mah fee	*mah mehr*	*mohng pehr*

my sister	**my brother**	
ma soeur	mon frère	
mah suhr	*mohng frehr*	

Have you children?
 Avez-vous des enfants?
 Ah-veh-voo deh zawn-fawng?

How beautiful!
 Comme c'est beau!
 Kohm seh boh!

Very interesting.
 Comme c'est intéressant.
 Kohm seh tehn-teh-reh-sawng.

Would you like a cigarette?
 Voulez-vous une cigarette?
 Voo-leh-voo zewn see-gah-reht?

something to drink?	**to eat?**
quelque chose à boire?	à manger?
kehl-kuh shoz ah bwahr	*ah mawn-zheh*

Sit down, please.
 Asseyez-vous, je vous en prie.
 Ah-seh-yeh-voo, zhuh voo-zawn-pree.

Make yourself at home.
 Faites comme chez vous.
 Feht kohm sheh voo.

Good luck!	**To your health!**
Bonne chance!	À votre santé!
Bonn shawns!	*Ah vohtr sawn-teh!*

When can I see you again?
 Quand puis-je vous revoir?
 Kawng pweezh voor vwahr?

Where shall we meet?
 Où est-ce qu'on se retrouve?
 Oo ehs kohns ruh-troov?

Here is my address.
 Voici mon adresse.
 Vwah-see mohn nah-dress.

What is your address?
 Quelle est votre adresse?
 Kehl eh vohtr ah-dress?

What is your phone number?
 Quel est votre numéro de téléphone?
 Kehl eh vohtr' new-meh-roh duh teh-leh-fonn?

May I speak to ... ?
 Est-ce que je peux parler à ... ?
 Ehs kuhzh puh pahr-leh ah ...?

Would you like to have lunch?
 Voulez-vous déjeuner?
 Voo-leh-voo deh-zhuh-neh?

  to have dinner? **to have a drink?**
   dîner?   prendre un verre?
   dee-neh?   *prawn-druhn vehr?*

  to go to the movies? **the theatre?**
   aller au cinéma?   au théâtre?
   ah-leh oh see-neh-mah? *oh teh-ahtr?*

  the beach?
   sur la plage?
   sewr lah plahzh?

  to take a walk?
   faire une promenade (à pied) ?
   fehr ewn promm-nahd ah p'yeh?

With great pleasure!
 Avec grand plaisir!
 Ah-vehk grawn pleh-zeer!

I am sorry.   **I cannot.**
 Je regrette beaucoup. Je ne peux pas.
 Zhuh ruh-greht boh-koo. *Zhuhnn puh pah.*

Another time.
 Une autre fois.
 Ewn ohtr' fwah.

I must go now.
Il faut que je m'en aille tout de suite.
Eel fohk zhuh mawn na'y tood sweet.

Thank you for a wonderful time.
Merci beaucoup, c'était charmant.
Mehr-see boh-koo, seh-teh shahr-mawng.

Thank you for an excellent dinner ...
Merci beaucoup pour cet excellent diner ...
Mehr-see boh-koo poor seh tehk-seh-lawng dee-neh ...

> **lunch**
> déjeuner
> *deh-zhuh-neh*

This is for you.
Quelque chose pour vous.
Kell-kuh shohz poor voo.

A little souvenir.
Un petit souvenir.
Uhng p'tee soov-neer.

You are very kind.
Vous êtes bien aimable.
Voo zeht b'yehn neh-mahbl.

It's nothing really.
Ça n'est vraiment pas grand chose.
Sah neh vreh-mawng pah grawn-shohz.

With best regards.
Avec nos sincères salutations.
Ah-vehk noh sehn-sehr sah-lew-tah-s'yohng.

Congratulations!
Félicitations!
Feh-lee-see-tah-s'yohng!

7. EMERGENCIES

Help!
Au secours!
Ohs-coor!

Police!
Police!
Poh-lees!

Fire!
Au feu!
Oh-fuh!

Stop that man!
Arrêtez-le!
Ah-reh-teh-luh!

Stop that woman!
Arrêtez-la!
Ah-reh-teh-lah!

I have been robbed!
On m'a volé!
Ohng mah voh-leh!

Look out!
Attention!
Ah-tawn-s'yohng!

Wait a minute!
Attendez!
Ah-tawn-deh!

Stop!
Arrêtez!
Ah-reh-teh!

Get out!
Sortez!
Sohr-teh!

Hurry up!
Dépêchez-vous!
Deh-peh-sheh-voo!

Don't bother me!
Laissez-moi tranquille!
Leh-seh mwah trawn-keel!

What is going on?
Qu'est-ce qui se passe?
Kehs keess pass?

Entrance
Entrée
Awn-treh

Exit
Sortie
Sohr-tee

Ladies
Dames
Damm

Gentlemen
Messieurs
Meh-s'yuh

Danger!
Danger!
Dawn-zheh!

Keep out!
Défense d'entrer!
Deh-fawns dawn-treh!

No smoking
Défense de fumer
Deh-fawns duh few-meh

No parking
Défense de stationner
Deh-fawns duh stah-s'yoh-neh

Dead end
Sans issue
Sawng zee-sew

One way
Sens unique
Sawng sew-neek

I am ill.
 Je suis souffrant.
 Zhuh swee soo-frawng.

It hurts here.
 J'ai mal là.
 Zheh mahl lah.

Please, call a doctor.
 S'il vous plaît, faites venir un médecin.
 Seel voo pleh, feht vuh-neer uhng mehd-sehng.

Take me to the hospital.
 Transportez-moi à l'hôpital.
 Trawns-pohr-teh-mwah ah loh-pee-tahl.

Where is a drugstore?
 Où y a-t-il une pharmacie?
 Oo-yah-teel ewn fahr-mah-see?

Where is a dentist?
 Où y a-t-il un dentiste?
 Oo-yah-teel uhng dawn-teest?

I have lost my bag.
 J'ai perdu mon sac.
 Zheh pehr-dew mohng sack.

 my wallet
  mon portefeuille
  mohng pohr-tuh-fuh'y

 my passport
  mon passeport
  mohng pahs-pohr

 my camera
  mon appareil photographique
  mohn nah-pah-reh'y foh-toh-grah-feek

I am an American.
 Je suis américain.
 Zhuh swee zah-meh-ree-kehng.

Where is the American Consulate?
 Où est le Consulat des Etats-Unis?
 Oo eh luh kohn-sew-lah deh zeh-tah-zew-nee?

Don't get excited!
 Calmez-vous!
 Kahl-meh-voo!

Everything is all right.
 Tout va bien.
 Too vah b'yehng.

SPANISH

Facts About Spanish

Spanish is spoken by more than 150 million people in Spain, in the Spanish Mediterranean islands, in all the countries of Central and South America (with the exception of Brazil and the Guianas) and in the Caribbean islands of Cuba, Puerto Rico, and the Dominican Republic. In addition, it is spoken in the Philippine Islands and the western part of North Africa. In the United States it is still widely used in the southwestern states as well as in the Spanish communities of New York and other eastern cities.

Because of its great international importance, Spanish has been adopted as one of the five official languages of the United Nations.

Spanish is a Romance language, derived from Latin. As it is spoken in so many countries, there are regional differences in pronunciation. However, the Spanish used here will be understood throughout the Spanish-speaking world.

A popular misconception is that Castilian Spanish is different from Latin American Spanish. Actually, there is less difference than there is between American and British English.

Advice on Accent

The Spanish lisp sound, more accentuated in
Spain than in Latin America, has been rendered in our phonetics by **th**. This sound is
given to **z** and **c** (before *e* or *i*) to differentiate
them from the letter *s*.

h in Spanish is always silent.
j is pronounced like the English **h.**
ñ is pronounced as **ny** in *canyon*.
ll is pronounced as **lli** in *million*.
r is trilled, and **rr** is strongly trilled.

You Already Know Some Spanish

Many Spanish and English words share a
common descent from Latin, although the pronunciation is often strange to the English ear:

Almost all English words ending in *-tion* end
in Spanish in *-ción:* revolution *revolución,* constitution *constitución,* institution *institución.*

Most adverbs ending in *-ly* in English end in
-mente in Spanish: naturally *naturalmente,* generally *generalmente,* rapidly *rápidamente.*

English words ending in *-ble* end in *-ble* in
Spanish: possible *posible,* honorable *honorable.*

Many English nouns ending in *-ty* exist in
Spanish but end in *-ad:* facility *facilidad,* quality
cualidad.

Many Spanish words have entered English
from western folklore. Most Americans will have
no difficulty in recognizing the following: *loco*
(crazy), *hombre* (man), *caballero* (gentleman),
rancher (from *ranchero*), lasso (from *lazo*—knot),
and vamoose (from *vamos*—let's go).

1. FIRST CONTACT

Yes.
Sí.
See.

No.
No.
Noh.

Good.
Bueno.
BWEH-*noh.*

Thank you.
Gracias.
GRAH-*th'yahs.*

You are welcome.
De nada.
Deh NAH-*dah.*

Excuse me.
Dispénseme.
*Dees-*PEHN-*seh-meh.*

It's all right.
Está bien.
*Ehs-*TAH *b'yehn.*

Please.
Por favor.
*Pohr fah-*VOHR.

I would like ...
Me gustaría ...
*Meh goos-tah-*REE-*yah ...*

What?
¿Qué?
Keh?

This.
Esto.
EHS-*toh.*

Where?
¿Dónde?
DOHN-*deh?*

Here.
Aquí.
*Ah-*KEE.

When?
¿Cuándo?
KWAHN-*doh?*

Now.
Ahora.
*Ah-*OH-*rah.*

Later.
Luego.
L'WEH-*goh.*

Who?
¿Quien?
K'yehn?

I
yo
yoh

you
usted (Vd.)
*oos-*TEHD

he
él
ehl

she
ella
EH-*l'yah*

Your name?
¿Su nombre?
Soo NOHM-*breh?*

Good morning.
Buenos días.
BWEH-*nohs* DEE-*ahs.*

Good evening.
Buenas noches.
BWEH-*nahs* NOH-*chehs.*

Good night.
Buenas noches.
BWEH-*nahs* NOH-*chehs.*

Good-by.
Adiós.
*Ah-d'*YOHS.

How are you?
¿Cómo está usted?
KOH-*moh ehs*-TAH *oos*-TEHD?

Very well, thank you. And you?
Muy bien, gracias. ¿Y usted?
Mooy b'yehn, GRAH-*th'yahs. Ee oos*-TEHD?

How much?
¿Cuánto es?
KWAHN-*toh ehs?*

I do not understand. Please repeat.
No comprendo. Repita, por favor.
Noh kohm-PREHN-*doh. Reh*-PEE-*tah, pohr fah*-
VOHR.

one	two	three	four
uno	dos	tres	cuatro
oo-noh	*dohs*	*trehs*	KWAH-*troh*

five	six	seven	eight
cinco	seis	siete	ocho
THEEN-*koh*	SEH-*ees*	*s'YEH-teh*	OH-*choh*

nine	ten	eleven	twelve
nueve	diez	once	doce
NWEH-*veh*	*d'*YEHTH	OHN-*theh*	DOH-*theh*

2. ACCOMMODATIONS

Where is a good hotel?
¿Dónde hay un buen hotel?
DOHN-*deh eye oon bwehn oh*-TEHL?

I want a room ...
Deseo una habitación ...
Deh-SEH-*oh* OO-*nah ah-bee-tah-th'*YOHN ...

    for one person
    para una persona
    PAH-*rah* OO-*nah pehr*-SOH-*nah*

for two persons
para dos personas
PAH-rah dohs pehr-SOH-nahs

with bath
con baño
kohn BAH-n'yoh

for two days
por dos días
pohr dohs DEE-ahs

for a week
por una semana
pohr OO-nah seh-MAH-nah

till Monday
hasta lunes
AHS-tah LOO-nehs

Tuesday
martes
MAHR-tehs

Wednesday
miercoles
m'YEHR-koh-lehs

Thursday
jueves
HWEH-vehs

Friday
viernes
v'YEHR-nehs

Saturday
sábado
SAH-bah-doh

Sunday
domingo
Doh-MEEN-goh

How much is it?
¿Cuánto es?
KWAHN-toh ehs?

Here are my bags.
Aquí están mis maletas.
Ah-KEE ehs-TAHN mees mah-LEH-tahs.

Here is my passport.
Aquí está mi pasaporte.
Ah-KEE ehs-TAH mee pah-sah-POHR-teh.

I like it.
Me gusta.
Meh GOOS-tah.

I do not like it.
No me gusta.
Noh meh GOOS-tah.

Show me another.
Enséñeme otro.
Ehn-SEH-n'yeh-meh OH-troh.

Where is the toilet?
¿Dónde está el excusado?
DOHN-*deh* ehs-TAH *ehl ehs-koo*-SAH-*doh?*

Where is the men's room?
¿Dónde está el cuarto para señores?
DOHN-*deh* ehs-TAH *ehl* KWAHR-*toh* PAH-*rah seh-n'*YOH-*rehs?*

Where is the ladies' room?
¿Dónde está el cuarto para damas?
DOHN-*deh* ehs-TAH *ehl* KWAHR-*toh* PAH-*rah* DAH-*mahs?*

hot water	**a towel**
agua caliente	una toalla
AH-*gwah kah-l'*YEHN-*teh*	OO-*nah* TWAH-*l'yah*

soap
jabón
hah-BOHN

Come in!
¡Entre!
EHN-*treh!*

Please have this washed.
Por favor, esto es para lavar.
Pohr fah-VOHR, EHS-*toh es* PAH-*rah lah*-VAHR.

pressed	**cleaned**
planchar	limpiar
plahn-CHAHR	*leem-p'*YAHR

When will it be ready?
¿Cuándo estará listo?
KWAHN-*doh ehs-tah-*RAH LEES-*toh?*

I need it for tonight.
Lo necesito para esta noche.
*Loh neh-theh-*SEE-*toh* PAH-*rah* EHS-*tah* NOH-*cheh.*

for tomorrow
>   para mañana
>   PAH-*rah mah-n'*YAH-*nah*

My key, please.
>   Mi llave, por favor.
>   *Mee l'*YAH-*veh, pohr fah-*VOHR.

Any mail for me?
>   ¿Hay cartas para mí?
>   *Eye* KAHR-*tahs* PAH-*rah mee?*

>   **Any packages?**
>   >   ¿Algún paquete?
>   >   *Ahl-*GOON *pah-*KEH-*teh?*

I want five airmail stamps for the USA.
>   Deseo cinco sellos (estampillas) para los Estados
>   Unidos.
>   *Deh-*SEH-*oh* THEEN-*koh* SEH-*l'yohs (ehs-tahm-*PEE-
>   *l'yahs)* PAH-*rah lohs Ehs-*TAH-*dohs Oo-*NEE-*dohs.*

Have you postcards?
>   ¿Tiene tarjetas postales?
>   T'YEH-*neh tahr-*HEH-*tahs pohs-*TAH-*lehs?*

I want to send a telegram.
>   Quiero mandar un telegrama.
>   K'YEH-*roh mahn-*DAHR *oon teh-leh-*GRAH-*mah.*

Call me at seven in the morning.
>   Llámeme a las siete de la mañana.
>   L'YAH-*meh-meh ah lahs s'*YEH-*teh deh lah mah-
>   n'*YAH-*nah.*

Where is the telephone?
>   ¿Dónde está el teléfono?
>   DOHN-*deh ehs-*TAH *ehl teh-*LEH-*foh-noh?*

Hello!
>   ¡Hola! (or) ¡Diga!
>   OH-*lah!* (or) DEE-*gah!*

Send breakfast to room 702.
　　Mande el desayuno al cuarto setecientos dos.
　　MAHN-*deh ehl deh-sah-*YOO*-noh ahl* KWAHR*-toh
　　*seh-teh-th'*YEHN*-tohs dohs.*

orange juice
　　jugo de naranja
　　HOO*-goh deh nah-*RAHN*-hah*

ham and eggs
　　jamón y huevos
　　hah-MOHN *ee* WEH*-vohs*

rolls and coffee
　　panecillos y café
　　*pah-neh-*THEE*-l'yohs ee kah-*FEH

I am expecting a friend.
　　Estoy esperando un amigo.
　　Ehs-TOY *ehs-peh-*RAHN*-doh oon ah-*MEE*-goh.*

Tell him (her) to wait.
　　Dígale que espere.
　　DEE*-gah-leh keh ehs-*PEH*-reh.*

If anyone calls I will be back at six.
　　Si alguien llama estaré de vuelta a las seis.
　　See AHL*-g'yehn l'*YAH*-mah ehs-tah-*REH *deh* VWEHL*-
　　tah ah lahs* SEH*-ees.*

Tell me, please, where is there a restaurant.
　　Dígame, por favor, dónde hay un restaurante.
　　DEE*-gah-meh, pohr fah-*VOHR, DOHN*-deh eye oon
　　rehs-tow-*RAHN*-teh.*

　　a barber shop
　　　　una barbería
　　　　OO*-nah bahr-beh-*REE*-ah*

　　a beauty parlor
　　　　un salón de belleza
　　　　*oon sah-*LOHN *deh beh-l'*YEH *thah*

a drug store
una farmacia
oo-*nah* fahr-MAH-*th'yah*

What is the telephone number?
¿Cuál es el número de teléfono?
Kwahl ehs ehl NOO-*meh-roh deh* teh-LEH-*foh-noh?*

What is the address?
¿Cuál es la dirección?
*Kwahl ehs lah dee-rehk-th'*YOHN?

I want to change some money.
Deseo cambiar dinero.
*Deh-*SEH-*oh kahm-b'*YAHR *dee-*NEH-*roh.*

What is the rate for dollars?
¿A comó está el cambio del dólar?
Ah KOH-*moh ehs-*TAH *ehl* KAHM-*b'yoh dehl* DOH-*lahr?*

thirteen	fourteen	fifteen
trece	catorce	quince
TREH-*theh*	kah-TOHR-*theh*	KEEN-*theh*

sixteen	seventeen
diez y seis	diez y siete
d'YEHTH *ee* SEH-*ees*	d'YEHTH *ee s'*YEH-*teh*

eighteen	nineteen
diez y ocho	diez y nueve
d'YEHTH *ee* OH-*choh*	d'YEHTH *ee* NWEH-*veh*

twenty	thirty	forty
veinte	treinta	cuarenta
VAIN-*teh*	TRAIN-*tah*	kwah-REHN-*tah*

fifty	sixty
cincuenta	sesenta
theen-KWEHN-*tah*	seh-SEHN-*tah*

seventy	eighty	ninety
setenta	ochenta	noventa
seh-TEHN-*tah*	oh-CHEHN-*tah*	noh-VEHN-*tah*

hundred
  cien (ciento)
  *th'*YEHN (*th'*YEHN-*toh*)

two hundred
  doscientos
  *dohs-*TH'YEHN-*tohs*

three hundred
  trescientos
  *trehs-th'*YEHN-*tohs*

four hundred
  cuatrocientos
  KWAH-*troh-th'*YEHN-*tohs*

five hundred
  quinientos
  *keen-*YEHN-*tohs*

six hundred
  seiscientos
  *seh-ees-th'*YEHN-*tohs*

seven hundred
  setecientos
  *seh-teh-th'*YEHN-*tohs*

eight hundred
  ochocientos
  OH-*choh-th'*YEHN-*tohs*

nine hundred
  novecientos
  *noh-veh-th'*YEHN-*tohs*

thousand
  mil
  meel

ten thousand
  diez mil
  *d'*YEHTH *meel*

hundred thousand
  cien mil
  *th'*YEHN *meel*

My bill, please.
  Mi cuenta, por favor.
  Mee KWEHN-*tah, pohr fah-*VOHR.

3. EATING

Where is a good restaurant?
  ¿Dónde hay un buen restaurante?
  DOHN-*deh eye oon bwehn rehs-tow-*RAHN-*teh?*

A table for two, please.
  Una mesa para dos, por favor.
  OO-*nah* MEH-*sah* PAH-*rah dohs, pohr fah-*VOHR.

Waiter!
  ¡Camarero!
  *Kah-mah-*REH-*roh!*

Waitress!
  ¡Camarera!
  *Kah-mah-*REH-*rah!*

The menu, please.
  El menú, por favor.
  Ehl meh-NOO, *pohr* fah-VOHR.

What's good today?
  ¿Qué hay de bueno hoy?
  Keh eye deh BWEH-*noh oy?*

Is it ready?
  ¿Está listo?
  Ehs-TAH LEES-*toh?*

How long will it take?
  ¿Cuánto tiempo tardará?
  KWAHN-*toh t'*YEHM-*poh tahr-dah-*RAH?

This, please ...
  Esto, por favor ...
  EHS-*toh, pohr fah-*VOHR ...

and this
  y esto
  ee EHS-*toɪ.*

Bring me ...
  Tráigame ...
  TRY-*gah-meh* ...

water
  agua
  AH-*gwah*

milk
  leche
  LEH-*cheh*

    a glass of beer
     un vaso de cerveza
     oon VAH-*soh deh thehr-*VEH-*thah*

    red wine
     vino tinto
     VEE-*noh* TEEN-*toh*

    white wine
     vino blanco
     VEE-*noh* BLAHN-*koh*

    a cocktail
     un coctel
     oon kohk-TEHL

    whisky soda
     whisky soda
     whisky SOH-*dah*

    soup
     sopa
     SOH-*pah*

    fish
     pescado
     *pehs-*KAH-*doh*

    meat
     carne
     KAHR-*neh*

    bread and butter
     pan y mantequilla
     *pahn ee mahn-teh-*KEE-*l'yah*

a sandwich
  un bocadillo
  *oon boh-kah-*DEE-*l'yoh*

steak...
bistec...
BEES-*tehk*...

rare
poco asado
POH-*koh ah*-SAH-*doh*

medium
mediano
*meh-d'*YAH-*noh*

well done
muy asado
mwee ah-SAH-*doh*

chicken
pollo
POH-*l'yoh*

veal
ternera
tehr-NEH-*rah*

pork
cerdo
THER-*doh*

lamb
cordero
kohr-DEH-*roh*

lamb chop
chuleta de cordero
choo-LEH-*tah deh kohr*-DEH-*roh*

rice with chicken
arroz con pollo
ah-ROHTH *kohn* POH-*l'yoh*

pan fried rice, fish and meat
paella Valenciana
pah-EH-*l'yah vah-lehn-th'*YAH-*nah*

roast suckling pig
lechón asado
leh-CHOHN *ah*-SAH-*doh*

stuffed spicy corn-meal roll
enchilada
ehn-chee-LAH-*dah*

with potatoes...
con papas...
kohn PAH-*pahs*...

rice
arroz
ah-ROTH

And what vegetables?
Y ¿qué verduras?
Ee keh vehr-DOO-*rahs?*

peas
guisantes
ghee-SAHN-*tehs*

beans
habichuelas
*ah-bee-ch'*WEH-*lahs*

carrots
zanahorias
tha-nah-OH-*r'yahs*

onions
cebollas
theh-BOH-*l'yahs*

a salad
   una ensalada
   OO-*nah* ehn-sah-LAH-*dah*

lettuce	**tomatoes**
lechuga	tomates
leh-CHOO-*gah*	*toh*-MAH-*tehs*

Please bring me another fork.
   Tráigame otro tenedor, por favor.
   TRY-*gah-meh* OH-*troh teh-neh*-DOHR, *pohr fah*-VOHR.

knife	**spoon**
cuchillo	cuchara
koo-CHEE-*l'yoh*	*koo*-CHAH-*rah*

glass	**plate**
vaso	plato
VAH-*soh*	PLAH-*toh*

What is there for dessert?	**fruit**
¿Que tiene de postre?	fruta
*Keh t'*YEH-*neh deh* POHS-*treh?*	FROO-*tah*

pastry	**cake**
pastel	torta
pahs-TEHL	TOHR-*tah*

ice cream	**cheese**
helado	queso
eh-LAH-*doh*	KEH-*soh*

Some coffee, please.
   Un poco de café, por favor.
   Oon POH-*koh deh kah*-FEH, *pohr fah*-VOHR.

sugar	**cream**
azucar	crema
ah-THOO-*kahr*	KREH-*mah*

tea with lemon	**mineral water**
té con limon	agua mineral
teh kohn lee-MOHN	AH-*gwah mee-neh*-RAHL

The check, please.
  La cuenta, por favor.
  Lah KWEHN-*tah, pohr fah-*VOHR.

Is the tip included?
  ¿Está incluída la propina?
  *Ehs-*TAH *een-kloo·ee-dah lah proh-*PEE-*nah?*

It was very good.
  Estaba muy bueno.
  *Ehs-*TAH-*bah mwee* BWEH-*noh.*

4. SHOPPING

I would like to buy this . . .
  Desearía comprar esto . . .
  *Deh-seh-ah-*REE-*ah kohm-*PRAHR EHS-*toh . . .*

    that
      aquello
      *ah-*KEH-*l'yoh*

I am just looking round.
  Estoy mirando.
  *Ehs-*TOY *mee-*RAHN-*doh.*

Where is the section for . . .
  ¿Dónde está la sección de . . .
  DOHN-*deh ehs-*TAH *lah sehk-th'*YOHN *deh . . .*

    men's clothing
      trajes de caballero
      TRAH-*hehs deh kah-bah-l'*YEH-*roh*

    women's clothing
      trajes de señora
      TRAH-*hehs deh seh-n'*YOH-*rah*

hats	**gloves**
sombreros	guantes
*sohm-*BREH-*rohs*	GWAHN-*tehs*

underwear
ropa interior
ROH-*pah een-teh-r'*YOHR

shoes
zapatos
*thah-*PAH*-tohs*

stockings
medias
MEH-*d'yahs*

shirts
camisas
*kah-*MEE*-sahs*

socks
calcetines
*kahl-theh-*TEE*-nehs*

My size in America is . . .
Mi medida en America es . . .
*Mee meh-*DEE*-dah ehn Ah-*MEH*-ree-kah ehs . . .*

toys
juguetes
*hoo-*GHEH*-tehs*

perfumes
perfumes
*pehr-*FOO*-mehs*

jewelry
joyería
*hoh-yeh-*REE*-ah*

watches
relojes
*reh-*LOH*-hehs*

toilet articles
artículos de tocador
*ahr-*TEE*-koo-lohs deh toh-kah-*DOHR

sport articles
artículos de deporte
*ahr-*TEE*-koo-lohs deh deh-*POHR*-teh*

films
rollos de película
ROH-*l'yohs deh peh-*LEE*-koo-lah*

souvenirs
recuerdos
*reh-*KWEHR*-dohs*

Show me . . .
Muéstreme . . .
MWEHS-*treh-meh*

something less expensive
algo menos caro
AHL-*goh* MEH-*nohs* KAH-*roh*

another one
otro
OH-*troh*

better quality
mejor calidad
meh-HOHR *kah-lee*-DAHD

larger
más grande
mahs GRAHN-*deh*

smaller
más pequeño
mahs peh-KEH-*n'yoh*

I do not like the color.
No me gusta el color.
Noh meh GOOS-*tah ehl koh*-LOHR.

I want one . . .
Quiero uno . . .
K'YEH-*roh* OO-*noh* . . .

in green
en verde
ehn VEHR-*deh*

yellow
amarillo
ah-mah-REE-*l'yoh*

blue
azul
ah-THOOL

red
rojo
ROH-*hoh*

black
negro
NEH-*groh*

white
blanco
BLAHN-*koh*

gray
gris
grees

pink
color rosa
koh-LOHR ROH-*sah*

brown
pardo
PAHR-*doh*

I will take it with me.
Lo llevaré conmigo.
Loh l'yeh-vah-REH *kohn*-MEE-*goh*.

The receipt, please.
La cuenta, por favor.
Lah KWEHN-*tah, pohr fah*-VOHR.

Please send it to this address.
Por favor, mándelo a esta dirección.
Pohr fah-VOHR, MAHN-*deh-loh ah* EHS-*tah dee-rehk-th'*YOHN.

Where is there a flower shop?
¿Dónde hay una tienda de flores?
DOHN-*deh eye* OO-*nah t'*YEHN-*dah deh* FLOH-*rehs?*

Where is there a bookstore?
 ¿Dónde hay una librería?
 DOHN-*deh eye* OO-*nah lee-breh*-REE-*ah?*

Where is there a food market?
 ¿Dónde hay un mercado?
 DOHN-*deh eye* oon *mehr*-KAH-*doh?*

5. TRANSPORTATION

Taxi!
 ¡Taxi!
 TAHK-*see!*

Take me to the airport.
 Lleveme al aéropuerto.
 L'YEH-*veh-meh* ahl *ah-eh-roh*-PWEHR-*toh.*

Turn right. left
 Tome a la derecha. izquierda.
 TOH-*meh ah lah deh*-REH-*chah.* *eeth-k'*YEHR-*dah*

Straight ahead. **Not so fast!**
 Siga derecho. ¡No tan rápido!
 SEE-*gah deh*-REH-*choh.* *Noh tahn* RAH-*pee-doh!*

Hurry! **Stop here!**
 ¡Apúrese! ¡Pare aquí!
 Ah-POO-*reh-seh!* PAH-*reh ah*-KEE!

Wait for me.
 Espéreme.
 Ehs-PEH-*reh-meh.*

How much will it cost to . . . ?
 ¿Cuánto cuesta hasta . . . ?
 KWAHN-*toh* KWEHS-*tah* AHS-*tah . . . ?*

and back?
 ¿y vuelta?
 ee VWEHL-*tah?*

How much by the hour?   **by the day?**

¿Cuánto por hora?   ¿al día?

KWAHN-*toh pohr* OH-*rah?*   *ahl* DEE-*ah?*

Show me the sights.

Muéstreme los puntos de interés.

MWEHS-*treh-meh lohs* POON-*tohs deh een-teh-*REHS.

What is that building?

¿Qué edificio es ése?

*Keh eh-dee-*FEE-*th'yoh ehs* EH-*seh?*

Can it be visited?

¿Se puede visitar?

Seh PWEH-*deh vee-see-*TAHR?

I want to see the Cathedral.

Quiero ver la Catedral.

K'YEH-*roh vehr lah Kah-teh-*DRAHL.

To the railroad station.

A la estación.

*Ah lah ehs-tah-th'*YOHN.

Porter!   **I have two bags.**

¡Maletero!   Tengo dos maletas.

*Mah-leh-*TEH-*roh!*   TEHN-*goh dohs mah-*LEH-*tahs.*

A ticket to Guadalajara.

Un billete para Guadalajara.

*Oon bee-l'*YEH-*teh* PAH-*rah Gwah-dah-lah-*HAH-*rah.*

one way   **round trip**

ida   ida y vuelta

EE-*dah*   EE-*dah ee* VWEHL-*tah*

first class   **second class**

primera clase   segunda clase

*pree-*MEH-*rah* KLAH-*seh*   *seh-*GOON-*dah* KLAH-*seh*

Where is the train to Puebla?

¿De dónde sale el tren de Puebla?

Deh DOHN-*deh* SAH-*leh ehl trehn deh* PWEH-*blah?*

When does it leave?
¿A qué hora sale?
Ah keh OH-*rah* SAH-*leh?*

Is this the train for Burgos?
¿Es éste el tren de Burgos?
Ehs EHS-*teh ehl trehn deh* BOOR-*gohs?*

When do we get to Madrid?
¿Cuándo llegaremos a Madrid?
KWAHN-*doh l'yeh-gah-*REH-*mohs ah Mah-*DREED?

Where is the dining car?
¿Dónde está el coche comedor?
DOHN-*deh ehs-*TAH *ehl* KOH-*cheh koh-meh-*DOHR?

Open the window, please.
Abra la ventanilla, por favor.
AH-*brah lah vehn-tah-*NEE-*l'yah, pohr fah-*VOHR.

Close the window, please.
Cierre la ventanilla, por favor.
*Th'*YEH-*rreh lah vehn-tah-*NEE-*l'yah, pohr fah-*VOHR.

Is this the bus to Callao?
¿Es éste el autobús de Callao?
Ehs EHS-*teh ehl ow-toh-*BOOS *deh Kah-l'*YOW?

I want to go to Buena Vista.
Quiero ir a Buena Vista.
K'YEH-*roh eer ah* BWEH-*nah* VEES-*tah.*

Please tell me where to get off.
¿Dónde debo bajar?
DOHN-*deh* DEH-*boh bah-*HAHR?

Where is a gas station?
¿Dónde hay una estación de gasolina?
DOHN-*deh eye* OO-*nah ehs-tah-th'*YOHN *deh gah-soh-*LEE-*nah?*

Fill it up.
Llene el tanque.
L'YEH-*neh ehl* TAHN-*keh.*

Check the oil.
Examine el aceite.
*Ehk-sah-*MEE*-neh ehl ah-*THAY*-teh.*

water	tires
el agua	las llantas
ehl AH*-gwah*	*lahs l'*YAHN*-tahs*

Something is wrong with the car.
El automóbil no funciona bien.
*Ehl ow-toh-*MOH*-beel noh foon-th'*YOH*-nah b'yehn.*

Can you fix it?
¿Puede arreglarlo?
PWEH*-deh ah-rreh-*GLAHR*-loh?*

How long will it take?
¿Cuánto tiempo tardará?
KWAHN*-toh t'*YEHM*-poh tahr-dah-*RAH*?*

Is this the road to Barcelona?
¿Es éste el camino de Barcelona?
Ehs EHS*-teh ehl kah-*MEE*-noh deh Bahr-theh-*LOH*-nah?*

Have you a map?
¿Tiene Vd. un mapa?
T'YEH*-neh oos-*TEHD *oon* MAH*-pah?*

Is this the boat to Mallorca?
¿Es éste el barco de Mallorca?
Ehs EHS*-teh ehl* BAHR*-koh deh Mah-l'*YOHR*-kah?*

When does it leave?
¿Cuándo sale?
KWAHN*-doh* SAH*-leh?*

6. MAKING FRIENDS

Good day!	**My name is ...**
¡Buenos días!	Me llamo ...
BWEH*-nohs* DEE*-ahs!*	*Meh l'*YAH*-moh ...*

What is your name, Sir?
¿Cómo se llama Vd., señor?
KOH-*moh seh* L'YAH-*mah oos*-TEHD, *seh-n'*YOHR?

What is your name, Madam?
¿Cómo se llama Vd., señora?
KOH-*moh seh* L'YAH-*mah oos*-TEHD, *seh-n'*YOH-*rah?*

What is your name, Miss?
¿Cómo se llama Vd., señorita?
KOH-*moh seh* L'YAH-*mah oos*-TEHD, *seh-n'yoh-*REE-
tah?

I am delighted to meet you.
Encantado de conocerle.
*Ehn-kahn-*TAH-*doh deh koh-noh-*THEHR-*leh.*

Do you speak English?
¿Habla Vd. inglés?
AH-*blah oos*-TEHD *een*-GLEHS?

I speak only a little Spanish.
Hablo solamente un poco de español.
AH-*bloh soh-lah-*MEHN-*teh oon* POH-*koh deh ehs-
pah-n'*YOHL.

I am from New York.
Soy de Nueva York.
Soy deh NWEH-*vah Yohrk.*

Where are you from?
¿De dónde es Vd.?
Deh DOHN-*deh ehs oos*-TEHD?

I like your country.
Me gusta su país.
Meh GOOS-*tah soo pah-*EES.

I like your city.
Me gusta su ciudad.
Meh GOOS-*tah soo th'yoo-*DAHD.

Have you been in America?
¿Ha estado en América?
*Ah ehs-*TAH-*doh ehn Ah-*MEH-*ree-kah?*

This is my first visit here.
Es mi primera visita por aquí.
*Ehs mee pree-*MEH-*rah vee-*SEE-*tah pohr ah-*KEE.

May I sit here?
¿Puedo sentarme aquí?
PWEH-*doh sehn-*TAHR-*meh ah-*KEE?

May I take your picture?
¿Me deja sacar una foto de Vd.?
Meh DEH-*hah sah-*KAHR OO-*nah* FOH-*toh deh oos-*
TEHD?

This is a picture of my wife.
Esta es una fotografía de mi esposa.
EHS-*tah ehs* OO-*nah foh-toh-grah-*FEE-*ah deh mee*
*ehs-*POH-*sah.*

my husband mi esposo *mee ehs-*POH-*soh*	**my son** mi hijo *mee* EE-*hoh*
my daughter mi hija *mee* EE-*hah*	**my mother** mi madre *mee* MAH-*dreh*
my father mi padre *mee* PAH-*dreh*	**my sister** mi hermana *mee ehr-*MAH-*nah*
my brother mi hermano *mee ehr-*MAH-*noh*	

Have you children?
¿Tiene Vd. hijos?
*T'*YEH-*neh oos-*TEHD EE-*hohs?*

How beautiful!
 ¡Qué bonito!
 *Keh boh-*NEE*-toh!*

Very interesting.
Muy interesante.
*Mooy een-teh-reh-*SAHN*-teh.*

Would you like a cigarette?
 ¿Le gustaría un cigarrillo?
 *Leh goos-tah-*REE*-ah oon thee-gah-*REE*-l'yoh?*

Would you like something to eat?
 ¿Le gustaría comer algo?
 *Leh goos-tah-*REE*-ah koh-*MEHR AHL*-goh?*

Would you like something to drink?
 ¿Le gustaría beber algo?
 *Leh goos-tah-*REE*-ah beh-*BEHR AHL*-goh?*

Sit down, please.
 Siéntese, por favor.
 S'YEHN*-teh-seh, pohr fah-*VOHR*.*

Make yourself at home!
 ¡Está en su casa!
 *Ehs-*TAH *ehn soo* KAH*-sah!*

Good luck!
 ¡Buena suerte!
 BWEH*-nah* SWEHR*-teh!*

To your health!
 ¡A su salud!
 *Ah soo sah-*LOOD*!*

When can I see you again?
 ¿Cuándo puedo volver a verle?
 KWAHN*-doh* PWEH*-doh vohl-*VEHR *ah* VEHR*-leh?*

Where shall we meet?
 ¿Dónde nos veremos?
 DOHN*-deh nohs veh-*REH*-mohs?*

Here is my address.
 Aquí tiene mi dirección.
 *Ah-*KEE *t'*YEH*-neh mee dee-rehk-th'*YOHN*.*

What is your address?
 ¿Cuál es su dirección?
 *Kwahl ehs soo dee-rehk-th'*YOHN*?*

What is your phone number?
¿Cuál es su número de teléfono?
Kwahl ehs soo NOO-*meh-roh deh teh-*LEH-*foh-noh?*

May I speak to...
Puedo hablar con...
PWEH-*doh ah-*BLAHR *kohn...*

Mr.
Señor.
*Seh-n'*YOHR.

Mrs.
Señora.
*Seh-n'*YOH-*rah.*

Miss
Señorita
*Seh-n'yoh-*REE-*tah*

Would you like to have lunch?
¿Le gustaría almorzar?
*Leh goos-tah-*REE-*ah ahl-mohr-*THAHR?

to have dinner?
cenar?
*theh-*NAHR?

to go to the movies?
ir al cine?
eer ahl THEE-*neh?*

to go to the theatre?
ir al teatro?
*eer ahl teh-*AH-*troh?*

to go to the beach?
ir a la playa?
eer ah lah PLAH-*yah?*

to take a walk?
pasear?
*pah-seh-*AHR?

With great pleasure!
¡Con mucho gusto!
Kohn MOO-*choh* GOOS-*toh!*

I am sorry.
Lo siento.
*Loh s'*YEHN-*toh.*

I cannot.
No puedo.
Noh PWEH-*doh.*

Another time.
Otra vez.
OH-*trah vehth.*

I must go now.
Me tengo que ir ahora.
Meh TEHN-*goh keh eer ah-*OH-*rah.*

Thank you for a wonderful time.
Gracias para las horas magníficas.
GRAH-*th'yahs* PAH-*rah lahs* OH-*rahs mah-*GNEE-*fee-kahs.*

Thank you for an excellent dinner.
Gracias para la cena excelente.
GRAH-*th'yahs* PAH-*rah lah* THEH-*nah ehks-theh-*
LEHN-*teh.*

This is for you.
Esto es para Vd.
EHS-*toh ehs* PAH-*rah* oos-TEHD.

You are very kind.
Es Vd. muy amable.
Ehs oos-TEHD *mooy ah-*MAH-*bleh.*

It's nothing really.
No hay de qué.
Noh eye deh keh.

With best regards!
¡Con mis mejores recuerdos!
*Kohn mees meh-*HOH-*rehs reh-*KWEHR-*dohs!*

Congratulations!
¡Felicitaciones!
*Feh-lee-thee-tah-th'*YOH-*nehs!*

7. EMERGENCIES

Help!	**Police!**	**Fire!**
¡Socorro!	¡Policía!	¡Fuego!
*Soh-*KOH-*rroh!*	*Poh-lee-*THEE-*ah!*	FWEH-*goh!*

Stop that man!
¡Pare a ese hombre!
PAH-*reh ah* EH-*seh* OHM-*breh!*

Stop that woman!
¡Pare a esa mujer!
PAH-*reh ah* EH-*sah moo-*HEHR!

I have been robbed!	**Look out!**
¡Me han robado!	¡Cuidado!
*Meh ahn roh-*BAH-*doh!*	*Kwee-*DAH-*doh!*

Wait a minute!
    ¡Espérese un momento!
    *Ehs-*PEH*-reh-seh oon moh-*MEHN*-toh!*

Stop!	**Get out!**	**Hurry up!**
¡Pare!	¡Salga!	¡Apúrese!
PAH-*reh!*	SAHL-*gah!*	*Ah-*POO*-reh-seh!*

Don't bother me!   **What's going on?**
    ¡No me moleste!   ¿Qué pasa?
    *Noh meh moh-*LEHS*-teh!   Keh* PAH*-sah?*

Entrance   **Exit**
    Entrada   Salida
    *Ehn-*TRAH*-dah*   *Sah-*LEE*-dah*

Ladies
    Señoras (Damas)
    *Seh-n'*YOH*-rahs (*DAH*-mahs)*

Gentlemen
    Señores (Caballeros)
    *Seh-n'*YOH*-rehs (Kah-bah-l'*YEH*-rohs)*

Danger!   **Keep out!**
    ¡Peligro!   ¡Se prohibe la entrada!
    *Peh-*LEE*-groh! Seh proh-*EE*-beh lah ehn-*TRAH*-dah!*

No smoking
    Se prohibe fumar
    *Seh proh-*EE*-beh foo-*MAHR

No parking
    Se prohibe estacionar
    *Seh proh-*EE*-beh ehs-tah-th'yoh-*NAHR

One way
    Una vía
    OO*-nah* VEE*-ah*

I feel ill.
    Me siento mal.
    *Meh s'*YEHN*-toh mahl.*

Call a doctor!
  ¡Llame al doctor!
  *L'*YAH-*meh ahl dohk-*TOHR!

It hurts here.
  Me duele aquí.
  Meh DWEH-*leh ah-*KEE.

Where is the drugstore?
  ¿Dónde está la farmacia?
  DOHN-*deh ehs-*TAH *lah fahr-*MAH-*th'yah?*

Take me to the hospital!
  ¡Lléveme al hospital!
  *L'*YEH-*veh-meh ahl ohs-pee-*TAHL!

Where is there a dentist?
  ¿Dónde hay un dentista?
  DOHN-*deh eye oon dehn-*TEES-*tah?*

I have lost my bag ...
  He perdido mi bolsa ...
  *Eh pehr-*DEE-*doh mee* BOHL-*sah ...*

    my wallet
      mi portamonedas
      *mee pohr-tah-moh-*NEH-*dahs*

    my camera
      mi cámara
      mee KAH-*mah-rah*

    my passport
      mi pasaporte
      *mee pah-sah-*POHR-*teh*

I am an American.
  Soy americano.
  *Soy ah-meh-ree-*KAH-*noh.*

Where is the American Consulate?
  ¿Dónde está el Consulado Americano?
  DOHN-*deh ehs-*TAH *ehl Kohn-soo-*LAH-*doh Ah-meh-ree-*KAH-*noh?*

Don't worry.
  No se preocupe.
  *Noh seh preh-oh-*KOO-*peh.*

Everything is all right.
  Todo está bien.
  TOH-*doh ehs-*TAH *b'yehn.*

GERMAN

Facts About German

German is spoken by about 120 million people in Germany, Austria, Switzerland, Luxemburg, and Liechtenstein. It is widely spoken and understood throughout Central and Eastern Europe, and even survives as a spoken language in some parts of the United States such as Pennsylvania and Wisconsin and in German communities of southern Brazil.

An unusual feature of German is its apparent use of very long words, which are simply formed by joining several words together.

German, as a Teutonic language, is related directly to English as well as to Dutch and the Scandinavian languages of northern Europe.

There are many dialects in Germany, Austria, and Switzerland, but the basic German text in this book is written in the official High German (*Hochdeutsch*) and will serve you well in any German-speaking area.

Advice on Accent

Letters with an umlaut (two dots over vowels) are pronounced as follows: ä pronounced **ay**; ö pronounced **uh**; ü pronounced by pursing the lips as if whistling and saying **ew**.

v is pronounced like the English **f.**
w is pronounced like the English **v.**
We render the German guttural sound by **kh.**

It is an extremely frequent sound in German and is used even in the word for "I"—*ich.*

s is usually pronounced either as z or sh.

You Already Know Some German

English is descended directly from Saxon, an old German dialect. Therefore, a great majority of the short and common English words are more or less analogous to their German counterparts, although because of difference in pronunciation it may be difficult at first to recognize them. However, their presence is still a great help to English-speaking people when they speak German. Here are a few: *Haus* (house), *Mann* (man), *Maus* (mouse), *Hand* (hand), *Finger* (finger), *Schuh* (shoe), *Sohn* (son), *Arm* (arm), *Buch* (book), *Glas* (glass), *Bier* (beer), *Land* (land), *Wolf* (wolf), and very many others.

Besides the above words which closely resemble English, other German words in their original form have become part of our everyday language. You will certainly know the following: *Kindergarten* (children's garden), *Gesundheit* (health), *Dachshund* (badger hound), *Hamburger* (from Hamburg), *Wiener Schnitzel* (Viennese cutlet), *Sauerkraut* (sour cabbage), *auf Wiedersehn!* (to the seeing again).

1. FIRST CONTACT

Yes.
Ja.
Yah.

No.
Nein.
Nine.

Good.
Gut.
Goot.

Thank you.
Danke.
DAHN-*keh.*

You are welcome.
Bitte.
BIT-*teh.*

Excuse me.
Verzeihung.
*Fehr-*TSIGH-*hoonk.*

It's all right.
Geht in Ordnung.
Gait in OHRD-*noonk.*

Please.
Bitte.
BIT-*teh.*

I would like . . .
Ich möchte . . .
Ikh MUHKH-*teh . . .*

What?
Was?
Vahss?

This.
Das.
Dahss.

Where?
Wo?
Voh?

Here.
Hier.
Here.

When?
Wann?
Vahn?

Now.
Jetzt.
Yet'st.

Later.
Später.
SHPEH-*tehr.*

Who?
Wer?
Vehr?

I
ich
ikh

you
Sie
Zee

he
er
ehr

she
sie
zee

Your name, please?
Ihr Name, bitte?
Eer NAH-*meh,* BIT-*teh?*

Good day.
Guten Tag.
GOO-*t'n tahk.*

Good morning.
Guten Morgen.
GOO-*t'n* MOHR-*g'n.*

Good evening.
Guten Abend.
GOO-*t'n* AH-*bent.*

Good night.
Gute Nacht.
GOO-*teh nahkht.*

Good-by.
Auf Wiedersehen.
Owf VEE-*dehr-zehn.*

y well, thank you. And you?
Danke, sehr gut. Und Ihnen?
DAHN-*keh, zehr* goot.
Oont EE-*nehn?*

derstand, please repeat.
he nicht, bitte noch einmal.
-SHTEH-*heh nikht,* BIT-*teh nohkh* INE-

	two	three	four	five
	zwei	drei	vier	fünf
nss	tsvigh	dry	fear	fewnf

	seven	eight	nine	ten
	sieben	acht	neun	zehn
zehks	ZEE-*b'n*	ahkht	.noyn	tsehn

2. ACCOMMODATIONS

Where is a good hotel?
Wo ist ein gutes Hotel?
Voh isst ine GOO-*tess hoh-*TEHL?

I want a room for one.
Ich möchte ein Einzelzimmer.
Ikh MUHKH-*teh ine* INE-*tsehl-tsim-mehr.*

I want a room for two.
Ich möchte ein Doppelzimmer.
Ikh MUHKH-*teh ine* DOH-*p'l-tsim-mehr.*

I want a room with bath.
Ich möchte ein Zimmer mit Bad.
Ikh MUHKH-*teh ine* TSIM-*mehr mitt baht.*

for two days.	**for a week.**
auf zwei Tage.	auf eine Woche.
owf tsvigh TAH-*geh.*	*owf* EYE-*neh* VOH-

till Monday	**Tuesday**	**Wednesd**
Bis Montag	Dienstag	Mittwo
biss MOHN-*tahk*	DEENS-*tahk*	MITT-*vo*

Thursday	**Friday**
Donnerstag	Freitag
DOHN-*nehrs-tahk*	FRY-*tahk*

Saturday	**Sunday**
Samstag	Sonntag
ZAHMS-*tahk*	ZOHN-*tahk*

How much is it?	**Here are my bags.**
Was kostet es?	Hier ist mein Gepäck.
Vahss KOHS-*teht ess?*	*Here isst mine gay-*PECK.

Here is my passport.
Hier ist mein Pass.
Here isst mine pahs.

I like it.	**I don't like it.**
Es gefällt mir.	Es gefällt mir nicht.
*Ess gay-*FEHLT *meer.*	*Ess gay-*FEHLT *meer nikht.*

Show me another.
Zeigen Sie mir was anderes.
TSIGH-*g'n zee meer vahss* AHN-*deh-ress.*

Where is the toilet?
Wo ist die Toilette?
*Voh isst dee t'wah-*LET-*teh?*

Where is the men's room?
Wo ist die Herrentoilette?
Voh isst dee HEHR-*rehn-t'wah-*LET-*teh?*

Where is the ladies' room?
Wo ist die Damentoilette?
Voh isst dee DAH-*men-t'wah-*LET *teh?*

Hot water   **a towel**
   heisses Wasser   ein Handtuch
   HIGH-*sehs* VAHS-*sehr*   *ine* HAHNT-*tookh*

soap
   Seife
   ZIGH-*feh*

Come in!
   Herein!
   Hehr-INE!

Please have this washed.
   Bitte lassen Sie das waschen.
   BIT-*teh* LAHS-*s'n zee dahs* VAH-*sh'n*

     pressed.   **cleaned.**
     bügeln.   reinigen.
     BEW-*g'ln.*   RYE-*nee-g'n.*

When will it be ready?
   Wann wird's fertig sein?
   Vahn veert's FEHR-*tick zine?*

I need it for tonight.   **for tomorrow.**
   Ich brauche es heute abend.   morgen.
   Ikh BROW-*kheh ess* HOY-*teh* AH-*bent.*   MOHR-*g'n.*

My key, please.
   Meinen Schlüssel, bitte.
   MY-*nehn* SHLEW-*sehl,* BIT-*teh.*

Any mail for me?   **Any packages?**
   Post für mich da?   Packete?
   Pohst fewr mikh dah?   *pah-*KEH-*teh?*

I want five air mail stamps for the USA.
   Ich brauche fünf Luftpostmarken nach Amerika.
   Ikh BROW-*kheh fewnf* LOOFT-*pohst-mahr-ken*
     *nahkh ah-*MEH-*ree-kah.*

Have you postcards?
   Haben Sie Postkarten?
   HAH-*b'n zee* POHST-*kahr-ten?*

I want to send a telegram.
   Ich möchte ein Telegramm absenden.
   Ikh MUHKH-*teh ine teh-leh-*GRAM *AHP-zen-den.*

Call me at seven in the morning.
   Wecken Sie mich um sieben Uhr.
   VECK-*'n zee mikh oom* ZEE-*b'n oor.*

Where is the telephone?   **Hello.**
   Wo ist ein Telefon?   Hallo.
   *Voh isst ine teh-leh-*PHOHN?   *Hah-*LOH.

Send breakfast to room 702.
   Schicken Sie mein Frühstück aufs Zimmer sieben-
      hundertzwei.
   SHICK-*k'n zee mine* FREW-*shtewk owfs* TSIM-*mehr*
      ZEE-*b'n hoon-dehrt-tsvigh.*

orange juice   **ham and eggs**
   Orangensaft   ham and eggs
   *oh-*RAHN-*zhen-zahft*

rolls and coffee
   Brötchen und Kaffee
   BRUHT-*khen oont kah-*FEH

I am expecting someone.
   Ich erwarte jemand.
   *Ikh ehr-*VAHR-*teh* YEH-*mahnt.*

Tell him to wait.
   Er soll auf mich warten.
   Ehr zohl owf mikh VAHR-*ten.*

Did anyone call?
   Hat jemand angerufen?
   Haht YEH-*mahnt* AHN-*gay-roo-f'n?*

I'll be back at six.
   Ich bin um sechs zurück.
   *Ikh been oom zehks tsoo-*REWK.

Where is a restaurant?
Wo ist ein Restaurant?
*Voh isst ine res-toh-*RAHNG*?*

Where is a barber shop?
Wo ist ein Raseur?
*Voh isst ine rah-*ZUHR*?*

Where is a beauty shop?
Wo ist ein Damenfriseur?
Voh isst ine DAH-*men-free-zuhr?*

Where is a drugstore?
Wo ist eine Drogerie?
Voh isst EYE-*neh droh-gheh-*REE*?*

What is the telephone number?
Was für Telefonnummer?
*Vahss fewr teh-leh-*FOHN-*noom-mehr?*

What is the address, please?
Welche Adresse, bitte?
VEHL-*kheh ah-*DRESS-*seh,* BIT-*teh?*

I want to change some money.
Ich möchte Geld wechseln.
Ikh MUHKH-*teh gehlt* VEHK-*sehln.*

What is the rate for dollars?
Wie steht der Dollar?
Vee shteht dehr DOHL-*lahr?*

ten	eleven	twelve
zehn	elf	zwölf
tsehn	*ehlf*	*tsvuhlf*

thirteen	fourteen	fifteen
dreizehn	vierzehn	fünfzehn
DRY-*tsehn*	FEAR-*tsehn*	FEWNF-*tsehn*

sixteen	seventeen	eighteen
sechzehn	siebzehn	achtzehn
ZEKH-*tsehn*	SEEP-*tsehn*	AHKHT-*tsehn*

nineteen
neunzehn
NOYN-*tsehn*

twenty
zwanzig
TSVAHN-*tsik*

thirty
dreissig
DRY-*sik*

forty
vierzig
FEAR-*tsik*

fifty
fünfzig
FEWNF-*tsik*

sixty
sechzig
ZEHKH-*tsik*

seventy
siebzig
SEEP-*tsik*

eighty
achtzig
AHKHT-*sik*

ninety
neunzig
NOYN-*tsik*

hundred
hundert
HOON-*dehrt*

My bill, please.
Meine Rechnung, bitte.
MY-*neh* REHKH-*noonk,* BIT-*teh.*

3. EATING

Where is a good restaurant?
Wo ist ein gutes Restaurant?
Voh isst ine GOO-*tess rehs-toh-*RAHNG?

A table for two, please.
Einen Tisch für zwei, bitte.
EYE-*nehn tish fewr tsvigh,* BIT-*teh.*

Waiter!
Herr Ober!
Hehr OH-*behr!*

Waitress!
Fräulein!
FROY-*line!*

The menu, please.
Die Speisekarte, bitte.
Dee SHPY-*zeh-kahr-teh,* BIT-*teh.*

What's especially good today?
Etwas Besonderes heute?
ETT-*vahss beh-*ZOHN-*deh-ress* HOY-*teh?*

Is it ready?
Ist es fertig?
Isst ess FEHR-*tick?*

How long will it take?
Wie lange wird es dauern?
Vee LAHN-*geh veert ehss* DOW-*ehrn?*

This here... **and this.**
Das hier... und das.
Dahss here... *oont dahss.*

Bring me...
Bringen Sie mir...
BREEN-*g'n zee meer...*

water	**milk**	**a glass of beer**
Wasser	Milch	ein Glas Bier
VAHS-*sehr*	*meelkh*	*ine glahs beer*

red wine	**white wine**
Rotwein	Weisswein
ROHT-*vine*	VICE-*vine*

a cocktail	**whisky soda**
einen Cocktail	Whiskey mit Soda
EYE-*nehn* COHK-*tehl*	*whiskey mitt* ZOH-*dah*

soup	**fish**	**meat**
Suppe	Fisch	Fleisch
ZOOP-*peh*	*Fish*	*Fly'sh*

bread and butter	**a sandwich**
Brot und Butter	ein belegtes Brot
Broat oont BOOT-*tehr*	*ine beh-*LEHK-*tess broat*

steak...	**rare**
ein Steak...	englisch
ine steak...	EHN-*glish*

medium
halb durchgebraten
hahlp DOORKH-*geh-brah-ten*

well done
durchgebraten
DOORKH-*geh-brah-ten*

chicken	**veal**	**pork**
Huhn	Kalb	Schwein
Hoon	*Kahlp*	*Shvine*

lamb	**lamb chop**
Lamm	Lammskotelett
Lahm	LAHMS-*koht-let*

Sauerbraten with dumplings
Sauerbraten mit Knödel
ZOW-*ehr-brah-ten* mitt K'NUH-*dehl*

Leg of veal with little dumplings
Kalbsstelze mit Spätzle
KAHLPS-*shtehl-tseh* mitt SHPETTS-*leh*

Creamschnitzel with mushrooms and egg noodles
Rahmschnitzel mit Champignons und Eiernudeln
RAHM-*shneet-sehl* mitt SHAHM-*peen-yohns* oont
EYE-*ehr-nood'ln*

No sauce for me.
Keine Tunke für mich.
KIGH-*neh* TOON-*keh fewr mikh.*

with potatoes...
mit Kartoffeln...
*mitt kahr-*TOHFF-*l'n ...*

rice	**an omelet**
Reis	eine Omelette
Rice	EYE-*neh ohm-*LET-*teh*

And what vegetables?	**peas**
Und was für Gemüse?	Erbsen
*Oont vahss fewr gay-*MEW-*zeh?*	EHR-*psehn*

beans	**carrots**	**onions**
Bohnen	Karrotten	Zwiebeln
BOH-*nehn*	*kah-*ROHT-*ten*	TSVEE-*behln*

a salad
  einen Salat
  EYE-*nehn sah*-LAHT

lettuce
  Kopfsalat
  KOHPF-*sah-laht*

tomatoes
  Tomaten
  Toh-MAH-*ten*

Please bring me another fork.
  Bitte bringen Sie mir eine andre Gabel.
  BIT-*teh* BRIN-g'n *zee meer* EYE-*neh* AHN-*dreh*
  GAH-*b'l.*

knife
  Messer
  MESS-*sehr*

spoon
  Löffel
  LUHF-*f'l*

glass
  Glas
  Glahs

plate
  Teller
  TEHL-*lehr*

What is there for dessert?
  Was gibt's zum Nachtisch?
  Vahss geept's tsoom NAHKH-*tish?*

fruit
  Obst
  ohpst

pastry
  Bäckerei
  *behk-keh-*RYE

cake
  Kuchen
  KOOH-*khehn*

ice cream
  Gefrorenes
  *Geh-*FROH-*reh-ness*

cheese
  Käse
  KAY-*zeh*

Some coffee, please.
  Kaffee, bitte.
  KAHF-*feh,* BIT-*teh.*

sugar
  Zucker
  TSOOK-*kehr*

cream
  Sahne
  ZAH-*neh*

tea with lemon
  Tee mit Zitrone
  *Teh mitt tsee-*TROH-*neh*

mineral water
  Mineralwasser
  *Mee-neh-*RAHL-*vahs-sehr*

More, please.
　Noch, bitte.
　Nohkh, BIT-*teh.*

That's enough.
　Genug.
　Gay-NOOK.

The check, please!
　Zahlen!
　TSAH-*l'n!*

Is the tip included?
　Ist die Bedienung inbegriffen?
　*Isst dee beh-*DEE-*noonk* IN-*beh-griff'n?*

It was very good.
　Es war sehr gut.
　Ess vahr zehr goot.

4. SHOPPING

I would like to buy this... that.
　Ich möchte gerne das hier kaufen... das dort.
　Ikh MUHKH-*teh* GEHR-*neh dahss here* KOW-*f'n...*
　　dahss dohrt.

I am just looking around.
　Ich möchte mich nur umsehen.
　Ikh MUHKH-*teh meekh noor* OOM-*zeh-hen.*

Where is the section for...
　Wo ist die Abteilung für...
　*Voh isst dee ahp-*TIE-*loonk fewr...*

men's clothing	**women's clothing**
Männerkleidung	Damenkleidung
MEN-*nehr-kligh-doonk*	DAH-*men-kligh-doonk*

hats	**gloves**	**underwear**
Hüte	Handschuhe	Unterwäsche
HEW-*teh*	HAHNT-*shoo-heh*	OON-*tehr-veh-sheh*

shoes	**stockings**	**shirts**
Schuhe	Strümpfe	Hemden
SHOO-*heh*	SHTREWM-*pfeh*	HEM-*den*

My size in America is...
In Amerika habe ich Grösse...
In ah-MEH-ree-kah HAH-beh ikh GRUH-seh...

toys	**perfumes**
Spielwaren	Parfumerien
SHPEEL-*vah-rehn*	*Pahr-few-meh-*REE-*ehn*

jewelry	**watches**
Juwelen	Uhren
*Yoo-*VEH-*lehn*	OO-*rehn*

toilet articles	**sport articles**
Toilette-Artikel	Sportwaren
*Twah-*LET-*ahr-tee-k'l*	SHPOHRT-*vah-rehn*

films	**souvenirs**
Filme	Andenken
FILL-*meh*	AHN-*den-ken*

Show me...
Zeigen Sie mir...
TSIGH-*g'n zee meer*...

another one
etwas Anderes
ETT-*vahss* AHN-*deh-ress*

something less expensive
etwas Billigeres
ETT-*vahss* BEEL-*lee-geh-ress*

a better quality
etwas Besseres
ETT-*vahss* BESS-*seh-ress*

bigger
grösser
GRUHS-*sehr*

smaller
kleiner
KLIGH-*nehr*

I don't like the color.
Die Farbe gefällt mir nicht.
Dee FAHR-*beh geh-*FEHLT *meer nikht.*

I want one...
Ich möchte es gerne...
Ikh MUHKH-*teh ess* GEHR-*neh*...

in green	in yellow	in blue
in grün	in gelb	in blau
in grewn	*in gehlp*	*in* BLAH-*oo*

red	black	white
rot	schwarz	weiss
roht	*shvahrts*	*vice*

grey	pink	brown
grau	rosa	braun
GRAH-*oo*	ROH-*zah*	*brown*

I will take it with me.
Ich werde es mitnehmen.
Ikh VEHR-*deh ess* MITT-*neh-men.*

The receipt, please.
Die Quittung, bitte.
Dee QUIT-*toonk,* BIT-*teh.*

Please send it to this address.
Bitte senden Sie es an diese Adresse.
BIT-*teh* ZEHN-*den zee ehss ähn* DEE-*zeh ah-*DRESS-*seh.*

Where is there a flower shop?
Wo ist ein Blumenladen?
Voh isst ine BLOO-*men-lah-den?*

Where is there a bookstore?
Wo ist eine Buchhandlung?
Voh isst EYE-*neh* BOOKH-*hahnd-loonk?*

Where is there a food shop?
Wo ist ein Lebensmittelgeschäft?
Voh isst ine LEH-*bens-mitt-tel-geh-shehft?*

5. TRANSPORTATION

Taxi!	**Take me to the airport.**
Taxi!	Zum Flughafen.
TAHK-*see!*	*Tsoom* FLOOK-*hah-fehn.*

Turn right.
  Biegen Sie rechts ein.
  BEE-g'n zee rehkhts ine.

Turn left.
  Biegen Sie links ein.
  BEE-g'n zee links ine.

Not so fast!
  Nicht so schnell!
  Nikht zoh shnehl!

Hurry up!
  Schneller!
  SHNEHL-lehr!

Stop here!
  Halten Sie hier!
  HAHL-ten zee here!

Wait for me!
  Warten Sie auf mich!
  VAHR-ten zee owf meekh!

How much is it?
  Wieviel macht es aus?
  Veel-FEEL mahkht ess ows?

How much is it to . . . ?
  Was kostet es bis . . . ?
  Vahss KOHS-teht ess bis . . . ?

  and back?
  und zurück?
  oont tsoo-REWK?

How much by the hour?
  Wieviel kostet es per Stunde?
  Vee-FEEL KOHS-teht ehss pehr SHTOON-deh?

  by the day?
    per Tag?
    pehr tahk?

Show me the sights.
  Zeigen Sie mir die Sehenswürdigkeiten.
  TSIGH-gehn zee meer dee ZEH-hens-vewr-dig-kite'n.

What is that building?
  Was für ein Gebäude ist das?
  Vahss fewr ine geh-BOY-deh isst dahss?

Can I go in?
  Kann man hineingehen?
  Kahn mahn heen-INE-gain?

I want to see the city hall.
  Ich möchte das Rathaus sehn.
  Ikh MUHKK-teh dahss RAHT-house zehn.

Porter!
   Träger!
   TRAY-*ghehr!*

I have two bags.
   Ich habe zwei Koffer.
   Ikh HAH-*beh tsvigh* KOHF-*fehr.*

A ticket to ...
   Eine Fahrkarte nach ...
   EYE-*neh* FAHR-*kahr-teh nahkh ...*

   one way
      einfach
      INE-*fahkh*

   round trip
      hin—und zurück
      *heen oont tsoo-*REWK

   first class
      erster Klasse
      EHR-*stehr* KLAHS-*seh*

   second class
      zweiter Klasse
      TSVIGH-*tehr* KLAHS-*seh*

When does it leave?
   Wann fährt er ab?
   Van fehrt ehr ahp?

Where is the train to Munich?
   Wo ist der Zug nach München?
   Voh isst dehr tsook nahkh MEWN-*khen?*

Is this the train for Frankfurt?
   Ist das der Zug nach Frankfurt?
   Isst dahss dehr tsook nahkh FRAHNK-*foort?*

When do we get to Vienna?
   Wann kommen wir in Wien an?
   Vahn KOHM-*men veer in veen ahn?*

Where is the dining car?
   Wo ist der Speisewagen?
   Voh isst dehr SHPY-*zeh-vah-g'n?*

Open the window.
   Machen Sie das Fenster auf.
   MAH-*khen zee dahss* FEHN-*stehr owf.*

Close the window.
   Machen Sie das Fenster zu.
   MAH-*khehn zee dahss* FEHN-*stehr tsoo.*

Where is the bus to the municipal park?
Wo ist der Obus zum Stadtpark?
Voh isst dehr OH-*boos tsoom* SHTAHT-*pahrk?*

I want to go to the broadcasting tower.
Ich möchte zum Funkturm fahren.
Ikh MUHKH-*teh tsoom* FOONK-*toorm* FAH-*r'n.*

Please tell me where to get off.
Bitte sagen Sie mir, wo ich aussteigen muss.
BIT-*teh* ZAH-*g'n zee meer voh ikh* OWS-*shty-g'n
mooss.*

Where is a gas station?
Wo ist eine Tankstelle?
Voh isst EYE-*neh* TAHNK-*shtehl-leh?*

Fill it up.
Machen Sie den Tank voll.
MAH-*khen zee den tahnk fohl.*

Check the oil.
Sehen Sie das Öl nach.
ZEH-*hen zee dahss uhl nahkh.*

water	tires
das Wasser	die Reifen
dahss VAHS-*sehr*	*dee* RYE-*fehn*

Something is wrong with the car.
Etwas ist mit dem Wagen los.
ETT-*vahss isst mitt dehm* VAH-*g'n lohs.*

Can you fix it?
Können Sie ihn reparieren?
KUHN-*nehn zee een reh-pah-*REE-*ren?*

How long will it take?
Wie lange wird es dauern?
Vee LAHN-*geh veert ess* DAH-*oo-ehrn?*

Is this the road to Bayreuth?
Ist das die Strasse nach Bayreuth?
Isst dahss dee SHTRAH-*seh nahkh bye-*ROIT?

Have you a map?
  Haben Sie eine Strassenkarte?
  HAH-*ben zee* EYE-*neh* SHTRAH-*s'n-kahr-teh?*

Where is the boat to . . . ?
  Wo ist das Boot nach . . . ?
  Voh isst dahss boat nahkh . . . ?

When does it leave?
  Wann geht es ab?
  Van geht ess ahp?

6. MAKING FRIENDS

Good day!   **My name is . . .**
  Guten Tag!   Mein Name ist . . .
  GOO-*ten tahk!*   *Mine* NAH-*meh isst . . .*

What is your name, Sir?
  Wie ist Ihr Name, mein Herr?
  Vee isst eer NAH-*meh, mine hehr?*

    Madam?   **Miss?**
      meine Dame?   Fräulein?
      MY-*neh* DAH-*meh?*   FROY-*line?*

I am delighted to meet you.
  Sehr erfreut.
  *Zehr ehr-*FROYT.

Do you speak English?   **A little.**
  Sprechen Sie Englisch?   Ein wenig.
  SHPREH-*khehn zee* EHN-*glish?*   *Ine* VEH-*nick.*

Do you understand?   **Please speak slowly.**
  Verstehn Sie?   Bitte langsamer.
  *Fehr-*SHTEHN *zee?*   BIT-*teh* LAHNK-*zah-mehr.*

I speak only a little German.
  Ich spreche nur ein wenig Deutsch.
  Ikh SHPREH-*kheh noor ine* VEH-*nick doytsh.*

I am from New York. **Where are you from?**
Ich komme aus New York. Woher sind Sie?
Ikh KOHM-*meh ows New York.* *Voh-*HAIR *zint zee?*

I like your country.
Ihr Land gefällt mir.
*Eer lahnt geh-*FEHLT *meer.*

I like your city.
Ihre Stadt gefällt mir.
EE-*reh shtaht geh-*FEHLT *meer.*

Have you been in America?
Waren Sie in Amerika?
VAH-*rehn zee in ah-*MEH-*ree-kah?*

This is my first visit here.
Ich bin das erste Mal hier.
Ikh been dahss EHR-*steh mahl here.*

May I sit here?
Kann ich mich hersetzen?
Kahn ikh meekh HAIR-*zeht-sen?*

Come here.
Kommen Sie her.
KOHM-*men Zee hehr.*

May I take your picture?
Darf ich Sie photographieren?
*Dahrf ikh zee foh-toh-grah-*FEE-*rehn?*

This is a picture of my wife.
Das ist ein Bild meiner Frau.
Dahss isst ine beelt MY-*nehr frow.*

>   **of my husband**
>   meines Mannes
>   MY-*nehs* MAHN-*ness*

>   **of my son** **of my daughter**
>   meines Sohnes meiner Tochter
>   MY-*nehss* ZOH-*nehss* MY-*nehr* TOHKH-*tehr*

of my mother
  meiner Mutter
  MY-*nehr* MOOT-*tehr*

of my father
  meines Vaters
  MY-*nehss* FAH-*tehrs*

of my sister
  meiner Schwester
  MY-*nehr* SHVESS-*tehr*

of my brother
  meines Bruders
  MY-*nehss* BROO-*dehrs*

Have you children?
  Haben Sie Kinder?
  HAH-*ben* zee KIN-*dehr?*

How beautiful!
  Wie schön!
  Vee shuhn!

Very interesting.
  Sehr interessant.
  *Zehr in-teh-reh-*SAHNT.

Would you like a cigarette?
  Zigarette gefällig?
  *Tsee-gah-*RET-*teh geh-*FEHL-*lick?*

Would you like something to drink?
  Möchten Sie etwas trinken?
  MUHKH-*ten zee* ETT-*vahss* TRIN-*ken?*

Would you like something to eat?
  Möchten Sie etwas essen?
  MUHKH-*ten zee* ETT-*vahss ess'n?*

Sit down, please.
  Nehmen Sie Platz, bitte.
  NEH-*men zee plahts,* BIT-*teh.*

Make yourself at home!
  Machen Sie sich's bequem!
  MAH-*khen zee zeekhs beh-*KVEHM!

Good luck!
  Viel Glück!
  Feel glewk!

To your health!
  Zum Wohl!
  Tsoom vohl!

When can I see you again?
  Wann kann ich Sie wiedersehen?
  Vahn kahn ikh zee VEE-*dehr-zeh-hen?*

Where shall we meet?
  Wo können wir uns treffen?
  Voh KUHN-*nehn veer oons* TREHF-*f'n?*

Here is my address.
  Hier ist meine Adresse.
  Here isst MY-*neh ah-*DRESS-*seh.*

What is your address?
  Wie ist Ihre Adresse?
  Vee isst EE-*reh ah-*DRESS-*seh?*

What is your phone number?
  Wie ist Ihre Telephonnumer?
  Vee isst EE-*reh teh-leh-*FOHN-*noom-mehr?*

May I speak to ...	**Mr.**
Ich möchte ...	Herrn
Ikh MUHKH-*teh ...*	*Hehrn*

Mrs.	**Miss**
Frau	Fräulein
Frow	FROY-*line*

Would you like to have lunch?
  Möchten Sie zu Mittag essen?
  MUHKH-*ten zee tsoo* MITT-*tahk ess'n?*

  to have dinner?
    zu Abend essen?
    tsoo AH-*bent* ESS'*n?*

go to the movies?	**go to the theatre?**
ins Kino gehn?	ins Theater gehn?-
inss KEE-*no gehn?*	*inss teh-*AHT'*r gehn?*

  go to the beach?
    an den Strand gehn?
    ahn dehn shtrahnt gain?

  take a walk?
    spazieren gehn?
    *shpah-*TSEE-*ren gain?*

With great pleasure.
Mit Vergnügen.
*Mitt fehr-*GNEW*-g'n.*

I am sorry
Ich bedauere.
*Ikh beh-*DAH*-oo-eh-reh.*

I cannot.
Ich kann nicht.
Ikh kahn nikht.

Another time.
Ein anderes Mal.
Ine AHN*-deh-ress mahl.*

I must go now.
Ich muss jetzt gehn.
Ikh mooss yehtst gain.

Thank you for a wonderful time.
Es war sehr schön. Ich danke Ihnen.
Ess vahr zehr shuhn. Ikh DAHN*-keh* EE*-nehn.*

Thank you for an excellent dinner.
Danke für das gute Diner.
DAHN*-keh fewr dahss* GOO*-teh dee-*NEH.

This is for you.
Das ist für Sie.
Dahss isst fewr zee.

You are very kind.
Sie sind sehr liebenswürdig.
Zee zint zehr LEE*-bens-vewr-dick.*

It's nothing, really.
Nicht der Rede wert.
Nikht dehr REH*-deh vehrt.*

With best regards.
Mit besten Grüssen.
Mitt BESS*-ten* GREW*-sehn.*

Congratulations!
Meinen Glückwunsch!
MY*-nehn* GLEWK*-voonsh!*

7. EMERGENCIES

Help!   **Police!**   **Fire!**
Zu Hilfe!   Polizei!   Feuer!
Tsoo HEEL-feh!   *Poh-lee-TSIGH!*   FOY-*ehr!*

Stop that man! (woman)   **Hurry up!**
Aufhalten!   Schnell!
OWF-*hahl-ten!*   *Shnell!*

I have been robbed!
Man hat mich bestohlen!
*Mahn haht meekh beh-*SHTOH-*len!*

Look out!   **Wait a minute!**
Aufpassen!   Einen Moment!
OWF-*pahs-sen!*   EYE-*nen moh-*MEN

Stop!   **Get out!**   **What's going on?**
Halt!   Hinaus!   Was ist los?
Hahlt!   *Heen-*OWSS!   *Vahss isst lohs?*

Entrance   **Exit**
Eingang   Ausgang
INE-*gahnk*   OWSS-*gahnk*

Ladies   **Gentlemen**
Damen   Herren
DAH-*men*   HEHR-*ren*

Danger!   **Keep out!**
Gefahr!   Eintritt verboten!
*Geh-*FAHR!   INE-*tritt fehr-*BOH-*ten!*

No smoking   **No parking**
Nichtraucher   Parken verboten
NIKHT-*row-khehr*   PAHR-*ken fehr-*BOH-*ten*

One way
Einbahnstrasse
INE-*bahn-shtrah-seh*

I am ill.
   Ich bin krank.
   Ikh been krahnk.

Call a doctor!
   Rufen Sie einen Arzt!
   ROO-*fehn zee* EYE-*nehn ahrtst!*

It hurts here.
   Es tut hier weh.
   Ehss toot here vay.

Where is the drugstore?
   Wo ist die Apotheke?
   *Vo isst dee ah-poh-*TEH-*keh?*

Take me to the hospital.
   Bringen Sie mich ins Spital.
   BRIN-*gehn zee mikh inss shpee-*TAHL.

Where is there a dentist?
   Wo ist ein Zahnarzt?
   Vo isst ine TSAHN-*ahrtst?*

I have lost my bag.
   Ich habe meinen Koffer verloren.
   Ikh HAH-*beh* MY-*nehn* KOHF-*fehr fehr-*LOH-*ren.*

my wallet
   meine Brieftasche
   MY-*neh* BREEF-*tah-sheh*

my camera
   meine Kamera
   MY-*neh* KAH-*meh-rah*

my passport
   meinen Pass
   MY-*nehn pahss*

I am an American.
   Ich bin Amerikaner.
   *Ikh been ah-meh-ree-*KAH-*nehr.*

Where is the American consulate?
   Wo ist das amerikanische Konsulat?
   *Voh isst dahss ah-meh-ree-*KAH-*nee-sheh kohn-soo-*LAHT?

Don't get excited.
   Nur keine Aufregung.
   Noor KIGH-*neh* OWF-*reh-goonk.*

Everything is all right.
   Alles ist in Ordnung.
   AHL-*less isst in* OHRD-*noonk.*

ITALIAN

Facts About Italian

Italian is spoken by about 60 million people in Italy and southern Switzerland, in Tunisia, Lybia, Somaliland, and Ethiopia, in some islands of the Mediterranean, in many communities of the United States and Argentina and other South American countries.

Almost all Italian words end in a vowel. This makes Italian an ideal language for singing and has resulted in the predominance of Italian in musical studies.

Italian is a Romance language, that is, descended directly from Latin. Although there exist certain regional dialects in various parts of Italy, the Italian used in this book will serve you wherever Italian is spoken.

Advice on Accent

Particular attention should be paid to the following Italian letters:

r is trilled on the front teeth and **rr** trilled more.
c before *i* and *e* has the sound of **ch** in English, and **ch** has the sound of the English **k**.
sc before *i* and *e* is always like **sh** in English.
gh is always like **g** in *get;* **gli** followed by a vowel is like **lli** in *million*.
gn like **ny** in *canyon*.
z sounds like **ts**.

You Already Know Some Italian

Many Italian and English words share a common descent from Latin, although almost all English words ending in *-tion* end in Italian in *-zione:* revolution *revoluzione,* constitution *costituzione,* institution *istituzione.*

Many adverbs ending in *-ly* in English are the same in Italian but end in *-mente:* naturally *naturalmente,* generally *generalmente,* rapidly *rapidamente.*

English words ending in *-ment* end in *-mento* in Italian: compliment *complimento,* regiment *regimento.*

English words ending in *-ble* end in *-bile* in Italian: possible *possibile,* honorable *onorabile,* etc.

Many English nouns ending in *-ty* exist in Italian but end in *-tà:* quality *qualità,* liberty *libertà,* city *città.*

Besides words such as those referred to above, you are no doubt familiar with many Italian words pertaining to the arts or cuisine which have become a part of English. Everyone will recognize such words as *fortissimo* (very strong), *allegro* (lively), *opera* (work), *spaghetti* (strings), and *bravo!* (brave).

1. FIRST CONTACT

Yes.	**No.**	**Good.**
Sí.	No.	Bene.
See.	*No.*	BEH-*neh.*

Thank you.
Grazie.
GRAH-*ts'yeh.*

You are welcome.
Prego.
PREH-*goh.*

Excuse me.
Scusi.
SKOO-*zee.*

It's all right.
Va bene.
Vah BEH-*neh.*

Please.
Per piacere.
Pehr p'yah-CHEH-*reh.*

I would like ...
Vorrei ...
Vohr-RAY ...

What?
Che cosa?
Keh KOH-*sah?*

This.
Questo.
Kwess-toh.

Where?
Dove?
DOH-*veh?*

There.
Lì, là.
Lee, lah.

When? **Now.** **Later.**
Quando? Adesso. Più tardi.
KWAHN-*doh?* *Ah-*DES-*soh.* *P'yoo* TAHR-*dee.*

Who? **I** **you** **he** **she**
Chi? io Lei egli ella
Kee? EE-*oh* *lay* EHL-*yee* EHL-*lah*

Your name?
Il Suo nome?
Eel swoh NOH-*meh?*

Good morning, good day.
Buon giorno.
Bwohn DJOHR-*noh.*

Good evening.
Buona sera.
BWOH-*nah* SEH-*rah.*

Good night.
  Buona notte.
  BWOH-*nah* NOHT-*teh.*

Good-by.
  Arrivederci.
  *Ahr-ree-veh-*DEIIR-*chee.*

How are you?
  Come sta?
  KOH-*meh stah?*

Very well, thank you. And you?
  Benissimo, grazie. E Lei?
  *Beh-*NEES-*see-moh,* GRAH-*ts'yeh. Eh lay?*

How much?
  Quanto?
  KWAHN-*toh?*

I do not understand, please repeat.
  Non capisco, ripeta, per piacere.
  *Nohn kah-*PEES-*koh, ree-*PEH-*tah, pehr p'yah-*CHEH-
  reh.

One	**two**	**three**
uno	due	tre
OO-*noh*	DOO-*eh*	*treh*

four	**five**	**six**
quattro	cinque	sei
KWAHT-*troh*	CHIN-*kweh*	*say*

seven	**eight**	**nine**
sette	otto	nove
SET-*teh*	OHT-*toh*	NOH-*veh*

ten	**eleven**	**twelve**
dieci	undici	dodici
*d'*YEH-*chee*	OON-*dee-chee*	DOH-*dee-chee*

2. ACCOMMODATIONS

Where is a good hotel?
  Dov'è un buon albergo?
  *doh-*VEH *oon bwohn ahl-*BEHR-*goh?*

I want a room for one person.
Desidero una camera per una persona.
*Deh-*SEE*-deh-roh* OO-*nah* KAH-*meh-rah per* OO-*nah
per-*SOH*-nah.*

I want a room for two.
Desidero una camera per due.
*Deh-*SEE*-deh-roh* OO-*nah* KAH-*meh-rah pehr* DOO-*eh.*

I want a room with bath.
Desidero una camera con bagno.
*Deh-*SEE*-deh-roh* OO-*nah* KAH-*meh-rah kohn* BAH-*
n'yoh.*

I want a room for two days.
Desidero una camera per due giorni.
*Deh-*SEE*-deh-roh* OO-*nah* KAH-*meh-rah pehr* DOO-*eh*
DJOHR-*nee.*

I want a room for a week.
Desidero una camera per una settimana.
*Deh-*SEE*-deh-roh* OO-*nah* KAH-*meh-rah pehr* OO-*nah
set-tee-*MAH*-nah.*

till Monday fino a lunedì FEE-*noh ah loo-neh-*DEE	**Tuesday** martedì *mahr-teh-*DEE
Wednesday mercoledì *mehr-koh-leh-*DEE	**Thursday** giovedì *djoh-veh-*DEE
Friday venerdì *veh-nehr-*DEE	**Saturday** sabato SAH-*bah-toh*
Sunday domenica *doh-*MEH*-nee-kah*	

How much is it?
Quanto costa?
KWAHN-*toh* KOHS-*tah?*

Here are my bags.
    Ecco le mie valige.
    EHK-*koh leh* MEE-*eh vah-*LEE-*djeh.*

Here is my passport.
    Ecco il mio passaporto.
    EHK-*koh eel* MEE-*oh pahs-sah-*POHR-*toh.*

I like it.	**I do not like it.**
Mi piace.	Non mi piace.
*Mee p'*YAH-*cheh.*	*Nohn mee p'*YAH-*cheh.*

Show me another, please.
    Me ne mostri un'altra, prego.
    Meh neh MOHS-*tree oon* AHL-*trah,* PREH-*goh.*

Where is the toilet?
    Dov'è il gabinetto?
    *Doh-*VEH *eel gah-bee-*NET-*toh?*

Where is the men's room?
    Dov'è la toeletta per signori?
    *Doh-*VEH *lah toh-eh-*LET-*tah pehr see-n'*YOH-*ree?*

Where is the ladies' room?
    Dov'è la toeletta per signore?
    *Doh-*VEH *lah toh-eh-*LET-*tah per see-n'*YOH-*reh?*

hot water	**a towel**
acqua calda	un asciugamani
AHK-*kwah* KAHL-*dah*	*oon ah-shoo-gah-*MAH-*nee*

soap
    sapone
    *sah-*POH-*neh*

Please have this washed.
    Per piacere, mi faccia lavare questo.
    *Pehr p'yah-*CHEH-*reh mee* FAHT-*chah lah-*VAH-*reh*
    KWESS-*toh.*

cleaned	**pressed**
lavare a secco	stirare
*lah-*VAH-*reh ah* SEHK-*koh*	*stee-*RAH-*reh*

When will it be ready?
Quando sarà pronto?
KWAHN-*doh sah*-RAH PROHN-*toh?*

I need it for tonight.
Lo voglio per questa sera.
Loh VOH-*l'yoh pehr* KWESS-*tah* SEH-*rah.*

> **for tomorrow**
> per domani
> *pehr doh*-MAH-*nee*

My key, please.
La mia chiave, per piacere.
Lah MEE-*ah k'*YAH-*veh pehr p'yah*-CHEH-*reh.*

Any letters for me?
C'è posta per me?
Cheh POHS-*tah pehr meh?*

I want five airmail stamps for the United States.
Vorrei cinque francobolli per via aerea per gli
Stati Uniti.
Vohr-RAY CHEEN-*kweh frahn-koh*-BOHL-*lee pehr*
VEE-*ah ah*-EH-*reh-ah pehr l'yee* STAH-*tee* OO-NEE-
tee.

Have you any postcards?
Ha cartoline postali?
Ah kahr-toh-LEE-*neh poh*-STAH-*lee?*

I would like to send a telegram.
Vorrei spedire un telegramma.
Vohr-RAY *speh*-DEE-*reh oon teh-leh*-GRAHM-*mah.*

Call me at seven in the morning.
Mi chiami alle sette della mattina.
*Mee k'*YAH-*mee* AHL-*leh* SEHT-*teh* DEHL-*lah maht-*
TEE-*nah.*

Where is the telephone?   **Hello!**
Dov'è il telefono?   Pronto!
Doh-VEH *eel teh*-LEH-*foh-noh?*   PROHN-*toh!*

Please bring breakfast to room 702.
  Per piacere, mi porti la colazione nella camera
  settecento due.
  *Pehr p'yah-*CHEH*-reh, mee* POHR*-tee lah koh-lah-*
  TS'YOH*-neh* NEHL*-lah* KAH*-meh-rah set-teh-*CHEN*-*
  toh DOO*-eh.*

orange juice
  succo di arancia
  SOOK*-koh dee ah-*RAHN*-chah*

ham and eggs
  uova con prosciutto
  WOH*-vah kohn proh-*SHOOT*-toh*

rolls and coffee
  panini e caffè
  *pah-*NEE*-nee eh kahf-*FEH

I am expecting a friend.
  Attendo un amico, una amica.
  *Aht-*TEHN*-doh oon ah-*MEE*-koh,* OO*-nah ah-*MEE*-*
  kah.

Tell him (her) to wait.
  Gli (Le) dica di aspettare.
  L'yee (Leh) DEE*-kah dee ahs-peht-*TAH*-reh.*

Tell me, please, where is a restaurant.
  Mi dica, per piacere, dov'è un ristorante.
  Mee DEE*-kah pehr p'yah-*CHEH*-reh doh-*VEH *oon*
  *ree-stoh-*RAHN*-teh.*

  a barber shop   **a hairdresser**
    un barbiere   un parrucchiere
    *oon bahr-*B'YEH*-reh*   *oon pahr-rook-*K'YEH*-reh*

  a drugstore
    una farmacia
    OO*-nah fahr-mah-*CHEE*-ah*

What is the address?
 Qual'è l'indirizzo?
 *Kwahl-*EH *leen-dee-*REET*-tsoh?*

What is the telephone number?
 Qual'è il numero telefonico?
 *Kwahl-*EH *eel* NOO*-meh-roh teh-leh-*FOH*-nee-koh?*

I would like to change some money.
 Vorrei cambiare del denaro.
 *Vohr-*RAY *kahm-*B'YAH*-reh dehl deh-*NAH*-roh.*

What is the rate for dollars?
 Qual'è il cambio per dollaro?
 *Kwahl-*EH *eel* KAHM*-b'yoh pehr* DOHL*-lah-roh?*

thirteen tredici TREH-*dee-chee*	**fourteen** quattordici *kwaht-*TOHR-*dee-chee*
fifteen quindici KWEEN-*dee-chee*	**sixteen** sedici SEH-*dee-chee*
seventeen diciasette *dee-chahs-*SET-*teh*	**eighteen** diciotto *dee-*CHOHT-*toh*

nineteen diciannove *dee-chahn-*NOH-*veh*	**twenty** venti VEHN-*tee*	**twenty-one** ventuno *vehn-*TOO-*noh*
thirty trenta TREHN-*tah*	**forty** quaranta *kwah-*RAHN-*tah*	**fifty** cinquanta *cheen-*KWAHN-*tah*
sixty sessanta *seh-*SAHN-*tah*	**seventy** settanta *seht-*TAHN-*tah*	**eighty** ottanta *oht-*TAHN-*tah*
ninety novanta *noh-*VAHN-*tah*	**one hundred** cento CHEHN-*toh*	**two hundred** duecento *dweh-*CHEHN-*toh*

three hundred	one thousand	two thousand
trecento	mille	duemila
*treh-*CHEHN*-toh*	MEEL*-leh*	*dweh-*MEE*-lah*

ten thousand	one hundred thousand
diecimila	centomila
*d'yeh-chee-*MEE*-lah*	*chehn-toh-*MEE*-lah*

one million
un milione
*oon mee-*L'YOH*-neh*

My bill, please.
Il conto, per piacere.
Eel KOHN*-toh, pehr p'yah-*CHEH*-reh.*

3. EATING

Where is a good restaurant?
Dov'è un buon ristorante?
*Doh-*VEH *oon bwohn ree-stoh-*RAHN*-teh?*

A table for two, please.
Una tavola per due, per piacere.
OO*-nah* TAH*-voh-lah pehr-*DOO*-eh, pehr p'yah-*CHEH*-reh.*

Waiter!	**Waitress!**
Cameriere!	Cameriera!
*Kah-meh-*R'YEH*-reh!*	*Kah-meh-*R'YEH*-rah!*

The menu, please.
La lista, per piacere.
Lah LEE*-stah, pehr p'yah-*CHEH*-reh.*

What is good today?	**Is it ready?**
Che c'è di buono oggi?	È pronto?
Keh cheh dee BWOH*-noh* OH*-dgee?*	*Eh* PROHN*-toh?*

How long will it take?
Quanto tempo ci vuole?
KWAHN-*toh* TEHM-*poh chee* VWOH-*leh?*

This, please ...   **and this**
Questo, per piacere ...   e questo
KWEH-*stoh, pehr* p'yah-CHEH-*reh* ...   *eh* KWEH-*stoh*

Bring me ...   **water**   **milk**
Mi porti ...   acqua   latte
Mee POHR-*tee* ...   AHK-*kwah*   LAHT-*teh*

    a glass of beer
    un bicchiere di birra
    oon beek-K'YEH-*reh dee* BEER-*rah*

red wine   **white wine**
vino rosso   vino bianco
VEE-*noh* ROHS-*soh*   VEE-*noh* B'YAHN-*koh*

a cocktail   **whisky soda**
un cocktail   un whiskey soda
oon cocktail   *oon whiskey soda*

soup   **fish**   **meat**
zuppa   pesce   carne
tsoop-pah   PEH-*sheh*   KAHR-*neh*

a sandwich   **bread and butter**
un panino   pane e burro
oon pah-NEE-*noh*   PAH-*neh eh* BOOR-*roh*

vegetable soup
minestrone
mee-ness-TROH-*neh*

steak ...   **rare**   **medium**
bistecca ...   al sangue   media
bee-STEH-*kah* ...   *ahl* SAHN-*gveh*   MEH-*d'yah*

    well done   **salt and pepper**
    ben cotta   sale e pepe
    behn KOHT-*tah*   SAH-*leh eh* PEH-*peh*

roast chicken
pollo arrosto
POHL-*loh* ahr-ROH-*stoh*

veal cutlet
cotoletta di vitello
*koh-toh-*LET-*tah dee vee-*TEHL-*loh*

lamb chop
costoletta di agnello
*kohs-toh-*LET-*tah dee ah-*N'YEHL-*loh*

pork roast
arrosto di maiale
*ahr-*ROH-*stoh dee mah-*YAH-*leh*

sole meunière
sogliola alla mugnaia
SOH-*l'yoh-lah* AHL-*lah moo-*N'YAH-*yah*

filet of veal
filetto di vitello
*fee-*LEHT-*toh dee vee-*TEHL-*loh*

with potatoes...	fried	mashed
con patate...	fritte	purée
*kohn pah-*TAH-*teh* ...	FREET-*teh*	*pew-*REH

boiled	an omelet	rice
bollite	una frittata	riso
*bohl-*LEE-*teh*	OO-*nah freet-*TAH-*tah*	REE-*zoh*

And what vegetables?	peas
E quali legumi?	piselli
Eh KWAH-*lee leh-*GOO-*mee?*	*pee-*ZEHL-*lee*

carrots	beans	onions
carote	fagioli	cipolle
*kah-*ROH-*teh*	*fah-*JOH-*lee*	*chee-*POHL-*leh*

mushrooms
funghi
FOON-*ghee*

a salad
una insalata
OO-*nah een-sah-*LAH-*tah*

lettuce
lattuga
*laht-*TOO-*gah*

tomatoes
pomodori
*poh-moh-*DOH-*ree*

cucumber
cetriolo
*cheh-tree-*OH-*loh*

Please bring me another fork.
Per piacere, mi porti un'altra forchetta.
*Pehr p'yah-*CHEH-*reh, mee* POHR-*tee oon* AHL-*trah fohr-*KEHT-*tah.*

knife
coltello
*kohl-*TEHL-*loh*

spoon
cucchiaio
*kook-*K'YAH-*yoh*

a glass
un bicchiere
*oon beek-*K'YEH-*reh*

a plate
un piatto
oon P'YAHT-*toh*

What is there for dessert?
Che c'è per dessert?
Keh CHEH *pehr dehs-*SEHR?

cheese
formaggio
*fohr-*MAH-*djoh*

fruit
frutta
FROOT-*tah*

pastry
pasticceria
*pah-stee-cheh-*REE-*ah*

cake
torta
TOHR-*tah*

ice cream
gelato
*jeh-*LAH-*toh*

Some coffee, please.
Caffè, per piacere.
*Kahf-*FEH, *pehr p'yah-*CHEH-*reh.*

cream
crema
KREH-*mah*

sugar
zucchero
TZOOK-*keh-roh*

tea with lemon
tè con limone
*teh kohn lee-*MOH-*neh*

mineral water
acqua minerale
AHK-*kwah mee-neh-*RAH-*leh*

A little more, please.
Un po' di più, per piacere.
*Oon poh dee p'yoo, pehr p'yah-*CHEH*-reh.*

That's enough.
Basta.
BAH-*stah.*

The check, please.
Il conto, per piacere.
Eel KOHN-*toh, pehr p'yah-*CHEH*-reh.*

Is the service included?
Il servizio è incluso?
*Eel sehr-*VEE*-ts'yoh eh een-*KLOO*-zoh?*

It was very good!
Tutto era buonissimo!
Toot-toh EH-*rah bwoh-*NEES*-see-moh!*

4. SHOPPING

I would like to buy this . . .
Vorrei comprare questo . . .
*Vohr-*RAY *kohm-*PRAH*-reh* KWEH-*stoh . . .*

and that
e quello
eh KWEHL-*loh*

I am just looking around.
Sto guardando in giro.
*Stoh gwahr-*DAHN*-doh een* JEE-*roh.*

Where is the department for . . .
Dov'è il reparto di . . .
*Dohv-*EH *eel reh-*PAHR*-toh dee . . .*

men's clothing
abiti per signore
AH-*bee-tee pehr see-*N'YOH*-reh*

women's clothing
abiti per signora
AH-*bee-tee pehr see-*N'YOH-*rah*

underwear
biancheria
*b'yahn-keh-*REE-*ah*

stockings	**shirts**	
calze	camice	
KAHL-*tseh*	*kah-*MEE-*cheh*	

shoes	**hats**	**gloves**
scarpe	cappelli	guanti
SKAHR-*peh*	*kahp-*PEHL-*lee*	GWAHN-*tee*

My size in America is . . .
Il mio numero in America è . . .
Eel MEE-*oh* NOO-*meh-roh een ah-*MEH-*ree-kah*
eh . . .

toys	**perfumes**
giocattoli	profumi
*joh-*KAHT-*toh-lee*	*proh-*FOO-*mee*

jewelry	**watches**
gioielli	orologi
*joh-*YEHL-*lee*	*oh-roh-*LOH-*jee*

toilet articles
articoli da toletta
*ahr-*TEE-*koh-lee dah toh-*LEHT-*tah*

sports articles
articoli da giuoco
*ahr-*TEE-*koh-lee dah joo-*OH-*koh*

films	**souvenirs**
pellicole	ricordi
*pehl-*LEE-*koh-leh*	*ree-*KOHR-*dee*

Show me . . .	**another one**
Mi mostri . . .	un altro, un'altra
*mee-*MOH-*stree . . .*	*oon* AHL-*troh, oon* AHL-*trah*

something less expensive
qualcosa di più a buon mercato
*kwahl-*KOH*-zah dee p'yoo ah bwohn mehr-*
KAH-toh

a better quality
una migliore qualità
OO*-nah mee-*L'YOH*-reh kwah-lee-*TAH

larger
più largo, larga
p'yoo LAHR*-goh,* LAHR*-gah*

smaller
più piccolo, piccola
p'yoo PEEK*-koh-loh,* PEEK*-koh-lah*

I don't like the color.
Non mi piace il colore.
*Nohn mee p'*YAH*-cheh eel koh-*LOH*-reh.*

I want one ...
Ne voglio uno ...
Neh VOH*-l'yoh* OO*-noh ...*

in green
in verde
een VEHR*-deh*

in yellow
in giallo
een JAHL*-loh*

in blue
in azzurro
*een aht-*TSOO*-roh*

red
rosso
ROHS*-soh*

black
nero
NEH*-roh*

white
bianco
B'YAHN*-koh*

grey
grigio
GREE*-joh*

pink
rosa
ROH*-zah*

brown
marrone
*mahr-*ROH*-neh*

I shall take it with me.
Lo prendo con me.
Loh PREHN*-doh kohn meh.*

Send it to this address.
Lo mandi a questo indirizzo.
Loh MAHN*-dee ah* KWEH*-stoh een-dee-*REE*-tsoh.*

A receipt, please.
  Una ricevuta, per piacere.
  oo-*nah ree-cheh-*voo-*tah, pehr p'yah-*CHEH-*reh.*

Where is a flower shop?
  Dov'è un fioraio?
  *Dohv-*EH *oon f'yoh-*RAH-*yoh?*

  a food market?
    negozio di generi alimentari?
    *neh-*GOH-*ts'yoh dee* JEH-*neh-ree ah-lee-men-*
    TAH-*ree?*

5. TRANSPORTATION

Taxi!
  Tassì!
  *Tahs-*SEE!

Take me to the airport.
  Mi conduca all'aeroporto.
  *Mee kohn-*DOO-*kah ahl-lah-eh-roh-*POHR-*toh.*

Turn left.
  Giri a sinistra.
  JEE-*ree ah see-*NEE-*strah.*

Turn right.
  Giri a destra.
  JEE-*ree ah* DEH-*strah.*

Not so fast!
  Non così presto!
  *Nohn koh-*SEE PREH-*stoh!*

Hurry up!
  Faccia presto!
  FAH-*chah* PREH-*stoh!*

Stop here!
  Fermi qui!
  FEHR-*mee kwee!*

Wait for me!
  Mi aspetti!
  *Mee ah-*SPEHT-*tee!*

How much is it?
  Quanto è?
  KWAHN-*toh eh?*

How much is it to . . . ?
  Quanto è per . . . ?
  KWAHN-*toh eh pehr . . . ?*

and back?
  e ritorno?
  *eh ree-*TOHR-*noh?*

How much by the hour?   by the day?
    Quanto per ora?   per giorno?
    KWAHN-*toh pehr* OH-*rah?*   *pehr* JOHR-*noh?*

Show me the sights.
    Mi mostri le cose da vedere.
    Mee MOH-*stree leh* KOH-*seh dah veh*-DEH-*reh.*

What is that building?
    Che edificio è questo?
    Keh eh-dee-FEE-*choh eh* KWESS-*toh?*

May I visit it?
    Si può visitare?
    *See pwoh vee-see-*TAH-*reh?*

I would like to see the Coliseum.
    Vorrei vedere il Colosseo.
    Vohr-RAY *veh*-DEH-*reh eel koh*-LOHS-*seh-oh.*

To the railroad station, please.
    Alla stazione, per piacere.
    AHL-*lah stah-*TS'YOH-*neh, pehr p'yah-*CHEH-*reh.*

Porter!   **I have two bags.**
    Facchino!   Ho due valige.
    Fahk-KEE-*noh!*   *Oh* DOO-*eh vah*-LEE-*jeh.*

A ticket to . . .
    Un biglietto per . . .
    *Oon bee-l'*YET-*toh pehr . . .*

one way   **round trip**
    andata soltanto   andata e ritorno
    ahn-DAH-*tah sohl*-TAHN-*toh*   *eh ree*-TOHR-*noh*

first class   **second class**
    prima classe   seconda classe
    PREE-*mah* KLAHS-*seh*   *seh*-KOHN-*dah* KLAHS-*seh*

Where is the train to Florence?
    Dov'è il treno per Firenze?
    Dohv-EH *eel* TREH-*noh pehr fee*-REHN-*tseh?*

When does it leave?
  Quando parte?
  KWAHN-*doh* PAHR-*teh?*

Is this the train to Venice?
  È questo il treno per Venezia?
  Eh KWEH-*stoh eel* TREH-*noh pehr veh*-NEH-*ts'yah?*

When do we get to Milan?
  Quando arrivamo a Milano?
  KWAHN-*doh ahr-ree-*VAH-*moh ah mee-*LAH-*noh?*

Where is the dining car?
  Dov'è la carrozza ristorante?
  *Dohv-*EH *lah kahr-*ROHT-*tsah ree-stoh-*RAHN-*teh?*

Open the window.
  Apra il finestrino.
  AH-*prah eel fee-neh-*STREE-*noh.*

Close the window.
  Chiuda il finestrino.
  K'YOO-*dah eel fee-neh-*STREE-*noh.*

Where is the bus to the Villa d'Este?
  Dov'è l'autobus per la villa d'Este?
  *Dohv-*EH *lah-oo-toh-boos pehr la* VEEL-*lah* DEH-*steh?*

I would like to go to . . .
  Vorrei andare a . . .
  *Vohr-*RAY *ahn-*DAH-*reh ah . . .*

Please, tell me where to get off.
  Per piacere, mi dica dove scendere.
  *Pehr p'yah-*CHEH-*reh, mee* DEE-*kah* DOH-*veh* SHEHN-*deh-reh.*

Where is a gas station?
  Dov'è un'autorimessa?
  *Dohv-*EH *oon'ah-oo-toh-ree-*MEHS-*sah?*

Fill it up!
Faccia il pieno!
FAH-*tchah eel* P'YEH-*noh!*

Check the oil . . .
Verifichi l'olio . . .
*Veh-*REE-*fee-kee* LOH-*l'yoh* . . .

water	tires
l'acqua	le ruote
LAHK-*kwah*	*leh* RWOH-*teh*

Something is wrong with the car.
C'è qualche cosa che non va.
Cheh KWAHL-*keh* KOH-*sah keh nohn vah.*

Can you fix it?
Si può ripararlo?
*See pwoh ree-pah-*RAHR-*loh?*

Is this the road to Naples?
È questa la strada per Napoli?
Eh KWEH-*stah lah* STRAH-*dah pehr* NAH-*poh-lee?*

Where is the boat to . . .
Dov'è la nave per . . .
*Dohv-*EH *lah* NAH-*veh pehr* . . .

When does it leave?
Quando parte?
KWAHN-*doh* PAHR-*teh?*

6. MAKING FRIENDS

Good day.
Buon giorno.
Bwohn JOHR-*noh.*

How do you do?
Come sta?
KOH-*meh stah?*

My name is . . .
Il mio nome è . . .
Eel MEE-*oh* NOH-*meh eh* . . .

What is your name, Sir?
  Quale è il Suo nome, signore?
  KWAH-*leh eh eel* SOO-*oh* NOH-*meh see-n'yOH-reh?*

What is your name, Madam?
  Quale è il Suo nome, signora?
  KWAH-*leh eh eel* SOO-*oh* NOH-*meh see-n'yOH-rah?*

What is your name, Miss?
  Quale è il Suo nome, signorina?
  KWAH-*leh eh eel* SOO-*oh* NOH-*meh see-n'yoh-*REE-
    nah?

I am delighted to see you.
  Piacere di vederLa.
  *P'yah-*CHEH-*reh dee veh-*DEHR-*lah.*

Do you speak English?
  Parla inglese?
  PAHR-*lah een-*GLEH-*seh?*

A little.   **Do you understand?**
  Un poco.   Capisce?
  Oon POH-*koh.*   *Kah-*PEE-*sheh?*

Please speak slowly.
  Parli lentamente.
  PAHR-*lee lehn-tah-*MEHN-*teh.*

I speak only a little Italian.
  Parlo solamente un poco italiano.
  PAHR-*loh soh-lah-*MEN-*teh oon* POH-*koh ee-tah-*
    l'yAH-noh.

I am from New York.
  Vengo da Nuova York.
  VEHN-*goh dah Noo-*OH-*vah York.*

Where are you from?
  Da dove viene?
  Dah DOH-*veh v'yEH-neh?*

I like your country ... your city.
   Mi piace il suo paese ... la sua città.
   Mee p'YAH-cheh eel soo-*oh pah-*EH-*zeh ... lah* soo-*ah cheet-*TAH.

Have you been in America?
   È stato in America?
   Eh STAH-*toh een Ah-*MEH-*ree-kah?*

This is my first visit here.
   Ci sono per la prima volta.
   Chee SOH-*noh pehr lah* PREE-*mah* VOHL-*tah.*

May I sit here?
   Posso sedermi qui?
   POHS-*soh seh-*DEHR-*mee kwee?*

May I take your picture?
   Posso farLe una foto?
   POHS-*soh* FAHR-*leh* OO-*nah* FOH-*toh?*

Come here.
   Venga qui.
   VEHN-*gah* KWEE.

This is a picture of my wife.
   Questa è la foto di mia moglie.
   KWESS-*tah eh lah* FOH-*toh dee* MEE-*ah* MOH-*l'yeh.*

my husband
  mio marito.
  MEE-*oh mah-*REE-*toh*
	my son
	  mio figlio
	  MEE-*oh* FEE-*l'yoh*

my daughter
  mia figlia
  MEE-*ah* FEE-*l'yah*
	my mother
	  mia madre
	  MEE-*ah* MAH-*dreh*

my father
  mio padre
  MEE-*oh* PAH-*dreh*
	my sister
	  mia sorella
	  MEE-*ah soh-*REHL-*lah*

my brother
  mio fratello
  MEE-*oh frah-*TEHL-*loh*	

Have you children?
  Ha bambini?
  *Ah bahm-*BEE-*nee?*

What a beautiful child!
  Che bel bambino!
  *Keh behl bahm-*BEE-*noh!*

Very interesting!
  Molto interessante!
  MOHL-*toh een-teh-rehs-*SAHN-*teh!*

Would you like a cigarette?
  Vuole una sigaretta?
  VWOH-*leh oo-nah see-gah-*RET-*tah?*

Would you like something to drink?
  Qualche cosa da bere?
  KWAHL-*keh* KOH-*sah dah* BEH-*reh?*

Would you like something to eat?
  Qualche cosa da mangiare?
  KWAHL-*keh* KOH-*sah dah mahn-*JAH-*reh?*

Sit down please.
  Prego si accomodi.
  PREH-*goh see ahk-*KOH-*moh-dee.*

Good luck!
  Buona fortuna!
  BWOH-*nah fohr-*TOO-*nah!*

To your health!
  Salute!
  *sah-*LOO-*teh!*

When can I see you again?
  Quando posso rivederLa?
  KWAHN-*doh* POHS-*soh ree-veh-*DEHR-*lah?*

Where shall we meet?
  Dove ci incontreremo?
  DOH-*veh chee een-kohn-treh-*REH-*moh?*

Here is my address.
  Ecco il mio indirizzo.
  EHK-*koh eel* MEE-*oh een-dee-*REET-*tsoh.*

What is your address?
Qual'è il Suo indirizzo?
*Kwahl-*EH *eel* SOO-*oh een-dee-*REET-*tsoh?*

What is your phone number?
Qual'è il Suo numero del telefono?
*Kwahl-*EH *eel* SOO-*oh* NOO-*meh-roh del teh-*LEH-*foh-noh?*

May I speak to ...
Posso parlare a ...
POHS-*soh pahr-*LAH-*reh* ah ...

Would you like to have lunch?
Vuole fare colazione?
VWOH-*leh* FAH-*reh koh-laht-see-*OH-*neh?*

have dinner?
vuole pranzare?
VWOH-*leh prahn-*TSAH-*reh?*

go to the movies?
andare al cinema?
*ahn-*DAH-*reh ahl* CHEE-*neh-mah?*

go to the theatre?
andare a teatro?
*ahn-*DAH-*reh ah teh-*AH-*troh?*

go to the beach?
andare alla spiaggia?
*ahn-*DAH-*reh* AHL-*lah sp'*YAHD-*jah?*

take a walk?
fare una passeggiata?
FAH-*reh oo-nah pahs-sehd-*JAH-*tah?*

With great pleasure!
Volentieri!
*Voh-len-t'*YEH-*ree!*

I am sorry.
Mi dispiace.
*Mee dee-sp'*YAH-*cheh.*

I cannot.
Non posso.
Nohn POHS-*soh.*

Another time.
Un'altra volta.
*Oon-*AHL*-trah* VOHL*-tah.*

I must go now.
Devo andare.
DEH*-voh ahn-*DAH*-reh.*

Thank you for a wonderful time.
Grazie della bell'ora trascorsa insieme.
GRAH*-ts'yeh* DEHL*-lah behl-*OH*-rah tra-*SKOHR*-sah*
*een-s'*YEH*-meh.*

Thank you for an excellent dinner.
Grazie per l'eccelente pranzo.
GRAH*-ts'yeh per l'eht-cheh-*LEN*-teh* PRAHN*-tsoh.*

This is for you.
Questo è per lei.
KWESS*-toh eh per lay.*

You are very kind.
Lei è molto gentile.
Lay eh MOHL*-toh jehn* IEE*-leh.*

It's nothing really.
Non è niente.
*Nohn eh nee-*EHN*-teh.*

With best regards!
Con i migliori saluti!
*Kohn ee mee-l'*YOH*-ree sah-*LOO*-tee!*

Congratulations!
Congratulazioni!
*Kohn-grah-too-lah-ts'*YOH*-nee!*

7. EMERGENCIES

Help!
Aiuto!
*Ah-*YOO*-toh!*

Police!
Polizia!
*Poh-lee-*TSEE*-ah!*

Fire!
Fuoco!
*Foo-*OH*-koh!*

Stop that man!
Fermi quell'uomo!
FEHR*-mee 'kwehl-*WOH*-moh!*

Stop that woman!
Fermi quella donna!
FEHR-*mee* KWEHL-*lah* DOHN-*nah!*

I have been robbed!
Sono stato derubato!
SOH-*noh* STAH-*toh* deh-roo-BAH-*toh!*

Look out!
Attenzione!
*At-ten-ts'*YOH-*neh!*

Wait a minute!
Aspetti un minuto!
*Ahs-*PET-*tee* oon mee-NOO-*toh!*

Stop!	**Get out!**	**Hurry up!**
Fermi!	Fuori!	Presto!
FEHR-*meeh!*	*Foo-*OH-*ree!*	PREHS-*toh!*

Don't bother me!	**What's going on?**
Non mi disturbi!	Che succede?
*Nohn mee dee-*STOOR-*bee!*	*Keh soot-*CHEH-*deh?*

Entrance	**Exit**
Entrata	Uscita
*Ehn-*TRAH-*tah*	*Oo-*SHEE-*tah*

Ladies	**Gentlemen**
Signore	Signori
*See-n'*YOH-*reh*	*See-n'*YOH-*ree*

Danger!	**No smoking**
Pericolo!	Vietato fumare
*Peh-*REE-*koh-loh!*	*V'yeh-*TAH-*toh foo-*MAH-*reh*

Keep out!
Vietato l'ingresso!
*V'yeh-*TAH-*toh l'een-*GREHS-*soh!*

No parking	**One way**
Divieto di sosta .	Senso unico
*Dee-v'*YEH-*toh dee* SOHS-*tah*	SEHN-*soh* OO-*nee-koh*

I am ill.
  Sono malato.
  SOH-*noh mah-*LAH-*toh.*

It hurts here.
  Fa male qui.
  Fah MAH-*leh kwee.*

Call a doctor!
  Chiami un dottore!
  *K'*YAH-*mee oon doht-*TOH-*reh!*

Take me to the hospital!
  Mi conduca all'ospedale!
  *Mee kohn-*DOO-*kah ahl ohs-peh-*DAH-*leh!*

Where is there a dentist?
  Dov'è un dentista?
  *Doh-*VEH *oon den-*TEES-*tah?*

I have lost my bag.
  Ho perduto la mia valigia.
  *Oh per-*DOO-*toh lah* MEE-*ah vah-*LEE-*djah.*

    my wallet.
      il mio portafoglio.
      eel MEE-*oh pohr-tah-*FOH-*l'yoh.*

    my camera.
      la mia macchina fotografica.
      lah MEE-*ah* MAHK-*kee-nah foh-toh-*GRAH-*fee-kah.*

    my passport.
      il mio passaporto.
      eel MEE-*oh pah-sah-*POHR-*toh.*

I am an American.
  Sono americano.
  SOH-*noh ah-meh-ree-*KAH-*noh.*

Where is the American Consulate?
  Dov'è il consolato americano?
  *Doh-*VEH *eel kohn-soh-*LAH-*toh ah-meh-ree-*KAH-*noh?*

Don't get excited!
  Non si ecciti!
  Nohn see EHT-*chee-tee!*

Everything is all right!
  Tutto va bene!
  TOOT-*toh vah* BEH-*neh!*

RUSSIAN

Facts About Russian

Russian is spoken by more than 200 million people throughout Russia and the thirteen other affiliated republics that comprise the Soviet Union, all of which have Russian as their official language while at the same time conserving their own regional tongue. In addition, Russian is widely studied as a foreign language in schools in many countries of eastern Furope as well as in China and Mongolia.

Russian is a Slavic language, closely related to Polish, Bulgarian, Serbo-Croat, Slovene, Czech, and Slovak. A traveler who speaks Russian will find that he can communicate, to a degree, with natives of other Slavic countries, especially those of Yugoslavia and Bulgaria.

Once you have met a Russian, it is expected that you will address him or her by the first name and patronymic (that is, the first name of his or her father). John, the son of John, e.g., is said *Ivan Ivanovich*.

Advice On Accent

Since we have rendered the Russian sounds in phonetics instead of following the Russ an (Cyrillic) alphabet, there are certain sounds that the reader should pay special attention to, in order to be understood.

The letter y at the end of a syllable should be pronounced deep in the throat, as for example the i in the English word "girl."

The phonetic sh'ch represents a special Russian letter and should be said exactly as indicated: sh as in "hush" and ch as in "child." A good example of this letter can be found in the word Khrushchev, which is approximately pronounced as *khroo-sh'choff*.

How Russian Is Written

Russian has an alphabet of 33 letters, mainly adopted from ancient Greek through the influence of the Byzantine Empire on the emerging Russian nation. This large alphabet is quite phonetic and makes Russian comparatively easy to write.

Here is an example of some Russian words written in the Cyrillic alphabet. They mean "Entrance," "Exit," and "No Admittance," words especially useful to travelers.

Вход

Выход

Вход воспрещен

You Already Know Some Russian

Although well disguised, by the Russian alphabet, many Russian and English words of common Latin and Greek origin are similar—for example, *telegraf, telefon, teatr* (theatre), and many others.

In addition, many Russian words have crept into our daily English vocabulary. Here are some examples, along with their original Russian meanings: *troika* (three-horse team), *vodka* (little water), *soviet* (advisory council), *bolshevik* (derived from "person who wants *more*"), *samovar* (boils by itself), *sputnik* (one who goes along with—satellite). In addition, almost everyone is familiar with the Russian word for "no"—*n'yet*.

1. FIRST CONTACT

Yes.	No.	Good.
Dah.	*N'yet*	*Hah-rah-*SHOH.

Thank you.
*Spa-*SEE-*boh.*

You are welcome.
N'YEH *zah shtoh.*

Excuse me.
*Eez-vee-*NEE-*t'yeh.*

It's all right.
*Nee-cheh-*VOH.

Please.
*Pah-*ZHAHL-*stah.*

I would like ...
MOZH-*nah ...*

What?	This.	Where?
Shtoh?	EH-*toh.*	*G'd'yeh?*

Here.	When?	Now.
Z'd'yes.	*Kahk-*DAH?	*T'yeh-p'*YEHR.

Later.	Who?
*Pah-*TOHM.	*Ktoh?*

I	you	he	she
Yah	*vee*	*ohn*	*ah-*NAH

Your name?
VAH-*sheh* EE-*m'yah?*

Good morning (Good day.)
DOHB-*ree d'yen.*

Good evening.
DOHB-*ree v'*YEH-*chehr.*

Good night.
*Poh-*KOY-*noy* NOH-*chee.*

Good-by.
*Doh svee-*DAH-*n'yah.*

How are you?
*Kahk poh-zhee-*VAH-*yeh-t'yeh?*

Very well, thank you. And you?
*Hah-rah-*SHOH, *spah-*SEF-*boh. Ah kahk vee?*

I do not understand, please repeat.
*Yah n'yeh poh-nee-*MAH-*you, pah-*ZHAHL-*stah
pahf-tah-*REE-*t'yeh.*

How much?
SKOHL-*koh?*

one	two	three	four
*ah-*DEEN	*dvah*	*tree*	*cheh-*TEE-*r'yeh*

five	six	seven	eight
p'yaht	*shest*	*s'yem*	VOH-*sem*

nine		ten	
D'YEH-*v'yaht*		DEH-*s'yaht*	

eleven		twelve	
*ah-*DEE-*nah-tsaht*		*dveh-*NAHT-*saht*	

2. ACCOMMODATIONS

Where is a good hotel?
*G'd'yeh hah-*ROH-*shah-yah gohs-*TEE-*nee-tsah?*

I want a room for one person.
Yah hoh-choo KOHM-*nah-too dl'yah ohd-noh-*VOH.

I want a room for two persons.
Yah hoh-choo KOHM-*nah-too dl'yah dvoh-*EEKH.

I want a room with bath.
Yah hoh-choo KOHM-*nah-too s* VAHN-*noy.*

for two days	**for a week**
nah dvah d'nyah	*nah n'yeh-d'*YEH-*l'yoo*

till Monday
*doh poh-n'yeh-d'*YEL-*nee-kah*

Tuesday	**Wednesday**
FTOHR-*nee-kah*	*sr'yeh-*DEE

Thursday
chet-v'yehr-GAH

Friday
p'YAHT-nee-tsee

Saturday
soo-BOH-tee

Sunday
vohs-kr'yeh-s'YEH-n'yah

How much is it?
SKOHL-*koh?*

Here are my bags.
Voht moy bah-GAHZH.

Here is my passport.
Voht moy PAHS-*port.*

I like it.
M'n'yeh EH-*toh* NRAH-*veet-sah.*

I don't like it.
M'n'yeh EH-*toh n'yeh* NRAH-*veet-sah.*

Show me another.
*Poh-kah-*ZHEE-*t'yeh m'n'yeh droo-*GOO-*yoo.*

Where is the toilet?
*G'd'yeh oo-*BOHR-*nah-yah?*

Where is the men's room?
*G'd'yeh moosh-*SKAH-*yah oo-*BOHR-*nah-yah?*

Where is the ladies' room?
G'd'yeh DAHM-*skah-yah oo-*BOHR-*nah-yah?*

hot water
*gah-r'*YAH-*chay vah-*DEE

a towel
*poh-loh-*T'YEN-*tseh*

soap
MEE-*lah*

Come in!
*Vigh-*DEE-*t'yeh!*

Please have this washed.
MOHZH-*noh* EH-*toh* VEES-*tee-rat.*

Please have this pressed.
MOHZH-*noh* EH-*toh poh-*GLAH-*deet.*

Please have this cleaned.
MOHZH-*noh* EH-*toh poh*-CHEES-*teet.*

When will it be ready?
Kahk-DAH *eh-toh* BOO-*d'yet goh*-TOH-*voh?*

I need it for tonight.
M'n'yeh EH-*toh* NOOZH-*noh k v'*YEH-*cheh-roo.*

    for tomorrow
    nah ZAHF-*trah*

My key, please.
Moy klee'ooch, pah-ZHAHL-*stah.*

Any mail for me?
Yest PEES-*mah d'l'yah m'yeh-n'*YAH?

Any packages?
Pah-KEH-*tee?*

I want five airmail stamps for the U.S.A.
Yah hah-CHOO *p'yaht* MAH-*rock vohz*-DOOSH-*noy*
POHCH-*tee d'l'yah seh-sheh*-AH.

Have you postcards?
Oo vahs yest aht-KREET-*kee?*

I want to send a telegram.
Yah hah-CHOO *pohs*-LAHT *teh-leh*-GRAH-*moo.*

Call me at seven in the morning.
Rahz-boo-DEE-*t'yeh m'yeh-n'*YAH *f s'yem oo*-TRAH.

Where is the telephone?   **Hello!**
G'd'yeh teh-leh-FOHN?   *Ah*-LOH!

Send breakfast to room number . . .
Poh-SHLEE-*t'yeh* ZAHF-*trahk v* NOH-*mehr . . .*

orange juice
ah-pehl-SEE-*noh-vah-voh* SOH-*kah*

ham and eggs
yah-EETS *s veh-chee*-NOY

rolls and coffee
    KOH-*feh ee* BOO-*loh-check*

I am expecting a friend.
    *Yah ah-zhee-*DAH-*you pree-*YAH-*t'yeh-l'yah.*

Tell him (her) to wait.
    *Skah-*ZHEE-*t'yeh yeh-*MOO *chtob ohn poh-doh-*
    ZH'DAHL.

If anyone calls
    YES-*lee* KTOH-*nee-bood pohz-*VOH-*neet*

I'll be back at six.
    *Skah-*ZHEE-*t'yeh chtoh yah v'yehr-*NOOS *f shest.*

Tell me, please, where is a restaurant?
    *Skah-*ZHEE-*t'yeh m'n'yeh pah-*ZHAHL-*stah g'd'yeh*
    *res-toh-*RAHN?

Tell me, please, where is a barber shop?
    *Skah-*ZHEE-*t'yeh m'n'yeh pah-*ZHAHL-*stah g'd'yeh*
    *pah-rick-*MAH-*hehr-skah-yah?*

Tell me, please, where is a beauty parlor?
    *Skah-*ZHEE-*t'yeh m'n'yeh pah-*ZHAHL-*stah g'd'yeh*
    DAHM-*skah-yah pah-rick-*MAH-*hehr-skah-yah?*

Tell me, please, where is the drug store?
    *Skah-*ZHEE-*t'yeh m'n'yeh pah-*ZHAHL-*stah g'd'yeh*
    *ahp-t'*YEH-*kah?*

What is the telephone number?
    *Kah-*KOY EH-*toh* NOH-*mehr teh-leh-*FOH-*nah?*

What is the address?
    *Kah-*KOY EH-*toh* AH-*dress?*

I want to change some money.
    *Yah hah-*CHOO *rahz-m'yeh-n'*YAHT D'YEN-*ghee.*

What is the rate for dollars?
    *Kah-*KOY *koors zah* DOH-*lahr?*

twelve
*dveh-*NAH*-tsaht*

thirteen
*tree-*NAH*-tsaht*

fourteen
*cheh-*TEER*-nah-tsaht*

fifteen
*p'yaht-*NAH*-tsaht*

sixteen
*shest-*NAH*-tsaht*

seventeen
*s'yem-*NAH*-tsaht*

eighteen
*voh-sem-*NAH*-tsaht*

nineteen
*d'yeh-v'yaht-*NAH*-tsaht*

twenty
DVAH*-tsaht*

thirty
TREE*-tsaht*

forty
SOH*-rock*

fifty
*p'yaht-d'yeh-*S'YAHT

sixty
*shest-d'yeh-*S'YAHT

seventy
S'YEM*-deh-s'yaht*

eighty
VOH*-s'yehm-deh-s'yaht*

ninety
*deh-v'yah-*NOH*-stoh*

hundred
stoh

two hundred
*d'v'*YES*-tee*

three hundred
TREE*-stah*

four hundred
*cheh-*TEE*-rehs-tah*

five hundred
*p'yaht-*SOHT

six hundred
*shest-*SOHT

seven hundred
*s'yem-*SOHT

eight hundred
*voh-s'yehm-*SOHT

nine hundred
*d'yeh-v'yaht-*SOHT

thousand
TEE*-s'yah-chah*

ten thousand
d'yeh-s'yat TEE*-s'yahch*

hundred thousand
stoh TEE*-s'yahch*

My bill, please.
*Pah-*ZHAHL*-stah, moy s'choht.*

3. EATING

Where is a good restaurant?
*G'd'yeh hah-*ROH-*shee rehs-toh-*RAHN?

A table for two, please.
*Stohl dlia dvoh-*EEKH, *pah-*ZHAHL-*stah.*

Waiter!	**The menu, please.**
*Ah-fee-ts'*YAHNT!	*Pah-*ZHAHL-*stah, meh-*NEW.

What's good today?
*Chtoh s'yeh-*VOH-*dn'yeh hah-*ROH-*sheh-voh?*

Is it ready?
*Eh-toh goh-*TOH-*voh?*

How long will it take?
SKOHL-*koh vr'*YEM-*m'yeh-nee* NAH-*doh* EH-*toh-voh
zhdaht?*

This, please ...	**and this**
EH-*toh, pah-*ZHAHL-*stah ...*	*ee* EH-*toh*

Bring me ...
*Pree-n'yeh-*SEE-*t'yeh m'n'yeh ...*

water	**milk**
*vah-*DEE	*mah-lah-*KAH

a glass of beer
*stah-*KAHN PEE-*vah*

red wine
KRAHS-*nah-voh vee-*NAH

white wine	**a cocktail**
*b'*YEH-*lah-voh vee-*NAH	*kohk-*TAIL

whisky soda
VEES-*kee s* SOH-*doy*

soup	**fish**	**meat**
SOO-*pah*	REE-*bee*	M'YAH-*sah*

bread and butter
  *h'l'*YEH-*bah ee* MAHS-*lah*

a sandwich
  *boo-ter-*BROHD

steak . . .
  *beef-*SHTEX . . .

rare
  s KROH-*view*

medium
  *n'yeh-proh-*ZHAH-*r'yeh-nee*

well done
  *proh-*ZHAH-*r'yeh-nee*

chicken
  *tsee-pl'*YOHN-*kah*

veal
  *ee-*KREE

pork
  *svee-*NEE-*nee*

lamb
  *bah-*RAH-*nee-nee*

lamb chop
  VOHT-*kee*

No sauce for me.
  Mn'yeh bez SOW-*sah.*

with potatoes . . .
  *s kahr-*TOSH-*koy*

rice
  rees

an omelet
  *yah-*EECH-*nee-tsah*

And what vegetables?
  *Ah kah-*KEE-*yeh* OH-*vosh-chee?*

peas
  *goh-*ROH-*shek*

beans
  *boh-*BEE

carrots
  *mohr-*KOHV

onions
  look

a salad
  *sah-*LAHT

tomatoes
  *toh-*MAH-*tee*

Please bring me another fork.
  *Pah-*ZHAHL-*stah,* DIGH-*t'yeh mn'yeh droo-*GOO-*you*
  VEEL-*koo.*

knife
  nohzh

spoon
  LOHZH-*koo*

glass
  *stah-*KAHN

plate
  *tah-r'*YELL-*koo*

What is there for dessert?
Chtoh yest nah SLAHD-*koh-yeh?*

fruit
FROOK-*tee*

  pastry
  *pee-*ROHZH*-noh-yeh*

cake
*bis-*KVIT

  ice cream
  *moh-*ROH*-zheh-noh-yeh*

cheese
seer

Some coffee, please.
KOH-*feh, pah-*ZHAHL*-stah*

sugar
SAH-*har*

cream
SLEEF-*kee*

tea with lemon
*chigh s lee-*MOH-*nom*

mineral water
*mee-neh-*RAHL*-noy vah-*DEE

More, please.
*Yesh-*SHOH*, pah-*ZHAHL*-stah.*

That's enough.
*Doh-*VOHL*-noh.*

The check, please.
*Pah-*ZHAHL*-stah, s'*CHOHT.

Is the tip included?
*Chah-yeh-*VEE*-yeh f'k'lew-cheh-*NEE?

It was very good!
BEE-*loh* OH-*chen hoh-roh-*SHOH!

4. SHOPPING

I would like to buy this . . .   **that**
*Yah hah-*T'YEHL *bee koo-*PEET *EH-toh . . .*   *toh*

I am just looking around.
Yah TOHL-*koh smoh-*TREW.

Where is the section for . . .
*G'd'yeh ot-d'*YELL . . .

  men's clothing
  *moosh-*SKOH*-voh* PLAH-*t'yah*

women's clothing
ZHEN-*skoh-voh* PLAH-*t'yah*

hats
shliap

gloves
pehr-CHAH-*tok*

underwear
NEEZH-*n'yeh-voh* b'yeh-L'YAH

shoes
boh-TEE-*nok*

stockings
chew-LOHK

shirts
roo-BAH-*shek*

The size in America is . . .
Ah-meh-ree-KAHN-*skee rahz-m'*YEHR NOH-*mehr* . . .

toys
eeg-ROOSH-*kee*

perfumes
doo-HEE

jewelry
yoo-v'yeh-LEER-*nee-yeh eez-d'*YEH-*lee-yah*

watches
chah-SEE

toilet articles
pahr-few-M'YEH-*ree-yah*

sport articles
d'l'yah SPOHR-*tah*

films
*p'l'*YOHN-*kee*

souvenirs
poh-DAHR-*kee*

Show me . . .
Poh-kah-ZHEE-*t'yeh m'n'yeh* . . .

something less expensive
CHTOH-*nee-bood poh-d'yeh*-SHEV-*l'yeh*

another one
CHTOH-*nee-bood droo*-GOH-*yeh*

a better quality
LOOT-*cheh-voh* KAH-*chess-tvah*

bigger
BOHL-*sheh*

smaller
M'YEHN-*sheh*

I don't like the color.
  M'n'yeh n'yeh NRAH-*vee-tsah tsvet.*

I want one ...
  *Yah hah-t'*YELL *bee* EH-*toh zheh* ...

  in green
    *zeh-l'*YOH-*noh-voh* TSV'YEH-*tah*

  in yellow
    ZHOHL-*toh-voh* TSV'YEH-*tah*

  in blue
    SEE-*n'yeh-voh* TSV'YEH-*tah*

  red
    KRAHS-*noh-voh* TSV'YEH-*tah*

  black
    CHOHR-*noh-voh* TSV'YEH-*tah*

  white
    B'YEH-*loh-voh* TSV'YEH-*tah*

  grey
    S'YEH-*roh-voh* TSV'YEH-*tah*

  pink
    ROH-*zoh-voh-voh* TSV'YEH-*tah*

  brown
    *koh-*REECH-*n'yeh-voh-voh* TSV'YEH-*tah*

I will take it with me.
  Yah EH-*toh vohz-MOO s soh-*BOY.

I will return later.
  *Yah v'yehr-*NOOS.

The receipt, please.
  *Pah-*ZHAHL-*stah, rahs-*PEES-*koo.*

Please send it to this address.
  *Pah-*ZHAHL-*stah, poh-*SHLEE-*t'yeh* EH-*toh nah* EH-
  tot AHD-*ress.*

Where is the market?
　　G'd'yeh REE-*nok?*

Where is there a flower shop?
　　G'd'yeh MOHZH-*noh koo-*PEET *tsv'yeh-*TEE?

Where is there a bookstore?
　　G'd'yeh KNEEZH-*nee mah-gah-*ZEEN?

Where can I buy food?
　　G'd'yeh MOHZH-*noh koo-*PEET *proh-doh-*VOHLST-
　　vee-yeh?

5. TRANSPORTATION

Taxi! 　TAHK-*see!*	**Take me to the airport.** 　*Nah ah-eh-roh-*POHRT.
Turn right. 　*Nah-*PRAH-*voh.*	**Turn left.** 　*Nah-l'*YEH-*voh.*
Straight ahead. 　*Pr'*YAH-*moh.*	**Not so fast!** 　*N'yeh tahk* SKOH-*roh!*
Hurry up! 　*Skoh-r'*YEH-*yeh!*	**Stop here!** 　*Ohs-tah-noh-*VEE-*t'yes zd'yes!*

Wait for me!
　*Pah-dah-*ZHDEE-*t'yeh m'yeh-n'*YAH!

How much is it?
　SKOHL-*koh?*

How much is it to . . . ?
　SKOHL-*koh* STOH-*eet prah-*KAHT *doh . . . ?*

　　and back?
　　　*ee nah-*ZAHD?

How much by the hour?
　SKOHL-*koh vee b'yeh-r'*YOH-*t'yeh zah chahs?*

　　by the day?
　　　zah d'yen?

Show me the sights.
*Poh-kah-*ZHEE*-t'yeh m'n'yeh dohs-toh-pree-m'yeh-*
*   *CHAH*-t'yell-nohs-tee.*

What is that building?
Chtoh EH*-toh zah* ZDAH*-nee-yeh?*

May I go in?
MOHZ*-noh voy-*TEE*?*

I want to see the Kremlin.
*Yah hoh-*CHOO VEE*-d'yet Kreml.*

To the railroad station.
*Nah vokh-*ZAHL*.*

Porter!
*Nah-*SEEL*-sh'chick!*

I have two bags.
*Oo m'yeh-n'*YAH *dvah cheh-moh-*DAH*-nah.*

A ticket to . . .   **one way**
*Bee-*LET *v . . .*   TOHL*-koh too-*DAH

   round trip
   *too-*DAH *ee ob-*RAHT*-noh*

   first class
   *p'*YEHR*-voh-voh* KLAH*-sah*

   second class
   *ftoh-*ROH*-voh* KLAH*-sah*

When does it leave?
*Kahk-*DAH POH*-yezd oht-*HOH*-deet?*

Where is the train to Leningrad?
*G'd'yeh l'yeh-neen-*GRAHD*-skee* POH*-yezd?*

Is this the train for Kiev?
EH*-toh* KEE*-eff-skee* POH*-yezd?*

When do we get to Kharkov?
*Kahk-*DAH *mee* BOO*-d'yem v* HAHR*-koh-v'yeh?*

How long do we stop here?
SKOHL-*koh* vr'YEH-*meh-nee* BOO-'yem *zd'yes stoh-*
YAHT?

Open the window.
*Aht-*KROY-*t'yeh ahk-*NOH.

Close the window.
*Zah-*KROY-*t'yeh ahk-*NOH.

Where is the bus to Krasnoe Selo?
G'd'yeh *ahf-*TOH-*boos ee-*DOOSH-*chee* v KRAHS-*noh-*
*yeh s'yeh-*LOH?

I want to go to the University.
*Yah hah-*CHOO *poh-*YEH-*hat* v *oo-nee-vehr-see-*
T'YET.

Please tell me where to get off.
*Skah-*ZHEE-*t'yeh mn'yeh pah-*ZHAHL-*stah* g'd'yeh
*soy-*TEE.

Where is a gas station?
G'd'yeh STAHN-*tsee-yah behn-*ZEE-*nah?

Fill it up.
*Nah-*POHL-*nee-t'yeh bahk.*

Check the oil ...
*Proh-v'*YEHR-*t'yeh* MAHS-*loh* ...

water	tires
VOH-*doo*	SHEE-*nee*

Something is wrong with the car.
CHTOH-*toh* v *mah-*SHEE-*n'yeh n'yeh* f *poh-r'*YAHT·
keh.

Can you fix it?
Vee MOH-*zheh-t'yeh* EH-*toh poh-chee-*NEET?

How long will it take?
SKOHL-*koh* EH-*toh zigh-m'*YOHT?

Is this the road to Yalta?
 EH-toh doh-ROH-gah v YAHL-too?

Have you a map?
 Oo vahs yest KAHR-tah?

Where is the boat to . . . ?
 G'd'yeh SOOD-noh ee-DOOSH-sheh-yeh v . . . ?

When does it leave?
 Kahk-DAH oh-NOH oht-HOH-deet?

6. MAKING FRIENDS

How do you do!
 OH-chen pree-YAHT-noh!

My name is . . .
 Mah-YOH EE-m'yah . . .

What is your name, Sir?
 Kahk VAH-sheh EE-m'yah?

I am delighted to meet you.
 OH-chen pree-YAHT-noh s VAH-mee pohz-nah-KOH-meet-sah.

Do you speak English?
 Vee goh-voh-REE-t'yeh poh-ahn-GLEE-skee?

A little.   **Do you understand?**
 N'yeh-MNOH-goh.   *Poh-nee-MAH-yeh-t'yeh?*

Please speak slowly.
 Goh-voh-REET-yeh MEHD-len-noh, pah-ZHAHL-stah.

I speak only a little Russian.
 Yah OH-chen n'yeh-MNOH-goh goh-voh-r'YOO poh-ROOS-kee.

I am from New York.   **Where are you from?**
 Yah eez New YORK-ah.   *Vee oht-KOO-dah?*

I like your country.
  M'n'yeh NRAH-*veet-sah vahsh* GOH-*rod.*

Have you been in America?
  Vee BEE-*lee v ah-*MEH-*ree-keh?*

This is my first visit here.
  EH-*toh moy* P'YEHR-*vee pree-*YEZD *sew-*DAH.

May I sit here?
  MOHZH-*noh zd'yes sest?*

May I take your picture?
  MOHZH-*noh vahs sniat?*

Come here.
  *Ee-*DEE-*t'yeh s'yoo-*DAH.

This is my wife . . .
  EH-*toh mah-*YAH *zheh-nah . . .*

> **my husband**
>   *moy muzh*
>
> **my son**
>   *moy sin*
>
> **my daughter**
>   *mah-*YAH *dotch*
>
> **my mother**
>   *mah-*YAH *maht*
>
> **my father**
>   *moy ot-*YETS
>
> **my sister**
>   *mah-*YAH *ses-*TRAH
>
> **my brother**
>   *moy braht*

Have you children?
  Oo vahs yest D'YEH-*tee?*

How beautiful!
  *Kahk krah-*SEE*-voh!*

Very interesting!
  OH*-chen een-t'yeh-*R'YES*-noh!*

Would you like a cigarette?
  *Hah-*TEE*-t'yeh pah-pee-*ROH*-soo?*

Would you like something to drink?
  *Hah-*TEE*-t'yeh ch'yeh-*VOH*-nee-bood* VEE*-peet?*

Would you like something to eat?
  *Hah-*TEE*-t'yeh* CH'YEM*-nee-bood zah-koo-*SEET*?*

Sit down, please.
  *Pree-*SAH*-zhee-vigh-t'yes.*

Make yourself at home!
  BOOD*-t'yeh kahk* DOH*-mah!*

Good luck!
  *Zheh-*LAH*-yoo oo-*DAH*-chee!*

To your health!
  Zah VAH*-sheh zdoh-*ROH*-v'yeh!*

When can I see you again?
  *Kahk-*DAH *yah vahs smoh-*GOO *oh-p'*YAHT *oo-vee-
    d'yet?*

Where shall we meet?
  *G'd'yeh mee f'str'*YEH*-teem-sah?*

Here is my address.
  Voht moy AHD*-ress.*

What is your address?
  *Kah-*KOY *vahsh* AH*-dress?*

What is your phone number?
  *Kah-*KOY *vahsh* NOH*-mehr t'yeh-leh-*FOH*-nah?*

May I speak to . . .
  *Yah hah-*CHOO *gah-vah-*REET *s . . .*

Would you like to have lunch?
*Hah-*TEE*-t'yeh poh-oh-*B'YEH*-daht?*

    have dinner?
    *poh-*OO*-zhee-naht?*

Would you like to go to the movies?
*Hah-*TEE*-t'yeh poy-*TEE *v kee-*NOH*?*

    go to the theatre?
    *poy-*TEE *v teh-*AHTR*?*

Would you like to go to the beach?
*Hah-*TEE*-t'yeh poh-*YEH*-haht nah pl'yazh?*

    take a walk?
    *proh-goo-*L'YAHT*-sah?*

With great pleasure!
*S oo-doh-*VOHL*-stvee-yem!*

I am sorry.   **I cannot.**
M'n'yeh OH*-chen zhahl*   *Yah n'yeh moh-*GOO*.*

Another time.   **I must go now.**
*Droo-*GOY *rahz.*   *M'n'yeh poh-*RAH *eed-*TEE*.*

Thank you for a wonderful time.
*Spah-*SEE*-boh zah* LAHS*-koo.*

Thank you for an excellent dinner.
*Spah-*SEE*-boh zah* CHOOD*-nee ah-*B'YED*.*

This is for you.
EH*-toh vahm.*

You are very kind.
Vee OH*-chen l'you-*B'YEZ*-nee.*

It's nothing really.
EH*-toh nee-cheh-*VOH*.*

With best regards.
*Pree-v'*YET*.*

Congratulations!   **Have a good trip!**
*Pohz-drahv-l'*YAH*-you!*   *V* DOH*-bree chahs!*

7. EMERGENCIES

Help!
*Poh-moh-*GHEE*-t'yeh!*

Police!
*Mee-*LEE*-ts'yah!*

Fire!
*Poh-*ZHAHR*!*

Stop that man!
*Ohs-tah-noh-*VEE*-t'yeh yeh-*VOH*!*

Stop that woman!
*Ohs-tah-noh-*VEE*-t'yeh yeh-*YOH*!*

I have been robbed!
*M'yeh-n'*YAH *ah-*GRAH*-bee-lee!*

Look out!
*Smoh-*TREE*-t'yeh!*

Wait a minute!
*Poh-dohzh-*DEE*-t'yeh!*

Stop!
STOY*-t'yeh!*

Get out!
*Poh-*SHOHL *vohn!*

Hurry up!
*Skoh-*R'YEH*-yeh!*

Don't bother me!
*N'yeh m'yeh-*SHY*-t'yeh!*

What's going on?
*Chtoh proh-ees-*HOH*-deet?*

Entrance
Fhot

Exit
VEE*-hot*

Ladies
DAH*-mee*

Gentlemen
*Moosh-*CHEE*-nee*

Danger!
*Oh-*PAHS*-nost!*

Keep out!
*N'yeh fhoh-*DEE*-t'yeh!*

No smoking
*Koo-*REET *zah-presh-*CHIGH*-yet-sah*

No parking
*Stoh-*YAHN*-kah zah-presh-cheh-*NAH

One way
  Oh-DNOH *nah-pralv*-L'YEH-*nee-yeh*

I am ill.
  Yoh PLOH-*hoh s'yeh-*B'YAH CHOOST-*voo-yoo.*

Call a doctor!
  *Poh-zoh-*VEE-*t'yeh vrah-*CHAH!

It hurts here.   **Where is the drug store?**
  *Toot bah-*LEET.   *G'd'yeh ahp-t'*YEH-*kah?*

Take me to the hospital.
  *Oht-v'yeh-*ZEE-*t'yeh m'yeh-*N'YAH *v bohl-*NEE-*tsoo.*

Where is there a dentist?
  *G'd'yeh yest zoob-*NOY *vrahtch?*

I have lost my bag.
  *Yah poh-t'yeh-*R'YAHL *cheh-moh-*DAHN.

   my wallet
     *boo-*MAHZH-*nick*

   my camera
     *photo-ah-pah-*RAHT

   my passport
     PAHS-*pohrt*

I am an American.
  *Yah ah-meh-ree-*KAH-*nets* (fem. *ah-meh-ree-*KAHN-*kah).*

Where is the American Consulate?
  *G'd'yeh ah-meh-ree-*KAHN-*skoh-yeh* KOHN-*sool-stvoh?*

Don't get excited!
  *N'yeh vohl-*NOOY-*t'yes!*

Everything is all right.
  *F's'yoh f poh-*R'YAHD-*k'yeh.*

PORTUGUESE

Facts About Portuguese

Portuguese is spoken by over 74 million people in Portugal and Brazil, the Azores, Madeira and Cape Verde Islands, in Portuguese-speaking areas in Africa, such as Angola and Mozambique, and in Asia, such as Macao and Timor. It is widely understood in northern Spain, where the regional dialect is similar to Portuguese.

Portuguese is a Romance language derived from Latin. Although there are certain regional differences in accent, the Portuguese offered in this section is standard and you will be readily understood wherever Portuguese is spoken.

Advice on Accent

ç is pronounced as **ss**.

g is pronounced as **g** in *get,* when it occurs before *a, o,* or *u*.

g is pronounced softly, like **s** in *pleasure,* when it occurs before *e* or *i*.

s between vowels is pronounced as **z**.

x is pronounced sometimes as **sh**, sometimes as **s**, sometimes as **x**, and sometimes as **z**. Simply follow our phonetics for correct pronunciation.

The mark ~ is called a *til;* you should pronounce the vowel over which it is placed as if you were holding your nose.

You Already Know Some Portuguese

Many Portuguese and English words share a common descent from Latin, although the pronunciation is often strange to the English ear.

Almost all English words ending in *-tion* end in Portuguese in *-ção:* nation *nação;* revolution *revolução;* constitution *constituição;* institution *instituição.*

Most adverbs ending in *-ly* in English end in *-mente* in Portuguese: naturally *naturalmente;* generally *geralmente;* rapidly *ràpidamente.*

English words ending in *-ble* end in *-vel* in Portuguese: possible *possível;* incredible *incrível.*

Many English nouns ending in *-ty* exist in Portuguese, but end in *-dade:* facility *facilidade;* quality *qualidade;* liberty *liberdade.*

1. FIRST CONTACT

Yes.	**No.**	**Good.**
Sim.	Não.	Bom.
Seengh.	*Nowngh.*	*Bongh.*

Pardon.
Perdão.
*Pehr-*DOWNGH.

It's all right.
Está bem.
*Ehs-*TAH *bengh.*

Please.
Faça favor.
FAH-*sah faH-*VOHR.

I would like ...
Gostaria de ...
*Gohs-tah-*REE'*yah deh ...*

What?
(O) Quê?
(*Oh*) KEH?

This. That.
Isto. Isso.
EES-*toh.* EE-*soh.*

Where?
Onde?
OHN-*deh?*

Here. There.
Aquí. Alí.
*Ah-*KEE. *Ah-*LEE.

When?
Quando?
KWAHN-*doh?*

Now. Later.
Agora. Logo.
*Ah-*GOH-*rah.* LOH-*goh.*

Who?	**I**	**you**	**he**	**she**
Quem?	Eu	Você	Ele	Ela
Kengh?	EH'*oo*	*Voh-*SEH	EH-*leh*	EH-*lah*

Your name?
(O) Seu nome?
(*Oh*) SEH'*oo* NOH-*meh?*

Good morning. (Good day.)
Bom dia.
Bongh DEE'*yah.*

Good afternoon.
Boa tarde.
BOH-*ah* TAHR-*deh.*

Good evening. (Good night.)
Boa noite.
BOH-*ah* NOY-*teh.*

Good-by.
Adeus.
*Ah-*DEH'*oos.*

How are you?
Como está?
KOH-*moh ehs*-TAH?

Very well, thank you, and you?
Muito bem, obrigado (a) , e o senhor (a) ?
MUEEN-*toh bengh*, oh-bree-GAH-*doh* (dah) , *ee oh*
seh-n'YOHR (rah) ?

How much is it?
Quanto é?
KWAHN-*toh* EH?

I do not understand, please repeat.
Não compreendo, repita, faça favor.
*Nowngh kongh-pree-*EHN-*doh, reh-*PEE-*tah*, FAH-*sah*
fah-VOHR.

One	Two	Three	Four
um	dois	três	quatro
oongh	*doys*	*trehs*	KWAH-*troh*

Five	Six	Seven	Eight
cinco	seis	sete	oito
SEENGH-*koh*	*seys*	SEH-*teh*	OY-*toh*

Nine	Ten	Eleven	Twelve
nove	dez	onze	doze
NOH-*veh*	*dehs*	OHN-*zeh*	DOH-*zeh*

2. ACCOMMODATIONS

I want a room for one person (two persons).
Quero um quarto para uma pessoa (duas pessoas) .
KEH-*roh oongh* KWAHR-*toh* PAH-*rah* OO-*mah peh-*
SOH-*ah* (DOO-*ahs peh-*SOH-*ahs*) .

I want a room with bath.
Quero um quarto com casa de banho.
KEH-*roh oongh* KWAHR-*toh kongh* KAH-*zah deh*
BAH-*n'yoh*.

for two days
  por dois dias
  pohr doys DEE'*yahs*

for a week
  por uma semana
  pohr OO-*mah seh*-MAH-*nah*

till Monday
  até Segunda-feira
  ah-TEH *seh*-GOON-*dah* FAY-*rah*

Tuesday	**Wednesday**
Têrça-feira	Quarta-feira
TEHR-*sah* FAY-*rah*	KWAHR-*tah* FAY-*rah*

Thursday	**Friday**
Quinta-feira	Sexta-feira
KEEN-*tah* FAY-*rah*	SAYSH-*tah* FAY-*rah*

Saturday	**Sunday**
Sábado	Domingo
SAH-*bah-doh*	*doh*-MEENGH-*goh*

Here are my bags.
  Aquí estão as minhas malas.
  Ah-KEE *ehs*-TOWNGH *ahs* MEE-*n'yahs* MAH-*lahs.*

Here is my passport.
  Aquí está o meu passaporte.
  Ah-KEE *ehs*-TAH *oh* MEH'*oo pah-sah-*POHR-*teh.*

I like it (room).	**I don't like it (room).**
Gosto dele.	Não gosto dele.
GOHS-*toh* DEH-*leh.*	*Nowngh* GOHS-*toh* DEH-*leh.*

Show me another.
  Mostre-me outro.
  MOHS-*treh-meh* OH-*troh.*

Where is the bathroom?
  Onde está o quarto de banho?
  OHN-*deh ehs*-TAH *oh* KWAHR-*toh deh* BAH-*n'yoh?*

Where is the men's (ladies') room?
  Onde está o toilette?
  OHN-*deh* ehs-TAH *oh twah*-LEH-*teh?*

hot water
  água quente
  AH-*gwah* KEHN-*teh*

a towel
  uma toalha
  OO-*mah* TWAH-*l'yah*

soap
  sabonete
  sah-boh-NEH-*teh*

Come in!
  Entre!
  EHN-*treh!*

Please have this washed.
  Isto é para lavar, faça favor.
  EES-*toh* EH PAH-*rah* lah-VAHR, FAH-*sah fah*-VOHR.

Please have this pressed.
  Isto é para engomar.
  EES-*toh* EH PAH-*rah ehn-goh*-MAHR.

Please have this cleaned (dry).
  Isto é para limpar (a sêco).
  EES-*toh* EH PAH-*rah leengh*-PAHR (*ah* SEH-*koh*).

When will it be ready?
  Quando estará pronto?
  KWAHN-*doh ehs-tah*-RAH PROHN-*toh?*

I need it for tonight
  Preciso dele para esta noite
  Preh-SEE-*zoh* DEH-*leh* PAH-*rah* EHS-*tah* NOY-*teh*

  for tomorrow
    para àmanhã
    PAH-*rah* AH-*mah-n'*YANGH

My key, please.
  A minha chave, por favor.
  Ah MEE-*n'yah* SHAH-*veh, pohr fah*-VOHR.

Any mail for me?
  Algum correio para mim?
  Ahl-GOONGH *koh*-RRAY'*yoh* PAH-*rah meengh?*

Any packages?
Algum pacote?
*Ahl-*GOONGH *pah-*KOH-*teh?*

I want five airmail stamps for the U. S.
Quero cinco sêlos de avião para os Estados Unidos.
KEH-*roh* SEENGH-*koh* SEH-*lohs deh ah-v'*YOWNGH
PAH-*rah ohs Ehs-*TAH-*dohs Oo-*NEE-*dohs.*

Have you postcards?
Tem bilhetes postais?
*Tengh bee-l'*YEH-*tehs pohs-*TIGHS*?*

I want to send a telegram (cablegram).
Quero mandar um telegrama (cabograma) .
KEH-*roh mahn-*DAHR *oongh teh-leh-*GRAH-*mah*
(*kah-boh-*GRAH-*mah*) .

Call me at seven in the morning.
Chame-me às sete da manhã.
SHAH-*meh-meh* AHS SEH-*teh dah mah-n'*YANGH.

Where is the telephone? **Hello!**
Onde está o telefone? Está!
OHN-*deh ehs-*TAH *oh teh-leh-*FOH-*neh?* *ehs-*TAH!

Send breakfast to room 702.
Mande o café ao quarto setecentos e dois.
MAHN-*deh oh kah-*FEH AH'*oo* KWAHR-*toh seh-teh-*
SEHN-*tohs ee doys.*

> **orange juice**
> sumo de laranja
> soo-*moh deh lah-*RAHN-*jah*

> **ham and eggs**
> ovos com presunto
> OH-*vohs kongh preh-*ZOON-*toh*

> **rolls and coffee**
> pãezinhos e café
> *pengh-*ZEE-*n'yohs ee kah-*FEH

I am expecting a friend.
Espero um amigo (a) .
*Ehs-*PEH*-roh oongh ah-*MEE*-goh (gah) .*

Tell him (her) to wait.
Diga-lhe que espere.
DEE*-gah-l'yeh keh ehs-*PEH*-reh.*

If anyone calls ...
Se alguem chamar ...
*Seh ahl-*GENGH *shah-*MAHR ...

I'll be back at six.
Voltarei às seis.
*Vohl-tah-*RAY AHS *seys.*

Tell me, please, where is a barber shop.
Diga-me onde há uma barbearia, faça favor.
DEE*-gah-meh* OHN*-deh* AH OO*-mah bahr-bee-ah-*REE*'yah,* FAH*-sah fah-*VOHR.

Tell me, please, where is a beauty parlor.
Diga-me onde há um salão de beleza, faça favor.
DEE*-gah-meh* OHN*-deh* AH *oongh sah-*LOWNGH *deh beh-*LEH*-zah,* FAH*-sah fah-*VOHR.

Tell me, please, where is a drug store.
Diga-me onde há uma farmácia, faça favor.
DEE*-gah-meh* OHN*-deh* AH OO*-mah fahr-*MAH*-see'yah,* FAH*-sah fah-*VOHR.

What is the telephone number?
Qual é o número de telefone?
Kwahl EH *oh* NOO*-meh-roh deh teh-leh-*FOH*-neh?*

What is the address?
Qual é a direcção?
Kwahl EH *ah dee-reh-*SOWNGH?

I want to change some money.
Quero trocar algum dinheiro.
KEH*-roh troh-*KAHR *ahl-*GOONGH *dee-n'*YEH*-roh.*

What is the rate for dollars?
Qual é o câmbio do dólar?
Kwahl EH *oh* KAHM-*bee'yoh doh* DOH-*lahr?*

ten	eleven	twelve	thirteen
dez	onze	doze	treze
dehs	OHN-*zeh*	DOH-*zeh*	TREH-*zeh*

fourteen	fifteen	sixteen
catorze	quinze	dezasseis
*kah-*TOHR-*zeh*	KEENGH-*zeh*	*deh-zah-*SEYS

seventeen	eighteen
dezassete	dezoito
*deh-zah-*SEH-*teh*	*deh-*ZOY-*toh*

nineteen	twenty	thirty
dezanove	vinte	trinta
*deh-zah-*NOH-*veh*	VEEN-*teh*	TREEN-*tah*

forty	fifty
quarenta	cinquenta
*kwah-*REHN-*tah*	*seengh-*KWEHN-*tah*

sixty	seventy	eighty
sessenta	setenta	oitenta
*seh-*SEHN-*tah*	*seh-*TEHN-*tah*	*oy-*TEHN-*tah*

ninety	hundred	two hundred
noventa	cem	duzentos
*noh-*VEHN-*tah*	*sengh*	*doo-*ZEHN-*tohs*

three hundred	four hundred
trezentos	quatrocentos
*treh-*ZEHN-*tohs*	*kwah-troh-*SEHN-*tohs*

five hundred	six hundred
quinhentos	seiscentos
*kee-n'*YEHN-*tohs*	*seys-*SEHN-*tohs*

seven hundred	eight hundred
setecentos	oitocentos
*seh-teh-*SEHN-*tohs*	*oy-toh-*SEHN-*tohs*

nine hundred
  novecentos
  *noh-veh-*SEHN*-tohs*

thousand
  mil
  meel

ten thousand
  dez mil
  dehs meel

hundred thousand
  cem mil
  sengh meel

My bill, please.
  A minha conta, faça favor.
  Ah MEE*-n'yah* KOHN*-tah,* FAH*-sah fah-*VOHR*.*

3. EATING

Where is a good restaurant?
  Onde há um bom restaurante?
  OHN*-deh* AH *oongh bongh rehs-tah'oo-*RAHN*-teh?*

A table for two, please.
  Uma mesa para dois, faça favor.
  OO*-mah* MEH*-zah* PAH*-rah doys,* FAH*-sah fah-*VOHR*.*

Waiter!
  Môço! (Empregado!)
  MOH*-soh!* (*ehm-preh-*GAH*-doh!*)

Waitress!
  Empregada! (Criada!)
  *Ehm-preh-*GAH*-dah!* (*Kree-*AH*-dah!*)

The menu, please.
  O menú, por favor.
  *Oh meh-*NOO*, pohr fah-*VOHR*.*

What's good today?
  Que há de bom para hoje?
  Keh AH *deh bongh* PAH*-rah* OH*-jeh?*

Is it ready?
  Está pronto?
  *Ehs-*TAH PROHN*-toh?*

How long will it take?
Quanto tempo levará?
KWAHN-*toh* TEHM-*poh leh-vah-*RAH?

This, please ...
Isto, faça favor ...
EES-*toh*, FAH-*sah fah-*VOHR ...

and this
e isto
ee EES-*toh*

Bring me ...
Traga-me ...
TRAH-*gah-meh* ...

a glass of water
um copo de água
oongh KOH-*poh deh* AH-*gwah*

milk
leite
LAY-*teh*

a beer
uma cerveja
OO-*mah sehr-*VEH-*jah*

red wine
vinho tinto
VEE-*n'yoh* TEEN-*toh*

white wine
vinho branco
VEE-*n'yoh* BRAHN-*koh*

a cocktail
um coquetel
*oongh kohk-*TEHL

a whisky soda
um whisky soda
oongh whisky SOH-*dah*

soup
sopa
SOH-*pah*

fish
peixe
PAY-*sheh*

meat
carne
KAHR-*neh*

bread and butter
pão e manteiga
*powngh ee mahn-*TAY-*gah*

a sandwich
uma sanduiche
OO-*mah* SAHN-*dweesh*

steak ...
bife (filé) ...
BEE-*feh* (*fee-*LEH) ...

rare
mal passado
*mahl pah-*SAH-*doh*

medium
médio
MEH-*d'yoh*

well done
bem passado
*bengh pah-*SAH-*doh*

chicken
  galinha
  *gah-*LEE*-n'yah*

veal
  vitela
  *vee-*TEH*-lah*

pork (meat)
  carne de porco
  KAHR*-neh deh* POHR*-koh*

lamb
  carneiro
  *kahr-*NAY*-roh*

lamb chop
  costeleta de carneiro
  *kohs-teh-*LEH*-tah deh kahr-*NAY*-roh*

cod fish with potatoes, oil, onions, tomatoes, garlic, bay leaf
  bacalhau à Gomes de Sá
  *bah-kah-l'*YOW *AH* GOH*-mehs deh* SAH

rice made with small clams
  arroz de ameijoas
  *ah-*RROJ *deh ah-*MAY*-jwahs*

stew with specially prepared squid
  lulas de caldeirada
  LOO*-lahs deh kahl-day-*RAH*-dah*

bean, sausage, pork dish
  feijoada
  *fay-j'*WAH*-dah*

barbecue "Gaucho" style
  churrasco à Gaúcha
  *shoo-*RRAHS*-koh AH gah-oo-shah*

very light, fluffy doughnuts
  sonhos
  SOH*-n'yohs*

delicate cheese cakes
  queijadas
  *kay-*JAH*-dahs*

guava paste
  goiabada
  *goya-*BAH*-dah*

No sauce for me.
  Não quero môlho.
  Nowngh KEH*-roh* MOH*-l'yoh.*

with potatoes ...
  com batatas ...
  *kongh bah-*TAH*-tahs ...*

fried
  fritas
  FREE*-tahs*

rice
 arroz
 *ah-*RROJ

an omelet
 uma omeleta
 *oo-mah oh-meh-*LEH*-tah*

And what vegetables?
 E que legumes?
 *Ee keh leh-*GOO*-mehs?*

peas
 ervilhas
 *ehr-*VEE*-l'yahs*

beans
 feijão
 *fay-*JOWNGH

carrots
 cenouras
 *seh-*NOH*-rahs*

onions
 cebôlas
 *seh-*BOH*-lahs*

a salad
 uma salada
 *oo-mah sah-*LAH*-dah*

lettuce
 alface
 *ahl-*FAH*-seh*

tomatoes
 tomates
 *toh-*MAH*-tehs*

More, please.
 Mais, faça favor.
 Mighs, FAH*-sah fah-*VOHR*.*

That's enough.
 É suficiente.
 EH *soo-fee-s'*YEHN*-teh.*

Please bring me another fork.
 Traga-me outro garfo, faça favor.
 TRAH*-gah-meh* OH*-troh* GAHR*-foh,* FAH*-sah fah-*VOHR*.*

knife   **spoon**   **glass**
 faca   colher   copo
 FAH*-kah*   *koh-l'*YEHR   KOH*-poh*

plate   **cup**
 prato   chávena (chícara)
 PRAH*-toh*   SHAH*-veh-nah* (SHEE*-kah-rah*)

What is there for dessert?
 Que há para sobremesa?
 Keh AH PAH*-rah soh-breh-*MEH*-zah?*

fruit	pastry	cake
fruta	dôces	bôlo
FROO-*tah*	DOH-*sehs*	BOH-*loh*

ice cream	cheese
sorvete	queijo
sohr-VEH-*teh*	KAY-*joh*

Some coffee, please.   cream

Café, por favor.   creme

Kah-FEH, *pohr fah*-VOHR.   KREH-*meh*

sugar	tea with lemon
açúcar	chá com limão
ah-SOO-*kahr*	*shah kongh lee*-MOWNGH

mineral water

água mineral

AH-*gwah mee-neh*-RAHL

The check, please.

A conta, faça favor.

Ah KOHN-*tah,* FAH-*sah fah*-VOHR.

Is the tip included?

Está incluída a gorgeta?

Ehs-TAH *eengh-kloo*-EE-*dah ah gohr*-JEH-*tah?*

It was very good!

Estava muito bom!

Ehs-TAH-*vah* MUEEN-*toh bongh!*

4. SHOPPING

I would like to buy this...

Gostaria de comprar isto...

Gohs-tah-REE'*yah deh kongh*-PRAHR EES-*toh*...

that	I am just looking round.
aquilo	Só estou a ver.
ah-KEE-*loh*	SOH *ehs*-TOH *ah vehr.*

Where is the section for ...
  Onde fica a secção de ...
  OHN-*deh* FEE-*kah ah sehk*-SOWNGH *deh* ...

    men's clothing
      roupas de homem
      ROH-*pahs deh* OH-*mengh*

    women's clothing
      roupas de senhora
      ROH-*pahs deh seh-n'*YOH-*rah*

hats	**gloves**
chapeus	luvas
shah-PEH'*oos*	LOO-*vahs*

underwear	**shoes**
roupa interior	sapatos
ROH-*pah eengh-teh-r'*YOHR	*sah*-PAH-*tohs*

stockings	**shirts**
meias	camisas
MAY-*ahs*	*kah*-MEE-*zahs*

The size in America is ...
  Na América a medida é ...
  Nah Ah-MEH-*ree-kah ah meh*-DEE-*dah* EH ...

toys	**perfumes**
brinquedos	perfumes
breengh-KEH-*dohs*	*pehr*-FOO-*mehs*

jewelry	**watches**
jóias	relógios
JOH-*yahs*	*reh*-LOH-*j'yohs*

    toilet articles
      artigos de toilette
      ahr-TEE-*gohs deh twah*-LEH-*teh*

    sport articles
      artigos de desporto
      ahr-TEE-*gohs deh dehs*-POHR-*toh*

films
   filmes
   FEEL-*mehs*

souvenirs
   lembranças
   lehm-BRAHN-*sahs*

Show me ...
  Mostre-me ...
  MOHS-*treh-meh* ...

  something less expensive
   qualquer coisa mais barata
   kwahl-KEHR KOY-*zah mighs bah*-RAH-*tah*

  another one
   outro (a)
   OH-*troh* (*ah*)

  a better quality
   melhor qualidade
   *meh-l'*YOHR *kwah-lee*-DAH-*deh*

  bigger
   maior
   mah-YOHR

  smaller
   mais pequeno (a)
   mighs peh-KEH-*noh* (*ah*)

I don't like the color.
  Não gosto da côr.
  Nowngh GOHS-*toh dah kohr.*

I want one ...
  Quero um ...
  KEH-*roh oongh* ...

in green
  em verde
  engh VEHR-*deh*

  yellow
   amarelo
   ah-mah-REH-*loh*

  blue
   azul
   ah-ZOOL

  black
   preto
   PREH-*toh*

  red
   vermelho
   vehr-MEH-*l'yoh*

  white
   branco
   BRAHN-*koh*

  pink
   rosa
   ROH-*zah*

  grey
   cinzento
   seengh-ZEHN-*toh*

  brown
   castanho
   kahs-TAH-*n'yoh*

I will take it with me.
  Levo-o comigo.
  LEH-*voh-oh koh*-MEE-*goh.*

The receipt, please.
    O recibo, faça favor.
    *Oh reh-*SEE*-boh,* FAH*-sah fah-*VOHR.

Please send it to this address.
    Mande-o para esta direcção, faça favor.
    MAHN*-deh-oh* PAH*-rah* EHS*-tah dee-reh-*SOWNGH,
        FAH*-sah fah-*VOHR.

Where is there a bookstore?
    Onde há uma livraria?
    OHN*-deh* AH OO*-mah lee-vrah-*REE*'yah?*

Where is there a flower shop?
    Onde há um florista?
    OHN*-deh* AH *oongh floh-*REES*-tah?*

5. TRANSPORTATION

Taxi!
    Taxi!
    TAH*-xee!*

Take me to the airport.
    Leve-me ao aeroporto.
    LEH*-veh-meh* AH*'oo ah-eh-roh-*POHR*-toh.*

Turn right.
    Volte à direita.
    VOHL*-teh* AH *dee-*RAY*-tah.*

Turn left.
    Volte à esquerda.
    VOHL*-teh* AH *ehs-*KEHR*-dah.*

Straight ahead.
    Sempre a direito.
    SEHM*-preh ah dee-*RAY*-toh.*

Not so fast!
    Não tão depressa!
    *Nowngh towngh deh-*PREH*-sah!*

Hurry up!
 Depressa!
 *Deh-*PREH*-sah!*

Stop here!
 Pare aquí!
 PAH*-reh ah-*KEE!

Wait for me!
 Espere por mim!
 *Ehs-*PEH*-reh pohr meengh!*

How much is it?
 Quanto é?
 KWAHN*-toh* EH?

How much is it to . . . ?
 Quanto é até . . . ?
 KWAHN*-toh* EH *ah-*TEH . . . ?

and back?
 ir e vir?
 eer ee veer?

How much by the hour?
 Quanto é por hora?
 KWAHN*-toh* EH *pohr* OH*-rah?*

by the day?
 por dia?
 pohr DEE*'yah?*

  a car
   um carro
   oongh KAH*-rroh*

a boat
   um barco
   oongh BAHR*-koh*

  a bicycle
   uma bicicleta
   OO*-mah bee-see-*KLEH*-tah*

  a horse
   um cavalo
   *oongh kah-*VAH*-loh*

a donkey
   um burro
   oongh BOO*-rroh*

Show me the sights.
 Mostre-me os lugares de interêsse.
 MOHS*-treh-meh ohs loo-*GAH*-rehs deh eengh-teh-*
 REH*-seh.*

What is that building?
 Que edifício é aquele?
 *Keh eh-dee-*FEE*-s'yoh* EH *ah-*KEH*-leh?*

Can I go in?
 Posso entrar?
 POH*-soh ehn-*TRAHR?

I want to see the Tower of Belem.
 Quero ver a Tôrre de Belem.
 KEH*-roh vehr ah* TOH*-rreh deh Beh-*LENGH.

To the railroad station!
  À estação ferroviária (de trens) !
  AH *ehs-tah-*SOWNGH *feh-rroh-v'*YAH-*r'yah (deh trenghs) !*

Porter!
  Carregador!
  *Kahr-gah-*DOHR!

I have two bags.
  Tenho duas malas.
  TEH-*n'yoh* DOO-*ahs* MAH-*lahs.*

A ticket to ...
  Um bilhete para ...
  *Oongh bee-l'*YEH-*teh* PAH-*rah ...*

one way
  ida
  EE-*dah*

round trip
  ida e volta
  EE-*dah ee* VOHL-*tah*

first class
  primeira classe
  *pree-*MAY-*rah* KLAH-*seh*

second class
  segunda classe
  *seh-*GOON-*dah* KLAH-*seh*

When does it leave?
  Quando parte?
  KWAHN-*doh* PAHR-*teh?*

Where is the train to São Paulo?
  Onde fica o trem para São Paulo?
  OHN-*deh* FEE-*kah oh trengh* PAH-*rah Sowngh* PAH*'oo-loh?*

Is this the train for Santos?
  É êste o trem para Santos?
  EH EHS-*teh oh trengh* PAH-*rah* SAHN-*tohs?*

When do we get to Rio de Janeiro?
  Quando chegaremos ao Rio de Janeiro?
  KWAHN-*doh sheh-gah-*REH-*mohs* AH*'oo* REE*'yoh deh Jah-*NAY-*roh?*

Open the window, please.
  Abra a janela, faça favor.
  AH-*brah ah jah-*NEH-*lah,* FAH-*sah fah-*VOHR.

Close the window.

Feche a janela.

FEH-*sheh ah jah-*NEH-*lah.*

Where is the bus to Sintra?

Onde está a camionete (o ónibus) para Sintra?

OHN-*deh* ehs-TAH *ah kah-m'yoh-*NEH-*teh* (*oh* OH-*nee-boos*) PAH-*rah* SEENGH-*trah?*

I want to go to the Corcovado.

Quero ir ao Corcovado.

KEH-*roh eer* AH'*oo kohr-koh-*VAH-*doh.*

Please tell me where to get off.

Diga-me, faça favor, onde devo sair.

DEE-*gah-meh,* FAH-*sah fah-*VOHR, OHN-*deh* DEH-*voh sah-*EER.

Where is a gas station?

Onde há um pôsto de gasolina?

OHN-*deh* AH *oongh* POHS-*toh deh gah-zoh-*LEE-*nah?*

Fill it up.

Encha-o.

EHN-*shah-oh.*

Check the oil . . .

Verifique o óleo . . .

*Veh-ree-*FEE-*keh oh* OH-*l'yoh* . . .

water	tires
a água	os pneus
ah AH-*gwah*	*ohs* PNEH'*oos*

Something is wrong with the car.

Há alguma coisa avariada no carro.

AH *ahl-*GOO-*mah* KOY-*zah ah-vah-r'*YAH-*dah noh* KAH-*rroh.*

What's the matter?   **Can you fix it?**

O que é?   Pode arranjá-lo?

Oh keh EH?   POH-*deh ah-rrahn-*JAH-*loh?*

How long will it take?
　Quanto tempo levará?
　KWAHN-*toh* TEHM-*poh leh-vah-*RAH?

Is this the road to Petrópolis?
　É êste o caminho para Petrópolis?
　EH EHS-*teh oh kah-*MEE-*n'yoh* PAH-*rah Peh-*TROH-
　poh-lees?

Have you a map?
　Tem um mapa?
　Tengh oongh MAH-*pah?*

Where is the boat to Madeira?
　Onde está o barco para a Madeira?
　OHN-*deh ehs-*TAH *oh* BAHR-*koh* PAH-*rah ah Mah-*
　DAY-*rah?*

When does it leave?
　Quando parte?
　KWAHN-*doh* PAHR-*teh?*

6. MAKING FRIENDS

How are you?
　Como está?
　KOH-*moh ehs-*TAH?

My name is...
　Chamo-me...
　SHAH-*moh-meh* ...

What is your name, Sir?
　Qual é o seu nome, cavalheiro?
　Kwahl EH *oh* SEH'oo NOH-*meh, kah-vah-l'*YEH-*roh?*

Madam?	**Miss?**
minha senhora?	senhorita?
MEE-*n'yah seh-n'*YOH-*rah?*	seh-n'yoh-REE-*tah?*

I am delighted to meet you.
Muito prazer em conhecê-lo (la).
MUEEN-*toh* prah-ZEHR *engh* koh-n'yeh-SEH-*loh*
(*lah*).

Do you speak English?   A little.
Fala inglês?   Um pouco.
FAH-*lah* een-GLEHS?   *Oongh* POH-*koh*.

Do you understand?
Compreende?
Kongh-pree-EHN-*deh?*

I speak only a little Portuguese.
Falo pouco português.
FAH-*loh* POH-*koh* pohr-too-GEHS.

Please speak slowly.
Fale devagar, faça favor.
FAH-*leh* deh-vah-GAHR, FAH-*sah* fah-VOHR.

I am from New York.
Eu sou de Nova York.
EH'*oo soh deh* NOH-*vah* Yohrk.

Where are you from?
Donde é?
DOHN-*deh* EH?

I like your country.
Gosto do seu país.
GOHS-*toh doh* SEH'*oo* pah-EES.

I like your city.
Gosto da sua cidade.
GOHS-*toh dah* SOO-*ah* see-DAH-*deh*.

Have you been in America?
Já esteve na América?
JAH *ehs*-TEH-*veh nah* Ah-MEH-*ree-kah?*

This is my first visit here.
É a minha primeira visita aquí.
EH *ah* MEE-*n'yah* pree-MAY-*rah* vee-ZEE-*tah* ah-KEE.

May I sit here?
  Posso sentar-me aquí?
  POH-*soh* sehn-TAHR-*meh* ah-KEE?

Come here, please.
  Venha cá, faça favor.
  VEH-*n'yah* KAH, FAH-*sah* fah-VOHR.

May I take your picture?
  Posso tirar a sua fotografia?
  POH-*soh* tee-RAHR *ah* SOO-*ah* foh-toh-grah-FEE'*yah*?

This is my wife.
  É minha mulher.
  EH MEE-*n'yah* moo-l'YEHR.

>   **my husband**
>   meu marido
>   MEH'*oo* mah-REE-*doh*
>
>   **my children**
>   meus filhos
>   MEH'*oos* FEE-*l'yohs*

my son meu filho MEH'*oo* FEE-*l'yoh*	**my daughter** minha filha MEE-*n'yah* FEE-*l'yah*
my mother minha mãe MEE-*n'yah* mengh	**my father** meu pai MEH'*oo* pie
my sister minha irmã MEE-*n'yah* eer-MANGH	**my brother** meu irmão MEH'*oo* eer-MOWNGH

Have you children?
  Tem filhos?
  Tengh FEE-*l'yohs*?

How beautiful!
  Que belo!
  Keh BEH-*loh*!

Very interesting!
Muito interessante!
MUEEN-*toh eengh-teh-reh*-SAHN-*teh!*

Would you like a cigarette?
Quere um cigarro?
KEH-*reh oongh see*-GAH-*rroh?*

Would you like something to eat (to drink)?
Quere comer (beber) alguma coisa?
KEH-*reh koh*-MEHR (*beh*-BEHR) *ahl*-GOO-*mah*
KOY-*zah?*

Sit down, please.
Sente-se, por favor.
SEHN-*teh-seh, pohr fah*-VOHR.

Make yourself at home.
Esteja à vontade.
Ehs-TEH-*jah* AH *vohn*-TAH-*deh.*

Good luck!   **To your health!**
Boa sorte!   À sua saùde!
BOH-*ah* SOHR-*teh!*   AH *soo*-*ah sah*-OO-*deh!*

When can I see you again?
Quando posso tornar a vê-lo (la)?
KWAHN-*doh* POH-*soh tohr*-NAHR *ah* VEH-*loh* (*lah*)?

Where shall we meet?
Onde nos encontraremos?
OHN-*deh nohs ehn-kohn-trah*-REH-*mohs?*

Here is my address.
Aquí está a minha direcção.
Ah-KEE *ehs*-TAH *ah* MEE-*n'yah dee-reh*-SOWNGH.

What is your address?
Qual é a sua direcção?
Kwahl EH *ah* SOO-*ah dee-reh*-SOWNGH?

What is your phone number?
Qual é o seu número de telefone?
Kwahl EH *oh* SEH'*oo* NOO-*meh-roh deh teh-leh*-
FOH-*neh?*

May I speak to ...
Posso falar com ...
POH-*soh fah*-LAHR *kongh* ...

Would you like to have lunch?
Gostaria de almoçar?
Gohs-tah-REE'*yah deh ahl-moh*-SAHR?

dinner?	**go to the movies?**
jantar?	ir ao cinema?
jahn-TAHR?	*eer* AH'*oo see*-NEH-*mah?*

go to the theatre?	**go to the beach?**
ir ao teatro?	ir à praia?
eer AH'*oo t'*YAH-*troh?*	*eer* AH PRAH'*yah?*

take a walk?
dar um passeio?
dahr oongh pah-SAY-*oh?*

With great pleasure!
Com muito prazer.
Kongh MUEEN-*toh prah*-ZEHR.

I'm sorry, I can't.
Tenho muita pêna, não posso.
TEH-*n'yoh* MUEEN-*tah* PEH-*nah, nowngh* POH-*soh.*

Another time.
Outra vez.
OH-*trah vehs.*

I must go now.
Tenho que partir agora.
TEH-*n'yoh keh pahr*-TEER *ah*-GOH-*rah.*

Thank you for a wonderful time.
Obrigado(a) por umas horas muito agradáveis.
Oh-bree-GAH-*doh(ah) pohr* OO-*mahs* OH-*rahs*
MUEEN-*toh ah-grah*-DAH-*vays.*

Thank you for an excellent dinner.
Obrigado(a) por um jantar delicioso.
Oh-bree-GAH-*doh(ah) pohr oongh jahn*-TAHR *deh-
lee-s'*YOH-*zoh.*

This is for you.
    Isto é para sí.
    EES-toh EH PAH-*rah see.*

You are very kind!
    Que amável é!
    *Keh ah-*MAH-*vehl* EH!

It's nothing, really.
    Não é nada, realmente.
    Nowngh EH NAH-*dah, r'yahl-*MEHN-*teh.*

Congratulations!
    Parabéns!
    *Pah-rah-*BENGHS!

With best regards!
    Com muitas saùdades!
    Kongh MUEEN-*tahs sah-oo-*DAH-*dehs!*

7. EMERGENCIES

Help!
    Socôrro!
    *Soh-*KOH-*rroh!*

Police!
    Polícia!
    *Poh-*LEE-*s'yah!*

Fire!
    Fôgo!
    FOH-*goh!*

Stop that man!
    Pare esse homem!
    PAH-*reh* EH-*seh* OH-*mengh!*

Stop that woman!
    Para essa mulher!
    PAH-*reh* EH-*sah moo-l'*YEHR!

I have been robbed!
    Roubaram-me!
    *Rroh-*BAH-*rowngh-meh!*

Look out!
    Cuidado!
    *Kuee-*DAH-*doh!*

Wait a minute!
    Espere um momento!
    *Ehs-*PEH-*reh oongh moh-*MEHN-*toh!*

Stop!
    Pare!
    PAH-*reh!*

Get out!
    Saia!
    SAH'*yah!*

Hurry up!
    Apresse-se!
    *Ah-*PREH-*seh-seh!*

Don't bother me!
Não me importune!
*Nowngh meh eengh-pohr-*TOO*-neh!*

What's going on?
Que se passa?
Keh seh PAH*-sah?*

Entrance	**Exit**
Entrada	Saída
*Ehn-*TRAH*-dah*	*Sah-*EE*-dah*

Ladies
Senhoras
*Seh-n'*YOH*-rahs*

Gentlemen
Cavalheiros (Senhores)
*Kah-vah-l'*YEH*-rohs (Seh-n'*YOH*-rehs)*

Danger!	**Keep out!**
Perigo!	Entrada proibida!
*Peh-*REE*-goh!*	*Ehn-*TRAH*-dah proh-ee-*BEE*-dah!*

No smoking!
É proibido fumar!
EH *proh-ee-*BEE*-doh foo-*MAHR*!*

No parking!
É proibido estacionar!
EH *proh-ee-*BEE*-doh ehs-tah-s'yoh-*NAHR*!*

One way!
Direcção única!
*Dee-reh-*SOWNGH OO*-nee-kah!*

I am ill.
Estou doente.
*Ehs-*TOH *d'*WEHN*-teh.*

Call a doctor!
Chame um médico!
SHAH*-meh oongh* MEH*-dee-koh!*

It hurts here.
Doi-me aquí.
DOY-*meh ah*-KEE.

Take me to the hospital.
Leve-me para o hospital.
LEH-*veh-meh* PAH-*rah oh ohs-pee*-TAHL.

Where is there a dentist?
Onde há um dentista?
OHN-*deh* AH *oongh dehn*-TEES-*tah?*

I have lost my bag (suitcase).
Perdí a minha mala de viagem.
Pehr-DEE *ah* MEE-*n'yah* MAH-*lah deh* V'YAH-*jengh.*

  my handbag
  a minha mala de mão
  ah MEE-*n'yah* MAH-*lah deh mowngh*

  my camera
  a minha máquina fotográfica
  ah MEE-*n'yah* MAH-*kee-nah foh-toh*-GRAH-*fee-kah*

  my passport
  o meu passaporte
  oh MEH'*oo pah-sah*-POHR-*teh*

I am an American.
Sou americano.
Soh ah-meh-ree-KAH-*noh.*

Where is the American Consulate?
Onde fica o Consulado Americano?
OHN-*deh* FEE-*kah oh Kongh-soo*-LAH-*doh Ah-meh-ree*-KAH-*noh?*

Don't be upset.
Não se preocupe.
Nowngh seh pree-oh-KOO-*peh.*

Everything is all right.
Está tudo bem.
Ehs-TAH TOO-*doh bengh.*

SWEDISH

Facts About Swedish

Swedish is spoken by approximately 7 million people in Sweden and the metropolitan parts of Finland. Swedish is also widely understood in other Scandinavian countries such as Denmark and Norway. Swedish was chosen as the Scandinavian language to be included in the *Berlitz World-Wide Phrase Book* inasmuch as Swedish has more native speakers than either of the other two main Scandinavian languages as well as being widely spoken in Finland.

Swedish is a Teutonic language, belonging to the same group as English. Swedish, Danish, and Norwegian are closely related, and although they are distinctly different languages, with different pronunciation emphasis, they can be said to be mutually comprehensible, both in speaking and writing. Therefore, this book will serve you in the other Scandinavian countries as well as in Sweden.

Advice on Accent

å in Swedish is like the **aw** in *saw*.

ä is pronounced as the **ai** in *air*.

ö is like the **u** in *fur*.

The Swedish **u** has been represented in our phonetic system by the combination **ew**. To make this sound more exact, pronounce this with the lips pursed as if to whistle.

You will find that many Swedish words end in *et* or *en*. In general this *et* or *en* simply means "the" and is attached to the noun instead of being placed in front of it.

You Already Know Some Swedish

As English is a cousin of Swedish in the interlingual family relationships, you will be pleased to find many words that closely resemble English. As their pronunciation is somewhat different, however, you will need a little practice before you recognize them. In general, they resemble the similarities listed in German.

In addition, certain Swedish words have become familiar in English. Here are some, with their original meanings: *smörgåsbord* (hot and cold buffet—literally "sandwich table"); *ski* (pronounced *she* in Swedish); *slalom* (skiing term—literally "a curve"); *skål* ("To your health"). It is interesting to note that the original meaning of *skål* was "skull," and the word came into use because of the ancient Viking custom of drinking out of the silver-lined skulls of their erstwhile enemies.

1. FIRST CONTACT

Yes.
Ja.
Yaw.

No.
Nej.
Nay.

Good.
God.
Good.

Thank you.
Tack.
Tack.

You are welcome.
För all del.
Fur all dehl.

Excuse me.
Förlåt.
Fur-LOHT.

It's all right.
Det är bra.
Deh ehr brah.

Please.
Var så god.
Vahr so good.

I would like . . .
Jag vill gärna ha . . .
Yawg veel yehr-nah hah . . .

What?
Vad?
Vah?

This.
Detta.
DET-*tah.*

Where?
Var?
Vahr?

Here.
Här.
Hair.

When?
När?
Nair?

Now.
Nu.
New.

Later.
Senare.
SEH-*nah-reh.*

Who?
Vem?
Vem?

I
Jag
Yawg

you
ni
nee

he
han
hahn

she
hon
hohn

Your name?
Ert namn?
Ehrt NAH-*mn?*

Good morning.
God morgon.
GOH MOHR-*gone.*

Good evening.
God afton.
Good AHF-*tohn.*

Good night.
God natt.
Good naht.

Good-by.
Adjö.
*Ad-*YUH.

How are you?
Hur står det till?
Hewr store det till?

Very well, thank you! And you?
  Tack, mycket bra, och hur står det till med Er?
  Tack, MEW-*keh brah, ohg hewr store det till meh ehr?*

How much?
  Hur mycket?
  Hewr MEW-*keh?*

I do not understand, please repeat.
  Jag förstår inte, var så god att upprepa det hela.
  *Yawg fur-*STORE *in-teh, vahr so good aht* OOP-REH-*pah deh heh-lah.*

one	two	three	four
ett	två	tre	fyra
ett	*tvoh*	*treh*	FEW-*rah*

five	six	seven	eight
fem	sex	sju	åtta
fem	*sex*	*shew*	OHT-*tah*

	nine	ten	
	nio	tio	
	nee-yoh	*tee-yoh*	

2. ACCOMMODATIONS

Where is a good hotel?
  Var finns det ett bra hotell?
  *Vahr fins deh eht brah hoh-*TEL?

I want a room for one person.
  Jag vill ha ett rum för en person.
  *Yawg veel hah eht room fur ehn per-*SOHN.

I want a room for two persons.
  Jag vill ha ett rum för två personer.
  *Yawg veel hah eht room fur tvoh per-*SOH-*nehr.*

I want a room with bath.
  Jag vill ha ett rum med bad.
  Yawg veel hah eht room meh bahd.

for two days	**for a week**
för två dagar	för en vecka
fur tvoh DAH-*gahr*	*fur ehn vek-*KAH

till Monday	**Tuesday**
till Måndag	Tisdag
teel MOHN-*dahg*	TEES-*dahg*

Wednesday	**Thursday**	**Friday**
Onsdag	Torsdag	Fredag
OONS-*dahg*	TOHRS-*dag*	FREH-*dahg*

Saturday	**Sunday**
Lördag	Söndag
LUHR-*dahg*	SUHN-*dahg*

How much is the room?
  Vad kostar rummet?
  Vah KOH-*star* ROOM-*met?*

Here are my bags.
  Här är mina koffertar.
  Hair ehr mee-nah KOHF-*fehr-tahr.*

Here is my passport.
  Här är mitt pass.
  Hair ehr mitt pass.

I like it.
  Jag tycker om det.
  Yawg TEWK-*kehr ohm deh.*

I don't like it.
  Jag tycker inte om det.
  Yawg TEWK-*kehr* IN-*teh ohm deh.*

Show me another.
  Var vänlig att visa mig ett annat.
  Vahr VEHN-*leeg aht* VEE-*sah may eht* AHN-*naht.*

Where is the toilet?
 Var är toaletten?
 *Vahr ehr toh-ah-*LET-*ten?*

Where is the men's room?
 Var är herrtoaletten?
 Vahr ehr HERR-*toh-ah-*LET-*ten?*

Where is the ladies' room?
 Var är damtoaletten?
 Vahr ehr DAHM-*toh-ah-*LET-*ten?*

hot water	**a towel**	**soap**
varmvatten	en handduk	tvål
*vahrm-*VAHT-*ten*	*ehn hahnd-dewk*	*tvohl*

Come in!	**Please have this washed.**
Stig in!	Var vänlig att tvätta detta.
Steeg in!	*Vahr* VEHN-*leeg aht* TVET-*tah* DET-*tah.*

Please have this pressed.
 Var vänlig pressa detta.
 Vahr VEHN-*leeg* PRESS-*ah* DET-*tah.*

Please have this cleaned.
 Var vänlig kemiskt tvätta detta.
 Vahr VEHN-*leeg* SHEH-*miskt* TVET-*tah* DET-*tah.*

When will it be ready?
 När blir det färdigt?
 Nehr bleer deh FEHR-*digt?*

I need it for tonight.
 Jag behövar detta i kväll.
 *Yawg beh-*HUH-*vahr* DET-*tah ee kvehl.*

I need it for tomorrow.
 Jag behövar detta i morgon.
 *Yawg beh-*HUH-*vahr* DET-*tah ee* MOHR-*gohn.*

My key, please.
 Var så god: nyckeln.
 Vahr soh good NEWK-*keln.*

Any mail for me?
Något brev för mig?
NOH-*got brave fur may?*

Any package for me?
Något paket för mig?
NOH-*got pah-*KATE *fur may?*

I want five airmail stamps for the U.S.
Fem luftpostfrimärken till America.
*Fehm luft-post-free-mehr-kehn teel ah-*MEH-*ree-kah.*

Have you postcards?
Har Ni vykort?
*Hahr nee vew-*KOHRT?

I want to send a telegram.
Jag vill skicka ett telegram.
Yawg veel SHICK-*kah eht teh-leh-*GRAM.

Call me at seven in the morning.
Ring mig upp klockan sju på morgonen.
Ring may up KLOCK-*kahn shew poh* MOHR-*goh-nehn.*

Where is the telephone?   **Hello! Hello!**
Var är telefonen?   Hallo! Hallo!
*Vahr ehr teh-leh-*FOH-*nehn?*   *Hallo! Hallo!*

Send breakfast to the room.
Vill ni vara vänlig och skicka upp frukost till rummet.
Veel nee VAH-*rah* VEHN-*leeg ohg* SHICK-*kah up* FREW-*kohst teel* ROOM-*met.*

orange juice   **ham and eggs**
apelsin juice   skinka med ägg
*ah-pehl-*ZEEN *yoos*   SHIN-*kah meh egg*

rolls and coffee
bröd och kaffe
bruhd ohg KAHF-*feh*

I am expecting a friend.
Jag väntar en vän.
Yawg vehn-tahr ehn vehn.

Tell him to wait.
Var vänlig och be honom vänta.
Vahr VEEN-*leeg ohg beh hoh-nohm* VEHN-*tah.*

Where is the restaurant?
Var är restaurangen?
*Vahr ehr res-toh-*RAHN-*gen?*

Where is a barber shop?
Var är herrfrisören?
*Vahr ehr herr-free-*ZUH-*ren?*

Where is a beauty parlor?
Var är damfriseringen?
Vahr ehr DAHM-*free-zeh-rin-gain?*

Where is a drug store?
Var finns det ett apotek?
*Vahr fins deht ett ah-poh-*TEHK*?*

What is the telephone number?
Vad är telefon-numret?
*Vah ehr teh-leh-fohn-*NEWM-*ret?*

What is the address?
Vad är adressen?
*Vah ehr ad-*RES-*sen?*

I want to change some money.
Jag vill växla pengar.
Yawg veel vex-lah pen-gahr.

What is the rate for dollars?
Vad är dollar-kursen?
Vah ehr DOHL-*lahr koor-sen?*

eleven	twelve	thirteen
elva	tolv	tretton
*ehl-*VAH	*tohlv*	*treht-*TON

fourteen
 fjorton
 f'yohr-TON

fifteen
 femton
 fem-TON

sixteen
 sexton
 sex-TON

seventeen
 sjutton
 shew-TON

eighteen
 arton
 ahr-TON

nineteen
 nitton
 nit-TON

twenty
 tjugo
 tshew-GOH

thirty
 trettio
 *treht-t'*YOH

forty
 fyrtio
 *fur-t'*YOH

fifty
 femtio
 *fem-t'*YOH

sixty
 sextio
 *sex-t'*YOH

seventy
 sjuttio
 *shew-t'*YOH

eighty
 åttio
 *oht-t'*YOH

ninety
 nittio
 *nit-t'*YOH

one hundred
 ett hundra
 ett hoon-DRAH

two hundred
 två hundra
 tvoh hoon-DRAH

three hundred
 tre hundra
 treh hoon-DRAH

four hundred
 fyra hundra
 few-RAH *hoon*-DRAH

five hundred
 fem hundra
 fem hoon-DRAH

six hundred
 sex hundra
 sex hoon-DRAH

seven hundred
 sju hundra
 shew hoon-DRAH

eight hundred
 åtta hundra
 oht-TAH *hoon*-DRAH

nine hundred
 nio hundra
 nee-yoh hoon-DRAH

one thousand
 ett tusen
 ett TEW-*sen*

ten thousand
 tio tusen
 tee-oh TEW-*sen*

hundred thousand
 hundra tusen
 hoon-DRAH TEW-*sen*

My bill, please.
Var vänlig ge mig räkningen.
Vahr VEHN-*leeg yeh may* REHK-*nin-gen.*

3. EATING

Where is a good restaurant?
Var finns det en bra restaurang?
*Vahr finns deh ehn brah res-toh-*RAHNG?

A table for two.
Ett bord för två personer.
*Eht board fur tvoh pehr-*SOH-*nehr.*

Waiter!   **Waitress!**
Vaktmästare!   Fröken!
VAHKT-*meh-stah-reh!*   FRUH-*ken!*

The menu, please.
Var vänlig ge mig matsedeln.
Vahr VEHN-*leeg yeh may* MAHT-*sed-ehln.*

What's good today?
Vad kan Ni rekommendera i dag?
*Vah kahn nee reh-kohm-mahn-*DEH-*rah ee dahg?*

Is it ready?
Är detta färdigt?
Ehr DET-*tah* FEHR-*deeght?*

How long will it take?
Hur länge dröjer det?
Hewr LEHN-*geh* DRUH-*yehr deh?*

This please ...   **and this**
Detta ...   och detta
DET-*tah* ...   *ohg* DET-*tah*

water	**milk**	**a glass of beer**
vatten	mjölk	ett glas öl
VAHT-*ten*	*m'yulk*	*eht glahs uhl*

red wine
rödvin
ruhd-veen

white wine
vitt vin
veet vin

a cocktail
en cocktail
ehn cocktail

whisky soda
whisky soda
whisky soda

soup	**fish**	**meat**
soppa	fisk	kött
sop-pah	*fisk*	*shutt*

bread and butter
bröd och smör
bruhd ohg smuhr

a sandwich
en smörgås
ehn smuhr-gohs

steak . . .	**rare**	**medium**
stek . . .	rå	lättstekt
steak . . .	*row*	LET-*steaked*

well done
väl stekt
vail steaked

chicken	**veal**
kyckling	kalvkött
SHEWK-*ling*	KAHLF-*shutt*

pork	**lamb**	**lamb chop**
svinkött	lammkött	lammkotlett
SVEEN-*shutt*	LAHM-*shutt*	LAHM-*koht-let*

meatballs with cowberries
Köttbullar med lingon
SHUTT-*bool-lahr meh lin-gone*

hash with potatoes
Pytt i panna
Pewt ee PAHN-*nah*

No sauce for me.
Ingen sås för mig.
IN-*gehn sauce fur may.*

with potatoes . . .	**rice**	**an omelet**
med potatis . . .	ris	en omelett
*meh poh-*TAH-*tees . . .*	*rees*	*ehn ohm-let*

And what vegetables?
Och vilka grönsaker?
Ohg veel-kah GRUHN-*sah-kehr?*

peas	beans	carrots
ärtor	bönor	morötter
AIR-*tohr*	BUH-*nohr*	*moh*-RUT-*tehr*

onions	a salad
lök	sallad
luhk	SAHL-*lahd*

lettuce	tomatoes
grön sallad	tomater
gruhn SAHL-*lahd*	*toh*-MAH-*tehr*

Please bring me another fork.
Var vänlig ge mig en annan gaffel.
Vahr VEHN-*leeg yeh may ehn* AHN-*nahn* GAHF-*f'l.*

knife	spoon
kniv	sked
k'neev	*shed*

glass	plate
glas	tallrik
glahs	TAHL-*reek*

What is there for dessert?
Vad har Ni för dessert?
Vah hahr nee fur dehs-SEHR?

fruit	pastry	cake
frukt	bakelser	kaka
frewkt	BAH-*kehl-zehr*	KAH-*kai*

ice cream	cheese
glass	ost
glahs	*oost*

Some coffee, please.
Var vänlig: en kaffe.
Vahr VEHN-*leeg: ehn* KAHF-*feh.*

sugar
  socker
  SOHK-*kehr*

cream
  grädde
  GRED-*deh*

tea with lemon
  te med citron
  *teh meh see-*TROHN

mineral water
  mineralvatten
  *min-neh-*RAHL-VAHT-*ten*

More, please.
  Var vänlig ge mig mera.
  Vahr VEHN-*lee yeh may* MEH-*rah.*

That's enough.
  Det är nog.
  Deht air noog.

The check, please.
  Var vänlig ge mig räkningen.
  Vahr VEHN-*leeg yeh may* REHK-*neen-gehn.*

Is the tip included?
  Är drickspengar inberäknade?
  Air DRICK-*spen-gahr in-beh-*REHK-*nah-deh?*

It was very good!
  Det var mycket bra!
  Deh vahr MEW-*keh brah!*

4. SHOPPING

I would like to buy this ...
  Jag skulle vilja köpa det här ...
  Yawg SKOOL-*leh* VEEL-*yah* SHUH-*pah deh hair ...*

I am just looking around.
  Jag bara ser mig omkring.
  Yawg BAH-*rah sehr may* OHM-*kring.*

Where is the section for ... ?
  Var är ... avdelningen?
  *Vahr ehr ... ahv-*DEHL-*neen-gen?*

  men's clothing
    herrkläder
    HERR-KLAY-*dehr*

  women's clothing
    damklänningar
    DAHM-*klehn-nin-gahr*

hats
hattar
haht-tahr

gloves
handskar
hahnd-skahr

underwear
underkläder
OON-*dehr-klay-dehr*

shoes
skor
skoor

stockings
strumpor
STREWM-*pohr*

shirts
skjortor
SHOHR-*tohr*

The size in America is ...
Det amerikanska numret för detta är ...
*Deh ah-meh-ree-*KAHN-*skah* NEWM-*ret fur* DET-*tah
ehr ...*

toys
leksaker
lehk-zack-ehr

perfumes
parfumer
*pahr-*FEW-*mehr*

jewelry
smycken
SMEW-*ken*

watches
klockor
*klohk-*KOHR

toilet articles
toalettartiklar
*toh-ah-*LET-*ahr-tick-*LAHR

films
filmrullar
film-ruhl-lahr

souvenirs
minnesgåvor
MINN-*ness-goh-vohr*

sport articles
sportartiklar
*sport-ahr-tick-*LAHR

Show me ...
Vahr vänlig visa mig ...
Vahr VEHN-*leeg* VEE-*sah may ...*

something less expensive
något mindre dyrt
NOH-*got* MIN-*dreh dewrt*

another one
ett annat
eht AHN-*naht*

a better quality
någon bättre kvalité
NOH-*gone* BETT-*reh kvah-lee-*TEH

bigger	**smaller**
större	mindre
STUHR-*reh*	MIN-*dreh*

I don't like the color.
Jag tycker inte om färgen.
Yawg TEW-*kehr* IN-*teh ohm* FEHR-*yen.*

I want one ...   **in green**
Jag vill ha en ...   i grönt
Yawg veel hah ehn ...   *ee gruhnt*

in yellow	**in blue**	**in red**
i gult	i blått	i rött
ee gewlt	*ee bloht*	*ee ruht*

in black	**in white**	**in grey**
i svart	i vitt	i grått
ee svahrt	*ee veet*	*ee groht*

in pink	**in brown**
i rosa	i brunt
ee ROH-*sah*	*ee brewnt*

I will take it with me.
Jag tar det med mig.
Yawg tahr deh meh may.

The receipt, please.
Var vänlig: kvittot.
Vahr VEHN-*leeg: Quit-toht.*

Please send it to this address.
Var vänlig sänd detta till den här adressen.
Vahr VEHN-*leeg send* DET-*tah teel dehn hair ah-*
DRESS'*n.*

Where is there a flower shop?
Var finns det en blomsterhandel?
Vahr finns deh ehn BLOHM-*stehr-hahn-d'l?*

Where is there a bookstore?
Var finns det en bokhandel?
Vahr finns deh ehn BOHK-*hahn-d'l?*

Where is there a food shop?
Var finns det en livsmedelsaffär?
Vahr finns deh ehn LEEVS-*meh-d'ls-ahf-*FAIR?

5. TRANSPORTATION

Taxi!   **Take me to the airport.**
Taxi!   Kör mig till flygplatsen.
TAH-*ksee!*   *Shuhr may teel* FLEWK-*plaht-sen.*

Turn right.   **Turn left.**
Gå till höger.   Gå till vänster.
Goh teel HUH-*gehr.*   *Goh teel* VEHN-*stehr.*

Not so fast!   **Hurry up!**
Inte så hastigt!   Skynda er!
In-teh soh HAHS-*tick'd!*   SHEWN-*dah ehr!*

Stop here!   **Wait for me.**
Stanna här!   Vänta på mig.
STAHN-*nah hair!*   VEHN-*tah poh may.*

How much is it?
Hur mycket kostar det?
Hewr MEWK-*keh* KOHS-*tahr deh?*

How much is it to ... ?
Hur mycket kommer det att kosta till ... ?
Hewr MEWK-*keh* KOHM-*mehr deh aht* KOHS-*tah
teel ... ?*

    and back?
      och tillbaka?
      ohg TEFL-*bah-kah?*

How much by the hour?
   Hur mycket kommer det att kosta per timme?
   Hewr MEWK-*keh* KOHM-*mehr deh aht* KOHS-*tah per*
   TIM-*meh?*

    by the day?
     per dag?
     per dahg?

Show me the sights.
   Var vänlig visa mig sevärdheterna.
   Vahr VEHN-*lee* VEE-*sah may* SEH-*vaird-heh-tahr-*
   nah.

What is that building?
   Vad är den där byggnaden?
   Vah ehr den dehr BEWG-*nah-den?*

Can I go in?
   Får jag gå in?
   For yawg goh in?

I want to see Katarinahissen. Strömparterren.
   Jag vill se Katarinahissen. Strömparterren.
   *Yawg veel seh kah-tah-*REE-*nah-hiss'n.* STRUHM-
   *pahr-*TEHR-*ren.*

To the railroad station.
   Till järnvägsstationen.
   Teel YEHRN-*vehgs-stah-*SHOH-*nehn.*

Porter!	**I have two bags.**
Bärare!	Jag har två väskor.
BEH-*rah-reh!*	*Yawg hahr tvoh* VESS-*kohr.*

A ticket to Malmö.
   Jag vill ha en biljett till Malmö.
   *Yawg veel hah ehn bill-*YET *teel Mahl-muh.*

one way	**round trip**
enkel	tur och retur
EHN-*k'l*	*tewr ohg reh-*TEWR

first class	second class
första klass	andra klass
FUHR-*stah klahs*	AHN-*drah klahs*

When does the train leave?
Når går tåget?
Nair gohr TOH-*get?*

Where is the train to Linköping?
Var är tåget till Linköping?
Vahr ehr TOH-*get teel leen-*SHUH-*pink?*

Is this the train to Södertälje?
Är det här tåget till Södertälje?
Ehr deh hair TOH-*get teel suh-dehr* TAIL-*yeh?*

When do we get to Göteborg?
Når ankommer vi till Göteborg?
Nair AHN-*kohm-mehr vee teel* YUH-*teh-bohrg?*

Open the window.	**Close the window.**
Öppna fönstret.	Stäng fönstret.
UHP-*nah* FUHN-*streht.*	*Steng* FUHN-*streht.*

Where is the bus to Drottningholm?
Var är bussen till Drottningholm?
*Vahr ehr buss'n teel droht-ning-*HOHLM?

I want to go to Gävle.
Jag vill resa till Gävle.
Yawg veel REH-*sah teel* YEHV-*leh.*

Please tell me where to get off.
Var vänlig säg mig var jag skall gå av.
Vahr VEHN-*lee sehg may vahr yawg skahl goh ahv.*

Where is a gas station?
Var finns det en bensinstation?
*Vahr finns deh ehn ben-*ZEEN-*stah-*SHOHN?

Fill it up.	**Check the oil.**
Fyll tanken.	Kontrollera oljan.
Fewl TAHN-*ken.*	*Kohn-troh-*LEH-*rah* OHL-*yan.*

water	tires
vatten	däcken
VAHT-*ten*	*deck'n*

Something is wrong with the car.
Det måste vara något fel med bilen.
Deh MOHS-*teh* VAH-*rah* NOH-*got fehl meh* BEE-*lehn.*

Can you fix it?
Kan Ni reparera detta?
*Kahn nee reh-pah-*REH-*rah* DET-*tah?*

How long will it take?
Hur lång tid kommer det att ta?
Hewr lohng teed KOHM-*mehr deh aht tah?*

Is this the road to Norrköping?
Är detta vägen till Norrköping?
Ehr DET-*tah* VEH-*gehn teel* NOHR-*shup-ping?*

Have you a map?
Har Ni en vägkarta?
Hahr nee ehn VEHG-*kahr-tah?*

Where is the boat to ... ?	**When does it leave?**
Var är båten till ... ?	När går båten?
Vahr ehr BOH-*ten teel ...?*	*Nair gohr* BOH-*ten?*

6. MAKING FRIENDS

Good day.
God dag.
Good DAW.

My name is ...	**What is your name, Sir?**
Mitt namn är ...	Vad är Ert namn?
Mitt nahm'n ehr ...	*Vah ehr ehrt nahm'n?*

What is your name, madam?
Vad är damens namn?
Vah ehr DAH-*mens nahm'n?*

What is your name, Miss?
Vad är frökens namn?
Vah ehr FRUH-*kens nahm'n?*

I am delighted to meet you.
Det var roligt att träffas.
Deh vahr ROH-*leekht aht* TREHF-*ahs.*

Do you speak English?   **A little.**
Talar Ni engelska?   Litet.
TAH-*lahr nee* EHN-*gehl-skah?*   LEE-*teh.*

Do you understand?
Förstår ni?
*Fur-*STOHR *nee?*

Please speak slowly.
Var vänlig tala långsammare.
Vahr VEHN-*lee* TAH-*lah* LOAN-*sah-mah-ruh.*

I speak only a little Swedish.
Jag talar bara litet svenska.
Yawg TAH-*lahr* BAH-*rah* LEE-*teh* SVEN-*skah.*

I am from New York.
Jag kommer från New York.
Yawg KOHM-*mehr frohn New York.*

Where are you from?
Varifrån kommer Ni?
*Vah-ree-*FROHN KOHM-*mehr nee?*

I like your country.
Jag tycker om Ert land.
Yawg TEWK-*kehr ohm ehrt lahnd.*

I like your city.
Jag tycker om Er stad.
Yawg TEWK-*kehr ohm ehr stahd.*

Have you been in America?
  Har Ni varit i Amerika?
  Hahr nee VAH-*rit ee ah-*MEH-*ree-kah?*

This is my first visit here.
  Det är mitt första besök här.
  *Deh ehr mitt fur-stah beh-*SUHK *hair.*

May I sit here?
  Får jag sitta här?
  For yawg SIT-*tah hair?*

May I take your picture?   **Come here.**
  Får jag ta en bild av Er?   Kom hit.
  For yawg tah ehn build ahv ehr?   *Kohm hit.*

This is my wife.
  Det här min fru.
  Deh hair meen frew.

my husband	son	daughter
min man	son	dotter
meen mahn	*sohn*	DOHT-*tehr*

mother	father	sister	brother
mor	far	syster	bror
mohr	*fahr*	SEWS-*tehr*	*brohr*

Have you children?
  Har Ni några barn?
  Hahr nee NOH-*grah barn?*

Thank you for a wonderful time.
  Tack för en underbar tid.
  Tahk fur ehn OON-*dehr-bahr teed.*

Thank you for an excellent dinner.
  Tack för en utmärkt middag.
  Tahk fur ehn EWT-*mehrkt* MID-*dawg.*

This is for you.   **You are very kind.**
  Det är för Er.   Ni är mycket vänlig.
  Deh ehr fur ehr.   *Nee ehr* MEW-*keh* VEHN-*lee.*

It's nothing really.
Det är verkligen ingenting.
Deh ehr VEHR-*klee-gehn* IN-*gen-ting.*

With best regards.
Med de bästa hälsningar.
Meh deh BESS-*tah* HAILS-*nin-gahr.*

Congratulations!
Hjärtliga gratulationer!
YEHRT-*lee-gah grah-too-lah-*SHOH-*nehr!*

7. EMERGENCIES

Help!   **Police!**   **Fire!**
Hjälp!   Polis!   Det brinner!
Yehlp!   *Poh-*LEES!   *Deh* BRIN-*nehr!*

Stop that man!
Tag fast den där mannen!
Tah fahst dehn dehr MAHN-*nen!*

Stop that woman!
Tag fast den där kvinnan!
Tah fahst dehn dehr KVIN-*nahn!*

I have been robbed!
Jag har blivit bestulen!
Yawg hahr BLEE-*vit bess-*TEW-*lehn!*

Look out!   **Wait a minute!**
Se upp!   Vänta en minut!
Seh ohp!   VEHN-*tah ehn mee-*NEWT!

Stop!   **Get out!**   **Hurry up!**
Stanna!   Gå ut!   Skynda på!
STAHN-*nah!*   *Go ewt!*   SHEWN-*dah poh!*

Don't bother me!
Låt bli att besvära mig!
*Loht blee aht beh-*SVEH-*rah may!*

What's going on?
Vad är det som har hänt?
Vah ehr deh sohm hahr hent?

Entrance	**Exit**
Ingång	Utgång
*In-*GONG	*ewt-*GONG
Ladies	**Gentlemen**
Damer	Herrar
DAH-*mehr*	*Herr-rar*
Danger	**Keep out**
Fara	Håll Er utanför
FAH-*rah*	*Hohl ehr ew-tahn-*FUR

No smoking **No parking**
Rökning förbjuden Ej parkering
RUHK-*ning fur-*B'YEW-*den* *Ay pahr-*KEH-*ring*

One way
Enkelriktad trafik
EN-*kehl-reek-tahd trah-*FICK

I am ill. **It hurts here.**
Jag är sjuk. Det gör ont här.
Yawg ehr shewk. *Deh yuhr ohnt hair.*

Call a doctor.
Tillkalla en läkare.
TEEL-*kahl-lah ehn* LEH-*kah-reh.*

Where is the drugstore?
Var finns det ett apotek?
*Vahr finns deh eht ah-poh-*TEHK?

Take me to the hospital.
Kör mig till sjukhuset.
Shuhr may teel SHEWK-*hew-set.*

Where is a dentist?
Var finns det en tandläkare?
Vahr finns deh ehn TAHN-*leh-kah-reh?*

I have lost my bag.
　Jag har förlorat mitt bagage.
　*Yawg hahr fur-*LOH-*raht mitt bah-*GAHSH.

　　my wallet　　　　**my camera**
　　　min plånbok　　　　min kamera
　　　meen PLOHN-*bohk*　　*meen* KAH-*meh-rah*

　　my passport
　　　mitt pass
　　　mitt pahss

I am an American.
　Jag är amerikanare.
　*Yawg ehr ah-meh-ree-*KAH-*nah-reh.*

Where is the American Consulate?
　Var är amerikanska konsulatet?
　*Vahr ehr ah-meh-ree-*KAHN-*skah kohn-sew-*LAH-*teh?*

Do not get excited!　　**Take it easy!**
　Var inte orolig!　　　　Tag det lugnt!
　Vahr IN-*teh* OH-*roh-leeg!*　*Tah deh loog'n't!*

Everything is all right.
　Allt är i sin ordning.
　Ahlt ehr ee seen OHRD-*ning.*

DUTCH

Facts About Dutch

Dutch is spoken by about 12 million people in the Netherlands including Curaçao, Aruba in the Caribbean, and Dutch Guiana. Dutch is also widely understood in Indonesia and New Guinea. A language closely allied to Dutch is Flemish, one of the two official languages of Belgium. Afrikaans, another form of Dutch, is the official language of the Union of South Africa. The Dutch used in this book will enable you easily to be understood in the Flemish section of Belgium, the Union of South Africa and other places where Dutch is spoken.

Advice on Accent

Dutch is a Teutonic language and is closely related to English. It is characterized, even more so than German, by a guttural accent. The **g** especially should be pronounced very strongly in the back of the throat, roughly comparable to the **ch** of Loch Ness but more so. Other letters pronounced quite differently than in English include **j** pronounced like the y in "yes."

You Already Know Some Dutch

As Dutch may be considered a first cousin of English, many words will immediately become familiar to you and will be easy to remember once you jump the pronunciation barrier. Many words are strikingly similar. For example observe the following: you *u,* pen *pen,* paper *papier,* floor *vloer,* seven *zeven,* book *boek,* clock *klok,* half *half,* and a host of others.

One word familiar to all Americans, "Yankee," is derived directly from the Dutch word *Janke* meaning "Little John." This was a rather contemptuous name given to workers on Dutch farms in Colonial times and applied pejoratively by the British to all Americans, who, in turn, adopted it as a badge of honor.

1. FIRST CONTACT

Yes.	**No.**	**Good.**
Ja.	Neen.	Goed.
Yah.	*Nayn.*	*Khood.*

Thank you.
Dank U wel.
Dahnk EW *vehl.*

You are welcome.
Het is een genoegen.
*Heht is uhn khuh-*NOO-*khen.*

Excuse me.
Pardon.
*Pahr-*DOHN.

It's all right.
Het geeft niets.
Heht khehft neets.

Please.
Alstublieft.
*Ahl-stew-*BLEEFT

I would like.
Ik wil.
Ik veel.

What?	**This.**	**Where?**	**Here.**
Wat?	Dit.	Waar?	Hier.
Vaht?	*Ditt.*	*Vahr?*	*Here.*

When?	**Now.**	**Later.**
Wanneer?	Nu.	Later.
*Vahn-*NEHR?	*New.*	LAH-*tehr.*

Who?	**I**	**you**	**he**	**she**
Wie?	ik	U	hij	zij
Vee?	*ick*	*ew*	*hay*	*zay*

Your name?
Uw naam?
EW *nahm?*

Good morning.
Goeden morgen.
KHOO-*deh* MOHR-*khen.*

Good day.
Goeden dag.
KHOO-*den dahkh.*

Good evening.
Goeden avond.
KHOO-*den* AH-*vent.*

Good night.
Goede nacht.
KHOO-*deh nahkht.*

Good-by.
Vaarwel.
*Fahr-*VEHL.

How are you?   **Very well, thank you, and you?**
Hoe gaat het?   Heel goed, dank U, en U?
Hoo khaht heht?   *Hail khoot, dahnk* EW, *an ew?*

How much?
Hoeveel?
*hoo-*FAIL?

I do not understand, please repeat.
Ik versta het niet, zeg het nogeens.
*Ick fehr-*STAH *heht neet, zekh heht* NOHKH-*ains.*

one	two	three	four
een	twee	drie	vier
ain	*tvay*	*dree*	*fear*

five	six	seven	eight
vijf	zes	zeven	acht
fife	*zess*	ZEH-*ven*	*ahkht*

nine	ten	eleven	twelve
negen	tien	elf	twaalf
NEH-*khen*	*teen*	*ailf*	*tvahlf*

2. ACCOMMODATIONS

Where is a good hotel?
Waar is er een goed hotel?
*Vahr is uhr uhn khood hoh-*TEL?

I want a room for one person.
Ik wil een eenpersoons kamer.
Ick veel ain AIN-*pehr-sohns* KAH-*mer.*

I want a room for two persons.
Ik wil een kamer voor twee personen.
Ick veel ain KAH-*mer for tvay per-*SOH-*nen.*

I want a room with bath.
Ik wil een kamer met badkamer.
Ick veel ain KAH-*mer met* BAHT-*kah-mer.*

for two days	**for a week**
voor twee dagen	voor een week
for tvay DAH-*khen*	*for ain vehk*
till Monday	**Tuesday**
tot Maandag	Dinsdag
toht MAHN-*dahkh*	DINS-*dahkh*
Wednesday	**Thursday**
Woensdag	Donderdag
VOONS-*dahkh*	DOHN-*der-dahkh*
Friday	**Saturday**
Vrijdag	Zaterdag
FRAY-*dahkh*	ZAH-*tehr-dahkh*
Sunday	
Zondag	
ZOHN-*dahkh*	

How much is it?
Hoeveel kost het?
*Hoo-*FAIL *kohst ett?*

Here are my bags.
Hier zijn mijn koffers.
Here zayn main KOHF-*fehrs.*

Here is my passport.
Hier is mijn pas.
Here is main pass.

I like it.	**I don't like it.**
Het bevalt me.	Het bevalt me niet.
*Ett beh-*FAHLT *muh.*	*Ett beh-*FAHLT *muh* **neet**.

Show me another.
Laat U mij een andere zien.
Laht ew may uhn AHN-*deh-reh zeen.*

Where is the toilet?
Waar is de W.C.?
Vahr is duh vay say?

Where is the men's room?
Waar is de Heren?
Vahr is duh HEH-*ren?*

Where is the ladies' room?
Waar is de Dames?
Vahr is duh DAH-*mess?*

hot water	a towel	soap
warm water	een handoek	zeep
vahrm VAH-*tehr*	*uhn* HAHN-*dook*	*zape*

Come in!
Binnen!
BIN-*nen!*

Please have this washed.
Laat dit wassen. alstublieft.
Laht ditt VAHS-*sen, ahl-stew-*BLEEFT.

Please have this pressed.
Laat dit strijken, alstublieft.
Laht ditt STRIGH-*ken, ahl-stew-*BLEEFT.

Please have it cleaned.
Laat het stomen, alstublieft.
Laht ett STOH-*men, ahl-stew-*BLEEFT.

When will it be ready?
Wanneer is het klaar?
*Vahn-*NEHR *is ett klahr?*

Put it there.
Zet het daar.
Zeht hat dahr.

I need it for tonight.
Ik heb het vanavond nodig.
*Ick hep ett fahn-*AH-*vent* NOH-*dekh.*

for tomorrow
morgen
MOHR-*khen*

My key, please.
Mijn sleutel, alstublieft.
Main SLUH-*tehl, ahl-stew-*BLEEFT.

Any mail for me?
Is er post voor mij?
Is uhr pohst for may?

Any packages?
Pakjes?
PAHK-*yes?*

I want five airmail stamps for the United States.
Ik wil vijf luchtpostzegels hebben voor Amerika.
Ick veel fife LEWKHT-*pohst-zay-khels* HEB'n *for*
*ah-*MEH-*ree-kah.*

Have you postcards?
Hebt U briefkaarten?
Hept ew BREEF-*kahr-ten?*

I want to send a telegram.
Ik wil een telegram sturen.
*Ick veel uhn teh-leh-*KHRAHM STEW-*ren.*

Call me at seven in the morning.
Wek mij morgenochtend om zeven uur.
Veck may MOHR-*khen-*OHKH-*tend ohm* ZEH-*ven ewr.*

Where is the telephone?
Waar is de telefoon?
Vahr is deh TEH-*leh-fohn?*

Hello!
Hallo!
*Hah-*LOH!

Send breakfast to room 702.
Stuur ontbeit naar kamer zevenhondertwee.
*Stewr ohnt-*BAIT *nahr* KAHM-*mer* ZEH-*ven-*HOHN-
dehrt-tvay.

> **orange juice**
> sinasappelsap
> SEE-*nahs-ahp'l-sahp*

> **ham and eggs**
> ham en eieren
> *hahm ehn* AY-*ren*

> **rolls and coffee**
> broodjes en koffie
> BROHT-*yes ehn* KOHF-*fee*

I am expecting a friend.
Ik verwacht een vriend.
*Ick fehr-*VAHKHT *uhn freent.*

Tell him (her) to wait.
Zeg hem (haar) te wachten.
Zehkh hem (hahr) tuh VAHKH-*ten.*

If anyone calls I'll be back at six.
Als iemand naar mij vraagt ben ik terug om zes
uur.
Ahls EE-*mahnt nahr may frahkht ben ick tuh-*
RUHKH *ohm zess ewr.*

Tell me please where is a barber shop.
Kunt U me zeggen waar een herenkapper is.
Kuhnt ew muh ZEH-*khen vahr uhn* HEH-*ren-kahp-*
per is.

Tell me please where is a beauty parlor.
Zeg mij, alstublieft, waar is een dames salon.
*Zehkh may ahl-stew-*BLEEFT *vahr is ain* DAH-*mess-*
sah-lohn.

Tell me please where is a drug store.
Zeg mij, alstublieft, waar de apotheker is.
*Zehkh may ahl-stew-*BLEEFT *vahr duh ah-poh-*TEH-
ker is.

What is the telephone number?
Wat is het telefoonnummer?
*Vaht is ett teh-leh-*FOHN-*nuhm-mehr?*

What is the address?
Wat is het adres?
*Vaht is ett ah-*DRESS?

I want to change some money.
Ik wil geld wisselen.
Ick veel khehlt VISS-*seh-len.*

What is the rate for dollars?
Wat is de dollarkoers?
Vaht is duh DOHL-*lahr-koors?*

thirteen
dertien
DEHR-*teen*

fourteen
veertien
VARE-*teen*

fifteen
vijftien
FIFE-*teen*

sixteen
zestien
ZESS-*teen*

seventeen
zeventien
ZEH-*ven-teen*

eighteen
achttien
AHKHT-*teen*

nineteen
negentien
NEH-*khen-teen*

twenty
twintig
TVEN-*tahkh*

thirty
dertig
LEHR-*tahkh*

forty
veertig
FARŁ-*tahkh*

fifty
vijftig
FIFE-*tahkh*

sixty
zestig
ZESS-*tahkh*

seventy
zeventig
ZEH-*ven-tahkh*

eighty
tachtig
TAHKH-*tahkh*

ninety
negentig
NEH-*khen-tahkh*

hundred
honderd
HOHN-*dert*

two hundred
tweehonderd
TVAY-*hohn-dert*

three hundred
driehonderd
DREE-*hohn-dert*

four hundred
vierhonderd
FEAR-*hohn-dert*

five hundred
vijfhonderd
FIFE-*hohn-dert*

six hundred
zeshonderd
ZESS-*hohn-dert*

seven hundred
zevenhonderd
ZEH-*ven-hohn-dert*

eight hundred
achthonderd
AHKHT-*hohn-dert*

nine hundred
negenhonderd
NEH-*khen-hohn-dert*

thousand
duizend
DOY-*zent*

ten thousand
tien duizend
TEEN *doy-zent*

hundred thousand
honderd duizend
HOHN-*dert doy-zent*

My bill, please.
Mijn rekening, alstublieft.
Main REH-*keh-ning ahl-stew-*BLEEFT.

3. EATING

Where is a good restaurant?
Waar is een goed restaurant?
*Vahr is ain khood res-toh-*RAHNT?

A table for two, please.
Een tafel voor twee, alstublieft.
Ain TAH-*f'l for tvay ahl-stew-*BLEEFT.

Waiter!	**Waitress!**
Kelner!	Juffrouw!
KEHL-*nehr!*	YEW-*frow!*

The menu, please.
Het menu, alstublieft.
*Ett meh-*NEW, *ahl-stew-*BLEEFT.

What's good today?
Wat is lekker vandaag?
Vaht is LEK-*kehr fohn-*DAHKH?

Is it ready?
Is het klaar?
Is ett klahr?

How long will it take?
Hoe lang zal het duren?
Hoo lahng zahl ett DEW-*ren?*

This, please ...	**and that**
Dit, alstublieft ...	en dat
*Ditt, ahl-stew-*BLEEFT ...	*ehn datt*

Bring me ...	**water**	**milk**
Breng mij ...	water	melk
breng may ...	VAH-*tehr*	*mehlk*

a glass of beer
een glas bier
ehn khlahs beer

red wine
rode wijn
ROH-deh vine

white wine
witte wijn
VIT-teh vine

a cocktail
een cocktail
ehn cocktail

whisky soda
whisky soda
whisky soda

soup
soep
soop

fish
vis
viss

meat
vlees
flehs

bread and butter
brood en boter
broht ehn BOH-ter

a sandwich
een sandwich
ehn sandwich

steak . . .
biefstuk . . .
BEEF-stuhk . . .

rare
rauw
row

medium
half gaar
half khahr

well done
gaar
khahr

chicken
kip
kip

veal
kalfsvlees
KAHLPS-flehs

pork
varkensvlees
VAHR-kens-flehs

lamb
lamsvlees
LAHMS-flehs

lamb chop
lamscotelette
LAHMS-koht-let

green pea soup
snert
snehrt

mashed potatoes and apples
hete bliksem
HEH-teh BLEEK-some

herring salad
haringsla
HAH-ring-slah

salt herring
maatjes haring
MAHT-yes HAH-ring

smoked beef
rookvlees
ROHK-flehs

stew with vegetables
hutspot
HUT-spot

cheese
kaas (Edam, Gouda)
kahs (EH-*dahm*, KHOW-*dah*)

Indonesian rice dishes
Indise rijsttafel
IN-*dee-seh* RICET-*tah'f'l*

No sauce for me.
Geen jus voor mij.
Khehn jew for may.

with potatoes ...
met aardappelen ...
meht AHRD-*ahp-p'len* ...

rice
rijst
rice't

an omelet
en ommelet
*ehn oh-meh-*LET

And what vegetables?
en welke groenten?
ehn VEHL-*keh* KHROON-*ten?*

peas
erwtjes
EHRT-*yes*

beans
bonen
BOH-*nehn*

carrots
peentjes
PAINT-*yes*

onions
uien
OY-*ehn*

a salad
een sla
ehn slah

lettuce
kropsla
KROHP-*slah*

tomatoes
tomaten
*toh-*MAH-*ten*

Please bring me another fork.
Brengt U mij een andere vork, alstublieft.
Brengt ew may uhn AHN-*deh-reh fork, ahl-stew-*BLEEFT.

glass
glas
khlahs

knife
mes
mess

spoon
lepel
lehp'l

plate
bord
bohrt

What is there for dessert?
Wat is er voor dessert?
*Vaht is uhr for des-*SEHR?

fruit
vruit
froyt

pastry
gebak
*kheh-*BAHK

cake
koek
cook

icecream
ijs
ice

cheese
kaas
kahs

Some coffee, please.
    Een kop koffie, alstublieft.
    Ehn kohp KOHF-*fee ahl-stew-*BLEEFT.

sugar	**cream**
suiker	room
SOY-*kehr*	*roam*

tea with lemon	**mineral water**
tee met citroen	mineraal water
*teh met see-*TROHN	*mee-neh-*RAHL VAH-*tehr*

More, please.	**That's enough.**
Meer, alstublieft.	Het is genoeg.
*Mehr, ahls-tew-*BLEEFT.	*Hat is kheh-*NOOKH.

The check, please.
    De rekening, alstublieft.
    Duh REH-*keh-ning ahl-stew-*BLEEFT.

Is the tip included?
    Is de fooi inbegrepen?
    *Is duh foy in-buh-*KHREH-*pen?*

It was very good.
    Het was erg lekker.
    Ett vahs ehrkh LEK-*kehr.*

4. SHOPPING

I would like to buy this . . .	**that**
Ik wil dit kopen . . .	dat
Ick veel ditt kohp'n . . .	*daht*

Where is the section for . . .
    Waar is de afdeling van . . .
    Vahr is duh AHF-*deh-link fahn . . .*

men's clothing	**hats**
herenkleding	hoeden
HEH-*ren-kleh-dink*	*hood'n*

women's clothing
dameskleding
DAH-*mess-kleh-dink*

underwear
ondergoed
OHN-*dehr-khood*

stockings
kousen
KOW-*zen*

gloves
handschoenen
HAHND-*skhoo-nehn*

shoes
schoenen
SKHOO-*nehn*

shirts
hemden
hemd'n

The size in America is ...
De maat in Amerika is ...
*Duh maht in ah-*MEH-*ree-kah is ...*

toys
speelgoed
SPEHL-*khood*

perfume
parfum
*pahr-*FUHM

jewelry
juwelen
*yoo-*VEH-*len*

watches
horloges
*hohr-*LOH-*zhess*

toilet articles
toilet artikelen
*twa-*LET *ahr-tick-len*

sport articles
sports artikelen
SPORTS *ahr-tick-len*

films
filmen
FIHL-*men*

souvenirs
souvenirs
*soo-veh-*NEERS

Show me ...
Laat mij ...
laht may ...

something less expensive
zien iets goedkopers
*zeen eets khood-*KOH-*pehrs*

another one
iets anders
eets AHN-*dehrs*

a better quality
een betere kwaliteit
ehn BEH-*teh-reh kvah-lee-*TAIT

bigger	**smaller**
groter	kleiner
KHROH-*tehr*	KLAY-*nehr*

I don't like the color.
Ik houd niet van de kleur.
Ick howd neet fan deh kluhr.

I want one . . .	**in green**	**in yellow**
Ik wil een . . .	in groen	in geel
ick veel uhn . . .	*in khroon*	*in khehl*

in blue	**red**	**black**
in blauw	rood	zwart
in blah-oo	*road*	*zvahrt*

white	**grey**	**pink**	**brown**
wit	grijs	roza	bruin
vitt	*khrice*	ROH-*zah*	*bruyn*

Can I exchange it?
Kan ik het omruilen?
Kahn ick ett OHM-roy-len?

I will take it with me.
Ik zal het meenemen.
Ick zahl ett MAY-neh-men.

The receipt, please.
De kwitantie, alstublieft.
Duh kvee-TAHN-tsee, ahl-stew-BLEEFT.

Please send it to this address.
Stuur het alstublieft naar dit adres.
Stewr ett ahl-stew-BLEEFT nahr ditt ah-DRESS.

Where is the market?
Waar is de markt?
Vahr is duh mahrkt?

Where is there a flower shop?
Waar is een bloemist?
Vahr is ehn bloo-MIST?

Where is there a bookstore?
    Waar is een boekhandel?
    Vahr is ehn BOOK-*hahnd'l?*

Where is there a food shop?
    Waar is een kruidenier?
    *Vahr is ehn kruy-deh-*NEER?

5. TRANSPORTATION

Taxi!   **Take me to the airport.**
    Taxi!   Breng me naar de vlieghaven.
    Taxi!   *Breng may nahr deh* FLEEKH-*hah-f'n.*

Turn right.   **Turn left.**
    Keer rechtsom.   Keer linksom.
    Care REHKHTS-*ohm.*   *Care* LINKS-*ohm.*

Straight ahead.   **Not so fast!**
    Rechtdoor.   Niet zo vlug!
    *Rehkht-*DOHR.   *Neet zoh fluhkh!*

Hurry up!   **Stop here!**
    Schiet op!   Stop hier!
    *S'*KHEET *ohp!*   *Stop here!*

Wait for me!   **How much is it?**
    Wacht op me!   Hoeveel is het?
    Vahkht ohp muh!   *Hoo-*FAIL *is ett?*

How much is it to ... ?   **and back?**
    Hoeveel is het tot ...   en terug?
    *Hoo-*FAIL *is ett toad ...?*   *ehn tuh-*RUHKH?

How much by the hour?   **by the day?**
    Hoeveel per uur?   per dag?
    *Hoo-*FAIL *per ewr?*   *per dahkh?*

Show me the sights.
    Laat me de bezienswaardigheden zien.
    *Laht muh duh beh-zeens-*VAHR-*dehkh-heh-den*
    zeen.

What is that building?
　Wat is dat gebouw?
　Vaht is daht kheh-BOW?

Can I go in?
　Kan ik naar binnen gaan?
　Kahn ick nahr BIN-neh khahn?

I want to see the Palace on Dam Square.
　Ik will het Paleis op den Dam zien.
　Ick veel ett pah-LACE ohp den dahm zeen.

Porter!
　Kruier!
　KROY-ehr!

I have two bags.
　Ik heb twee valiezen.
　Ick hehp tvay fah-LEE-zen.

A ticket to . . .
　Een biljet naar . . .
　Eehn beel-YET nahr . . .

one way
　enkele reis
　EN-keh-leh rays

round trip
　rondreis
　ROHND-rays

first class
　eerste klasse
　EHR-steh KLAHS-seh

second class
　tweede klasse
　TVEH-deh KLAHS-seh

When does it leave?
　Wanneer vertrekt het?
　Vahn-NEHR fehr-TREKT ett?

Where is the train to Rotterdam?
　Waar is de trein naar Rotterdam?
　Vahr is duh train nahr ROHT-tehr-dahm?

When do we get to Delft?
　Wanneer komen we in Delft aan?
　Vahn-NEHR KOH-men vuh in dehlft ahn?

Where is the dining car?
　Waar is de restauratiewagen?
　Vahr is duh res-toh-RAH-see-vah-khen?

Open the window.
Maak het venster open.
Mahk ett FEN-*stehr ohp'n.*

Close the window.
Maak het venster dicht.
Mahk ett FEN-*stehr deekht.*

Where is the bus to Marken and Volendam?
Waar is de bus naar Marken en Volendam?
Vahr is duh buhs nahr MAHR-*ken ehn* FOH-*len-
dahm?*

Please tell me where to get off.
Zeg mij, alstublieft, waar ik moet uitstappen.
*Zehkh may ahls-tew-*BLEEFT *vahr ick moot* OYT-
stahp-pen.

Where is a gas station? **Fill it up.**
Waar is een garage? Vul het op.
*Vahr is ehn khah-*RAHZH? *Fewl ett ohp.*

Check the oil.
Controleer de olie.
*Kohn-troh-*LAIR *duh* OH-*lee.*

    water **tires**
     het water de banden
     ett VAH-*tehr* *duh* BAHN-*den*

Something is wrong with the car.
Er is iets niet in orde met de wagen.
Ehr is eets neet in OR-*der meht duh* VAH-*khen.*

Can you fix it?
Kan U het repareren?
*Kahn ew heht reh-pah-*REH-*ren?*

How long will it take?
Hoe lang zal het duren?
Hoo long zohl ett DEW-*ren?*

Is this the road to Arnhem?
Is dit de weg naar Arnhem?
Is ditt duh vehkh nahr ARN-*hem?*

Have you a map?
Hebt U een landkaart?
Hehpt ew ehn LAHNT-*kahrt?*

Where is the boat to . . . ?
Waar is de boot naar . . . ?
Vahr is duh boat nahr . . . ?

When does it leave?
Wanneer vertrekt het?
*Vahn-*NEHR *fehr-*TREK'T *ett?*

6. MAKING FRIENDS

Good day!
Goeden dag!
KHOO-*den dahkh!*

My name is . . .
Ik heet . . .
Ick hate . . .

What is your name, Sir?
Hoe heet U, Mijnheer?
Hoo hate EW, *main-*HEHR?

What is your name, Madam?
Hoe heet U, Mevrouw?
*Hoo hate ew, muh-*FROW?

What is your name, Miss?
Hoe heet U, Juffrouw?
Hoo hate EW, YEWF-*frow?*

I am delighted to meet you.
Het is me aangenaam U te leren kennen.
Ett is muh AHN-*kheh-nahm ew tuh* LEH-*rehn*
KEN-*nen.*

Do you speak English?
Spreekt U Engels?
Sprehkt ew EN-*ghels?*

A little.
Een beetje.
Ehn BAIT-*yeh.*

Do you understand?
  Verstaat U?
  *Fehr-*STAHT *ew?*

Please speak slowly.
  Spreek langzaam.
  Sprehk LAHNG-*zahm.*

I speak only a little Dutch.
  Ik spreek alleen een beetje Nederlands.
  *Ick sprehk ahl-*LEHN *ehn* BEHT-*yeh* NEH-*dehr-lands.*

I am from New York.
  Ik ben van New York.
  Ick behn fahn New York.

Where are you from?
  Waar bent U vandaan?
  *Vahr bent ew fahn-*DAHN?

I like your country.
  Uw land bevalt mij.
  *Ew lahnd buh-*FAHLT *muh.*

I like your city.
  Uw stad bevalt mij.
  *Ew stahd buh-*FAHLT *muh.*

Have you been in America?
  Bent U in Amerika geweest?
  *Bent ew in ah-*MEH-*ree-kah khuh-*VASTE?

This is my first visit here.
  Dit is mijn eerste bezoek hier.
  Ditt is mine EHR-*steh buh-*ZOOK *here.*

May I sit here?
  Mag ik hier zitten?
  Mahkh ick here ZIT-*ten?*

May I take your picture?
  Mag ik Uw foto nemen?
  Mahkh ick ew FOH-*toh* NEH-*men?*

Come here.
  Kom hier.
  Come here.

This is my wife.
  Dit is mijn vrouw.
  Ditt is mine frow.

my husband
   mijn man
   mine mahn

my son
   mijn zoon
   mine zohn

my daughter
   mijn dochter
   mine DOHKH-*tehr*

my mother
   mijn moeder
   mine MOO-*dehr*

my father
   mijn vader
   mine FAH-*dehr*

my sister
   mijn zuster
   mine ZEW-*ster*

my brother
   mijn broeder
   mine BROO-*der*

Have you children?
   Hebt U kinderen?
   Hehpt ew KIN-*deh-ren?*

What a beautiful child!
   Wat een knap kind!
   Vaht ehn k'nahp kint!

How beautiful!
   Wat mooi!
   Vaht moy!

Very interesting.
   Erg interessant.
   *Ehrkh in-tehr-ess-*SAHNT.

Would you like a cigarette?
   Wilt U een sigaret?
   *Veelt ew ehn see-khah-*RET?

Would you like something to drink?
   Wilt U iets drinken?
   Veelt ew eets DRIN-*ken?*

Would you like something to eat?
   Wilt U iets eten?
   Veelt ew eets EH-*ten?*

Sit down, please.
   Gaat U zitten.
   Khaht ew ZIT-*ten.*

Make yourself at home!
   Doet U alsof U thuis bent!
   *Doot ew ahl-*SOFF *ew toys bent!*

Good luck! **To your health!**
 Veel succes!   Op Uw gezondheid!
 *Feel sewk-*SESS!   *Ohp ew kheh-*ZOHND-*hide!*

When can I see you again?
 Wanneer kan ik U terugzien?
 *Vahn-*NEHR *kahn ick ew tuh-*RUHKH-*zeen?*

Here is my address. **What is your address?**
 Hier is mijn adres.   Wat is Uw adres?
 *Here is main ah-*DRESS.   *Vaht is ew ah-*DRESS?

What is your phone number?
 Wat is Uw telefoonnummer?
 *Vaht is ew teh-leh-*FOHN-*new-mehr?*

May I speak to . . . ?
 Kan ik met . . . spreken?
 Kahn ick meht . . . SPREH-*ken?*

Would you like to have lunch? have dinner?
 Wilt U lunchen?   middageten?
 Veelt ew LUN-*chen?*   MID-*dahkh-eh-ten?*

Would you like to go to the movies?
 Wilt U naar de bioskoop gaan?
 *Veelt ew nahr duh b'yoh-*SKOHP *khahn?*

 go to the theatre?
  naar het theater gaan?
  *nahr ett teh-*AHTR *khahn?*

Would you like to go to the beach?
 Wilt U naar het strand gaan?
 Veelt ew nahr ett strahnd khahn?

 take a walk?
  gaan wandelen?
  khahn VAHN-*deh-len?*

With great pleasure! **I am sorry.**
 Met plezier!   Het spijt me.
 *Meht pleh-*ZEER!   *Ett spayt muh.*

I cannot.
  Ik kan niet.
  Ick kahn neet.

Another time.
  Een andere keer.
  Ehn AHN-*deh-reh care.*

I must go now.
  Ik moet nu weggaan.
  Ick moot new VEHKH-*khahn.*

Thank you for a wonderful time.
  Dank U voor de gezellige tijd.
  *Dahnk ew fohr duh kheh-*ZEHL-*kheh taid.*

Thank you for an excellent dinner.
  Dank U voor een uitstekende maaltijd.
  *Dahnk ew fohr ehn oyt-*STEH-*ken-deh* MAHL-*taid.*

This is for you.
  Dit is voor U.
  Ditt is fohr ew.

You are very kind.
  U bent heel vriendelijk.
  Ew bent hale FREEN-*duh-luhk.*

It's nothing really.
  Het is werkelijk niets.
  Ett is VEHR-*kuh-luhk neets.*

With best regards!
  Met hartelijke groeten!
  Meht HAHR-*teh-luh-keh* KHROO-*ten!*

Congratulations!
  Gefeliciteerd!
  *Kheh-feh-lee-see-*TEHRD!

7. EMERGENCIES

Help!   **Police!**   **Fire!**
  Hulp!   Politie!   Brand!
  Hewlp!   *Poh-*LEE-*see!*   *Brohnd!*

Stop that man!
Houdt die man!
Howt dee mahn!

Stop that woman!
Houdt die vrouw!
Howt dee frow!

I have been robbed!
Ik ben bestolen!
Ick ben beh-STOH-len!

Look out!
Kijk uit!
Kake oyt!

Wait a minute!
Wacht even!
Vahkht EH-ven!

Stop!
Halt!
Hahlt!

Get out!
Eruit!
Eh-ROYT!

Hurry up!
Een beetje vlug!
Ehn BEHT-yuh fluhkh!

Don't bother me!
Laat me met rust!
Laht meh met rust!

What's going on?
Wat gebeurt er?
Vaht kheh-BURT ehr?

Entrance
Ingang
IN-khahng

Exit
Uitgang
OYT-khahng

Ladies
Dames
DAH-mess

Gentlemen
Heren
HEH-rehn

Danger!
Gevaar!
Kheh-FAHR!

Keep out!
Buiten blijven!
BOY-ten BLAI-ven!

No smoking
Niet roken
Neet ROH-ken

No parking
Niet parkeren
Neet pahr-KEH-ren

One way
Een richting
Ehn REEKH-ting

I am ill.
Ik ben ziek.
Ick ben zeek.

Call a doctor.
Roep een dokter.
Roop ehn DOK-tohr.

It hurts here.
Het doet hier pijn.
Ett doot here pain.

Where is the drug store?
Waar is de apotheker?
*Vahr is duh ah-poh-*TEH*-kehr?*

Take me to the hospital.
Breng me naar het ziekenhuis.
Breng muh nahr ett ZEE*-ken-huis.*

Where is there a dentist?
Waar is een tandarts?
Vahr is ehn TAHN*-darts?*

I have lost my bag.
Ik heb mijn koffer verloren.
Ick hehp main KOHF*-fehr fur-*LOH*-ren.*

> **my wallet**
> mijn portefeuille
> *main pohr-tuh-*FUY

> **my camera**   **my passport**
> mijn camera   mijn paspoort
> *main* KAH*-meh-rah*   *main* PASS*-port*

I am an American.
Ik ben Amerikaans.
*Ick ben ah-meh-ree-*KAHNS*.*

Where is the American Consulate?
Waar is het Amerikaans Consulaat?
*Vahr is ett ah-meh-ree-*KAHNS *kohn-sew-*LAHT*?*

Don't get excited!   **Everything is all right!**
Windt U niet op!   Alles is in orde.
Vint ew neet ohp!   AHL*-less is in* OHR*-deh.*

GREEK

Facts About Greek

Greek is spoken by approximately 10 million people in Greece and the Greek Islands of the Mediterranean and is also an important commercial language because of the large Greek merchant marine and widespread Greek commercial interests overseas.

Ancient Greek is the direct ancestor of most European languages, including the three main divisions, Latin (Romance), Teutonic, and Slavic. Modern Greek resembles ancient Greek much more than, for example, Italian resembles Latin, and students of ancient Greek will be pleased to find that they can read modern street signs and newspapers from their studies of Homer. Americans speaking Greek should watch out for the Greek word for "yes," which is *ne*, pronounced like the old English negative, "nay," meaning "no."

Advice on Accent

Greek has the advantage of being extremely easy for English-speaking people to pronounce. The single exception is the difference between **th** and **thh**, which correspond to two different Greek letters.

th as written in the phonetics should be pronounced as in *"then."*

thh, however, should be pronounced as in *"think."*

You Already Know Some Greek

In fact, you know a lot of it. The majority of scientific words are Greek constructions—atom, philosophy, astronomy, physics, chemistry, mathematics, to name but a few.

Greek prefixes are also familiar to American ears: *eu* (always good) as in euphoria, euphemism, eucharist; *dys* (always bad), as in dyspepsia, dystrophy, dysentery; *sym* (or *syn*—meaning "together") as in symphony, symposium, synthesis, etc.

However you will often find these words stressed differently in Greek and also slightly changed in their last syllable.

As you practice speaking and listening to Greek you will find with pleasure that you recognize, in their native pronunciation, an increasing number of the thousands of words that Greek has given to our language.

1. FIRST CONTACT

Yes.	**No.**	**Good.**
Nay.	OH-*khee.*	*Kah-*LAH.

Thank you.   **You are welcome.**
*Eff-hah-rees-*TOH.   TEE-*poh-tah.*

Excuse me.   **It's all right.**
*Sing-*NOH-*mee.*   *Them bee-*RAH-*zee.*

Please.   **I would like . . .**
*Pah-rah-kah-*LOH.   *Thhah* EE-*thheh-lah . . .*

What?	**This.**	**Where?**	**Here.**
Tee?	*Ahf-*TOH.	*Poo?*	*Eh-*THOUGH.

When?	**Now.**	**Later.**
POH-*teh?*	TOH-*rah.*	EES-*teh-rah.*

Who?	**I**	**you**
P'yohs?	*Eh-*GOH	*seess*

he	**she**
*ahf-*TOHS	*ahf-*TEE

Your name?
*Toh-noh-*MAH-*sahs?*

Good morning. (Good day.)
*Kah-lee-*MEH-*rah.*

Good evening.   **Good night.**
*Kah-lee-*SPEH-*rah.*   *Kah-lee-*NIKH-*tah.*

Good-by.
*Ah-*DEE-*oh.*

How are you?
*Pohs-*EES-*thheh?*

Very well, thank you. And you?
*Poh-lee kah-*LAH, *eff-hah-ree-*STOH. *Keh seess?*

How much?
POH-*soh?*

I do not understand, please repeat.
*Then kah-*TAH*-lah-vah, eh-pah-nah-*LAH*-veh-teh,*
*pah-rah-kah-*LOH*.*

one	two	three
EH-*nah*	THEE-*oh*	TREE-*ah*

four	five	six
TESS-*seh-rah*	PEN-*deh*	EH-*xee*

seven	eight	nine
ehp-TAH	*ohk*-TOH	*eh*-NEH-*ah*

ten	eleven
THEH-*kah*	EN-*theh-kah*

2. ACCOMMODATIONS

Where is a good hotel?
Poo EE-*neh* EH-*nah kah*-LOH *xeh-noh-though-*
HEE-oh?

I want a room ...
THEH-*loh though*-MAH-*t'yoh ...*

   for one person.
   the EH-*nah* PROH-*soh-poh.*

   for two persons.
   th'yah THEE-*oh.*

   with bath.   **for two days.**
   meh loo-TROH.   *yah* THEE-*oh* MEH-*ress.*

   for a week.
   yah MEE-*ah ev-though-*MAH-*thah.*

   till Monday   **Tuesday**
   *ohs teen Thef-*TEH-*rah*   TREE-*tee*

Wednesday
*Teh-*TAHR*-tee*

Thursday
PEHM-*tee*

Friday
*Pah-rahs-keh-*VEE

Saturday
SAH-*vah-toh*

Sunday
*Kee-r'yah-*KEE

How much is it?
POH-*soh* KAH-*nee?*

Here are my bags.
*Ahf-*TESS EE-*neh ee ah-pohs-keh-*VESS *moo.*

Here is my passport.
*Ahf-*TOH EE-*neh toh th'yah-vah-*TEE-*r'*YOH *moo.*

I like it.
*Mah-*REH*-see.*

I don't like it.
*Then mah-*REH*-see.*

Show me another.
THEEX-*teh moo* EH-*nah* AH-*loh.*

Where is the toilet?
Poo EE-*neh toh ah-poh-hoh-ree-*TEE-*r'yoh?*

Where is the men's room?
Poo EE-*neh toh ah-poh-hoh-ree-*TEE-*r'yoh ahn-*THRON?

Where is the ladies' room?
Poo EE-*neh toh ah-poh-hoh-ree-*TEE-*r'yoh ghee-neh-*KOHN?

hot water
*zehs-*TOH *neh-*ROH

a towel
*peh-*TSEH-*tah*

soap
*sah-*POO-*nee*

Come in!
*Em-*BROSS!

Please have this . . .
*Ahf-*TAH EE-*neh yah . . .*

washed.
PLEE-*see-moh.*

pressed.   cleaned.
see-THEH-*roh-mah.*   *kah*-THHAH-*rees-mah.*

When will it be ready?
POH-*teh thah* EE-*neh* EH-*tee-mah?*

I need it for ...   tonight.   tomorrow.
Tah THHEH-*loh ...*   *ah*-POHP-*seh.*   AHV-*r'yoh.*

My keys, please.
Toh klee-THEE *moo, pah-rah-kah*-LOH.

Any mail for me?
*Ee-*PAHR-*hoon* GRAH-*mah-tah yah* MEH-*nah?*

Any packages?
THEH-*mah-tah?*

I want five airmail stamps for the U.S.
THEH-*loh* PEN-*deh ah-eh-roh-poh-ree-*KAH *grah-mah-*TOH-*see-mah yah tahs ee-noh-*MEH-*nahs poh-lee-*TEE-*ahs.*

Have you postcards?
EH-*heh-teh kahrt-pohs-*TAHL?

I want to send a telegram.
THHEH-*loh nah* STEE-*loh tee-leh-*GRAH-*fee-mah.*

Call me at seven in the morning.
*Xee-*PNEES-*teh meh stees ehp-*TAH *toh proh-*EE.

Where is the telephone?
Poo EE-*neh toh tee-*LEH-*foh-noh?*

Hello!
*Em-*BROSS!

Send breakfast to room 702.
Nah STEE-*leh-teh toh* PROH-*ghev-mah stoh doh-*MAH-*t'yoh.*

orange juice
*pohr-toh-kah-*LAH-*thah*

ham and eggs
*oh-meh-*LEH*-tah meh zahm-*BOHN

rolls and coffee
*kah-*FEH *keh frahn-zoh-*LAH*-k'yah*

I am expecting a friend.
*Peh-ree-*MEH*-noh* FEE*-loh.*

Tell him (her) to wait.
*Nah peh-ree-*MEH*-nee.*

If anyone calls, I'll be back at six.
*Eh-*AHN *tee-leh-foh-*NEE*-see kah-*NEES *thhah ghee-*REE*-soh stees* EH*-xee.*

Tell me, please, where is ...
PEE*-teh moo pah-rah-kah-*LOH *poo* EE*-neh ...*

    a restaurant.
    *toh ess-tee-ah-*TOH*-r'yoh.*

    a barbershop.
    *toh koo-*REE*-oh.*

    a beauty parlor.
    *toh koh-moh-*TEE*-r'yoh.*

    a drug store.
    *toh fahr-mah-*KEE*-oh.*

What is the telephone number?
Pohs EE*-neh oh ah-reethh-*MOSS *tee-leh-*FOH*-noo?*

What is the address?
Pohs EE*-neh ee thee-*EFF*-thin-siss?*

I want to change some money.
THHEH*-loh nah-*LAH*-xoh* HREE*-mah-tah.*

What is the rate for dollars?
POH*-soh* EH*-khee toh though-*LAH*-ree-oh?*

twelve	**thirteen**
THOUGH*-theh-kah*	*theh-kah-*TREE*-ah*

fourteen
  *theh-kah-*TEH-*seh-rah*

fifteen
  *theh-kah-*PEN-*deh*

sixteen
  *theh-kah-*EH-*xee*

seventeen
  *theh-kah-ehp-*TAH

eighteen
  *theh-kah-ohk-*TOH

nineteen
  *theh-kah-eh-*NEH-*ah*

twenty
  EE-*koh-see*

thirty
  *tree-*AHN-*dah*

forty
  *sah-*RAHN-*dah*

fifty
  *peh-*NEEN-*dah*

sixty
  *eh-*XEEN-*dah*

seventy
  *ehv-doh-*MEEN-*dah*

eighty
  *ohg-*DOHN-*dah*

ninety
  *eh-neh-*NEEN-*dah*

hundred
  *eh-kah-*TOH

two hundred
  *d'yah-*KOH-*sah*

three hundred
  *tr'yah-*KOH-*sah*

four hundred
  *teh-trah-*KOH-*sah*

five hundred
  *pen-dah-*KOH-*sah*

six hundred
  *ehk-sah-*KOH-*sah*

seven hundred
  *ep-tah-*KOH-*sah*

eight hundred
  *ohk-tah-*KOH-*sah*

nine hundred
  *eh-neh-ak-*KOH-*sah*

thousand
  HEEL-*yah*

ten thousand
  THEH-*kah hee-l'*YAH-*thess*

hundred thousand
  *eh-kah-*TOH-*hee-l'*YAH-*thess*

My bill, please.
  *Loh-gah-r'yahz-*MOHS, *pah-rah-kah-*LOH.

3. EATING

Where is a good restaurant?
  Poo EE-*neh* EH-*nah kah-*LOH *ess-t'yah-*TOH-*r'yoh?*

A table for two, please.
  *Trah-*PEH-*zee yah* THEE-*oh, pah-rah-kah-*LOH.

Waiter!
  *Gahr-*SOHN!

The menu, please.
  *Ton kah-*TAH-*loh-goh, pah-rah-kah-*LOH.

What's good today?
  *Tee kah-*LOH EH-*hee* SEE-*meh-rah?*

Is it ready?
  EE-*neh* EH-*tee-moh?*

How long will it take?
  POH-*see* OH-*rah* THHEH-*lee?*

This please . . .   **and this.**
  *Ahf-*TOH, *pah-rah-kah-*LOH . . .   *keh ahf-*TOH.

Bring me . . .   **water**   **milk**
  FEHR-*teh moo* . . .   *neh-*ROH   GAH-*lah*

   a glass of beer
     EH-*nah poh-*TEE-*ree* BEE-*rah*

   red wine   **white wine**
     MAHV-*roh krah-*SEE   AHS-*proh krah-*SEE

   a cocktail   **whisky and soda**
     EH-*nah cocktail*   *whisky meh soda*

   soup   **fish**   **meat**
     SOO-*pah*   PSAH-*ree*   KREH-*ahs*

   bread and butter
     *psoh-*MEE *keh* VOO-*tee-roh*

a sandwich
   EH-*nah sandwich*

More, please.
*Ah-*KOH-*mah, p*ı*h-rah-kah-*LOH.

That's enough.
FTHAH-*nee.*

steak ...
   *beef-*TEH-*kee* ...

rare
   *oh-*MOH

    medium
      MEH-*tree-oh*

well done
   *kah-*LAH *psee-*MEH-*noh*

chicken
   *koh-*TOH-*poo-loh*

veal
   *mohs-*HAH-*ree*

pork   lamb   lamb chop
   *hee-ree-*NOH   *ahr-*NEE   *pigh-*DAH-*k'yah*

skewered sausage
   *koh-koh-*REH-*tsee*

shish kebab
   *soo-*VLAH-*k'yah*

fish (red mullet)
   *bahr-*BOO-*nee* SKAH-*rahs*

brandy
   OO-*zoh*

with potatoes ...
   *meh pah-*TAH-*tess* ...

ıice
   REE-*zee*

an omelet
   *oh-meh-*LEH-*tah*

And what vegetables?
Keh tee HOHR-*tah?*

peas
   *bee-*ZEH-*l'yah*

beans
   *fah-soh-*LAH-*k'yah*

carrots
   *kah-*ROH-*tah*

onions
   *kreh-*MEE-*thee*

a salad
   *sah-*LAH-*tah*

lettuce
*mah-*ROO-*lee*

tomatoes
*doh-*MAH-*tess*

Please bring me another . . .
*Pah-rah-kah-*LOH *eh-nah* AH-*loh . . .*

fork.
*pee-*ROO-*nee.*

knife
*mah-*HEH-*ree*

spoon
*koo-*TAH-*lee*

glass
*poh-*TEE-*ree*

plate
*p'*YAH-*toh*

What is there for dessert?
Tee EH-*hee yah glee-*KOH?

fruit
FROO-*tah*

pastry
PAHS-*tah*

cake
TOOR-*tah*

ice cream
*pah-goh-*TOH

cheese
*tee-*REE

Some coffee, please.
*Kah-*FEH, *pah-rah-kah-*LOH.

sugar
ZAH-*hah-ree*

cream
KREH-*mah*

tea with lemon
*tsigh meh leh-*MOH-*nee*

4. SHOPPING

I would like to buy this . . .
THHEH-*loh nah-goh-*RAH-*soh ahf-*TOH . . .

that.
*eh-*KEE-*noh.*

I am just looking around.
*Kee-*TAH-*zoh* MOH-*noh.*

Where is the section for . . .
Poo EE-*neh toh t'*MEE-*mah yah . . .*

men's clothing
*ahn-dree-*KAH ROO-*hah*

women's clothing
*ghee-neh-*KEE-*ah* ROO-*hah*

hats
*kah-*PEH-*lah*

gloves
GAHN-*t'yah*

underwear
*eh-*SOH-*roo-hah*

shoes
*pah-*POO-*ts'yah*

stockings
KAHL-*tsess*

shirts
*poo-*KAH-*mee-sah*

The size in America is . . .
*Toh ah-meh-ree-kah-nee-*KOH NOO-*meh-roh*
EE-*neh . . .*

toys
*pehkh-*NEE-*d'yah*

perfume
*ah-*ROH-*mah-tah*

jewelry
*kohs-*MEE-*mah-tah*

watches
*oh-roh-*LOH-*yah*

toilet articles
*kah-leen-dee-*KAH

sport articles
*athh-lee-tee-*KAH EE-*thee*

films
*teh-*NEE-*ess*

souvenirs
*ehn-*THHEE-*m'yah*

Show me . . .
DIX-*teh moo . . .*

something less expensive
KAH-*tee f'thhee-*NOH-*teh-roh*

another one
EH-*nah* AH-*loh*

a better quality
*kah-*LEE-*teh-ree pee-*OH-*tee-tah*

bigger
*meh-gah-*LEE-*teh-roh*

smaller
*mee-*KROH-*teh-roh*

I don't like the color.
*Then mah-*REH-*see toh* KHROH-*mah.*

I want one . . .
Toh THHEH-*loh . . .*

in green
PRAH-*see-noh*

in yellow	in blue
KEE-*tree-noh*	*bleh*

red	black
KOH-*kee-noh*	MAHV-*roh*

white	gray
AHS-*proh*	*gree*

pink	brown
rohz	*kah-*FEH

I will take it with me.
Thhah toh PAH-*roh mah-*ZEE *moo.*

The receipt, please.
*Poh-rah-kah-*LOH, *m'yah ah-*POH-*thee-xee.*

Please send it to this address.
STEEL-*teh toh sahf-*TEE *tin thee-*EFF-*thin-see.*

Where is the market place?
Poo EE-*nay ee ah-goh-*RAH?

Where is there a flower shop?
Poo EE-*nay* EH-*nah ahn-thhoh-poh-*LEE-*oh?*

Where is there a book store?
Poo EE-*nay* EH-*nah veev-lee-oh-poh-*LEE-*oh?*

Where is there a food shop?
*Poo boh-*ROH *nah-goh-*RAH-*soh* TROH-*fee-mah?*

5. TRANSPORTATION

Taxi!	**Take me to the airport.**
*Tahk-*SEE!	*Stoh ah-eh-roh-*DROH-*m'yoh.*

Turn right.	**Turn left.**
*Theh-*X'YAH.	*Ah-rees-teh-*RAH.

Straight ahead.	**Not so fast!**
EE-*s'yah.*	OH-*khee* TOH-*soh* GREE-*goh-rah!*

Hurry up!
P'yoh GREE-*goh-rah!*

Stop here!
*Stah-*THIIEE-*teh eh-*THOUGH!

Wait for me!
*Nah meh peh-ree-*MEH-*neh-teh!*

How much is it?
POH-*soh* EE-*nay?*

How much is it to . . . ?
POH-*sah* PEHR-*neh-teh* MEHKH-*ree . . . ?*

    and back?
      keh PEE-*soh?*

How much . . .   **by the hour?**   **by the day?**
POH-*soh . . .*   *ee* OH-*rah?*   *ee ee-*MEH-*rah?*

donkey
*ghigh-*THOO-*ree*

Show me the sights.
DIX-*teh moo tah ah-xee-oh-*THHEH-*ah-tah.*

What building is that?
Tee EE-*nay ahf-*TOH *toh* KTEE-*r'yoh?*

Can I go in?
*Boh-*ROH *nah boh* MEH-*sah?*

I want to see the Acropolis.
THHEH-*loh nah ee-*THOUGH *teen ahk-*ROH-*poh-*lee.

To the railroad station.
*Stoh see-thee-roh-droh-mee-*KOH *stathh-*MOH.

I have two bags.
EH-*hoh* THEE-*oh vah-*LEE-*tsess.*

A ticket to . . .
EH-*nah ee-see-*TEE-*r'yoh yah . . .*

one way
AH-*neff eh-pee-stroh-*FISS

round trip
*meh eh-pee-stroh-*FEE

When does it leave?
POH-*teh ah-nah-hoh-*REE?

Where is the train to Corinth?
Poo EE-*nay toh* TREH-*noh yah teen* KOH-*reen-thhoh?*

Is this the train for Salonica?
*Ahf-*TOH EE-*nay toh* TREH-*noh yah teen Thheh-sah-loh-*NEE-*kee?*

When do we get to Patras?
POH-*teh f'thhah-noh-meh stahs* PAHT-*rahs?*

Where is the dining car?
Poo EE-*nay toh ehs-tee-ah-*TOH-*r'yoh?*

Open the window.
*Ah-*NIX-*teh toh pah-*RAH-*thhee-roh.*

Close the window.
KLISS-*teh toh pah-*RAH-*thhee-roh.*

Where is the bus to Faliro?
Poo EE-*nay toh leh-oh-foh-*REE-*oh yah toh* FAH-*lee-roh?*

I want to go to Lutraki.
THHEH-*loh nah* PAH-*oh stoh Loo-*TRAH-*kee.*

Please tell me where to get off.
PEE-*teh moo poo nah kah-*TEH-*voh.*

Where is the gas station?
Poo EE-*nay oh stahthh-*MOHS *ven-*ZEE-*nees?*

Fill it up.
*Gheh-*MEES-*teh toh.*

Check the oil.
*Kee-*TAXA-*teh toh* LAH-*thee.*

water	tires
toh neh-ROH	*tah* LAHS-*tee-hah*.

Something is wrong with the car.
 KAH-*tee seem*-VEH-*nee stoh ah*-MAH-*xee*.

Can you fix it?
 Boh-REE-*teh nah toh eh-pee-skeh*-VAH-*seh-teh?*

How long will it take?
 POH-*soh keh*-ROH *thah* PAH-*ree?*

Is this the road to Glyfada?
 EE-*nay ahf*-TOHS *oh* DROH-*mohs yah tee Glee*-FAH-*dah?*

Have you a map?
 EH-*heh-teh* HAHR-*tee?*

Where is the boat to . . .?
 Poo EE-*nah toh* PLEE-*oh yah . . .?*

When does it leave?
 POH-*teh* FEV-*ghee?*

6. MAKING FRIENDS

How do you do? (Introduction)
 HEH-*roh poh*-LEE?

My name is . . .
 *Toh-noh-*MAH *moo* EE-*nay . . .*

What is your name, Sir?
 Pohs LEH-*ghess-thheh,* KEE-*ree-eh?*

Madam	**Miss**
Kee-REE-*ah moo*	*Des-pee*-NISS

I am delighted to meet you.
 HEH-*roh poh*-LEE *yah teen gnoh-ree-*MEE-*ah sahs.*

Do you speak English?	**A little.**
Mee-LAH-*teh ahn-glee*-KAH?	LEE-*goh.*

I speak only a little Greek.
*Mee-*LOH *poh-*LEE LEE-*gah eh-lee-nee-*KAH.

Do you understand?
*Kah-tah-lah-*VEH*-neh-teh?*

Please speak slowly.
*Oh-meh-*LEE*-teh ahr-*GAH, *pah-rah-kah-*LOH.

I am from New York.
EE-*may ah-*POH *teen* NEH-*ah* YOHR-*kee.*

Where are you from?
*Ah-poh-*POO EES*-thheh?*

I like your country.
*Mah-*REH*-see ee* HOH-*rah sahs.*

I like your city.
*Mah-*REH*-see ee* POH-*lees sahs.*

Have you been in America?
Eh-kheh-teh PAH*-ee steen Ah-meh-ree-*KEE?

This is my first visit here.
EE-*nay ee* PROH-*tee moo eh-*PEES*-kehp-sees eh-*THOUGH.

May I sit here?
*Boh-*ROH *nah* KAH-*tsoh eh-*THOUGH?

May I take your picture?
*Boh-*ROH *nah sahs foh-toh-grah-*FEE*-soh?*

Come here.
*Eh-*LAH*-teh though.*

This is a picture of ...	**my wife**
Nah ...	*ee ghee-*NEH*-kah moo*
my husband	**my son**
oh AHN*-drahs moo*	*oh yohs moo*
my daughter	**my mother**
ee KOH*-ree moo*	*ee mee-*TEH*-rah moo*

my father
*oh pah-*TEH-*rahs moo*

my sister
*ee ah-thehl-*FEE *moo*

my brother
*oh ah-thehl-*FOHS *moo*

Have you children?
EH-*kheh-teh peh-*TH'YAH?

How beautiful!
*Tee oh-*REH-*ah!*

Very interesting.
*Poh-*LEE *ehn-th'yah-*FEH-*rohn.*

Would you like ...
THHEH-*leh-teh ...*

a cigarette?
*tsee-*GAH-*roh?*

something to drink?
*nah pee-*EE-*teh* KAH-*tee?*

something to eat?
nah FAH-*teh* KAH-*tee?*

Sit down, please.
*Kah-*THHEES-*thheh, pah-rah-kah-*LOH.

Make yourself at home.
KAHN-*teh* OH-*pohs stoh* SPEE-*tee sahs!*

Good luck!
*Kah-*LEE *TEE-khee!*

To your health!
*Ees ee-*GHEE-*ahn sahs!*

When can I see you again?
POH-*teh boh-*ROH *nah sahs xah-nah-*THOUGH?

Where shall we meet?
*Poo thhah see-nahn-dee-*THHOO-*meh?*

Here is my address.
*Ahf-*TEE EE-*nay ee thee-*EFF-*thhin-siss moo.*

What is your address?
P'yah EE-*nay ee thee-*EFF-*thhin-siss sahs?*

What is your phone number?
Pohs EE-*nay oh ah-reethh-*MOHS *tee-leh-*FOH-*noo sahs?*

May I speak to you?
*Boh-*ROH *nah sahs mee-*LEE-*soh ee?*

Would you like to . . .   have lunch?
THHEH-*leh-teh nah . . .   ghev-mah-*TEE-*seh-teh?*

   and dinner?
   *nah theep-*NEE-*seh-teh?*

   go to the movies?
   PAH-*meh ston kee-nee-mah-toh-*GRAH-*foh?*

   go to the theatre?   go to the beach?
   stoh THHEH-*ah-troh?   stoh ah-kroh-*YAH-*lee?*

   take a walk?
   *peh-*REE-*pah-toh?*

With great pleasure!
*Meh meh-*GAH-*lee eff-hah-*REES-*tee-see!*

I am sorry.   I cannot.
*Lee-*POO-*meh.   Then boh-*ROH.

Some other time.   I must go now.
AH-*lee foh-*RAH.   PREH-*pee nah pee-*GHEH-*noh.

Thank you for a wonderful time.
*Eff-hah-rees-*TOH *yah teen peh-ree-*PEE-*ee-see.*

Thank you for an excellent dinner.
*Eff-hah-rees-*TOH *yah toh thhav-*MAH-*s'yoh* THEEP-*noh.*

This is for you.
*Ahf-*TOH EE-*nay yah sahs.*

You are very kind.
EES-*thheh poh-*LEE *kah-*LOSS.

It's nothing really.
Then EE-nay TEE-*poh-teh.*

With best regards.   **Congratulations!**
*Heh-reh-*TEEZ-*mah-tah.*   *Seen-hah-ree-*TEE-*r'yah!*

7. EMERGENCIES

Help!   **Police!**
*Voh-*EETHH*'yah!*   *Ahs-tee-noh-*MEE-*ah!*

Fire!
*Peer-kah-*YAH!

Stop that man!   **Stop that woman!**
*Stah-mah-*TEES-*teh tohn!*   *Stah-mah-*TEES-*teh teen!*

I have been robbed!   **Look out!**
Meh LEES-*teh-psahn!*   *Proh-soh-*HEE!

Wait a minute!
*Peh-ree-*MEH-*neh-teh* LEE-*goh!*

Stop!   **Get out!**   **Hurry up!**
*Stah-mah-*TEES-*teh!*   EH-*xoh!*   GREE-*goh-rah!*

Don't bother me!   **What's going on?**
*Ah-*FEES-*teh meh!*   *Tee seem-*VEH-*nee?*

Entrance   **Exit**
EE-*soh-thos*   EH-*xoh-thos*

Gentlemen   **Ladies**
KEE-*ree-ee*   *Kee-*REE-*eh*

Danger
KEEN-*thee-nohs!*

Keep out!
*Ah-pah-goh-*REH-*veh-teh ee* EE-*soh-thos!*

No smoking
*Ah-pah-goh-*REH-*veh-teh toh* KAHP-*neez-mah*

No parking
*Ah-pah-goh-*REH*-veh-teh ee* STATHH*-meff-siss*

One way
MOH*-nee kah-*TEFF*-thhin-siss*

I am ill.
EE*-may* AH*-rohs-tohs.*

Call a doctor!
*Foh-*NAX*-teh yah-*TROH!

It hurts here.
*Poh-*NIGH *eh-*THOUGH.

Where is the drug store?
Poo EE*-nay toh fahr-mah-*KEE*-oh?*

Take me to the hospital.
Nah meh PAH*-teh stoh noh-soh-koh-*MEE*-oh.*

Where is there a dentist?
*Poo ee-*PAHR*-hee oh-thohn-*TEE*-ah-trohs?*

I have lost . . .
EH*-hah-sah . . .*

my bag.
teen DZAHN*-dah moo.*

my wallet
*toh pohr-toh-*FOH*-lee moo*

my camera
*teen foh-toh-grah-fee-*KEE *moo mee-hah-*NEE

my passport
*toh th'yah-vah-tee-r'*YOH *moo*

I am an American.
EE*-may ah-meh-ree-kah-*NOHS. (m)
EE*-may ah-meh-ree-kah-*NISS. (f)

Where is the American Consulate?
Poo EE*-nay toh ah-meh-ree-kah-nee-*KOH *proh-xeh-*
NEE*-oh?*

Don't get excited!
*Mee steno-hoh-*REES*-thheh!*

Everything is all right.
OH*-lah* EE*-nay ehn* TAH*-xee.*

HEBREW

Facts About Hebrew

Hebrew is spoken by about two million people in Israel and is studied and spoken by an increasing number of people throughout the world. It is a Semitic language closely related to Arabic and Aramaic, the language of the ancient Middle East.

Hebrew has come down to the present day practically unchanged from ancient times inasmuch as it was continuously used by Jewish communities throughout the world as a language of prayer and study. It is interesting to note that, despite its religious and cultural use, it did not reappear as a native language serving everyday needs until the return of large numbers of Jewish people to their ancient homeland.

After so many centuries of disuse as a tool of communication, Hebrew has had to form words of modern usage from ancient roots. The word "electricity," for instance—*hashmal*—was taken from the Biblical reference in Ezekiel 1:4 to the radiant halo the prophet saw in the vision of the Almighty which appeared to him.

An unusual feature of Hebrew is the exact linguistic differentiation between the sexes. This means that you must use different forms of the verb when speaking to a man or to a woman.

This distinction also applies to *you* when you speak; men use the masculine form, women the feminine. We have simplified this by putting a small (m) or (f) after each sentence where it is applicable.

A popular misconception is that there is a close connection between Yiddish and Hebrew. This is not true, as Yiddish was originally a medieval German dialect, interspersed with many Hebrew words, which through the years, according to the places where it was spoken, has picked up many words of Russian, Polish, Lithuanian, and even English origin.

Advice On Accent

The phonetics in this section have been developed to enable you to pronounce Hebrew immediately without the intervening step of learning the Hebrew alphabet. An important point to remember is to give a guttural sound to **ch,** as in the English ch of "Lo*ch* Ness." This pronunciation feature comes up frequently, often at the end of a word and at the beginning of the following word.

How Hebrew Is Written

Hebrew is written with an alphabet of 22 basic letters, 5 of which change their form when they are at the end of a word, as well as 4 alternate letters. It is customarily written without the vowel sounds, which are sometimes added to the basic consonants in the form of dots or small lines referred to as *nikkud*. Hebrew is written from right to left, exactly the reverse of English; for this reason, Hebrew books start where English books end: at the last page.

As Hebrew has no official transliteration into Roman letters, we have given here only the phonetic rendition of Hebrew, making it possible for you to express yourself and to understand replies without having to learn the Hebrew language.

As an example of written Hebrew, here are three signs, of especial interest to the traveler, which you will often see in Israel. They mean "Entrance," "Exit," and "Keep Out."

יציאה

כניסה

אין כניסה

You Already Know Some Hebrew

Some Hebrew words of religious connotation are no doubt already familiar to you. They include *Amen* (So be it), *Halleluja* (Hail to the Lord!), *cherubim* (angels), *shibboleth* (used in English as "slogan" or "password" but originally meaning "ears of corn," which, according to Judges 12, the fleeing Ephraimites were unable to pronounce correctly), *Kosher* (pronounced kah-SHER—meaning "fit," "proper," or "according to law"). In addition to these words, you may be familiar with the Hebrew word of greeting and parting—*Shalom!*—meaning simply "Peace!"

1. FIRST CONTACT

Yes.	No.	Good.
Kehn.	*Loh.*	*Tohv.*

Thank you very much.	You are welcome.
*Toh-*DAH *rah-*BAH.	*Ahl loh dah-*VAHR.

Excuse me.	It's all right.
*Slee-*KHAH.	*Zeh bes-*SEH*-dehr.*

Please.	I would like ...
*Beh-vah-kah-*SHAH.	*Ah-*NEE *roh-*TZEH ... (m)
	*Ah-*NEE *roh-*TZAH ... (f)

What?	This.	Where?
Mah?	*Zeh.*	*Eh-*FOH?

Here.	When?	Now.
Kahn (or) *Poh.*	*Mah-*TAH*-ee?*	*Ahkh-*SHAHV.

Later.	Who?	I
*Ah-*KHAHR*-kahkh.*	*Mee?*	*Ah-*NEE

you	he	she
*ah-*TAH (m)	*hoo*	*hee*
aht (f)		

Your name?
  *Mah-sheem-*KHAH? (m)
  *Mah-*SH'MEKH? (f)

Good morning.	Good evening.
BOH*-kehr tohv.*	EH*-rehv tohv.*

Good night.	Good-by.
LIE*-lah tohv.*	*Leh-hit-rah-*OHT.

How are you?
  *Mah-shlohm-*KHAH? (m)
  *Mah-shloh-*MEHKH? (f)

Very well, thank you, and you?
  *Toh-*DAH *tohv veh-ah-*TAH? (m)
  *Toh-*DAH *tohv veh-*AHT? (f)

How much?
  KAH-*mah?*

I do not understand, please repeat.
  *Eh-*NEH-*nee meh-*VEEN, *beh-vah-kah-*SHAH *lahkh-*
    ZOHR. (m)
  *Eh-*NEH-*nee meh-vee-*NAH, *beh-vah-kah-*SHAH
    *lahkh-*ZOHR. (f)

one	two	three
*ah-*KHAHT	SHTAH-*yeem*	*shah-*LOHSH

four	five	six
*ahr-*BAH	*hah-*MESH	*shesh*

seven	eight	nine
SHEH-*vah*	SHMOH-*neh*	TEH-*shah*

ten	eleven	twelve
ESS-*sehr*	*ah-*KHAHD-*ess-sehr*	SHTAYM-*ess-reh*

2. ACCOMMODATIONS

Where is a good hotel?
  *Eh-*FOH *bet mah-*LOHN *tohv?*

I want a room . . .
  *Ah-*NEE *roh-*TZEH KHEH-*dehr* . . . (m)
  *Ah-*NEE *roh-*TZAH KHEH-*dehr* . . . (f)

  for one person.
    *leh-*BEHN *ah-*DAHM *eh-*KHAHD.

  for two persons.   **with bath.**
    *lee-*SHNEH *ah-nah-*SHEEM.   *eem ahm-*BAT-*yah.*

  for two days.   **for a week.**
    *leh-yoh-*MAH-*yeem.*   *leh-shah-*VOO-*ah.*

till Monday	**Tuesday**
ahd yohm shay-NEE	*yohm shlee*-SHEE
Wednesday	**Thursday**
yohm reh-vee-EE	*yohm khah-mee*-SHEE
Friday	**Saturday**
yohm shee-SHEE	*yohm shah*-BAHT
Sunday	
yohm ree-SHOHN	

How much is it?
KAH-*mah zeh oh*-LEH?

Here are my bags.
Kahn hah-meez-vah-DOHT *sheh*-LEE.

Here is my passport.
Kahn hah-d'ahr-KOHN *sheh*-LEE.

I like it.
Zeh moh-TZEH *khehn beh-eh*-NAH-*ee.*

I don't like it.
Zeh loh moh-TZEH *khehn beh-eh*-NAH-*ee.*

Show me another.
Tah-REH *lee ah*-KHEHR. (m)
Tah-REE *lee ah*-KHEHR. (f)

Where is the toilet?
Eh-FOH *bait hah-shee*-MOOSH?

Where is the men's room?
Eh-FOH *khah*-DAHR *hah-g'vah*-RIM?

Where is the ladies' room?
Eh-FOH *khah*-DAHR *hah-g'vah*-ROHT?

hot water
mah-YEEM *khah*-MEEM

a towel	**soap**
mah-GAY-*vet*	*sah*-BONE

Come in!
  Yah-VOH!

Please have this washed.
  Beh-vah-kah-SHAH *lah*-TEHT *zoht leh-khee*-BOOS.

Please have this pressed.
  Beh-vah-kah-SHAH *lah*-TEHT *zoht leh-ghee*-HOOTS.

Please have this cleaned.
  Beh-vah-kah-SHAH *lah*-TEHT *zoht leh-nee*-KOO-*ee*.

When will it be ready?
  Mah-TAH-*ee zeh yee*-YEH *moo*-KHAHN?

I need it for ...
  Ah-NEE *tsah*-REEKH *zoht ...*

    tonight.   **tomorrow.**
      hah-LIE-*lah.*   *leh-mah*-KHAHR.

My key, please.
  Hah-mahf-TEH-*ahkh sheh*-LEE *beh-vah-kah*-SHAH.

Any mail for me?
  Hah-YESH *doh*-AHR *bish-vee*-LEE?

Any packages?   **Have you postcards?**
  Khah-vee-LAH?   *Hah*-YESH *gloo*-YOHT?

I want five airmail stamps for the U.S.A.
  Ah-NEE *roh*-TZEH *khah-mee*-SHAH *boo*-LAY *doh*-AHR
    ah-VEER *leh-ahr*-TZOHT *hah*-BRIT. (m).
  Ah-NEE *roh*-TZAH *khah-mee*-SHAH *boo*-LAY *doh*-AHR
    ah-VEER *leh-ahr*-TZOHT *hah*-BRIT. (f)

I want to send a telegram.
  Ah-NEE *roh*-TZEH *leesh-loh*-AHKH *mee*-VRAHK. (m)
  Ah-NEE *roh*-TZAH *leesh-loh*-AHKH *mee*-VRAHK. (f)

Call me at seven in the morning.
  Teh-tsahl-TSEHL-*nah eh*-LAH-*ee beh*-SHEH-*vah*
    bah-BOH-*kehr.*

Where is the telephone?
　*Eh-*FOH *hah teh-leh-*FOHN?

Hello!
　*Hahl-*LOH!

Send breakfast to room 702.
　*Tish-*LAHKH (m) *ah-roo-*KHAHT *hah-boh-kehr leh-*
　KHEH-*dehr sh'vah meh-*ODD *oo-*SHTAH-*yim.*
　*Tish-lah-*KHEE (f) *ah-roo-*KHAHT *hah-boh-kehr leh-*
　KHEH-*dehr sh'vah meh-*ODD *oo-*SHTAH-*yim.*

orange juice
　*meets tah-poo-*KHEH *zah-*HAHV

rolls and coffee
　*lahkh-*MAH *n'yoht vehk-kah-*FEH

I am expecting a friend.
　*Ah-*NEE *meh-khah-*KEH *leh-yeh-*DEED. (m)
　*Ah-*NEE *meh-khah-*KAH *leh-yeh-deed-*DAH. (f)

Tell him (her) to wait.
　*Tah-*GHEED *loh (lah) leh-khah-*KOHT.

If anyone calls, I'll be back at six.
　*Eem mee-sheh-*HOO *yee-tahl-*FEHN *ah-*NEE *ah-*
　*khah-*ZOHR *beh-shah-*AH *shesh.*

Tell me, please, where is the restaurant?
　*Tah-*GHEED *beh-vah-kah-*SHAH *eh-*FOH *hah-mis-sah-*
　DAH?

Tell me, please, where is the barber shop?
　*Tah-*GHEED *beh-vah-kah-*SHAH *eh-*FOH *mah-speh-*
　RAH?

Tell me, please, where is the beauty parlor?
　*Tah-*GHEED *beh-vah-kah-*SHAH *eh-*FOH *mah-speh-*
　RAH *leg-vah-*ROHT? (m)
　*Tah-*GHEED-*dee beh-vah-kah-*SHAH *eh-*FOH *mah-*
　*speh-*RAH *leg-vah-*ROHT? (f)

Tell me, please, where is the drugstore?
*Tah-*GHEED *beh-vah-kah-*SHAH *eh-*FOH *beht meer-kah-*KHAHT?

What is the telephone number?
*Mah miss-*PAHR *hah-teh-leh-*FOHN?

What is the address?
*Mah hahk-toh-*VET?

I want to change some money.
*Ah-*NEE *roh-*TSEH *leh-hahkh-*LEEF KEH-*seff.* (m)
*Ah-*NEE *roh-*TSAH *leh-hahkh-*LEEF KEH-*seff.* (f)

What is the rate for dollars?
Mah EH-*rekh hah-dohl-*LAHR?

thirteen *shloh-*SHAH-*ah-*SAHR	**fourteen** *ahr-bah-*AH-*ah-*SAHR
fifteen *hah-mee-*SHAH-*ah-*SAHR	**sixteen** *shee-*SHAH-*ah-*SAHR
seventeen *shee-*VAH-*ah-*SAHR	**eighteen** *shmoh-*NAH-*ah-*SAHR
nineteen *tee-*SHAH-*ah-*SAHR	**twenty** *ess-*REEM
thirty *shloh-*SHEEM	**forty** *ahr-bah-*EEM
fifty *khah-mee-*SHEEM	**sixty** *shee-*SHEEM
seventy *shee-*VEEM	**eighty** *shmoh-*NEEM
ninety *tish-*EEM	**hundred** *meh-*AH
two hundred *mah-*TAH-*yim*	**three hundred** *shlosh meh-*OHT

four hundred	five hundred
ahr-BAH *meh*-OHT	*hah*-MESH *meh*-OHT

six hundred	seven hundred
shesh meh-OHT	SHEH-*vah meh*-OHT

eight hundred	nine hundred
shmoh-NEH *meh*-OHT	TEH-*shah meh*-OHT

thousand	ten thousand
EH-*leff*	*ah*-SEH-*ret ah-lah*-FIM

hundred thousand	million
MEH-*ah* EH-*leff*	*meel*-YOHN

3. EATING

Where is a good restaurant?
Eh-FOH *miss-sah*-DAH *toh*-VAH?

A table for two, please.
Shool-KHAHN *leh*-SHNAY *ah-nah*-SHEEM *beh-vah-kah*-SHAH.

Waiter!	**Waitress!**
Mehl-TSAHR!	*Mehl-tsah*-REET!

The menu, please.
Hah-tah-FRIT *beh-vah-kah*-SHAH.

What's good today?
EH-*zay d-vah*-RIM *toh*-VIM *yesh hah*-YOHM?

Is it ready?
Zay moo-KHAHN?

How long will it take?
KAH-*mah zmahn zay yee*-KAHKH?

This, please ...	**and this.**
Zay beh-vah-kah-SHAH ...	*veh zay.*

Bring me ...	**water**	**milk.**
Tah-VEE *lee* ...	MAH-*yeem.*	*khah*-LAHF.

a glass of beer.
kohs BEE-*rah.*

red wine.   white wine.
   yah-YEEN *ah*-DOHM.   *yah*-YEEN *lah*-VAHN.

a cocktail.   whisky soda.
   kohk-TAIL.   VEES-*kee eem* SOH-*dah.*

More, please.   **That's enough.**
   Oht yoh-TEHR.   *Zeh mahs*-PICK.

soup   **fish**   **meat**
mah-RAHK   *dahg*   *bahs*-SAHR

bread and butter
LEH-*khehm veh khay*-MAH

a sandwich   **steak . . .**
sand-VITCH   *bahs*-SAHR *tsah*-LOOY . . .

   rare   **well done**   **medium**
     rahkh   *tsah*-LOOY *tohv*   *bay-noh*-NEE

chicken   **veal**   **pork**
ohf   EH-*ghel*   *khah*-ZEER

lamb   **lamb chop**
keh-VEHS   *keh*-VEHS *kah*-TSOOTS

stuffed vegetable sandwich   **meat on a skewer**
fah-LAHF'L   *kah*-BAHB

vegetable stew with gravy   **No sauce for me.**
KHOO-*moos*   *Blee* ROH-*tehf.*

With potatoes . . .   **rice**
Eem tah-poo-KHAY *ah-dah*-MAH . . .   OH-*ress*

And what vegetables?   **peas**
Veh-EH-*zay yee-rah*-KOT?   *ah-foo*-NAH

beans   **carrots**   **onions**
shoo-EET   GAY-*zah*   *bah*-TSAHL

a salad	lettuce	tomatoes
sah-LAHT	KHAHS-*sah*	*ah-g'vah-n'*YOHT

Please bring me . . .
 Beh-vah-kah-SHAH *tah*-VEE *lee* . . .

another fork	spoon
mahs-LEG *ah*-KHEHR	*kahf*

knife	plate	glass
sah-KIN	*tsah*-LAH-*khaht*	*kohs*

What is there for dessert?
 Mah YESH *leh-mah*-NAH *ah-khroh*-NAH?

fruit	pastry	cake
peh-ROHT	*pahsh-teh*-DAH	OO-GAH

ice cream	cheese
glee-DAH	*g'vee*-NAH

Some coffee, please.   **sugar**
 Kah-FEH *beh-vah-kah*-SHAH. SOO-KAHR

cream	tea with lemon
shah-MEH-*net*	*teh eem lee*-MOHN

mineral water
 MAH-*yeem mee-neh*-RAH-*lim*

The check, please.
 Hah-khesh-BOHN *beh-vah-kah*-SHAH.

Is the tip included?
 Zeh koh-LEHL *gahm sheh*-ROOT?

It was very good!
 Zeh hah-YAH *tohv meh*-OHD!

4. SHOPPING

I would like to buy . . .
 Hah-yee-TEE *roh*-TSEH *lik*-NOT . . . (m)
 Hah-yee-TEE *roh*-TSAH *lik*-NOT . . . (f)

this   that.
  zeh   *veh zeh.*

I am just looking around.
  *Ah-*NEE *rahk mis-tah-*KEHL. (m)
  *Ah-*NEE *rahk mis-tah-*KEH-*let.* (f)

There is the section for . . .
  *Yehsh mahkh-lah-*KAHT *leh . . .*

  men's clothing   women's clothing
    *bi-g*DAY *gvah-*RIM   *bi-g*DAY *gvah-*ROHT

  hats   gloves
    *koh-vah-*EEM   *kfah-*FOHT

  underwear   shoes
    *leh-veh-*NEEM   *nah-ah-*LAH-*yeem*

  stockings   shirts
    *gahr-*BAH-*yeem*   *khool-*TSOHT

The size in America is . . .
  *Hah-mee-*DAH *beh-ah-*MEH-*ree-kah hee . . .*

  toys   perfumes
    *tsah-ah-*tsOO-*EEM*   *tahm-roo-*KIM

  jewelry   watches
    *tahkh-shee-*TIM   *shah-oh-*NEEM

  toilet articles   sports articles
    *dee-*VRAY *toy-*LET   *dee-*VRAY *spohrt*

  films   souvenirs
    FIL-*meem*   *mass-keh-*ROHT

Show me . . .
  *Tah-*RAY *lee . . .* (m)
  *Tah-*REE *lee . . .* (f)

  something less expensive.
    MAH-*sheh-hoo yoh-*TEHR *beh-*ZOHL.

  another one.
    *ah-*KHEHR.

a better quality.
mean meh-shoo-BAHKH *yoh*-TEHR.

bigger.   **smaller.**
yoh-TEHR *gah*-DOHL.   *yoh*-TEHR *kah*-TAHN.

I don't like the color.
Ah-NEE *loh oh*-HEHV *eht hah*-TSAY-*vah.* (m)
Ah-NEE *loh oh*-HEH-*vet eht hah*-TSAY-*vah.* (f)

I want one ...
Ah-NEE *roh*-TSEH *ay*-KHAHD ... (m)
Ah-NEE *roh*-TSAH *ay*-KHAHD ... (f)

in green   **in yellow**
beh-TSEH-*vah yah*-ROCK   *tsah*-HOHV

in blue   **in red**
kah-KHOHL   *ah*-DOHM

in black   **in white**
shah-KHOHR   *lah*-VAHN

in grey   **in pink**   **in brown**
ah-FOOR   *vah*-ROHD   *khoom*

I will take it with me.
Eh-KAHKH *ayt zeh ee*-TEE.

The receipt, please.
Hah-kah-bah-LAH *beh-vah-kah*-SHAH.

Please send it to this address.
Beh-vah-kah-SHAH *leesh*-LOH-*ahkh zeh leck*-TOH-*vet zoo.*

Where is there a flower shop?
Eh-FOH *khah*-NOOT *prah*-KHEEM?

Where is there a book shop?
Eh-FOH *khah*-NOOT *sfah*-RIM?

Where is there a food shop?
Eh-FOH *khah*-NOOT *mah*-KOH-*let?*

5. TRANSPORTATION

Taxi!
*Moh-*NEET!

Take me to the airport.
*Kahkh oh-*TEE *lehs-*DAY *teh-oo-*FAH.

Turn right.   **Turn left.**
*Pneh yeh-*MEE-*nah.*   *Pneh s-*MOH-*lah.*

Not too fast!
*Loh yoh-tehr mee-*DAH-*yee mah-*HEHR!

Hurry up!   **Stop here!**
*Mah-*HEHR!   *Tah-*TSOHR *kahn!*

Wait for me!
*Khah-*KAY *lee!*

How much is it?
KAH-*mah zeh oh-*LAY?

How much is it to ...?   **... and back?**
*Kah-mah zeh oh-*LAY *leh ...?*   *... ve khah-*ZOHR?

How much ...   **by the hour?**
KAH-*mah zeh oh-*LAY *...*   *leh shah-*AH?

   by the day?
    *leh-*YOHM?

Show me the sights.
*Tah-*REH *lee eht hah-meh-koh-*MOHT *hah-meh-*
AHN-*yeh-*NEEM. (m)
Tah REE *lee eht hah-meh-koh-*MOHT *hah-meh-*
AHN-*yeh-*NEEM. (f)

What is this building?
MAH-*hah-bin-*YAHN *hah-*ZEH?

Can I go in?
*Ah-*NEE *yeh-khohl leh-hee-kah-*NESS? (m)
*Ah-*NEE *yeh-khoh-*LAH *leh-hee-kah-*NESS? (f)

I want to go ...
 Ah-NEE *roh*-TSEH ... (m)
 Ah-NEE *roh*-TSAH ... (f)

  to the Mograbi. (central place in Tel-Aviv)
  leh-MOO-*grah*-*bee*.

  to the railroad station.
  leh-tah-khah-NAHT *hah-rah*-KAY-*vet*.

Porter!   **I have two bags.**
 Sah-BAHL!   *Yesh*-LEE *shtay mis-vah*-DOT.

A ticket to ...
 Kahr-TISS *leh* ...

  one way   **round trip**
  kee-VOON *ay*-KHAHD *tee*-YOOL

  first class
  mahkh-LAY-*keht ree-shoh*-NAH

  second class
  mahkh-LAY-*keht shnee*-YAH

When does it leave?
 Mah-TAH-*ee yoh*-TSEHT *hah-rah*-KAY-*vet?*

Where is the train to Haifa?
 Eh-FOH *hah-rah*-KAY-*vet leh khah-ee*-FAH?

Is this the train to Beer-Sheva?
 Zoo hee hah-rah-KAY-*vet leh beh-ehr*-SHEH-*vah?*

When do we get to Hedera?
 Mah-TAH-*ee nah*-GHEE-*ah leh-kheh*-DEH-*rah?*

Open the window.
 Tiff-TAHKH *eht hah-khah*-LOHN. (m)
 Tiff-tah-KHEE *eht hah-khah*-LOHN. (f)

Close the window.
 Tiss-GOHR *eht hah-khah*-LOHN. (m)
 Tiss-gheh-REE *eht hah-khah*-LOHN. (f)

Where is the bus to Tiberias?
Eh-FOH *hah-*OH-*toh-boos leh t'*VEH-*r'yah?*

I want to go to Ashkelon.
Ah-NEE *roh-*TSEH *lin-*SOH-*ah leh ash-keh-*LOHN. (m)
Ah-NEE *roh-*TSAH *lin-*SOH-*ah leh ash-keh-*LOHN. (f)

Please tell me where to get off.
*Beh-vah-kah-*SHAH *tah-*GHEED *lee eh-*FOH *lah-*RAY-*dett.*

Where is a gas station?
Eh-FOH *tah-khah-*NAHT *behn-*ZEEN?

Fill it up!
*Leh-mah-*LOT!

Check . . .	**the oil.**
*Teev-*DOCK . . .	*eht hah-*SHEH-*men.*
water.	tires.
MAH-*yeem.*	*tsmee-*GHEEM.

Something is wrong with the car.
MAH-*sheh-hoo loh bess-*SEH-*dehr eem hah-*OH-*toh.*

Can you fix it?
*Ah-*TAH *yeh-*KHOHL *leh-tah-*KEHN *eht zeh?*

How long will it take?
KAH-*mah z'mahn zeh yee-*KAHKH?

Is this the road to Elath?
*Zeh hah-*DAY-*raikh leh-eh-*LAHT?

Have you a map?
*Yesh leh-*KHAH *mah-*PAH? (m)
*Yesh lahkh mah-*PAH? (f)

Where is the boat to Ejn-Gev?
Eh-FOH *hah-see-*RAH *leh ayn-*GEFF?

When does it leave?
*Mah-*TAH-*yee hee nohs-*SAHT?

6. MAKING FRIENDS

Good day!
 *Shah-*LOHM!

My name is ...
 Shmee ...

What is your name, sir?
 *Mah sheem-*KHAH *ah-doh-*NEE?

What is your name, madame?
 *Mah shmehkh g'veer-*TEE?

What is your name, miss?
 *Mah shmehkh g'veer-*TEE?

I am delighted to meet you.
 *Ess-*MAHKH *meh-*OHD *leh-hah-*KEER *oht-*KHAH. (m)
 *Ess-*MAHKH *meh-*OHD *leh-hah-*KEER *oh-*TEHKH. (f)

Do you speak English?   **A little.**
 *Ah-*TAH *meh-dah-*BEHR *ahn-*GLIT? (m)   *K'tsaht.*
 *Aht meh-dah-*BEH*-reht ahn-*GLIT? (f)

I speak only a little Hebrew.
 *Ah-*NEE *meh-dah-*BEHR *ktsaht ee-*VRIT. (m)
 *Ah-*NEE *meh-dah-*BEH*-reht ktsaht ee-*VRIT. (f)

Do you understand?
 *Ah-*TAH *meh-*VEEN? (m)
 *Aht meh-vee-*NAH? (f)

Please speak slowly.
 *Teh-dah-*BEHR *leh-*AHT *beh-vah-kah-*SHAH. (m)
 *Teh-dah-*BREE *leh-*AHT *beh-vah-kah-*SHAH. (f)

I am from New York.
 *Ah-*NEE *mee New York.*

Where are you from?
 *Meh-*AH*-yeen ah-tah?* (m)
 *Meh-*AH*-yeen aht?* (f)

I like your country.
 *Ah-*NEE *oh-*HEHV *eht ahr-tseh-*KHAH. (m)
 *Ah-*NEE *oh-*HEH*-vet eht ahr-tseh-*KHAH. (f)

I like your city.
  Ah-NEE *oh*-HEHV *eht eer*-KHAH. (m)
  Ah-NEE *oh*-HEH-*vet eht eer*-KHAH. (f)

Have you been in America?
  Hah-EE-*tah beh-ah*-MEH-*ree-kah?* (m)
  Hah-EET *beh-ah*-MEH-*ree-kah?* (f)

This is my first visit here.
  Zeh bee-koo-REE *hah-ree*-SHOHN *kahn.*

May I sit here?
  Yeh-KHOHL *ah*-NEE *lah*-SHAY-*vet kahn?*

May I take your picture?
  Moo-TAHR *lee leh-tsah*-LEHM *oht*-KHAH? (m)
  Moo-TAHR *lee leh-tsah*-LEHM *oh*-TEHKH? (f)

Come here.
  Boh HAY-*nah.* (m)
  Boy HAY-*nah.* (f)

This is my wife.
  ZOO-*hee eesh*-TEE.

my husband.	**my son.**	**my daughter.**
bah-ah-LEE.	*beh*-NEE.	*bee*-TEE.
my mother.	**my father.**	**my sister.**
ee-MEE.	*ah*-VEE.	*ah-khoh*-TEE.

Have you children?
  Yesh-leh-KHAH *yeh-lah*-DIM? (m)
  Yesh-LAHKH *yeh-lah*-DIM? (f)

How beautiful!   **Very interesting!**
  KAH-*mah yahf*-FEH!   *Meh-ahn*-YEHN *meh*-OHD!

Would you like a cigarette?
  Ah-TAH *roh*-TSEH *see*-GAH-*ree-yah?* (m)
  Aht roh-TSAH *see*-GAH-*ree-yah?* (f)

Would you like something to drink?
  Ah-TAH *roh*-TSEH MAH-*sheh-hoo leesh*-TOHT? (m)
  Aht roh-TSAH MAH-*sheh-hoo leesh*-TOHT? (f)

Would you like something to eat?
   *Ah-*TAH *roh-*TSEH MAH-*sheh-hoo leh-eh-*KHOHL? (m)
   *Aht roh-*TSAH MAH-*sheh-noo leh-eh-*KHOHL? (f)

Sit down, please.
   *Shehv beh-vah-kah-*SHAH. (m)
   *Shvee beh-vah-kah-*SHAH. (f)

Make yourself at home.
   *Tahr-*GISH *eht ahts-meh-*KHAH *bah-*BAH-*yit.* (m)
   *Tahr-*GHEE-*shee eht ahts-*MEHKH *bah-*BAH-*yit.* (f)

Good luck!   **To your health!**
   *Mah-*ZAHL *tohv!*   *Leh* KHAH-*yeem!*

When can I see you again?
   *Mah-*TAH-*ee oo-*KHAHL *lee-*ROHT *oht-khah-*shoov?
   (m)
   *Mah-*TAH-*ee oo-*KHAHL *lee-*ROHT *oh-*TEKH-*shoov?* (f)

Where shall we meet?
   *Eh-*FOH *neet-pah-*GEHSH?

Here is my address.
   *Hee-*NEH *hahk-*TOH-*vet sheh-*LEE.

What is your address?
   *Mah ktoh-vaht-*KHAH?

What is your phone number?
   *Mah-mis-*PAHR *hah-tel-leh-*FOHN *shehl-*KHAH? (m)
   *Mah-mis-*PAHR *hah-tel-leh-*FOHN *sheh-*LAHKH? (f)

May I speak to . . .
   *Ah-*NEE *yah-*KHOHL *leh-dah-*BEHR *eem . . .*

Would you like to have lunch with me?
   *Ah-*TAH *roh-*TSEH *ee-*TEE *leh-eh-*KHOHL *ah-roo-*
   KHAHT *tsoh-hah-*RAH-*yeem?* (m)
   *Aht roh-*TSAH *ee-*TEE *leh-eh-*KHOHL *ah-roo-*KHAHT
   *tsoh-hah-*RAH-*yeem?* (f)

   dinner?
      *ah-roo-*KHAHT *eh-*rev?

Would you like to go to . . .
  *Ah-*TAH *roh-*TSEH *lah-*LAY*-kheht . . .*
  *Aht roh-*TSAH *lah-*LAY*-kheht . . .*

  the movies?   **the theater?**
    *leh-kohl-*NOH*-ah?* (m)   *leh-teh-ah-*TROHN?
    *leh-kohl-*NOH*-ah?* (f)

  the beach?   **for a walk?**
    *less-*FAHT *hah-*YAHM?   *leh-tah-*YEHL?

With great pleasure!
  *Beh-raht-*SOHN *rahv!*

I am sorry.
  *Ah-*NEE *meets-tah-*EHR. (m)
  *Ah-*NEE *meets-tah-eh-reht.* (f)

I cannot.   **Another time.**
  *Ehn-*NEE *yah-*KHOHL. (m)   *Pahm ah-*KHAY*-reht.*
  *Ehn-*NEE *yeh-khoh-*LAH. (f)

I must go now.
  *Ah-*NEE *tsah-*REEKH *lah-*LAY*-kheht ahkh-*SHAHV. (m)
  *Ah-*NEE *tsree-*KHAH *lah-*LAY*-kheht ahkh-*SHAHV. (f)

Thank you for a wonderful time.
  *Toh-*DAH *ah-*VOOR *hahz-*MAHN *hah-nah-*EEM.

Thank you for an excellent dinner.
  *Toh-*DAH *ah-*VOOR *ah-roo-*KHAHT *hah-*EH*-rev hah-
    teh-ee-*MAH.

This is for you.
  *Zeh bish-veel-*KHAH. (m)
  *Zeh bish-veel-*LEHKH. (f)

You are very kind.
  *Ah-*TAH *ah-*DEEV *meh-*OHD. (m)
  *Aht ah-dee-*VAH *meh-*OHD. (f)

It's nothing, really.
  *Ahl loh dah-*VAHR.

With best regards.
*Dree-*SHAHT *shah-*LOHM.

Congratulations!
*Mah-*ZAHL *tohv!*

Have a good trip!
*Ness-see-*YAH *toh-*VAH!

7. EMERGENCIES

Help!
*Hah-*TSEE-*loo!*

Police!
*Mish-tah-*RAH!

Fire!
*Sreh-*FAH!

Stop that man!
*Tah-*TSOHR *eht hah-*EESH!

. . . woman!
*. . . hah-ee-*SHAH!

I have been robbed!
*Shah-deh-*DOO *oh-*TEE!

Look out!
*Tee-zah-*HEHR! (m)
*Tee-zah-heh-*REE! (f)

Wait a minute!
*Khah-*KEH RAY-*gah!* (m)
*Khah-*KEE RAY-*gah!* (f)

Stop!
*Ah-*TSOHR!

Get out!
*Lekh mee-*KAHN! (m)
*Leh-*KHEE *mee-*KAHN! (f)

Hurry up!
*Mah-*HEHR!

Don't bother me!
*Ah-*ZOHV *oh-*TEE! (m)
*Ahz-*VEE *oh-*TEE! (f)

What's going on!
*Mah kah-*RAH!

Entrance
*K'nees-*SAH

Exit
*Yeh-tsee-*YAH

Ladies
*G'vah-*ROHT

Gentlemen
*G'vah-*RIM

Danger
*Sah-kah-*NAH

Keep out
*Loh leh-hee-kah-*NESS

No smoking
*Ahs-*SOOR *leh-ah-*SHEN

No parking
*Ayn khah-nee-*YAH

One way
*Kee-*VOON *ay-*KHAHD

I am ill.
Ah-NEE *khoh*-LAY. (m)
Ah-NEE *khoh*-LAH. (f)

It hurts here.
Zeh koh-EHV *kahn*.

Call a doctor!
Tick-RAH *leh-roh*-FEH! (m)
Tick-reh-EE *leh-roh*-FEH! (f)

Where is the drug store?
Eh-FOH *beht meer*-KAH-*khaht*?

Take me to the hospital!
Kahkh oh-TEE *leh beht khoh*-LEEM! (m)
K'khee oh-TEE *leh beht khoh*-LEEM! (f)

Where is the dentist?
Eh-FOH *roh*-FEH *sheh*-NAH-*yeem*?

I have lost . . .
Ee-BAH-*deh-tee* . . .

    my bag.
       eht hah-mis-vah-DAH *sheh*-LEE.

    my wallet.
       eht hah-ahr-NAHK *sheh*-LEE.

    my camera.
       eht hah-mahts-leh-MAH *sheh*-LEE.

    my passport.
       eht ah-dahr-KOHN *sheh*-LEE.

I am an American.
Ah-NEE *ah-meh-ree*-KAH-*ee*. (m)
Ah-NEE *ah-meh-ree*-KAH-*eet*. (f)

Where is the American Consulate?
Eh-FOH *hah-kohn*-SOO-*lee-yah hah-ah-meh-ree-*
    kah-EET?

Don't get excited!
Ahl-tit-rah-GESH! (m)
Ahl-tit-rahg-SHEE! (f)

Everything is all right.
Hah-KOHL *bess*-SEH-*dehr*.

ARABIC

Facts About Arabic

Arabic shares the distinction, with English, French, and Spanish, of being an international language that is spoken as a national language in the largest number of separate countries. It is spoken by more than 70,000,000 people throughout North Africa, in Morocco, Algeria, Tunis, Lybia, Egypt, Sudan, and the new countries of the Sahara; in the Middle East countries of Syria, Lebanon, Jordan, Iraq, Saudi Arabia, Aden, Yemen, Oman, Kuwait; and in the islands of the Red Sea and the Persian Gulf. It is a familiar idiom to millions more in Pakistan, Iran, Afghanistan, and other Asian countries, and even in parts of the U.S.S.R. and China, inasmuch as it is the language of the Koran and is taught to all young Moslems so that they may read the sacred book of Islam.

Arabic is a Semitic language, along with Hebrew and Aramaic, a language generally spoken in the Middle East in ancient times. It has kept to its original form more closely than other world languages largely through the influence of the Koran. The Koran can be said to hold the Arabic language together, because its style is the pillar of this tongue. Although there are some regional differences, radio programs, newspapers, and official documents are usually in classical Arabic, a close approximation of the language of the Koran.

Advice On Accent

Only two lines have been used in the Arabic section of this book—English phrases and the corresponding Arabic phonetics—as the Arabic alphabet would be of no practical value here. In order to approximate an unusual feature of Arabic, we have placed an apostrophe in many of our phonetic renditions. This apostrophe means that the speaker should hesitate slightly before pronouncing the following letter. A sort of catch in the voice would be nearly correct.

Whenever (m) or (f) appears after phonetic phrases, choose (m) when speaking to a man and (f) when speaking to a woman. This is very important for correct conversation.

How Arabic Is Written

Arabic is written from right to left, exactly the opposite from the way we write. It has an ancient and beautiful alphabetical script, but the letters have no recognizable similarity to ours. Here is how the signs *Entrance, Exit,* and *No Smoking* are written in Arabic:

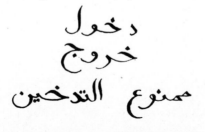

دخول

خروج

ممنوع التدخين

You Already Know Some Arabic

Besides our adapted version of Arabic numerals, a most important part of our daily life (we got these from the Arabs during the Middle Ages), there are some interesting English words which we owe to Arabic. Here are some of them with the original Arabic meanings: algebra, from *al jabr,* "putting together"; admiral, from *amir al bahr* (ruler of the sea); cipher, from *sifr,* "zero"; alcohol, from *al kohl,* "the powder"; Sahara, "desert"; asthma, "crisis." Perhaps the most picturesque is the fox-hunting expression "Tally ho!" It comes from the Arabic *Tala hon!* ("Come here!") and was introduced during the Crusades, when Crusaders brought the sport of falconry (and Arab falconers) back from the Holy Land.

1. FIRST CONTACT

Yes.	**No.**	**Good.**
Na'am.	*La.*	*M'leeh.*

Thank you.
SHOO-*kran.*

You are welcome.
AH'H-*lan wa sah'h-lan.*

Excuse me.
*Sa-*MIH-*nee.* (m)
*Sam-*HEEN-*ee.* (f)

It's all right.
TAH-*yib.*

Please.
*Ar-*JOOK. (m)
*Ar-*JOO-KEE. (f)

I would like ...
Ana b'reed ...

What?
Aysh? 1

This.
HA-*da.* (m)
HA-*dee.* (f)

Where?	**Here.**	**There.**
Wane? 2	*Hone.*3	*Hu-nak.*

When?	**Now.**	**Later.**
EM-*ta?*	HA-LAN.	*Ba'ad-*DANE.

Who?	**I**	**you**
Meen?	*Ana*	IN-*ta* (m)
		IN-*tee* (f)
		IN-*too* (plural)

he	**she**
HOO-*wa*	*hee-*YA

---

1 In Egypt, *Hay.*
2 In Egypt, *Fane.*
3 In Egypt, *Hehn-neh.*

Your name?
Iss-mak? (m)
Iss-mik? (f)

Good morning.
*Sah-*BAH'H *l'kheyr.*

Good night.
*Tiss-*BAH'HA*-la kheyr.*

Good day.
*Nah-*HAR*-kom sah-*EED.

Good evening.
Ma-sal' kheyr.

Good-by. (to one leaving)
MAH*-salamah.*

Good-by. (to one staying)
*B'*KHA*-tirr-koom.*

How are you?
Keef HA*-lahk?* (m)
Keef HA*-lik?* (f)

Very well, thank you (literally "Thanks to God"), and you?
*Mahb-*SOOT *ill-hahm-doo* LIL*-lah wa inta?* (m)
*Mah-*SOOT*-tah ill-hahm-doo* LIL*-ah wa intee?* (f)

I do not understand, please repeat.
Ma fa ham-tish, min fahd-lak EYE-EED *ta-nee.* (m)
Ma fa ham-tish, min fahd-lik EYE-EED-EE *ta-nee.* (f)

How much?
AD-AYSH?

one	two	three
WAH*-hid*	*it'nane*	*ta'*LA-TAH

four	five	six
*ar-bah-*AH	KHAM*-sah*	SIT*-tah*

seven	eight	nine
sab-ba'ah	*tama-nyah*	TISS*-a'ah*

ten	eleven
a'ah-sha-rah	EH-DA*-shar*

twelve
IT-NAH*-shahr*

2. ACCOMMODATIONS

Where is a good hotel?
Wane feeh oh-tell m'leeh?

I want a room . . .
Ana b'reed ood-dhaah . . .

for one person.
l'WA-hid.

for two persons.
l'tnane.

with bath
fee-ha hham-MAM

for two days
li y'o mane

for a week
li ESS-boo-ah

till Monday
li yom l'It-t'nane

Tuesday
It-tha-LAT

Wednesday
l'Arr ba'a

Thursday
il'Khah MEES

Friday
il'Jum-'aah

Saturday
iss'sapt

Sunday
il'A-hahd

How much will it be?
Ad-AYSH uj-RIT-ha?

Here are my bags.
HA-dee shun-AH-tee.

Here is my passport.
HAD-da pass-PORT-ee.

I like it.
B'ti-'jib-nee.

I don't like it.
Ma b'ti-jib-nee.

Show me another.
Fahr-rij-nee ghair-ha.

Where is the toilet?
Wane bate 'l-my'ah?

Where is the men's room?
Wane bate il-my'ah l'irri-jal?

Where is the ladies' room?
Wane bate il-my'ah lis-sayec-DAT?

hot water   **a towel**   **soap**
  my'ah SUKH-*nah*   *Man-sha-fah*   *sa-boon*

Come in!   **This is to be washed, please.**
  Ta-fad'dal! (m)   *Ar-jook ha-dee lil-gha-seel.*
  Ta-fad'da-lee! (f)

This is for pressing, please.
  *Ar-jook ha-dee lil-*KA-*we.*

This is to be cleaned, please.
  Ar-jook ha-dee LI'T-*tan-*ZEEF.

Where is the telephone?   **Hello!**
  Wane 'it-telefon?   *Al-lo!*

Send breakfast to room Number 702.
  *Ib-ba'at 'il-fu-toor lil-*OO-*dah nim-rit saba'a sifr
  it'nane.*

     orange juice   **boiled eggs**
       *a'a-*SEER *buir tu'am*   *beyd mass-look*

     bread and coffee
       khubz wa AH'*wah*

I am expecting a friend.
  *Ana bass-*TAN-*na sa-deek.* (m)
  *Ana bass-*TAN-*na sa-deek-ah.* (f)

Tell him to wait.   **Tell her to wait.**
  *Ull-uh yiss-*TAN-*na.*   *Ull-aha tiss-*TAN-*na.*

**If anyone calls on the telephone, I will be back at
six o'clock.**
  *I-za b'ye-*JEE-*nee telefon, ana b'arr-ja'a is-sa'ah
  sit-teh.*

Where is the restaurant, please?
  Min FAHD *la wane 'il-mah-ta'am?* (m)
  Min FAHD *li wane 'il-mah-ta'am?* (f)

Where is the barber shop?
 *Wane 'il-hal-*LA'A?

Where is the beauty shop?
 *Wane mah-*HAL *'it-tajmeel?*

Where is the drugstore?
 Wane iss-sah'yy-da-liy-yiah?

What is the telephone number?
 Aysh num-rat 'it-telefon?

What is the address?
 Aysh 'il-un-wan?

I want to change some money.
 *Ana b'reed a bad-*DILL *ma-sah-ree.*

What is the rate for dollars?
 Ad-aysh si'ir 'id-dular?

thirteen *ta lat-tashar*	**fourteen** *a-r-ba'a-*TA'A*-sha*
fifteen *khahm-ss-*TA*-sha*	**sixteen** *sit-*TA*-sha*

seventeen *saba'a-*TA*-sha*	**eighteen** *taman-*TA*-sha*	**nineteen** *tissa'a* TA*-sha*
twenty *'ish-reen*	**thirty** *tala-teen*	**forty** *ar-ba'a-*EEN
fifty *kham-*SEEN	**sixty** *sit-*TEEN	**seventy** *sab-*EEN
eighty *taman-yeen*	**ninety** *tiss'*EEN	**one hundred** *mi-y'ah*
two hundred *mi-tane*	**three hundred** *talat mi-y'ah*	**four hundred** *ar-ba'a mi-y'ah*
five hundred *khams mi-y'ah*	**six hundred** *sitt mi-y'ah*	**seven hundred** *saba'a mi-y'ah*

eight hundred	nine hundred	one thousand
taman mi-y'ah	*tissa'a mi-y'ah*	*al'f mi-y'ah*

My bill, please. **The receipt, please.**
Ar-jook 'il-hisab. *Ar-jook 'il-wassl.*

3. EATING

Where is a good restaurant?
Wane feeh muta'am KWAH-yiss?

A table for two, please.
Ar-JOOK tah'oolah l'tnane.

Waiter! **The menu, please.**
Gahr-SOHN! *Ar-JOOK LAY-hat at-ta'AM.*

What's good today? **Is it ready?**
Aysh feeh m'leeh el-YOHM? *H'ha-dir?*

How long will it take?
Ad-AYSH b'YAH-khood wa'at?

This please ... **and this.**
Ar-JOOK HA-da ... *wa HA-da.*

Bring me ... **water** **milk**
JEEB-lee ... *my-yah* *ha-LEEB*

    a glass of beer **brandy**
    kass BEER-ah *brandy*

    whisky and soda **More, please.**
    wisky wa soda *ba'ad SHWY-ee.*

That's enough.
Ta'a la hone.

    soup **fish** **meat**
    SHOOR-bah *SAM-ak* *LAH-hm*

bread and butter
khubz wa zib-dah

steak ...
SHAHR-*hat la-hm ...*

rare
mash-wee khafeef

medium
muss-muss

well done
mist-wee-yeh

chicken
far-rooje

lamb
DHAH-*nee*

lamb chop
SHAHR-*hat* DHAH-*nee*

shish kebab
LAH-H'*m* MASH-*wee*

cous-cous
koos-koos

potatoes ...
bah-tah-tis ...

rice
ruzz

an omelet
EJ-*jah*

peas
*baz-*ZEL-*lah*

beans
LOOB-*yah*

carrots
JAZ-*zar*

onions
BAH-*sahl*

a salad
SAH-*lah-tah*

lettuce
khass

tomatoes
*tah-*MAH-*tem*

dates
TAH-*m'rr*

Please bring one more fork.
*Ar-*JOOK JEEB-*lee* SHOO-*kah* TAN-*n'yah.*

knife
*sik-*KEEN

spoon
*mal-*A'A-*kah*

glass
*kub-*BA-*yah*

plate
SAH-*h'n*

What is there for dessert?
Aysh feeh l'il hel-ool?

fruit
*fa-*WA-*keh*

pastry
ha la-wiy'y-at

ice cream
ice cream

cheese
JIB-*nah*

Some coffee, please.   sugar
  *Ar-*JOOK AH'*wah.*   SUK-*kar*

mineral water   tea with lemon
  may'ah mah'a-da-nee yah   *shy bi lam-oon*

The check, please.
  *Ar-*JOOK *al his-*SAAB.

Is the tip included?
  *Il bakh-sheesh mahh-*SOOB?

It was very good!
  M'leeh k'teer!

4. SHOPPING

I would like to buy this . . .   that
  B'reed ISH-*tir-ree* HA-*da* . . .   *had-*DAK.

I am just looking around.
  *Ana bat-*FAR-RAJ.

Where is the section for . . .
  *Wane ma-*HAL . . .

    men's clothing   women's clothing
      *mal-*LA-*biss ri-*JAAL   *mal-*LA-*biss sa-yee-*DAAT

    hats   gloves
      *ba-ra-*NEET   *k'foof*

    underwear
      *mal-*LA-*biss tah'h-ta-*NEE-*yah*

    shoes   stockings   shirts
      ah-ziyah   *ja-*WAA-*rib*   *um-*SAAHN

The size in America is . . .
  Ill-k'yass fee america HOO-*wah* . . .

    toys   perfumes   jewelry
      lee'a'ab   *u'toor*   *see-ghah*

watches
   *sa'a-*AT

toilet articles
   a-da-wa'atzee nah

films
   *af-*FLAM

bracelets
   *as-*SA'A-*wir*

earrings
   hul-aam

in silver
   FID-*dhah*

gold
   da-hab

Show me . . .
   farr-ij-nee (m) . . .
   farr-ij-eenee (f) . . .

something less expensive
   shay ar-khass

   another one
      shay-tan-nee

   a better quality
      *shay-*AH-*san*

   bigger
      AK-*bar*

   smaller
      az-ghar

I don't like the color.
   *Ma b'hib ill-*LAH*'oon.*

I want one . . .
   breed WAH-*hed .* ∴.

in green
   AKH-*dhar*

   yellow
      ah-sfar

   blue
      AZ-*ra'a*

   red
      ah'h mar

   black
      a-swad

   white
      AB-*yad*

   gray
      *ra-*MA-*dee*

   pink
      zahri

   brown
      BOON-*nee*

I will take it with me.
   Ba'a-khdoo-uh ma'ee. (m)
   Ba'a-khdoo-ha ma'ee. (f)

The receipt, please.
   *Ar-*JOOK *il-wassl.*

Please send it to this address.
   *Ar-*JOOK *ib-ba'a-*TOO *lee hal-en-wan.* (m)
   *Ar-*JOOK *ib-ba'a-tee lee hal-en-wan.* (f)

Where is the market?
*Wane iss-*SOOK?

Where is there a flower shop?
*Wane mah-*HAL *zoo-*HOOR?

Where can I buy food?
Wane BISH-*tee-ree Ak'll?*

5. TRANSPORTATION

Taxi!   **Take me to the airport.**
TAK-*see!*   KHOOD-*nee l'il mat-'*TAR.

Turn right!   **Turn left!**
Haw'-id YA *meen!*   *Haw'-id shi-ma!*

Not so fast!   **Hurry up!**   **Stop here.**
Ma tiss-rah!   ISS-*ri!*   *Gif hone.*

Wait for me.
*Istan'*NA-*nee.*

How much do you want?
*Ad-*DAYSH *bit-*TREED?

How much is it to . . . ?
*Ad-*DAYSH *min hone lee . . . ?*

    and back?
     wa raji?

How much by the hour?   **by the day?**
*Ad-*DAYSH *bis-*SA-*ah?*   *Ad-*DAYSH *bil-yom?*

carriage   **horse**   **camel**
a'ar-abi-y'ah   *his-saahn*   JA'*mal*

    donkey
     *hee-*MAR

Show me the city.
Far-rij-nee 'il-ma-deenah.

What is that building?
*Aysh hal bin-*AY*-ah?*

Am I allowed to go in?
Mas-mooh-lee 'id-dookh-ool?

I want to see the Great Mosque.
*B'reed shoof 'il-*JAM*-ee-ah 'il-k'beer.*

To the railroad station!
*L'il mah-*HAT*-tah!*

Porter!   **I have two bags.**
Shay'-yal!   A'AN*-dee shanti-*TANE.

A ticket to Damascus.
Taz-karah li-Di-mishq.

one way   **round trip**
zi-haab   *zi-haab wa iya-ab*

first class   **second class**
da-ra-jah OO*-lah*   *da-ra-jah tan-yah*

When does it leave?
AIM*-tah biy'-sa-fir?*

Where is the train to Damascus?
Wane il-kit-tar lee Es-Shaams?

Is this the train to Cairo?
Ha-da il-kitar lee al KHAH*-ee-rah?*

When do we get to Riadh?
Aim-tah b'noow-sahl lee'R-ree-yahd?

Where is the dining car?
*Wane 'il-*MAT*-tahm?*

Open the window.   **Close the window.**
IF*-tahh ish-shu-*BAK.   SAK*-kir ish-shu-*BAK.

Where is the bus to Tripoli?
Wane 'il-bus lee Trab-luss?

I want to go to Beirut.
*B'reed aruh'h lee-Bay-*ROOT.

Please tell me where to get off.
*Ar-*JOOK *ulli wane an-zil.*

Where is a gas station?
*Wane may-*HAT-TA *'il-ben-*ZEEN?

Fill it up.
Imm' lah.

Check the oil.   water.   tires.
*Shoof iz-zate.   'il-my'ah.   'il-it-*TAH-*rat.*

Something is wrong with the car.
*Is-sa-*YA-*rah maa-*B'TIM-*shee m'leeh.*

Can you fix it?
B'TIH-*der sahl-lah'h-haa?*

How long will it take?
Ad-daysh b'takh-ud wa't?

Is this the road to Sidon?
HA-*a 'itahr-*REEQ *li-syahda?*

Have you a map?
A'EN-DAK KHAR-*tah?*

Where is the boat to Alexandria?
Wane 'il-ba-khi-rah l'Is-skin-di-riy'ah?

When does it leave?
AIM-*tah b'it-sa-fir?*

6. MAKING FRIENDS

Good day.   **How are you?**
*Nah-*HAH'*rak sa-*EED. (m)   *Keef* HAL-*lak?* (m)
*Nah-*HAH'*rik sa-*EED. (f)   *Keef* HAL-*lik?* (f)

My name is . . .   **What is your name, Sir?**
ISS-*mee . . .*   *Aysh iss-mak ya,* SA-*yid?*

What is your name, Madame?
  Aysh iss-mik ya SITT?

What is your name, Miss?
  Aysh iss-mik ya aa-nisah?

I am honored to meet you.
  *Ta'shar-*RAFT *bih mah-hah-rif-tahk.* (m)
  *Ta'shar-*RAFT *bih mah-hah-rif-tik.* (f)

Happy to see you again.
  *Ana sa-*EED *in-nee* SHOOF-*tu-koom tan-nee.* (m)
  *Ana sa-*EED-*ah in-nee* SHOOF-*tu-koom tan-nee.* (f)

Do you speak English?   **A little.**
  *B'tek'h-kee een-*GLEE-*zee?*   *Ah '*ILEE'L.

I speak only a little Arabic.   **Do you understand?**
  B'eh'h-kee a'Ar-a-bee shwey.   *Inta b'tif-ham?*

Please speak slowly.
  *Ar-*JOOK *eh'h-kee a'ala* MA-*h'l.*

I am from New York.   **Where are you from?**
  Ana min New York.   *Min wane in-ta?* (m)
                              Min wane IN-*tee?* (f)

I like your country.
  *Ana b'hib bil-*AD-*koom.*

I like your city.
  *Ana b'hib madee-*NET-*koom.*

Have you been in America?
  Kunt fee America? (m)
  Kun tee fee America? (f)

This is my first visit here.
  Ha-dee AH-*wal zee-*YAR-*ah lee hone.*

May I sit here?
  B'seer uh'ud hone?

May I take your picture?
*B'tiss-*MAH*-lee* AH*-hood* SOOR*-tak?* (m)
*B'tiss mah-*HEE*-lee* AH*-hood* SOOR*-tik?* (f)

This is a picture of my wife.
HA*-dee* SOO*-raht z'owj-tee.*

This is a picture of my husband.
HA*-dee* SOO*-raht z'ow-jee.*

my son	my daughter	my mother
IBB*-nee*	BIN*-tee*	UM*-mee*

my father	my sister	my brother
AB*-bee*	UKH*-tee*	AH*-khee*

Have you children?
A'an-dak au-oo-'laad? (m)
A'an-dik au-oo'laad? (f)

How beautiful!
*Ya ja-*MAL*-uh!* (m)
*Ya ja-*MAL*'-ha!* (f)

Would you like a cigarette?
*Bi-*TREED *see-gar-rah?* (m)
*Bi-*TREED*-ee see-gar-rah?* (f)

Would you like something to drink?
*Bi-*TREED *mash-*ROOB? (m)
*Bi-*TREED*-ee mash-*ROOB? (f)

Would you like something to eat?
*Bi-*TREED*-*AK*'ll?* (m)
*Bi-*TREED*-ee* AK*'ll?* (f)

Sit down, please.
T'fahd-dall er-ta'ah'h. (m)
T'fahd-dall-lee er-ta'a-hee. (f)

Make yourself at home! (This is your home!)
HA*-da bay-*TAK! (m)
HA*-da bay-tik!* (f)

Good luck!
  M'WAH-*ffak!*

To your health!
  Sih-HAHT-*ahk!* (sing.)
  Sih-HAHT-*koom!* (pl.)

When can I see you again?
  AIM-*tah ah-shoo fahk tah-nee?*

Where shall we meet?
  Wane b'nill-ta'ee?

Here is my address.
  Ha-da un-WA *nee.*

What is your address?
  Aysh un-wa'a-nak? (m)
  Aysh un-wa'a-nik? (f)

What is your phone number?
  Aysh NOM-*rat tele-fon-ak?* (m)
  Aysh NOM-*rat tele-fon-ik?* (f)

May I speak to ... ?
  Mumkin ah-kee ma'a ...?

Would you like to have lunch?
  Bi-TREED *tit-gha-dda?* (m)
  Bi-TREED-*ee tit-gha-ddee?* (f)

Would you like to have dinner?
  Bi-TREED *tit-a'*SHA*?* (m)
  Bi-TREED-*ee tit-a'*SHEE*?* (f)

Would you like to go to the movies?
  Bi-TREED *t'rooh' l'*SSEE-*neh-mah?* (m)
  Bi-TREE-*ee t'rooh'hee l'*SSEE-*nee-mah?* (f)

    theatre?
    l'ytee-A-*tro?*

Would you like to go to the seashore?
  Bi-TREED *t'rooh li'l-bah'r?* (m)
  Bi-TREE-*ee t'rooh'hee li'l-bah'r?* (f)

    for a walk?
    tit-MASH-*a?* (m)
    tit-MASH-*ee?* (f)

With great pleasure!
 Bi-KOOL *soo*-ROOR!

I am sorry.
 Mitt-ASS-*if.* (m)
 Mitt-ASSI-*feh.* (f)

I cannot.
 MA *bih'der.*

Another time.
 MAH-*rrah tan-yah.*

I must go.
 La-zim ARUH'H.

I enjoyed myself much!
 SHOOK-*ran, in-ba*-SAHT *k'teer!*

Thank you for an excellent dinner.
 SHOO-*kran a'ala* A'A-*shah.*

This is for you.
 HA-*da 'ala* SHAN-*ak.* (m)
 HA-*da 'ala* SHAN-*ik.* (f)

You are very kind.
 INTA *lah-teef k'teer.* (m)
 IN-*tee la*-TEEF-*ah k'teer.* (f)

You are welcome.
 AH-*lan wa* SAHH-*lan.*

Greetings!
 Sa-LAM-*at!*

Congratulations!
 Mah-brook!

7. EMERGENCIES

Help!
 Ya-HOO!

Police!
 Police!

Fire!
 Haree-'ah!

Stop that man!
 IM*sik ir*-RAJ-*il dah!*

Stop that woman!
 IM*sik iss*-SITT *deeh!*

I have been robbed!
 Ana in-sara't!

Look out!
 HA-*sib!*

Wait a moment.
 In-TAZ-*ir* LAH'-*zah.* (m)
 Intaziri LAH'-*zah.* (f)

Hurry up!
 Isri'! (m)
 Isri'-ee! (f)

Stop!   **What's going on?**   **Get out!**
  oo-*kuff!* (m)   *Aysh feeh?*   UKH-*ruj!* (m)
  oo-*kuf-fee!* (f)   UKH-*ruj-ee!* (f)

Entrance   **Exit**   **Keep out!**
  Du-khool   *Khu rooj*   *Mam-*NOO' *u'dduk* HOOL!

I am ill.   **Call a doctor!**
  *Ana marh-*EEDH. (m)   *Ihd-hir tah-*BEEB! (m)
  *Ana marh-*EEDH-*ah.* (f)   *Ihd-hir-ee tah-*BEEB! (f)

The pain is here.
  Al-waja' hone.

Where is the drug store?
  *Wane iss-*SAH'YY-*da-*LIY-*yiah?*

Take me to the hospital.
  *Wadd-eeni 'l-must-*ASH-*fa.*

Where is there a dentist?
  *Wane tah-*BEEB' *il-as-*NAAN?

I have lost my bag.   **my wallet**
  *Dh*A'A-*it minee shan-ti-tee.*   *mah'*FAZ-*tee*

  my camera   **my passport**
    kah-mahr-tee   *pass-portee*

I am an American.
  Ana amricanee. (m)
  *Ana am-ri-ca-*NEE-*yah.* (f)

Where is the American consulate?
  *Wane' il-unsu-*LI-*yyiah' il-Amrica-*NIY-*yah?* (m)
  *Wane' il-unsu-*LEE-*yyiah' il-Amrica-*NEYE-*yah?* (f)

Take it easy.   **Everything is all right.**
  Ta-'wil BAA-*lak.* (m)   *Kull-uh tamaam.*
  Tau-lee BAA-*lik.* (f)

SWAHILI

Facts About Swahili

Swahili is spoken by more than 25 million people throughout East and Central Africa and is a national language of Tanganyika, Ruanda-Urundi, Kenya, Uganda, Nyassaland, Zanzibar, and the Congo. As more African countries attain independence, Swahili will become increasingly important as an international language for East Africa.

Swahili was evolved from the original African Bantu languages mixed with a good deal of Arabic and was used for centuries by the African traders along the East Coast and in the interior. In fact, *Kiswahili,* the correct name of the language, means "Tongue of the Coast." It is still the language of safaris, and there will be someone who speaks it in any village of East or Central Africa.

When telling time in Swahili, you count from 6 A.M. which they consider 12 o'clock. Therefore 7 A.M. is 1 o'clock in the morning, our 8 A.M. is 2 o'clock. In other words, to know the hour in Swahili substract 6 hours from our time.

Advice On Accent

Swahili was formerly written in Arabic script but now is written in Roman letters. As the language is almost completely phonetic, you will find it pleasantly easy to pronounce.

You Already Know Some Swahili

Readers of literature about Africa and viewers of African adventure films have absorbed certain words that they will readily recognize in Swahili. These include *simba* (lion), *safari* (trip), *bwana* (master), *Bantu* (the men), and *askari* (gun bearer, soldier).

1. FIRST CONTACT

Yes.	No.	Good.
Ndiyo.	La.	Nzuri.
N'DEE-*yoh*.	*Lah*.	N'ZOO-*ree*.

Thank you.
Ahsante.
Ah-SAHN-*teh*.

You are welcome.
Marahaba.
Mah-rah-HAH-*bah*.

Excuse me.
Niwie radhi.
Nee-WEE-*eh* RAHD-*hee*.

It's all right.
Naam.
NAH-*ahm*.

Please.
Tafadhali.
Tah-fah-DAH-*lee*.

I would like ...
Ningependa ...
Neen-gheh-PEN-*dah* ...

What?
Nini?
NEE-*nee?*

This.
Hii.
HEE-*ee*.

Where?
Wapi?
WAH-*pee?*

Here.
Hapa.
HAH-*pah*.

When?	Now.	Later.
Lini?	Sasa.	Baadaye.
LEE-*nee?*	SAH-*sah*.	*Bah-ah*-DAH-*yeh*.

Who?	I	you	he (or) she
Nani?	Mimi	Wewe	Yeye
NAH-*nee?*	MEE-*mee*	WEH-*weh*	YEH-*yeh*

Your name?
Jina lako?
DJEE-*nah* LAH-*koh?*

Good day.
Hujambo.
Hoo-JAHM-*boh*.

Good evening.
Habari za jioni.
Hah-BAH-*ree zah jee*-OII-*nee*.

Good night.
    Ulale salama.
    *Oo-*LAH*-leh sah-*LAH*-mah.*

Good-by.
    Kwaheri.
    *Kwah-*HEH*-ree.*

How are you?
    U hali gani?
    Oo HAH*-lee* GAH*-nee?*

Very well, thank you, and you?
    Njema, ijapokuwa ya kwako?
    *N'*JEH*-mah, ee-jah-poh-*KOO*-wah yah* KWAH*-koh?*

How much?
    Kadiri gani?
    *Kah-*DEE*-ree* GAH*-nee?*

I do not understand, please repeat.
    Sifahami, tafadhali sema tena.
    *See-fah-*HAH*-mee, tah-fah-*DAH*-lee* SEH*-mah* TEH-
    nah.

one	**two**	**three**	**four**
moja	mbili	tatu	nne
MOH-*jah*	*m'*BEE-*lee*	TAH-*too*	*n'neh*

five	**six**	**seven**	**eight**
tano	sita	saba	nane
TAH-*noh*	SEE-*tah*	SAH-*bah*	NAH-*neh*

nine	**ten**	**eleven**	
tisa	kumi	kumi na moja	
TEE-*sah*	KOO-*mee*	KOO-*mee nah* MOH-*jah*	

2. ACCOMMODATIONS

Where is a good hotel?
    Hoteli nzuri iko wapi?
    *Hoh-*TEH*-lee n'*ZOO*-ree* EE*-koh* WAH*-pee?*

I want a room . . .
    Nataka chumba . . .
    *Nah-*TAH*-kah* CHOOM*-bah . . .*

for one person.
  cha mtu mmoja.
  *chah m'too m'*MOH-*jah.*

for two persons.
  cha watu wawili.
  chah WAH-*too wah-*WEE-*lee.*

with bath.
  kilicho na chumba cha kuogea.
  *kee-*LEE-*choh nah* CHOOM-*bah chah koo-oh-*
    GEH-*ah.*

for two days
  kwa siku mbili
  kwah SEE-*koo m'*BEE-*lee*

for a week
  kwa juma moja
  kwah JOO-*mah* MOH-*jah*

till Monday
  mpaka Jumatatu
  *m'*PAH-*kah Djoo-mah-*TAH-*too*

Tuesday	**Wednesday**
Jumanne	Jumatano
*Djoo-*MAHN-*neh*	*Djoo-mah-*TAH-*noh*

Thursday	**Friday**
Alhamisi	Ijumaa
*Ahl-hah-*MEE-*see*	*Ee-djoo-*MAH-*ah*

Saturday	**Sunday**
Jumamosi	Jumapili
*Djoo-mah-*MOH-*see*	*Djoo-mah-*PEE-*lee*

How much is it?
  Ni kiasi gani?
  *Nee kee-*AH-*see* GAH-*nee?*

Here are my bags.
  Mizigo yangu ni haya.
  *Mee-*ZEE-*go* YAHN-*goo nee* HAH-*yah.*

Here is my passport.
  Pasporti yangu ni hii.
  *Pass-*POHR*-tee* YAHN*-goo nee* HEE*-ee.*

I like it.   **I don't like it.**
  Ninakipenda.   Sikipendi.
  *Nee-nah-kee-*PEN*-dah.*   *See-kee-*PEN*-dee.*

Show me another.
  Nionyeshe kingine.
  *Nee-ohn-*YEH*-sheh ki-n'*GHEE*-neh.*

Where is the toilet?
  Choo kiko wapi?
  CHOH*-oh* KEE*-koh* WAH*-pee?*

Where is the men's room?
  Choo cha wanaume kiko wapi?
  CHOH*-oh chah wah-nah-oo-meh* KEE*-koh* WAH*-pee?*

Where is the ladies' room?
  Choo cha wanawake kiko wapi?
  CHOH*-oh chah wah-nah-*WAH*-keh* KEE*-koh* WAH*-pee?*

hot water   **a towel**
  maji ya moto   taulo
  MAH*-jee yah* MOH*-toh*   *tah-*OO*-loh*

soap
  sabuni
  *sah-*BOO*-nee*

Come in!
  Ingia!
  *In-*GHEE*-ah!*

Please have this washed.
  Tafadhali usafishe hii.
  *Tah-fah-*DAH*-lee oo-sah-*FEE*-sheh* HEE*-ee.*

Please have this pressed.
  Tafadhali upige hii pasi.
  *Tah-fah-*DAH*-lee oo-*PEE*-gheh* HEE*-ee* PAH*-see.*

Please have this cleaned.
Tafadhali utengeneze hii.
*Tah-fah-*DAH-*lee oo-ten-gheh-*NEH-*zeh* HEE-*ee.*

When will it be ready?
Itakuwa tayari saa ngapi?
*Ee-tah-*KOO-*wah tah-*YAH-*ree* SAH-*ah n'*GAH-*pee?*

I need it for tonight.
Nitaihitaji leo usiku.
*Nee-tah-ee-hee-*TAH-*jee* LEH-*oh oo-*SEE-*koo.*

for tomorrow	Put it there.
kwa kesho	Itie hapo.
kwah KEH-*shoh*	*Ee-*TEE-*heh* HAH-*poh.*

My key, please.
Tafadhali, funguo zangu.
*Tah-fah-*DAH-*lee, foo-*GOO-*oh* ZAHN-*goo.*

Any mail for me?
Baruwa yangu iko?
*Bah-*ROO-*wah* YAHN-*goo* EE-*koh?*

Any packages?
Je, kuna vibumba?
Jeh, KOO-*nah vee-*BOOM-*bah?*

I want five airmail stamps for the U.S.
Nataka sitampu tano za baruwa za ndege zina-
zokwenda Amerika.
*Nah-*TAH-*kah see-*TAHM-*poo* TAH-*noh zah bah-*ROO-
*wah zah n'*DEH-*gheh zee-nah-zohk-*WEN-*dah Ah-
*MEH-*ree-kah.*

Have you postcards?
Je, unazo postkadi?
*Jeh, oo-*NAH-*zoh* post-KAH-*dee?*

I want to send a telegram.
Nataka kutuma simu telegramu.
*Nah-*TAH-*kah koo-*TOO-*mah* SEE-*moo teh-leh-*GRAH-
moo.

Call me at seven in the morning.
　Uniite saa moja ya asubuhi.
　*Oo-nee-*EE-*teh* SAH-*ah* MOH-*djah yah a-soo-*BOO-*hee.*

Where is the telephone?
　Simu iko wapi?
　SEE-*moo* EE-*koh* WAH-*pee?*

Hello!
　Je!
　Jeh!

Send breakfast to room 702.
　Utume brekfasti kwa chumba nambari mia saba
　na mbili.
　*Oo-*TOO-*meh brehk-*FAHS-*tee kwah* CHOOM-*bah*
　*nahm-*BAH-*ree* MEE-*ah* SAH-*bah nah m'*BEE-*lee.*

orange juice
　maji ya michungwa
　MAJ-*jee yah mee-*CHOONG-*wah*

ham and eggs
　mayai na hemu
　*mah-*YAH-*ee nah* HEH-*moo*

rolls and coffee
　mikate na kahawa
　*mee-*KAH-*teh nah kah-*HAH-*wah*

I am expecting a friend.
　Ninaongoja rafiki kufika.
　*Nee-nah-ohn-*GOH-*jah rah-*FEE-*kee koo-*FEE-*kah.*

Tell him (her) to wait.
　Mwambie aongoje.
　*M'wahm-*BEE-*eh ah-ohn-*GOH-*djeh.*

If anyone calls,
　Kama nimeulizwa,
　KAH-*mah nee-meh-oo-*LEEZ-*wah,*

I'll be back at six.
 nitarudi saa kumi na mbili jioni.
 nee-tah-ROO-dee SAH-*ah* KOO-*mee nah* m'BEE-*lee*
 jee-OH-nee.

Tell me, please, where is a restaurant?
 Tafadhali unaweza kuniambia kwenye mkahawa?
 *Tah-fah-*DAH-*lee oo-nah-*WEH-*zah koo-nee-ahm-*
 BEE-*ah* KWEHN-*yeh m'kah-*HAH-*wah?*

Where is a barber shop?
 Unaweza kuniambia duka ya kinyozi?
 *Oo-nah-*VEH-*zah koo-nee-ahm-*BEE-*ah* DOO-*kah yah*
 *kin-*YOH-*zee?*

Where is a drugstore?
 Unaweza kuniambia duka ya dawa?
 *Oo-nah-*VEH-*zah koo-nee-ahm-*BEE-*ah* DOO-*kah yah*
 DAH-*wah?*

What is the telephone number?
 Nambari ya simu yako ni ngapi?
 *Nahm-*BAH-*ree yah* SEE-*moo* YAH-*koh nee* n'GAH-
 pee?

What is the address?
 Anwani yako je?
 *Ahn-*WAH-*nee* YAH-*koh jeh?*

I want to change some money.
 Nataka kubadilisha pesa.
 *Nah-*TAH-*kah koo-bah-dee-*LEE-*shah* PEH-*sah.*

What is the rate for dollars?
 Dolla moja ni shillingi ngapi?
 DOHL-*lah* MOH-*jah nee shil-*LIN-*ghee n'*GAH-*pee?*

twelve	thirteen
kumi na mbili	kumi na tatu
KOO-*mee nah* m'BEE-*lee*	KOO-*mee nah* TAH-*too*

fourteen
kumi na nne
KOO-*mee nah* n'neh

fifteen
kumi na tano
KOO-*mee nah* TAH-*noh*

sixteen
kumi na sita
KOO-*mee nah* SEE-*tah*

seventeen
kumi na saba
KOO-*mee nah* SAH-*bah*

eighteen
kumi na nane
KOO-*mee nah* NAH-*neh*

nineteen
kumi na tisa
KOO-*mee nah* TEE-*sah*

twenty
ishirini
*ee-shee-*REE-*nee*

thirty
thelathini
*teh-lah-*TEE-*nee*

forty
arubaini
*ah-roo-bah-*EE-*nee*

fifty
hamsini
*hahm-*SEE-*nee*

sixty
sitini
*see-*TEE-*nee*

seventy
sabini
*sah-*BEE-*nee*

eighty
themanini
*teh-mah-*NEE-*nee*

ninety
tisini
*tee-*SEE-*nee*

hundred
mia moja
MEE-*ah* MOH-*jah*

two hundred
mia mbili
MEE-*ah* m'BEE-*lee*

three hundred
mia tatu
MEE-*ah* TAH-*too*

four hundred
mia nne
MEE-*ah* n'neh

five hundred
mia tano
MEE-*ah* TAH-*noh*

six hundred
mia sita
MEE-*ah* SEE-*tah*

seven hundred
mia saba
MEE-*ah* SAH-*bah*

eight hundred
mia nane
MEE-*ah* NAH-*neh*

nine hundred
 mia tisa
 MEE-*ah* TEE-*sah*

thousand
 elfu moja
 EHL-*foo* MOH-*jah*

ten thousand
 elfu kumi
 EHL-*foo* KOO-*mee*

hundred thousand
 mia elfu
 MEE-*ah* EHL-*foo*

My bill, please.
 Nipatie hesabu yangu tafadhali.
 *Nee-pah-*TEE-*eh heh-*SAH-*boo* YAHN-*goo tah-fah-*
  DAH-*lee.*

3. EATING

Where is a good restaurant?
 Hoteli nzuri iko wapi?
 *Hoh-*TEH-*lee n'zoo-ree* EE-*koh* WAH-*pee?*

A table for two, please.
 Tafadhali utupatie meza kwa watu wawili.
 *Tah-fah-*DAH-*lee oo-too-pah-*TEE-*eh* MEH-*zah kwah*
  WAH-*too wah-*WEE-*lee.*

Waiter!
 Jamaa!
 *Jah-*MAH-*ah!*

The menu, please.
 Hebu menu.
 HEH-*boo* MEH-*noo.*

What's good today?
 Chakula gani nzuri leo?
 *Chah-*KOO-*lah* GAH-*nee n'zoo-ree* LEH-*oh?*

Is it ready?
 Iko tayari?
 EE-*koh tah-*YAH-*ree?*

How long will it take?
 Itachukua muda gani?
 EE-*tah-choo-koo-ah* MOO-*dah* GAH-*nee?*

This please ...   **and this.**
Tafadhali hii ...   na hii.
*Tah-fah-*DAH*-lee* HEE*-ee* ...   *nah* HEE*-ee.*

Bring me ...   **water**   **milk**
Uniletee ...   maji   maziwa
*Oo-nee-leh-*TEH*-eh* ...   MAH*-jee*   *mah-*ZEE*-wah*

a glass of beer
gilasi moja ya tembo
*gee-*LAH*-see* MOH*-jah yah* TEM*-boh*

red wine
divai nyekundu
*dee-*VAH*-ee n'yeh-*KOON*-doo*

white wine
divai nyeupe
*dee-*VAH*-ee n'yeh-*OO*-peh*

a cocktail   **whisky soda**
kokteli   whiskey na soda
*kohk-*TEH*-lee*   WEES*-kee nah* SOH*-dah*

More, please.
Ongeza, tafadhali.
*On-*GHEH*-zah, tah-fah-*DAH*-lee.*

That's enough.
Imetosha.
*Ee-meh-*TOH*-shah.*

soup   **fish**   **meat**
supu   samaki   nyama
SOO*-poo*   *sah-*MAH*-kee*   *n'*YAH*-mah*

bread and butter   **a sandwich**
mkate na siagi   sandwichi
*m'*KAH*-teh nah see-*AH*-ghee*   *sahnd-*WEE*-chee*

pork   **chicken**
nyama ya nguruwe   kuku
*n'*YAH*-mah yah n'goo-*ROO *weh*   KOO*-koo*

lamb
nyama ya kondoo
n'YAH-mah yah koh-n'DOH-oh

rice and mutton
mchele na nyama ya kondoo
m'CHEH-leh nah n'YAH-mah yah koh-n'DOH-oh

fish and patties
chapati na samaki
chah-PAH-tee nah sah-MAH-kee

steak	**with potatoes...**
siteki	na viazi ...
see-TEH-kee	*nah vee-AH-zee ...*

rice	**an omelet**
mchele	omeleti
m'CHEH-leh	*oh-meh-LEH-tee*

And what vegetables?
Na chakula gani tena?
Nah chah-KOO-lah GAH-nee TEH-nah?

peas	**beans**
piisi	maharagwe
pee-EE-see	*mah-hah-RAHG-weh*

carrots	**onions**
karoti	kitunguu
kah-ROH-tee	*kee-toon-GOO-oo*

a salad	**lettuce**	**tomatoes**
saladi	letasi	nyanya
sah-LAH-dee	*leh-TAH-see*	*n'YAH-n'yah*

Please bring me another fork.
Tafadhali uniletee uma ingine.
Tah-fah-DAH-lee oo-nee-leh-TEH-eh oo-mah een-GEE-neh.

knife
  kisu
  KEE-*soo*

spoon
  kijiko
  *kee-*JEE-*koh*

glass
  gilasi
  *gee-*LAH-*see*

plate
  sahani
  *sah-*HAH-*nee*

What is there for dessert?
  Maandazi gani ilioko?
  *Mah-ahn-*DAH-*zee* GAH-*nee ee-lee-*OH-*koh?*

fruit
  matunda
  *mah-*TOON-*dah*

pastry
  maandazi
  *mah-ahn-*DAH-*zee*

cheese
  chiisi
  *chee-*EE-*see*

cake
  keki
  KEH-*kee*

ice cream
  ais-krimu
  *ice-*KREE-*moo*

Some coffee, please.
  Tafadhali kahawa.
  *Tah-fah-*DAH-*lee kah-*HAH-*wah.*

cream
  kirimu
  *kee-*REE-*moo*

tea with lemon
  chai na mlimau
  CHAH-*ee nah m'lee-*MAH-*oo*

mineral water
  soda
  SOH-*dah*

The check, please.
  Lipizo tafadhali.
  *Lee-*PEE-*zoh tah-fah-*DAH-*lee.*

Is the tip included?
  Kilizo kiko ndani yake?
  *Kee-*LEE-*zoh* KEE-*koh n'*DAH-*nee* YAH-*keh?*

It was very good.
  Nimefurahiwa mno.
  *Nee-meh-foo-rah-*HEE-*wah m'noh.*

4. SHOPPING

I would like to buy this ...
Nataka kununua hii ...
*Nah-*TAH-*kah koo-noo-*NOO-*ah* HEE-*ee ...*

> **that**
> ile
> EE-*leh*

I am just looking around.
Natazama tu.
*Nah-tah-*ZAH-*mah too.*

Where is the section for ...
Wapi kwenye ...
*Wah-pee k'*WEHN-*yeh ...*

> **men's clothing**
> nguo za wanaume
> n'GOO-*oh zah wah-nah-*OO-*meh*

> **women's clothing**
> nguo za wanawake
> n'GOO-*oh zah wah-nah-*WAH-*keh*

> **hats**   **gloves**
> makofia   gilavu
> *mah-koh-*FEE-*yah*   *ghee-*LAH-*voo*

> **underwear**   **shoes**
> nguo za ndani   viatu
> n'GOO-*oh zah n'*DAH-*nee*   *vee-*AH-*too*

> **stockings**   **shirts**
> stokingi   shati
> *stoh-*KEE-*n'gee*   `SHAH-*tee*

The size in America is ...
Kipimo chake ki amerika ni ...
*Kee-*PEE-*moh* CHAH-*keh* **kee** *ah-*MEH-*ree-kah nee ...*

toys
vipuzi
*vee-*POO*-zee*

perfumes
manukato
*mah-noo-*KAH*-toh*

jewelry
majohari
*mah-joh-*HAH*-ree*

watches
saa
SAH*-ah*

toilet articles
vyombo vya kuogea
*v'*YOHM*-boh v'yah koo-oh-*GHEH*-ah*

sport articles
vitu vya sporti
VEE*-too v'yah* SPOHR*-tee*

films
mafilmu
*mah-*FEEL*-moo*

souvenirs
makumbukumbu
*mah-koom-boo-*KOOM*-boo*

Show me . . .
Nionyeshe . . .
*Nee-on-*YEH*-sheh* . . .

something less expensive
kitu kilicho rahisi kidogo
KEE*-too kee-*LEE*-choh rah-*HEE*-see kee-*DOH*-goh*

another one
kingine tena
*kee-n'*GEE*-neh* TEH*-nah*

a better quality
kilicho bora zaidi ya hiki
*kee-*LEE*-choh* BOH*-rah zah-*EE*-dee yah* HEE*-kee*

bigger
kikubwa kuliko hiki
*kee-*KOOB*-wah koo-*LEE*-koh* HEE*-kee*

smaller
kidogo kuliko hiki
*kee-*DOH*-goh koo-*LEE*-koh* HEE*-kee*

I don't like the color.
  Sipendi rangi yake.
  See PEN-*dee* RAHN-*ghee* YAH-*keh.*

I want one ...
  Nataka moja ...
  *Nah-*TAH-*kah* MOH-*djah ...*

   in green
     ya kijani kibichi
     *yah kee-*JAH-*nee kee-*BEE-*chee*

   in yellow
        ya kimanjano
        *yah kee-men-*JAH-*noh*

   in blue
     ya rangi samawiti
     *yah rah-n'*GEE *sah-mah-*WEE-*tee*

   red   **black**
     nyekundu   nyeusi
     *n'yeh-*KOO-*n'doo*   *n'yeh-*OO-*see*

   white   **gray**
     nyeupe   kijivu
     *n'yeh-*OO-*peh*   *kee-*JEE-*voo*

   pink
     nyekundu-nyeupe
     *n'yeh-*KOO-*n'doo-n'yeh-*OO-*peh*

   brown
     hudhurungi
     *hoo-thoo-*ROO-*n'gee*

I will take it with me.
  Nitaichukua mwenyewe.
  *Nee-tah-ee choo-*KOO-*ah m'weh-n'*YEH-*weh.*

The receipt, please.
  Tafadhali unipe risiti.
  *Tah-fah-*DAH-*lee oo-*NEE-*peh ree-*SFE-*tee.*

Please send it to this address.
 Tafadhali uitume kwa anwani hii.
 *Tah-fah-*DAH*-lee oo-ee-*TOO*-meh kweh ahn-*WAH*-nee*
 HEE*-ee.*

Where is there a flower shop?
 Wapi duka ya maua?
 WAH*-pee* DOO*-kah yah mah-*OO*-ah?*

Where is there a bookstore?
 Wapi duka ya vitabu?
 WAH*-pee* DOO*-kah yah vee-*TAH*-boo?*

Where is there a food shop?
 Wapi duka ya chakula?
 WAH*-pee* DOO*-kah yah chah-*KOO*-lah?*

5. TRANSPORTATION

Taxi!
 Teksi-ring!
 TEHK*-see-ring!*

Take me to the airport.
 Unipelike kiwanja cha ndege.
 *Oo-nee-peh-*LEE*-keh kee-*WAHN*-jah cheh n'*DEH*-*
 gheh.

Turn right.
 Fuata njia ya kulia.
 *Foo-*AH*-tah n'*JEE*-ah yah koo-*LEE*-ah.*

Turn left.
 Fuata njia ya kushoto.
 *Foo-*AH*-tah n'*JEE*-ah yah koo-sh*OH*-toh.*

Straight ahead.
 Endelea mbele.
 *Ehn-deh-*LEH*-ah m'*BEH*-leh.*

Not so fast!
  Pole-pole!
  POH-*leh*-POH-*leh!*

Hurry up!
  Haraka!
  Hah-RAH-*kah!*

Stop here!
  Simama hapa!
  See-MAH-*mah* HAH-*pah!*

Wait for me!
  Niongoje!
  Nee-ohn-GOH-*jeh!*

How much is it?
  Gharama gani?
  Ghah-RAH-*mah* GAH-*nee?*

How much is it to ... ?
  Gharama gani mpaka ...?
  Ghah-RAH-*:mah* GAH-*nee* m'PAH-*kah ...?*

  and back?
    na kurudi?
    nah koo-ROO-*dee?*

How much ...
  Gharama ni nini ...
  Ghah-RAH-*mah nee* NEE-*nee ...*

  by the hour?
    kwa saa?
    kwah SAH-*ah?*

  by the day?
    kwa siku?
    kwah SEE-*koo?*

a car	**a bicycle**	**a horse**
motokari	baisekeli	farasi
moh-toh-KAH-*ree*	*bye-seh*-KEH-*lee*	*fah*-RAH-*see*

a lion	**an elephant**	**a gazelle**
simba	tembo	shwara
SEE-*m'bah*	TEH-*m'boh*	SHWAH-*rah*

a leopard	**a zebra**
chui	punda milia
CHOO-*ee*	POON-*dah* mee-LEE-*ah*

Show me the sights.
  Nisafirishe unionyeshe mji.
  Nee-sah-fee-REE-*sheh oo-nee-ohn*-YEH-*sheh* m'jee.

Where are the wild animals?
  Wapi kwenye wanyama wa porini?
  WAH-*pee* k'WEH-*n'yeh* wah-n'YAH-*mah* wah poh-REE-*nee?*

What is that building?
  Hii ni nyumba gani?
  HEE-*ee* nee n'YOHM-*bah* GAH-*nee?*

Can I go in?
  Naweza kuigia ndani yake?
  Nah-WEH-*zah* koo-ee-GHEE-*ah* n'DAH-*nee* YAH-*keh?*

I want to see the Parliament Building.
  Nataka kuona mjengo wa Paliamenti.
  Nah-TAH-*kah* koo-OH-*nah* m'JEHN-go wah pah-l'yah-MEN-*tee.*

To the railroad station.
  Katika stesheni ya gari-moshi.
  Kah-TEE-*kah* steh-SHEH-*nee* yah gah-ree-MOH-*shee.*

Porter!
  Porter!
  POHR-*tah!*

I have two bags.
  Nina mizigo miwili.
  NEE-*nah* mee-ZEE-goh mee-WEE-*lee.*

A ticket to . . .
  Tikiti ya kwenda mpaka . . .
  Tee-KEE-*tee* yah KWEH-*n'dah* m'PAH-*kah* . . .

one way
  kwenda peke yake
  KWEH-*n'dah* PEH-*keh* YAH-*keh*

round trip
  kwenda na kurudi
  KWEH-*n'dah* nah koo-ROO-*dee*

first class
  klasi ya kwanza
  KLAH-*see yah* KWAHN-*zah*

second class
  klasi ya pili
  KLAH-*see yah* PEE-*lee*

When does it leave?
  Gari inatoka saa ngapi?
  GAH-*ree ee-nah-*TOH-*kah* SAH-*ah n'*GAH-*pee?*

Where is the train to Mombasa?
  Wapi gari ya Mombasa?
  WAH-*pee* GAH-*ree yah Mohm-*BAH-*sah?*

Is this the train for Kisumu? . . . .
  Je! Gari hii inakwenda mpaka Kisumu?
  Jeh! GAH-*ree* HEE-*ee in-ahk-*WEN-*dah m'*PAH-*kah Kee-soo-moo?*

When do we get to Voi?
  Tutafika Voi saa ngapi?
  *Too-tah-*FEE-*kah Voy* SAH-*ah n'*GAH-*pee?*

Open the window.
  Fungua dirisha.
  *Foon-*GOO-*ah dee-*REE-*shah.*

Close the window.
  Funga dirisha.
  FOON-*gah dee-*REE-*shah.*

Where is the bus to Kampala?
  Wapi teksi inayokwenda Kampala?
  WAH-*pee* TEHK-*see in-ah-yoh-*KWEHN-*dah Kahm-PAH-lah?*

I want to go to Moshi.
  Nataka kwenda Moshi.
  *Nah-*TAH-*kah* KWEN-*dah* MOH-*shee.*

Please tell me where to get off.
  Tafadhali uniambie ninakoshuka.
  *Tah-fah-*DAH-*lee oo-nee-ahm-*BEE-*eh nee-nah-koh-*SHOO-*kah.*

Where is there a gas station?
  Wapi stesheni ya petroli?
  WAH-*pee* steh-SHEH-*nee yah* peh-TROH-*lee?*

Fill it up.
  Jaza.
  JAH-*zah.*

Check the oil.	**water**	**tires**
Tazama oil.	maji	hewa
*Tah-*ZAH-*mah oil.*	MAH-*jee*	HEH-*wah*

Something is wrong with the car.
  Motokaa hii haiendi sawa.
  *Moh-toh-*KAH-*ah* HEE-*ee hah-ee-*EHN-*dee* SAH-*wah.*

Can you fix it?
  Unaweza kuitengeneza?
  *Oo-nah-*WEH-*zah koo-ee-ten-gheh-*NEH-*zah?*

How long will it take?
  Itachukua muda gani?
  *Ee-tah-choo-*KOO-*ah* MOO-*dah* GAH-*nee?*

Is this the road to Nakuru?
  Je! Hii ndiyo njia inayokwenda Nakuru?
  Jeh! HEE-*ee n'-*DEE-*yoh n'*JEE-*ah ee-nah-yoh-*KWEH-
  *n'dah Nah-*KOO-*roo?*

Have you a map?
  Una ramani?
  OO-*nah rah-*MAH-*nee?*

Where is the boat to . . . ?
  Wapi meli ya . . . ?
  WAH-*pee* MEH-*lee yah . . . ?*

When does it leave?
  Inaanza safari̧ saa ngapi?
  *In-ah-*AHN-*zah sah-*FAH-*ree* SAH-*ah n'*GAH-*pee?*

6. MALING FRIENDS

How do you do?
U hali gani?
Oo HAH-*lee* GAH-*nee?*

My name is . . .
Jina langu ni . . .
JEE-*nah* LAHN-*goo nee . . .*

What is your name, Sir?
Jina lako ni nani, Mzee?
JEE-*nah* LAH-*koh nee* NAH-*nee, m'*ZEH-*eh?*

What is your name, Madam?
Jina lako ni nani, Mama?
JEE-*nah* LAH-*koh nee* NAH-*nee,* MAH-*mah?*

What is your name, Miss?
Jina lako ni nani, Dada?
JEE-*nah* LAH-*koh nee* NAH-*nee,* DAH-*dah?*

I am delighted to see you.
Kukuona kumenifurahisha sana.
*Koo-koo-*OH-*nah koo-meh-nee-foo-rah-*HEE-*shah*
SAH-*nah.*

Do you speak English?
Unajua Kiingereza?
*Oo-noo-*JOO-*ah Kee-ee-n'geh-*REH-*zah?*

A little.
Kidogo.
*Kee-*DOH-*goh.*

I speak only a little Swahili.
Naweza kusema Kiswahili kidogo tu.
*Nah-*WEH-*zah koo-*SEH-*mah Kiss-wah-*HEE-*lee kee-*
DOH-*goh too.*

Do you understand?
 Unafahamu?
 *Oo-nah-fah-*HAH*-moo?*

Please speak slowly.
 Tafadhali sema pole-pole.
 *Tah-fah-*DAH*-lee* SEH*-mah* POH*-leh-*POH*-leh.*

I am from Dar es Salaam.
 Mimi nimetoka Dar es Salaam.
 MEE*-mee nee-meh-*TOH*-kah Dahr-*ESS*-sah-lah-ahm.*

Where are you from?
 Wewe umetoka wapi?
 WEH*-weh oo-meh-*TOH*-kah* WAH*-pee?*

I like your country.
 Napenda kwenu.
 *Nah-*PEN*-dah k'*WEH*-noo.*

I like your city.
 Napenda mji wenu.
 *Nah-*PEN*-dah m'jee* WEH*-noo.*

Have you been in America?
 Umepata kufika Amerika?
 *Oo-meh-*PAH*-tah koo-*FEE*-kah Ah-*MEH*-ree-kah?*

This is my first visit here.
 La. Hii ndiyo ugeni wangu wa kwanza.
 Lah. HEE*-ee n'*DEE*-yoh oo-*GHEH*-nee* WAHN*-goo wah k'*WAHN*-zah.*

May I sit here?
 Naweza kuketi hapa?
 *Nah-*WEH*-zah koo-*KEH*-tee* HAH*-pah?*

May I take your picture?
 Naweza kuchukua picha yako?
 *Nah-*WEH*-zah koo-choo-*KOO*-ah* PEE*-chah* YAH*-koh?*

Come here, please.
Njoo hapa, tafadhali.
Ndjoo HAH-*pah, tah-fah-*DAH-*lee.*

This is a picture of my wife
Hii ni picha ya bibi yangu
HEE-*ee nee* PEE-*chah yah* BEE-*bee* YAH-*n'goo.*

> **my husband**
> bwana wangu
> *b'*WAH-*nah* WAH-*n'goo*

> **my son**
> mwana wangu
> *m'*WAH-*nah* WAH-*n'goo*

> **my daughter**
> binti wangu
> BIN-*tee* WAH-*n'goo*

> **my mother**
> mama yangu
> MAH-*mah* WAH-*n'goo*

> **my father**
> baba yangu
> BAH-*bah* WAH-*n'goo*

> **my sister**
> dada yangu
> DAH-*dah* YAH-*n'goo*

> **my brother**
> ndugu yangu
> *n'*DOO-*goo* YAH-*n'goo*

Have you children?
Una watoto?
*Oo-nah wah-*TOH-*toh?*

How beautiful!
Salaala!
*Sah-*LAH-*ah-*LAH!

Very interesting.
Vizuri sana.
*Vee-*ZOO-*ree* SAH-*nah.*

Would you like a cigarette?
Unataka sigara?
*Oo-nah-*TAH-*kah see-*GAH-*rah?*

Would you like something to drink?
Ungependa kitu cha kunywa?
*Oon-gheh-*PEN-*dah* KEE-*too chah* KOON-*'y-wah?*

Would you like something to eat?
Ungependa chakula?
*Oon-gheh-*PEN-*dah chah-*KOO-*lah?*

Sit down, please.
     Tafadhali kaa kitako.
     *Tah-fah-*DAH-*lee* KAH-*ah kee-*TAH-*koh*

Make yourself at home.
     Starehe.
     *Stah-*REH-*heh.*

Good luck!
     Bahati njema!
     *Bah-*HAH-*tee n'ʋ*JEH-*mah!*

To your health!
     Kwa shukrani yako!
     *Kwah shoo-*KRAH-*nee* YAH-*koh!*

When can I see you again?
     Naweza kukuona tena lini?
     *Nah-*WEH-*zah koo-koo-oh-nah* TEH-*nah* LEF-*nee?*

Where shall we meet?
     Tutakutana wapi?
     *Too-tah-koo-*TAH-*nah* WAH-*pee?*

Here is my address.
     Anwani yangu ni hii.
     *Ahn-*WAH-*nee* YAHN-*goo nee* HEE-*ee.*

What is your address?
     Anwani yako ni nini?
     *Ahn-*WAH-*nee* YAH-*koh nee* NEE-*nee?*

What is your phone number?
     Simu yako ni nambari gani?
     SEE-*ɱoo* YAH-*koh nee nahm-*BAH-*ree* GAH-*nee?*

May I speak to . . .
     Naweza kusema na . . .
     *Nah-*WEH-*zah koo-*SEH-*mah nah* . . .

Would you like to have lunch?
     Utapenda chakula cha saa sita?
     *Oo-tah-*PEN-*dah chah-*KOO-*lah chah* SAH-*ah* SEE-
     tah?

have dinner?
cha usiku?
chah oo-SEE-*koo?*

Would you like to go to the movies?
Ungependa kwenda sinema?
*Oon-gheh-*PEN-*dah* KWEHN-*dah* see-NEH-*mah?*

go to the theatre?
kwenda kwa theata?
KWEHN-*dah kwah thee-*AH-*tah?*

Would you like to go to the beach?
Ungependa kwenda pwani?
*Oon-gheh-*PEN-*dah* KWEHN-*dah p'*WAH-*nee?*

take a walk?
kupunga hewa?
*koo-*POON-*gah* HEH-*wah?*

With great pleasure!
Kabisa!
*Kah-*BEE-*sah!*

I am sorry.	**I cannot.**
Niwie radhi.	Siwezi.
*Nee-*WEE-*eh* RAH-*thee.*	*See-*WEH-*zee.*

Another time.
Mara ingine.
MAH-*rah ee-n'*GEE-*neh.*

I must go now.
Sina budi kwenda sasa.
SEE-*nah* BOO-*dee k'*KWEHN-*dah* SAH-*sah.*

Thank you for a wonderful time.
Ahsante sana kwa shukrani yako.
*Ah-*SAHN-*teh* SAH-*nah kwah shoo-*KRAH-*nee* YAH-

Thank you for an excellent diner.
Ahsante sana kwa ukarimu wako.
*Ah-*SAHN-*teh* SAH-*nah k'wah oo-kah-*REE-*moo* WAH-
koh.

This is for you.
  Hii ni yako.
  HEE-*ee nee* YAH-*koh*.

You are very kind.
  U mfadhili sana.
  Oo m'fah-THEE-*lee* SAH-*nah*.

It's nothing really.
  Si kitu.
  See KEE-*too*.

With best regards.
  Kwa salama sana.
  Kwah sah-LAH-*mah* SAH-*nah*.

Congratulations!
  Pongezi!
  *Poh-n'*GHEH-*zee!*

7. EMERGENCIES

Help!	**Police!**	**Fire!**
Mnisaidie!	Polisi!	Moto!
*M'nee-sah-ee-*DEE-*eh!*	*Poh-*LEE-*see!*	MOH-*toh!*

Stop that man!
  Msimamishe huyo!
  *M'see-mah-*MEE-*sheh* HOO-*yoh!*

Stop that woman!
  Shika mwanamke huyo!
  SHEE-*kah m'wah-nah-M'keh* HOO-*yoh!*

I have been robbed!
  Nimenyanganywa!
  *Nee-men-yahn-*GAHN-*wah!*

Look out!
  Jihadhari!
  *Jee-hahd-*HAH-*ree!*

Wait a minute!
  Ngoja kidogo!
  *N'*GOH-*jah* KEE-*doh-goh!*

Stop!
  Simama!
  *See-*MAH-*mah!*

Get out!
  Toka nje!
  TOH-*kah N'jeh!*

Hurry up!
  Haraka!
  *Hah-*RAH-*kah!*

Don't bother me!
  Usinisumbue!
  *Oo-see-nee-soom-*BOO-*eh!*

What's going on?
Kitu gani hapa?
KEE-*too* GAH-*nee* HAH-*pah?*

Entrance
Mlango
*M'*LAHN-*goh*

Exit
Njia ya Kutokea
*N'*JEE-*ah yah koo-toh-*KEH-*ah*

Ladies
Wanawake
*Wah-nah-*WAH-*keh*

Gentlemen
Wanaume
Wah-nah-oo-meh

Danger!
Hatari!
*Hah-*TAH-*ree!*

Keep out!
Usiingie!
*Oo-see-ee-n'*GHEE-*eh!*

No smoking
Usivute sigara
*Oo-see-*voo-*teh see-*GAH-*rah*

No parking
Usiweke motokaa
*Oo-see-*WEH-*keh moh-toh-*KAH-*ah*

One way
Njia ya upande moja
*N'*JEE-*ah yah oo-*PAHN-*deh* MOH-*jah*

I am ill.
Naugua.
*Nah-oo-*GOO-*ah.*

Call a doctor.
Mwite mganga.
*M'*WEE-*teh m'*GAH-*n'gah.*

It hurts here.
Hapa pananiuma.
HAH-*pah pah-nah-nee-oo-mah.*

Where is the drugstore?
Wapi duka ya dawa?
WAH-*pee* DOO-*kah yah* DAH-*wah?*

Take me to the hospital!
Unipeleke hospitali!
*Oo-nee-peh-*LEH-*keh hohs-pee-*TAH-*lee!*

Where is there a dentist?
 Wapi daktari wa meno?
 WAH-*pee* dahk-TAH-*ree wah* MEH-*noh?*

I have lost my bag ...
 Nimepoteza mfuko wangu ...
 *Nee-meh-poh-*TEH*-zah m'*FOO*-koh* WAH-*n'goo* ...

   my camera
    kamera yangu
    *kah-*MEH*-rah* YAH-*n'goo*

I have lost my wallet.
 Nimepoteza kibeti changu.
 *Nee-meh-poh-*TEH*-zah kee-*BEH*-tee* CHAH-*n'goo.*

I have lost my passport.
 Nimepoteza pasporti yangu.
 *Nee-meh-poh-*TEH*-zah pahs-*POHR*-tee* YAH-*n'goo.*

I am an American.
 Mimi ni Mwamerika.
 MEE-*mee nee m'wah-*MEH*-ree-kah.*

Where is the American consulate?
 Wapi ofisi ya Konsuleti ya Kiamerika?
 WAH-*pee oh-*FEE*-see Kohn-soo-*LEH*-tee yah Kee-ah-*
    MEH*-ree-kah?*

Don't get excited!   **Everything is all right.**
 Tulia!   Kila kitu tamaam.
 *Too-*LEE*-ah!*   KEE-*lah* KEE-*too tah-*MAH*-ahm.*

URDU-HINDI

Facts About Urdu-Hindi

Urdu, the language of Pakistan, is spoken by about 60 million people. Hindi, a closely related language, is the tongue of approximately 150 million people in India. Other important languages exist in both these countries, but the above, with English, are the native languages. Urdu and Hindi used to be referred to, outside of India, as Hindustani, but this term is no longer used. Since the independence of Pakistan and India, Urdu and Hindi have tended to separate, Urdu tending more toward Persian and Arabic, and Hindi reaching back toward Sanskrit, the ancient language of India.

Despite certain differences in the two languages, the vocabulary selected for the Urdu-Hindi section of this book is common to both Pakistan and India and will serve you well in either nation.

Hindi is a much older term than Urdu. Urdu came into use during the reign of the Mogul emperor of India, Akbar, who discovered that his multilingual army had evolved a method of common communication composed of Hindi, Sanskrit, Persian, Turkish, Arabic, Pushtu, and other languages. He was so pleased with the new language popularized by his army that he made it the official language of his empire and named it Urdu, after the Turkish word for "army"—*ordu*—from which we, in turn, get the English word "horde."

Advice On Accent

There is a distinct nasal pronunciation in Urdu-Hindi which we have rendered in our phonetics as **nh**. When you see this, practice saying **nh** while holding your nose.

When **b, p, t, d, j**, and **ch** are followed by an **h**, it is advisable—to give a truly correct Urdu-Hindi pronunciation—to put a slight catch in your voice between the consonant and the following **h**.

How Urdu-Hindi Is Written

Urdu is written in the Persian script, which comes from Arabic but has been considerably modified. It is written from right to left. Hindi is written in Devanagari (literally "Country of the Gods") script, which has 33 consonants and 12 vowels. These in turn are capable of merging with other letters to form a considerable number of separate letters. The Devanagari script is the same as ancient Sanskrit script. Devanagari, unlike Urdu, is written from left to right. Here is an example of how "Keep Out" is written in Urdu and Hindi.

URDU: دُورِارہیو

HINDI: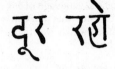

Both Urdu and Hindi have accepted versions in the Roman alphabet and for this reason we have included their Romanized versions directly above our phonetic rendition.

You Already Know Some Urdu-Hindi

Readers of Kipling as well as world travelers and students of India and Pakistan will have no difficulty recognizing the following Urdu-Hindi words which we have given here with their original spelling and original meaning: jungle (*jangal*—"woods"); jodhpur (riding pants named after the city of Jodhpur); khaki ("dust colored"); pajamas (*pyjama*—"covering for legs"); divan ("audience room"); sahib ("lord"); baksheesh ("kind gift"); verandah (*barandah*—"raised outer area of house"); thug (*thug*—pronounced "toog"); pundit ("learned man"); yogi (religious hermit). The Taj Mahal, perhaps the world's most beautiful building, means "The Jewel of Palaces." Its original name was *Mumtaz Mahal*, after the beautiful wife of the emperor, whose name in turn meant "The Select One."

1. FIRST CONTACT

Yes.
Hanh.

No.
*Nah-*HEENH.

Good.
*Ah-*TCHAH.

Thank you.
SHOO-*kree-yah.*

You are welcome.
MEH-*ehr-bah-nee.*

Excuse me.
*Moo-*AHF *kee-*JEE-*eh.*

It's all right.
KOH-*yee baht nah-*HEENH.

Please.
MEH-*hehr-bah-nee seh.*

I would like . . .
MOODJ *chah-hee-*YEH . . .

What?
K'yah?

This.
Yeh.

Where?
KAH-*hanh?*

Here.
YAH-*hanh.*

When?
Kahb?

Now.
Ahb.

Later.
Bahd-menh.

Who?
Cow'n?

I
mainh

you
ahp

he
voh

she
voh

Your name?
*Ahp-kah-*NAHM?

Greetings.
*Sah-*LAHM.

Good-by.
P'heer MEE-*len-geh.*

How are you?
*Ahp k'*EYE-*seh henh?*

Very well, thank you. And you?
*Mainh aht-*CHAH *hoon,* SHOO-*kree-yah. Our ahp?*

How much?
KIT-*NEH* PIE-*seh?*

I do not understand, please repeat.
*Mainh nah-*HEENH SAHM-*jah,* MEH-*ahr-bah-nee seh*
p'here KAY-*hee-yeh.*

one	**two**	**three**	**four**
ehk	*doh*	*teen*	*chahr*

five	**six**	**seven**	**eight**
pahnch	*ch'heh*	*saht*	*ahth*

nine	**ten**	**eleven**	**twelve**
now	*dahss*	*g'*YAH-*rah*	BAH-*rah*

2. ACCOMMODATIONS

Where is a good hotel?
*Koy-ee aht-*CHAH HOH-*tel* KAH-*hahnh hay?*

I want a room for one person.
*Moo-*JEH *ehk* KAHM-*rah* CHAH-*hee-yeh, ehk* AHD-
meh VAH-*lah.*

I want a room for two persons.
*Moo-*JEH *ehk* KAHM-*rah* CHAH-*hee-yeh, doh* AHD-
mee-yohn VAH-*lah.*

I want a room with bath.
*Moo-*JEH *ehk* KAHM-*rah* CHAH-*hee-yeh jees menh*
GOOSE-*ehl-*KAH-*nah hoh.*

　for two days
　　doh DEE-*nohnh keh* LEE-*yeh*

　for a week
　　*ehk hahf-*TEH *keh* LEE-*yeh*

till Monday	**Tuesday**
SOHM-*vahr tahk*	MAHN-*g'l tahk*

Wednesday	**Thursday**
Bood tahk	*Joo-mah-*RAHT *tahk*

Friday	Saturday
Joo-mah tahk	*Sah-NEE-chertahk*

Sunday
It-VAHR tahk

How much is it?
Kit-NEH PIE-seh?

Here are my bags.
Meh-RAH sah-MAHN yeh hay.

Here is my passport.
Yeh hay meh-RAH PAHS-pohrt.

I like it.
Moo-JEH pah-SAHNT hay.

I don't like it.
Moo-JEH pah-SAHNT nah-HEENH.

Show me another.
Koh-YEE our dick-HIGH-yeh.

Where is the toilet?
Pah-eh-KHAH-nah kah-HAHN hay?

Where is the men's room?
AHD-mee-yohn-kah KAHM-rah kah-HAHNH hay?

the ladies' room?
OUR-tohn kah?

hot water	a towel
GAH-rahm PAH-nee	*TOW-lee-yah*

soap
SAH-bahn

Come in!
AH-yeh!

Please have this washed.
Yeh d'hool-VAH denh.

Please have this pressed.
  Yeh IS-*tah-ree* KAHR-VAH *denh.*

Please have this cleaned.
  *Yeh sahf-kahr-*VAH *denh.*

When will it be ready?
  *Yeh kahb tay-*YAHR *hoh* JAH-*ee-gah?*

I need it for tonight.
  *Yeh moo-*JEH *ahdj raht keh lee-*YEH CHAH-*hee-yeh.*

  for tomorrow.
    *kahl keh lee-*YEH.

My key, please.
  MEH-*ree* CHAH-*bee.*

Any mail for me?
  MEH-*ree lee-*YEH *koh-*YEE *cheet-*HEE?

Any packages?
  *Koh-*YEE PAHR-*sel?*

I want five airmail stamps for the U.S.
  *Moo-*JEH *ahm-ree-*KAH *keh lee-*YEH *pahnch hah-*VIE
  dahk keh TEE-*kat chah-hee-*YENH.

I want to send a telegram.
  *Mainh tahr b'*HEHJ-*nah* CHAH-*tah hoon.*

Have you postcards?
  K'yah ahp keh pass POST-*card henh?*

Call me at seven in the morning.
  *Moo-*JEH *sah-*VEH-*reh saht bah-*YEH *hah-*GAH DEH-
  nah.

Where is the telephone?   **Hello!**
  TEH-*lee foon kah-*HAHNH *hay?*   *Hel-*LOH!

Send breakfast to room 702.
  *Kahm-*RAH NAHM-*buhr saht saw doh koh* NAHSH-
  *;ah b'*HEH-*joh.*

orange juice
nah-RAHN-*ghee kah-rahs*

toast and eggs
tosh our ahn-deh

rolls and coffee
ROH-*tee our* KAH-*fee*

I am expecting a friend.
*Mainh ehk dosht kah in-tah-*ZAHR *kahr* RAH-*hah*
hoonh.

Tell him (her) to wait.
*Oos seh kah-*HOH *keh t'*HIGH-*reh.*

If anyone calls, I'll be back at six.
*Ah-*GAHR *koh-*YEE POO-*cheh, mainh ch-heh bah-*
JEH VAH-*pass* AH-*oon-gah.*

Tell me, please, where is the restaurant?
*Mood-*JEH *bah-tah-*YEH, RES-*toh-rahn kah-*HAHN
hay?

Tell me, please, where is the barbershop?
*Mood-*JEH *bah-tah-*YEH, *hah-*JAHM *kee doo kah-*
JAHM *kee doo-*KAHN *hay?*

Tell me, please, where is the beauty parlor?
*Mood-*JEH *bah-tah-*YEH, *beauty parlor kah-*HAHN
hay?

Tell me, please, where is the drugstore?
*Mood-*JEH *bah-tah-*YEH, KEH-*mist kee doo-*KAHN
*kah-*HAHN *hay?*

What is the telephone number?
*Teh-lee-*FOON NAHM-*bahr k'yah hay?*

What is the address?
*Pah-*TAH *k'yah hay?*

I want to change some money.
Mainh kooch PIE-*sah bah-dahl-*NAH CHAH-*tah*
hoonh.

What is the rate for dollars?
    DAH-*lahr* kiss BHAH-*ho bah-dahl*-TEH *henh?*

thirteen	fourteen	fifteen
TEH-*rah*	CHOW-*dah*	PAHN-*drah*

sixteen	seventeen	eighteen
SOH-*lah*	SAHT-*rah*	AHT-*hah-rah*

nineteen	twenty	thirty	forty
oon-NEES	*bis*	*tees*	*chah*-LEES

fifty	sixty	seventy
pah-CHAHS	*sahth*	*saht*-TAHR

eighty	ninety	hundred	two hundred
AHS-*see*	*nah*-VEH	*sow*	*doh sow*

three hundred	four hundred	five hundred
tin sow	*chahr sow*	*pahnch sow*

six hundred	seven hundred	eight hundred
ch-heh sow	*saht sow*	*ahth sow*

nine hundred	thousand	ten thousand
now sow	*hah*-ZAHR	*dahs hah*-ZAHR

hundred thousand
    ehk lahkh

My bill, please.	The receipt, please.
MEH-*rah beel*, LAH-*oh*.	*Rah*-SEET *did*-JEH.

3. EATING

Where is a good restaurant?
    Koh-YEE *aht*-CHAH RESS-*toh-rahn* KAH-*hahn hay?*

A table for two, please.
    Doh kee ehk mehz CHAH-*hee-yeh.*

Waiter!	The menu, please.
By-RAH!	MEH-*noo* LAH-*oh*.

What's good today?
Ahdj KAH-*oon-sah* KHAH-*nah aht*-CHAH *hay?*

Is it ready?
K'yah voh teh-YAHR *hay?*

How long will it take?
KIT-*nee dehr lah-geh*-GHEE?

This, please ...	**and this.**
Yeh ...	*our yeh.*

Bring me ...	**water**
MEH-*reh lee*-YEH LAH-*oh*	PAH-*nee*

milk	**a glass of beer**
doodh	*beer kah ehk glahs*

red wine
lahl ahn-GOO-*ree shah*-RAHB

white wine
sah-FED *ahn*-GOO-*ree shah*-RAHB

a cocktail	**whisky soda**
kahk-tehl	*whisky soda*

More, please.	**That's enough.**
MEH-*hehr-bah-nee-seh, our.*	KAH-*fee high.*

soup	**fish**	**a sandwich**
SHOR-*bah*	*much*-LEE	*ehk sandwich*

meat	**bread and butter**
gohsh't	*roh*-TEE *our mac*-HAHN

steak ...	**rare**
steak ...	*bah*-HOOT *kahn* BHOO-*nah* HOO-AH

medium
dahr-mee-YAH-*nah dahr-*JEH *kah* BHOO-*nah*
HOO-*ah*

well done
aht-CHEE *tah*-RAH BHOO-*nah* HOO-*ah*

chicken
*moor-*GHEE *kah gohsht*

veal
*batch-*HREH *kah gohsht*

beef
GAH-*eh kah gohsht*

goat
*bah-*KREE *kah gohsht*

pork
s'wahr kah gohsht

lamb
bhehr kah gohsht

meat and rice cooked together
*pee-*LAH-*oo*

lentils
*mah-*SOOR

No sauce for me.
*Mood-*JEH CHAHSH-*nee nah-*HEENH *chah-hee-*YEH.

with potatoes . . .
AHL-*wohn keh sahth . . .*

peas
MAH-*tehr*

beans
P'HAH-*lee-yahn*

carrots
GAH-*jah-renh*

onions
p'yahz

a salad
*sah-*LAHT

tomatoes
*toh-*MAH-*tahr*

peppers
MEER-*chenh*

Please bring me another fork.
*Mood-*JEH *ehk our* KAHN-*tah lah denh.*

knife
*ch'hoo-*REE

spoon
CHAM-*chee*

glass
glass

plate
T'HAH-*lee*

What is there for dessert?
MEET-*hah k'yah hay?*

fruit
p'hahl

pastry
pastry

cake
cake

ice cream
*ice kah-*REEM

Some coffee, please.
KAH-*fee* LAY-*yeh.*

cream
*mah-*LAH-*yee*

sugar
   CHEE-*nee*

tea with lemon
   chah-ee our LEE-*moonh*

The check, please.
   Beel LAH-*ee-yeh.*

Is the tip included?
   Bahkh-SHEESH *sah*-MET?

It was very good.
   Bah-HOOT *aht*-CHAH *thah.*

4. SHOPPING

I would like to buy this ∴.
   Mainh yeh …

    and that.
      our voh k'hah-RID-*nah* CHAH-*tah hoonh.*

I am just looking around.
   Mainh seerf dehk rah-HAH *hoonh.*

Where is the section for … ?
   … kah HISS-*sah kah*-HAHN *hay?*

    men's clothing
      AHD-*mee-yohn keh kah*-PREH

    women's clothing
      OUR-*tohn keh kah*-PREH

    hats   **gloves**   **shoes**
      hat   *das*-TAH-*nee*   JOO-*teh*

    underwear
      NEE-*cheh pah*-HEN-*neh keh kah*-PREH

    stockings   **shirts**
      joo-RAH-*behn*   *kah-mee*-SEHN

The size in America is …
   Ahm-REE-*kah mehn nap hay …*

    toys   **perfumes**   **jewelry**
      khee-LOW-*neh*   AHT-*tahr*   ZEH-*vahr*

toilet articles
  *nah-*HAH*-neh-d'*HOH*-neh kee chee-*ZEHN

sport articles
  *k'*HEHL*-neh kee chee-*ZEHN

films	**souvenirs**
film	YAHD*-gah-ree kee chee-*ZEHN

Show me . . .
  *. . . moo-*JEH *deek-*HOW

  something less expensive
    koy kahm dahm kee cheese

another one	**a better quality**
koy our	*koy* BAHR*-hee-yah*

bigger	**smaller**
*bah-*REE	*ch-*HOH*-tee*

I don't like the color.
  *Moo-*JEH *rahng pah-*SAHND *nah-*HĘEN.

I want one . . .
  *Moo-*JEH *ehk chah-*HEE*-yeh . . .*

in green	**in yellow**
*hah-*REH *rahng mehn*	PEE*-leh rahng mehn*

in blue	**red**
NEE*-leh rahng mehn*	*lahl*

black	**white**	**grey**
*see-*YAH	*sah-*FED	*b'*HOO*-rah*

pink	**brown**
*goo-*LAH*-bee*	*bah-*DAH*-mee*

I will take it with me.
  Maynh EE*-seh saht leh* JAH*-oon-gah.*

The receipt, please.
  *Rah-*SEED *de-jec-*YEH.

Please send it to this address.
  Yeh is pah-TAH *pahr b'haij dehnh.*

Where is there a market?
  *Bah-*ZAHR *kah-*HAHN *hay?*

Where is there a flower stand?
  *P'hool kah-*HAHN *meel-*TEH *henh?*

Where is there a bookstore?
  *Kee-*TAH-*bohn kee doo-*KAHN *kah-*HAHN *hai?*

Where is there a grocery store/food shop?
  *K'*HAH-*neh* PEE-*neh kee* CHEE-*zohn kee doo-*KAHN
    *kah-*HAHN *hay?*

5. TRANSPORTATION

Taxi!
  TAH-*ksee!*

Take me to the airport.
  *Moo-*JEH *hah-vah-*yee *ad-*DEH *koh leh cheh-*LOH.

Turn right.
  DAH-*ehn* MOO-*roh.*
	Turn left.
	  BAH-*ehn* MOO-*roh.*

Straight ahead.
  SID-*hah ah-gay.*
	Not so fast!
	  IT-*nah tehz nah-*HEENH!

Hurry up!
  JEHL-*dee kah-*ROH!
	Stop here!
	  *Yah-*HAHN *TIE-roh!*

Wait for me!
  *Meh-*RAH *in-tah-*ZAHR *kah-*ROH!

How much is it?
  KIT-*neh* PIE-*seh?*

How much is it to . . . ?
. . . *tack* JAH-*neh keh* KIT-*neh* PIE-*seh?*

   and back?
   our VAHP-*see keh?*

How much by the hour?
Ehk G'HAHN-*teh keh* KIT-*neh* PIE-*seh?*

  by the day?   **car**
   ehk din keh?   MOH-*tahr keh*

  a bicycle   **a rickshaw**   **an elephant**
   bicycle keh   RICK-*shah keh*   *haht-*HEE *keh*

  a horse   **a camel**
   *g'*HOH-*reh keh*   *oont keh*

Show me the sights.
DECK-*neh keh* LAH-*eek jahg-*HENH *dick-*HAH-*oh.*

What is that building?
*Voh ee-*MAH-*ret* COW-*nsee hay?*

Can I go in?
K'yah main AHN-*dahr jah sahk-*TAH *hoonh?*

I want to see the Taj Mahal.
Main tadj MAH-*hahl* DEKH-*nah* CHAH-*tah hoonh.*

I want to see the Shalimar Gardens.
Main SHAH-*lee-mahr bahgh* DEKH-*nah* CHAH-*tah
hoonh.*

To the railroad station.
RAIL-*vay is-*TAH-*shon koh.*

Porter!   **I have two bags.**
KOO-*lee!*   MEH-*reh pass doh chee-*ZEHN *henh.*

A ticket to . . .
. . . *kah ehk* TEE-*kat*

one way   **round trip**
ehk TAH-*rahf kah*   VAHP-*see*

When does it leave?
  Yeh kahb CHEHL-*tee hay?*

Where is the train to Patna?
  PAHT-*nah* JAH-*neh-vah-lee gah-*REE *kah-*HAHN *hay?*

Is this the train for Lahore?
  *K'yah lah-*HUR JAH-*neh-vah-lee gah-*REE *yeh-*HEE
    hay?

When will it arrive there?
  *Yeh kahb vah-*HAHNH *pah-*HOHN-*cheh-ghee?*

When does it get to New Delhi?
  *Yeh nigh deel-*LEE *kahb pah-*HUNCH-*tee hay?*

Where is the dining car?
  K'HAH-*nah k'*HAH-*neh kah deeb-*BAH *kah-*HAHN *hay?*

Please open the window.
  *K'heer-*KEE *k'hohl did-*JEH.

Close the window.
  *K'heer-*KEE *bahnd kahr did-*JEH.

Where is the bus to Srinagar?
  SREE-*nah-gahr* JAH-*neh-vah-lee bahs kah-*HAHNH
    hay?

I want to go to Karachi.
  *Mainh Kah-*RAH-*chee* JAH-*nah* CHAH-*tah hoonh.*

Please tell me where to get off.
  *Bah-*TAH-*yeh moo-*JEH *kah-*HAHNH *oo-tahr-*NAH
    *chah-hee-*YEH.

Where is the gas station?
  *Pah-*TROHL *pump kah-*HAHNH *hay?*

Fill it up.
  *Ee-*SEH *b'hahr doh.*

Check the oil.   water   tires
  Tehl deck loh.   PAH-*nee   tire*

Something is wrong with the car.
MOH-*tahr mainh kooch-h khah*-RAH-*bee hay.*

What's the matter?
K'yah baht hay?

Can you fix it?
*K'yah toom ee-*SEH *t'heek kahr sahke-*TEH *hoh?*

How long will it take?
KIT-*neh dehr lah-geh-*GHEE?

Is this the road to Calcutta?
*K'yah kahl-*KAT-*tah* JAH-*neh-vah-lee yeh-*HEE *sah-*
RAHK *hay?*

Have you a map?
*K'yah toom-*HAH-*reh pass nahk-*SHAH *hay?*

Where is the boat to . . . ?
. . . JAH-*neh-vah-lah jah-*HAHZ *kah-*HAHN *hay?*

When does it leave?
*Yeh kahb chahl-*TAH *hay?*

6. MAKING FRIENDS

How do you do?
*Sah-*LAHM.

How are you?
Ahp KAH-*ee-seh henh?*

My name is . . .
MEH-*rah nahm hay . . .*

What is your name, Sir?
*Jah-*NAHB *ahp kah k'yah nahm hay?*

What is your name, Madam?
Jee, ahp kah k'yah nahm hay?

What is your name, Miss?
Miss ahp kah k'yah nahm hay?

I am delighted to see you.
*Mood-*JEH *ahp koh dekh kahr bah-*HOOT KHOO-*shee*
hooey.

Do you speak English?
*K'yah ahp ahn-*GREH-*zee* BOHL-*teh henh?*

A little.   **Do you understand?**
*Toh-*REE-*see.*   *Ahp sah-*MAHJ-*teh henh?*

Please speak slowly.
AH-*hiss-tah* AH-*hiss-tah boh-lee-*YEH.

I speak only a little Hindustani.
*Mainh seerf t'hoh-*REE-*see hin-doos-*TAH-*neh bohl*
*sahk-*TAH *hoonh.*

I am from New York.
Mainh New York seh hoonh.

Where are you from?
*Ahp kah-*HAHN *seh henh?*

I like your country.
*Mood-*JEH *ahp kah moolk pah-*SAHND *hay.*

I like your city.
*Mood-*JEH *ahp kah* SHEH-*hahr pah-*SAHND *hay.*

Have you been in America?
*K'yah ahp kahb-*HEE *ahm-*REE-*kah gah-*YEH?

This is my first visit here.
*Mainh yah-*HAHN PEH-*lee bahr* AH-*ya hoonh.*

May I sit here?
*Mainh yah-*HAHN *bah-*EETH *sahk-*TAH *hoonh?*

May I take your picture?
*Mainh ahp kee tahs-*VEER *oo-*TAHR *sahk-*TAH *hoonh?*

Come here.
*Yah-*HAHN *ah-*OO.

This is my wife.
  Yeh MEH-*ree* BEE-*vee hay.*

  my husband
    MEH-*reh* SHOW-*hahr hay*

  my son
    MEH-*rah* BEH-*tah hay*

  my daughter
    MEHR-*ree* BEH-*tee hay*

  my mother
    MEH-*ree mahn hay*

  my father
    MEH-*rah bahp hay*

  my sister
    MEH-*ree beh-*HAN *hay*

  my brother
    MEH-*rah* B'HAH-*yee hay*

Have you children?
  *K'yah ahp keh bah-*CHEH HEHNH*?*

How beautiful!
  *Kit-*NAH *k'hoob-*SOO-*raht!*

Very interesting!
  *Bah-*HOOT *deel-*CHAHSP*!*

Would you like a cigarette?
  K'yah ahp SIG-*rat pee-*YEN-*gay?*

Would you like something to drink?
  *K'yah ahp kooch-h pee-*YEN-*gay?*

Would you like something to eat?
  *K'yah ahp kooch-h k'*HAH *in-gay?*

Sit down, please.
  *Bah-*EET-*h jah-*YEH*.*

Make yourself at home.
  Meh-REH *g'hahr koh ahp*-NAH *g'hahr* SAH-*mahj-yeh.*

When can I see you again?
  Mainh ahp seh p'heer kahb meel saht-TAH *hoon?*

Where shall we meet?
  Hahm KAH-*hahn mee*-LEHN-*geh?*

Here is my address.
  Yeh hay meh-RAH *pah*-TAH.

What is your address?
  Ahp kah k'yah pah-TAH *hay?*

What is your phone number?
  Ahp kah tay-lee-foon NAHM-*bahr k'yah hay?*

May I speak to . . .
  K'yah mainh . . . seh baht kahr sahk-TAH-*hoon*

Would you like to have lunch?
  K'yah ahp dohpeh-hehr kah KHAH-*nah* KHAH-*nah pah*-SAHND *kah*-REN-*geh?*

> **dinner?**
>   *shahm kah* KHAH-*nah?*

Would you like to go to the movies?
  K'yah ahp SEE-*neh-mah* YAH-*nah pah*-SAHND *kah*-REHN-*geh?*

> **to the theatre?**
>   *theatre* JAH-*nah?*

Would you like to go to the beach?
  K'yah ahp sah-MOON-*dahr-kee-nah*-REH JAH-*nah pah*-SAHND *kah*-REHN-*geh?*

> **to the museum?**
>   *ah*-JAH-*eeb-g'hahr* JAH-*nah?*

Would you like to take a walk?
K'yah ahp sair kahr-NAH pah-SAHND kah-REHN-geh?

With great pleasure!   **I am sorry.**
Bah-REE khoo-SHEE-seh!   *Moo-JEH ahf-SOHS hay.*

I cannot.
Maynh nah-HEEN kahr sahk-TAH.

Another time.
P'heer kee-SEE vohkt sah-HEE.

I must go now.
Moo-JEH ahb JAH-nah chah-HEE-yeh.

Thank you for a wonderful time.
Bah-HOOT ah-CHEH vohkt kah shoo-KREE-yah.

Thank you for an excellent dinner.
Bah-HOOT mah-ZEH keh k'hah-NEH kah shoo-KREE-yah.

This is for you.
Yeh ahp keh lee-YEH hay.

You are very kind.
Ahp kee bah-REE MEH-hehr-bah-nee.

It's nothing really.
Koy khahs cheese toh nah-HEENH.

Congratulations!   **With best regards.**
Moo-BAH-rahk hoh!   *AH-dahb keh saht.*

7. EMERGENCIES

Help!   **Police!**
Mah-DAHD!   *Poh-LEES!*

Fire!
Ahg lag gah-YEE!

Stop that man!
Oos AHD-*mee koh* ROH-*koh!*

Stop that woman!
Oos OUR-*aht koh* ROH-*koh!*

I have been robbed!   **Look out!**
Maynh lot GAH-*yah!*   *Dehk keh!*

Wait a minute!   **Stop!**
Ehk MEE-*naht* TIE-*roh!*   TIE-*roh!*

Get out!
NEE-*kehl jah-oh!*

Hurry up!   **What's going on?**
JAHL-*dee kah-*ROH!   *K'yah hoh rah-*HAH *hay?*

Don't bother me!
*Mood-*JEH *nah-*HEENH *sah-*TAH-*oh!*

Entrance
DAHKH-*leh kah rahs-*TAH

Exit
BAH-*heer* NICH-*ehl-neh kah* RAHS-*tah*

Ladies
OUR-*tohn keh lee-*YEH

Gentlemen
AHD-*mee-yohn keh lee-*YEH

Danger!   **Keep out!**
KHAHT-*rah!*   *Door rah-*HOH!

No smoking
SIG-*ret* PEE-*nah* MAH-*nah hay*

No parking
MOH-*tahr* KHAH-*rah* KAHR-*nah* MAH-*nah hay*

One way
Ehk TAH-*rahf*

I am ill.
*Maynh bee-*MAHR* hoonh.*

Call a doctor!
DAHK-*tehr koh boo-*LAH-*oh!*

It hurts here.
*Yah-*HAHN* *DOOK-*tah hay.*

Where is a drugstore?
KEH-*mist kee doo-*KAHN* *KAH-*hahn hay?*

Take me to the hospital.
*Mood-*JEH* *hahs-pah-*TAHL* *leh jaw.*

Where is there a dentist?
DAHN-*tohn kah* DAHK-*tehr* *KAH-*hahn hay?*

I have lost my bag . . .
*meh-*RAH* *sah-*MAHN* *goom hoh gah-*YAH* *hay . . .*

my wallet	**my camera**
*meh-*RAH* BAHT-*vah*	*meh-*RAH* KEHM-*rah*
my passport	**my ticket**
*meh-*RAH* *pahs-port*	*mera tikat*

I am an American.
*Maynh ahm-*REE-*kee hoon.*

Where is the American Consulate?
*Ahm-*REE-*kee consulate* *KAH-*hahn hay?*

Don't get excited!
*G'hah-*BRAH-*oh nah-*HEENH!*

Everything is all right.
Sahb kooch teek hay.

MALAY-INDONESIAN

Facts About Malay-Indonesian

Malay and Indonesian are considered two different languages but are mutually comprehensible. Malay is spoken by about 14 million people in the Malay Peninsula, while Indonesian is spoken by approximately 70 million more in the Indonesian Archipelago.

Malay is descended largely from Sanskrit, the ancient language of India. In fact, the word *Melayu*, meaning "The Fleeing Ones," refers to groups fleeing from their enemies. Malay-Indonesian has also been largely influenced by Arabic through the adoption of the Islamic religion.

Although there are certain differences in construction and spelling between Malay and Indonesian, the sentences and phrases used in this section will be readily understood in any part of Malay or Indonesia.

You may occasionally be startled to see the figure 2 written after a noun. This means simply that the noun is said twice to indicate the plural.

Advice On Accent

Malay, formerly written in Arabic script, is now written in Roman letters. You will find it pleasantly easy to pronounce.

Indonesian, however, has the following exceptions:

The letter **j** is pronounced as the English **y**. To give the sound of the English **j**, **dj** must be used.

You Already Know Some Malay-Indonesian

Readers of literature about southeast Asia will readily recognize the following words (given here with their literal translation) which have entered into English: *Tuan* (master), *amok* (seizure of fury), *kris* (dagger), *sarong* (garment, literally "covering"), *kampong* (village), *topi* (hat), *Mata Hari* (the famous spy, whose name means "Eye of the Day" or, in other words, "The Sun").

1. FIRST CONTACT

Yes.	No.	Good.
Ja.	Tidak.	Baik.
Yah.	*Tee-DAHK.*	*Bike.*

Thank you. **You are welcome.**
Terima kasih. Kembali.
T'REE-mah KAH-see. *Kem-BAH-lee.*

Excuse me. **It's all right.**
Maaf. Tidak apa.
MAH-ahf. *Tee-dahk ahp-pah.*

Please. **I would like . . .**
Silahkan. Saja mau . . .
See-LAH-kahn. *SAH-yah mah'oo . . .*

What?	This.	That.
Apa?	Ini.	Itu.
AH-pah?	*Ee-nee.*	*Ee-too.*

Where?	Here.	There.
Dimana?	Disini.	Disitu.
Dee-MAH-nah?	*Dee-see-nee.*	*Dee-SEE-too.*

When?	Now.	Later.
Bila?	Sekarang.	Nanti.
BEE-lah?	*Seh-KAH-rahng.*	*Nahn-tee.*

Who?	I	he, she
Siapa?	Saja	ia
S'YAH-pah?	*Sah-yah*	*ee-yah*

you (if woman) **you (if man)**
saudari saudara
sah'oo-dah-ree *sah'oo-dah-rah*

you (if familiar)
engkau
ehn-kow

Your name? (to woman)
  Nama saudari?
  Nah-mah sah'oo-dah-ree?

Your name? (to man)
  Nama saudara?
  Nah-mah sah'oo-dah-rah?

Mr.	**Mrs.**	**Miss**
Tuan	Nona	Nyonya
Too-AHN	NOH-*nah*	N'YOHN-*yah*

(above three also used for "you")

Good morning.
  Selamat pagi.
  S'LAH-maht PAH-*ghee.*

Good evening.
  Selamat malam.
  S'LAH-maht MAH-*lahm.*

Good-by (if staying).
  Selamat djalan.
  S'LAH-maht djah-lahn.

Good-by (if leaving)
  Selamat tinggal.
  S'LAH-maht teeng-gal.

How are you?
  Apa kabar?
  AH-*pah kah-*BAR?

Very well, thank you, and you?
  Kabar baik, terima kasih, dan tuan?
  Kah-bar bike, teh-ree-mah kah-see, dahn too-ahn?

How much?
  Berapa?
  *Beh-*RAH-*pah?*

I do not understand, please repeat.
  Saja tidak mengerti, tjoba bitjara lagi.
  *Sah-yah tee-*DAHK *men-*HER-*tee, t'joh-bah bee-*CHAH-
  rah LAH-*ghee.*

one	**two**	**three**	**four**
satu	dua	tiga	ampat
sah-too	*doo-ah*	*tee-gah*	*ahm-paht*

five	**six**	**seven**
lima	anam	tudjuh
lee-mah	*ah-nahm*	*tood-joo*

eight	**nine**	**ten**
delapan	sembilan	sepuluh
*deh-*LAH-*pahn*	SEM-*bee-lahn*	*seh-*POO-*loo*

2. ACCOMMODATIONS

Where is a good hotel?
Dimana ada hotel jang baik?
*Dee-*MAH-*neh* AH-*dah hotel yahng bike?*

I want a room ...
Saja mau satu kamar ...
SAH-*yah mah'oo* SAH-*too* KAH-*mahr* ...

    for one person.
      untuk satu orang.
      OON-*took* SAH-*too* OH-*rahng.*

    for two persons.
      untuk dua orang.
      OON-*took* DOO-*ah* OH-*rahng.*

    with bathroom.
      dengan kamar mandi.
      DEN-*gahn* KAH-*mahr* MAHN-*dee.*

    for two days.
      untuk dua hari.
      OON-*took* DOO-*ah* HAH-*ree.*

    for a week.
      untuk satu minggu.
      OON-*took* SAH-*too* MEEN-*goo.*

    till Monday
      Sampai hari Senen
      *Sahm-*PIGH HAH-*ree* SEN-*en*

Tuesday	**Wednesday**
hari Selasa	hari Rabu
HAH-*ree seh-*LAH-*sah*	HAH-*ree* RAH-*boo*

Thursday	**Friday**
hari Kamis	hari Djumat
HAH-*ree* KAH-*mees*	HAH-*ree* DJOO-*maht*

Saturday	**Sunday**
hari Sabtu	hari Ahad
HAH-*ree* SAHB-*too*	HAH-*ree ah-*HAD

How much is it?
  Berapa sewanja?
  *Beh-*RAH-*pah seh-*WAHN-*yah?*

Here are my bags.
  Inilah tas-tas saja.
  EEN-*ee-lah tahs-tahs* SAH-*yah.*

Here is my passport.
  Ini paspor saja.
  EE-*nee* PAHS-*pohr sah-yah.*

I like it. (this)
  Saja suka. (ini)
  SAH-*yah* SOO-*kah.* (EE-*nee*)

I don't like it. (that)
  Saja tidak suka. (itu)
  SAH-*yah tee-*DAK SOO-*kah.* (EE-*too*)

Show me another.
  Kasi lihat kepada saja jang lain.
  KAH-*sih* LEE-*laht keh-*PAH-*dah* SAH-*yah yahng line.*

Where is the toilet?
  Dimana kamar-ketjil?
  Dee-mah-nah kah-mahr ket-jeel?

Where is the men's room?
  Dimana kamar-ketjil lelaki?
  Dee-mah-nah kah-mahr ket-jeel leh-lah-kee?

Where is the ladies' room?
Dimana kamar-ketjil wanita?
Dee-mah-nah kah-mahr ket-jeel wah-nee-tah?

hot water
air panas
ah-yer PAH-*nahs*

a towel
handuk
*hahn-*DOOK

soap
sabun
*sah-*BOON

Come in!
Masuk!
*Mah-*SOOK!

Please have this washed.
Tjoba tjutjikan ini.
*T'joh-bah t'choot-jee-*KAHN EE-*nee.*

pressed.
seterika.
*seh-teh-*REE-*kah.*

When will it be ready?
Bila akan selesai?
Bee-lah ah-kahn seh-lah-sigh?

I need it . . .
Saja perlu . . .
SAH-*yah* PER-*loo* . . .

for tonight.
untuk malam ini.
OON-*took* MAH-*lahm* EE-*nee.*

for tomorrow.
untuk besok.
OON-*took beh-sohk.*

Put it there.
Tarok disana.
TAH-*rohk dee-*SAH-*nah.*

Give me my key, please.
Tjoba kasi kuntji saja.
*T'*JOH-*bah* KAH-*see* KOONT-*jee sah-yah.*

Any mail for me?
Apakah ada surat-surat untuk saja?
Ah-pah-kah ah-dah soo-raht-soo-raht OON-*took sah-yah?*

Any packages?
Apakah ada bungkus-bungkusan?
Ah-pah-kah ah-dah boong-koos-boong-koos-ahn?

Five airmail stamps for the U.S.
Lima perangko pesawat-udara untuk ke Amerika Serikat.
Lee-mah peh-rahng-ko peh-sah-waht-oo-dah-rah OON-*took keh ah-meh-ree-kah seh-ree-kaht.*

Have you postcards?
Apakah saudara ada kartu-pos?
*Ah-*PAH-*kah sah'oo-*DAH-*rah* AH-*dah* KAHR-*too-pohs?*

I want to send a telegram.
Saja mau kirim telegram.
SAH-*yah mah'oo kee-reem teh-leh-grahm.*

Call me at seven in the morning.
Teleponlah saja pada djam tudjuh pagi.
Teh-leh-pohn-lah sah-yah pah-dah d'jahm too-joo pah-ghee.

Where is the telephone?   **Hello!**
Dimana telepon?   Halo!
*Dee-*MAH-*nah teh-leh-*POHN?   *hah-*LOH!

Send breakfast to room 702.
Antarkan makanan-pagi kekamar tudjuh nol dua.
*Ahn-*TAHR-*kahn mah-*KAH-*nahn* PAH-*ghee keh-kahmar too-joo nohl doo-ah.*

orange juice	bacon and fried eggs
air djeruk	speg dan telor goreng
*ah-yer d'*JEH-*rook*	*speg dahn teh-lohr goh-*RENG

bread and coffee	toast
roti dan kopi	roti panggang
roh-tee dahn koh-pee	*roh-tee pahng-gahng*

I am waiting for a friend.
Saja menunggu seorang teman.
SAH-*yah meh-noong-goo seh-oh-rahng teh-mahn.*

Tell him (or her) to wait for a while.
Kasi-tahu kepada ia, tunggu sebentar.
Kah-see tah-hoo keh-pah-dah ee-yah toong-goo
she-ben-tar.

Tell me, please, where is the restaurant?
Tolong kasi-tahu kepada saja, dimana rumah-
makan?
Toh-long kag-see tah-hoo keh-pah-dah sah-yah
dee-mah-nah ROO-*mah mah-*KAHN?

Where is there a drug store?
Dimana toko obat?
Dee-mah-nah TOH-*koh* OH-*baht?*

Where is there a barber shop?
Dimana tukang-tjukur?
*Dee-mah-nah too-kahng t'joo-*KOOR?

What is the telephone number?
Apa nomor teleponnja?
AH-*pah* NOH-*mohr teh-leh-*POHN-*n'yah?*

What is the address?
Apa alamatnja?
AH-*pah ah-lah-*MAHT-*n'yah?*

I want to change some money.
Saja mau menukarkan uang.
SAH-*yah* MAH'OO *meh-noo-*KAHR-*kahn wahng.*

What is the rate for U.S. dollars?
Berapakah kursnja untuk uang dollar Amerika
Serikat?
*Beh-*RAH-*pah-kah* KOORS-*n'yah oon-*TOOK *wahng*
*dollar ah-*MEH-*ree-kah* SEH-*ree-kaht?*

ten	eleven
sepuluh	sebelas
seh-poo-loo	SEH-*beh-lahs*

twelve
duabelas
DOO-*ah-beh-lahs*

thirteen
tigabelas
tee-gah-beh-lahs

fourteen
ampatbelas
ahm-paht-beh-lahs

fifteen
limabelas
lee-mahb-beh-lahs

sixteen
anambelas
ah-nahm-beh-lahs

seventeen
tudjuhbelas
tood-joo-beh-lahs

eighteen
delapanbelas
*deh-*LAH*-pahn-beh-lahs*

nineteen
sembilanbelas
SEM-*bee-lahn-beh-lahs*

twenty
duapuluh
*doo-*AH*-poo-loo*

thirty
tigapuluh
tee-gah-poo-loo

forty
ampatpuluh
ahm-paht-poo-loo

fifty
limapuluh
lee-mah-poo-loo

sixty
anampuluh
ah-nahm-poo-loo

seventy
tudjuhpuluh
tood-joo-poo-loo

eighty
delapanpuluh
deh-lah-pahn-poo-loo

ninety
sembilanpuluh
SEM-*bee-lahn-poo-loo*

one hundred
seratus
*seh-*RAH*-toos*

two hundred
dua ratus
*doo-*AH RAH-*toos*

three hundred
tiga ratus
tee-gah RAH-*toos*

four hundred
ampat ratus
ahm-paht RAH-*toos*

five hundred
lima ratus
lee-mah RAH-*toos*

six hundred
anam ratus
ah-nahm RAH-*toos*

seven hundred	**eight hundred**
tudjuh ratus	delapan ratus
tood-joo RAH-*toos*	*deh-lah-pahn* RAH-*toos*

nine hundred	**one thousand**
sembilan ratus	seribu
sehm-bee-lahn RAH-*toos*	*seh-ree-boo*

ten thousand	**one hundred thousand**
sepuluh ribu	seratus ribu
seh-poo-loo REE-*boo*	*seh-*RAH-*toos* REE-*boo*

Give me my bill, please.
Tjoba kasi rekening saja.
T'joh-bah KAH-*see reh-ken-in sah-yah.*

3. EATING

Where is a good restaurant?
Dimana ada rumah-makan jang baik?
*Dee-*MAH-*nah* AH-*dah* ROO-*mah-*MAH-*kahn yahng bike?*

I want a table for two, please.
Saja mau medja untuk dua orang.
SAH-*yah mah'oo* MED-*jah* OON-*took* DOO-*ah* OH-*rahng.*

Waiter!
Bung! (it means friend)
Bung!

Please give me the menu.
Tjoba kasi saja daftar makanan.
*T'*JOH-*bah* KAH-*see sah-yah* DAHF-*tar mah-*KAH-*nahn.*

What food is good today?
Makanan apa jang enak untuk hari ini?
*Mah-*KAH-*nahn ah-pah yahng eh-nak* OON-*took*
HAH-*ree* EE-*nee?*

Is it ready?
> Apakah sudah selesai?
> *Ah-*PAH-*kah soo-*DAH *seh-*LEH-*sigh?*

How long will it take?
> Berapa lama membikinnja?
> *Beh-*RAH-*pah* LAH-*mah mem-bee-*KEEN-*n'yah?*

This...   **and this.**
> Ini...   dan ini.
> EE-*nee...*   *dahn* EE-*nee.*

Bring me...
> Bawakkan untuk saja...
> *Bah-*WAHK-*kahn* OON-*took* SAH-*yah...*

     a glass of ice water   **milk**
>   satu gelas air es   susu
>   SAH-*too glahs ah-eer ehs*   *soo-soo*

     a bottle of beer   **orange juice**
>   satu botol bir   air djeruk
>   SAH-*too* BOH-*tohl beer*   AH-*eer d'*JEH-*rook*

     red wine   **white wine**
>   anggur merah   anggur putih
>   AHNG-*goor meh-*RAH   AHNG-*goor poo-*TIH

     soup   **fish**   **meat**
>   sop   ikan   daging
>   *sohp*   *ee-*KAHN   DAH-*gheeng*

     bread and butter   **cheese**
>   roti dan mentega   kedju
>   ROH-*tee dahn men-*TEH-*gah*   KED-*joo*

a sandwich   **steak...**
> satu sanwis   bistik...
> *sah-too* SAHN-*wees*   BEES-*teek...*

     rare   **medium**
>   setengah masak   sedang sedang
>   STEN-*gah mah-*SAHK   SEH-*dahng* SEH-*dahng*

well done
masak betul
mah-SAHK *beh*-TOOL

chicken
ajam
AH-*yahm*

veal
daging anak sapi
DAH-*ghing* AH-*nahk* SAH-*pee*

pork
daging babi
DAH-*ghing* BAH-*bee*

lamb
daging biri
DAH-*ghing bee-ree*

goat
daging kambing
DAH-*ghing kahm-beeng*

with potatoes...
dengan kentang...
den-gahn ken-tahng...

(Indonesian Specialties)

fried rice
nasi goreng
NAH-*see goh*-REHNG

sauce (spicy)
sambal
SAHM-*bahl*

shrimp chips
kerupuk
keh-roo-pook

salad
gado gado
GAH-*doh* GAH-*doh*

rice
nasi
nah-see

string beans
katjang buntjis
kaht-yahng BOONT-*jees*

carrots
wortel
WOR-*tel*

cabbage
kubis
KOO-*bis*

onions
bawang
BAH-*wahng*

tomatoes
tomat
toh-maht

cucumbers
ketimun
keh-TEE-*moon*

Please give me ...
  Tjoba kasi saja ...
  *T'*JOH-*bah* KAH-*see* SAH-*yah* ...

another fork.	**spoon**	**knife**
garpu lagi.	sendok	pisau
GAR-*poo* LAH-*ghee*.	*sen*-DOHK	*pee*-SAH'*oo*

cup	**plate**	**glass**
tjangkir	piring	gelas
CHAHNG-*keer*	PEE-*ring*	*glahs*

fruit	**pastry (cake)**	**ice cream**
buah	kue-kue	es krem
BOO-*ah*	*kweh kweh*	*ehs krehm*

coffee	**sugar**	**milk**
kopi	gula	susu
KOH-*pee*	GOO-*lah*	SOO-*soo*

More, please.
  Tjoba kasi lagi.
  *T'*JOH-*bah* KAH-*see* LAH-*ghee*.

That's enough.
  Itu tjukup.
  Ee-too CHOO-*koop*.

Please give me the check.
  Tjoba kasi saja bon.
  *T'*JOH-*bah* KAH-*see* sah-yah bohn.

Is the tip included?
  Apakah ini termasuk uang persennja?
  *Ah-pah-kah ee-nee ter-*MAH-*sook wahng per-*SEN-
  n'yah?

It was very delicious.
  Makanan itu enak sekali.
  Mah-kah-nahn ee-too eh-nahk seh-kahl-lee.

4. SHOPPING

I would like to buy this...   **that**
 Saja hendak membeli ini...   itu
 SAH-*yah hen-dahk mem-*BEH*-lee ee-nee* ...   EE-*too*

I am just (want to) looking around.
 Saja mau melihat-lihat sadja.
 SAH-*yah ma'oo meh-lee-haht-lee-haht* SAH-*jah.*

Where is the section for...
 Dimanakah bagian pendjualan untuk...
 *Dee-mahn-ah-kah bah-*GHEE*-ahn pen-d'joo-*AH*-*
 lahn OON-*took* ∴..

> **men's clothing**
> pakaian lelaki
> *pah-*KAH*-yahn leh-*LAH*-kee*

> **women's clothing**
> pakaian wanita
> *pah-*KAH*-yahn wah-*NEE*-tah*

> **hats**   **underwear**
> topi   tjelana dalam
> TOH-*pee*   *cheh-lah-nah* DAH-*lahm*

> **shoes**   **stockings**   **shirts**
> sepatu   kaos kaki   kemedja
> *seh-*PAH*-too* KAH-*ohs kah-ke*   *keh-*MEHD*-jah*

My size in America is...
 Ukuran saja di Amerika ialah...
 Oo-koo-rahn SAH-*yah dee ah-mee-ree-kah yah-*
 lah ...

> **toys**   **perfume**
> mainan   minjak wangi
> MIGH-*nahm*   MEEN-*yak* WAHN-*ghee*

jewelry
barang barang perhiasan permata
BAH-*rahng* BAH-*rahng* *per-h'yah-sahn* *per-*
MAH-*ta*

soap and toothpaste
sabun dan tapal-gigi
*sah-*BOON *dahn* TAH-*pahl* GHEE-*ghee*

sword	**Batik cloth**	**films**
pedang	kain batik	pilem
*p'*DAHNG	*kine bah-*TEEK	PEE-*lem*

Show me . . .
Tundjukkan kepada saja . . .
*Toond-*JOOK-*kahn keh-*PAH-*dah* SAH-*yah* . . .

something less expensive
jang tidak seberapa mahal
*yahng tee-*DAK *seh-beh-rah-pah mah-ahl*

another one	**a better quality**
jang lain	jang baik mutunja
yahng line	*yahng bike moo-*TOON-*yah*

larger	**smaller**
lebih besar	lebih ketjil
leh-bih beh-sar	*leh-bih ket-*JEEL

I don't like the color.
Saja tidak suka warnanja.
SAH-*yah tee-*DAK SOO-*kah wahr-*NAHN-*yah.*

I want one . . .
Saja mau satu . . .
SAH-*yah mah'oo* SAH-*too* . . .

in green
jang berwarna hidjau
*yahng ber-*WAHR-*nah heed-jow*

yellow	**blue**	**red**
kuning	biru	merah
KOO-*ning*	BEE-*roo*	MEH-*rah*

black	white	grey
hitam	putih	kelabu
HEE-*tam*	*poo*-TIH	*keh*-LAH-*boo*

brown	pink
tjokelat	merah-muda
choh-keh-LAHT	*meh*-RAH-MOO-*dah*

I will give you 50 rupiahs for it.

Saja kasi limapuluh rupiah untuk itu.

Sah-yah kah-see lee-mah-poo-loo roo-p'yah OON-*took* EE-*too.*

I will take it with me.

Saja akan bawak.

SAHN-*yah ah*-KAHN BAH-*wahk.*

The receipt, please.

Tjoba kasi saja rekeningnja.

*T'*JOH-*bah* KAH-*see* SAH-*yah* REH-*ken'ing-n'yah.*

Please send it to this address.

Tjoba kirimkan kepada alamat ini.

*T'*JOH-*bah kee*-REEM-*kahn keh*-PAH-*dah ah*-LAHM-*aht* EE-*nee.*

Where is the market?

Dimanakah pasar?

Dee-mah-NAH-*kah pah*-SAHR?

5. TRANSPORTATION

Taxi!
Taksi!
Tahk-see!

Trishaw! (bicycle cart)
Betjak!
Beht-jack!

I want to go to the airport.

Saja mau pergi kelapangan terbang.

Sah-jah mah'oo PER-*ghee keh-lah-pahn-gahn ter-bahng.*

How much is it?
  Berapa?
  *Beh-*RAH*-pah?*

Straight ahead.
  Terus.
  Troos.

Turn right.
  Menggok kekanan.
  MENG*-gok keh-kah-nan.*

Turn left.
  Menggok kekiri.
  MENG*-gok keh-kee-ree.*

Not so fast!
  Djangan begitu tjepat!
  *Djahn-gahn beh-*GHEE*-too t'yeh-paht!*

Slowly!
  Pelan-pelan!
  Plahn-plahn!

Hurry up!
  Lekas-lekas!
  LEE*-kahs-*LEE*-kahs!*

Stop here!
  Berhenti disini!
  *Ber-*HEN*-tee dee-*SEE*-nee!*

Wait for me!
  Tunggu saja!
  TOON*-goo* SAH*-yah!*

How much is it to . . . and back?
  Berapa harganja kembala kembali ke . . . ?
  *Beh-*RAH*-pah har-*GAHN*-yah kem-bah-lah kem-bah-*
  lee keh . . . ?

How much . . .
  Berapa . . .
  *Beh-*RAH*-pah . . .*

by the hour?
  sewanja satu djam?
  *seh-*WAHN*-yah sah-too d'jahm?*

  by tne day?
    satu hari?
    sah-too HAH*-ree?*

Show me the sights of this town.
  Tundjukkan saja pemandangan kota ini.
  Toon-d'jook-kahn SAH*-yah peh-mahn-dahn-gan*
  koh-tah ee-nee.

a car
  otomobil
  *oh-toh-*MOH*-beel*

a bicycle
  sepeda
  *seh-*PEH*-dah*

What is that building?
Gedung apakah itu?
*Gheh-doong ah-*PAH-*kah* EE-*too?*

Can I go in?
Bolehkah saja masuk?
*Boh-*LEH-*kah* SAH-*yah mah-*SOOK?

I want to see . . .
Saja mau melihat . . .
SAH-*yah mah'oo meh-*LEE-*hat . . .*

> **the Merdeka Palace. (the Presidential Palace)**
> Astana Merdeka.
> AHS-*tah-nah mer-*DEH-*kah.*

> **Borobudur Temple.**
> Tjandi Borobudur.
> CHAHN-*dee boh-roh-boo-*DOOR.

To the railroad station.
Ke stasiun Kereta Api.
*Keh stah-s'yoon keh-*REH-*tah* AH-*pee.*

Porter!
Saudara! (literally "brother")
Sow-dah-rah!

I have two bags.
Saja ada dua tas.
SAH-*yah ah-dah-doo-ah tahs.*

A ticket to . . .
Satu kartjis untuk ke . . .
SAH-*too kart-yees oon-took keh . . .*

> **round trip**
> kembala-kembali.
> *kem-*BAH-*lah-kem-*BAH-*lee.*

first class	**second class**
kelas satu	kelas dua
klahs sah-too	*klahs doo-ah*

When does it leave?
Bila akan berangkat?
BEE-*lah ah*-KAHN *beh*-RAHNG-*kaht?*

Where is the train to Bandung?
Dimanakah kereta-api untuk pergi ke Bandung?
Dee-mah-NAH-*kah keh-reh-tah-ah-pee oon-took
per-ghee keh bahn-doong?*

Is this the train for Surabaja?
Inikah kereta-api untuk pergi ke Surabaja?
EE-*nee-kah keh*-REH-*tah-ah-pee* OON-*took* PER-*ghee
keh Soo-rah*-BAH-*yah?*

When do we get to Djokjakarta?
Bila kita akan tiba di Djokjakarta?
BEE-*lah* KEE-*tah ah-kahn* TEE-*bah dee D'johk-jah-
kar-tah?*

Open the window.	**Close the window.**
Buka djendela.	Tutup djendela.
BOO-*kah d'jen*-DEH-*lah.*	TOO-*toop d'jen*-DEH-*lah.*

Where is the bus to Semarang?
Dimanakah bis untuk pergi ke Semarang?
Dee-mah-NAH-*kah bees oon-took per-ghee keh seh-*
MAH-*rahng?*

Please tell me where I have to get off.
Tolong kasi tahu kepada saja dimana saja harus
turun.
TOH-*long* KAH-*see* TAH-*hoo keh*-PAH-*dah* SAH-*yah
dee*-MAH-*nah* SAH-*yah* HAH-*roos too-roon.*

Where is a gas station?
Dimanakah ada tempat pendjual minjak bensin?
Dee-mah-NAH-*kah* AH-*dah* TEM-*paht pen-d'*JOO-*ahl
*MEEN-*yahk ben*-SEEN?

Fill it up.
Isilah sampai penuh.
Ee-see-lah sam-pigh peh-noo.

Please check ...
> Tjoba periksa ...
> *T'JOH-bah peh-*REEK*-sah ...*

> **the oil ...**
>> minjaknja ...
>> *meen-yahk-n'yah ...*

> **water**
>> airnja
>> *ire-n'yah*

> **tires**
>> bannja
>> *bahn-n'yah*

Something is wrong with the car.
> Mesin otomobil ini sedikit rusak.
> *Meh-sen oh-toh-moh-beel ee-nee seh-*DEE*-kit roo-*SAHK.

Can you fix it?
> Apakah saudara bisa membetulkannja?
> *Ah-*PAH*-kah sah'oo-dah-rah bee-sah mem-beh-*TOOL*-kahn-n'yah?*

How long will it take?
> Memakan tempo berapa lama?
> *Mem-mah-kahn* TEM*-poh beh-*RAH*-pah* LAH*-mah?*

Is this the road to Palembang?
> Apakah djalanan ini untuk pergi ke Palembang?
> *Ah-*PAH*-kah d'jah-*LAH*-nahn* EE*-nee* OON*-took* PER*-ghee keh pah-*LEM*-bahng?*

Have you a map?
> Apakah saudara ada peta?
> *Ah-*PAH*-kah sah'oo-dah-rah* AH*-dah peh-tah?*

Where is the boat to ... ?
> Dimanakah kapal jang akan berlajar ke ... ?
> *Dee-mah-*NAH*-kah kah-pahl yahng ah-kahn ber-lah-yar keh ... ?*

When does it leave?
> Bila akan bertolak?
> *Bee-lah ah-kahn ber-toh-lak?*

6. MAKING FRIENDS

How do you do?
 Apa kabar?
 Ah-pah KAH-*bahr?*

My name is ...
 Nama saja ...
 NAH-*mah* SAH-*yah* ...

What is your name, sir?
 Siapa nama, tuan?
 SYAH-*pah* NAH-*mah*, TOO-*ahn?*

What is your name, madam?
 Siapa nama, njonja?
 SYAH-*pah* NAH-*mah*, N'YOHN-*n'yah?*

What is your name, miss?
 Siapa nama, nona?
 SYAH-*pah* NAH-*mah*, NOH-*nah?*

Do you speak English?
 Apakah saudara bisa bitjara bahasa Inggeris?
 *Ah-*PAH-*kah sah'oo-*DAH-*rah bee-*SAH *beet-*JAH-*rah*
 *bah-*HAH-*sah* EEN-*gher-ees?*

A little.
 Sedikit.
 *Seh-*DEE-*kit.*

Do you understand?
 Apakah tuan mengerti?
 *Ah-*PAH-*kah too-*AHN *men-*GHER-*tee?*

Please speak slowly.
 Tjoba bitjara pelan-pelan.
 *T'*JOH-*bah beet-*JAH-*rah plahn-plahn.*

I speak only a little Indonesian.
 Saja bisa bitjara bahasa Indonesia hanja sedikit
 sadja.
 SAH-*yah bee-*SAH *beet-*JAH-*rah bah-*HAH-*sah Een-*
 *doh-*NEH-*s'yah* HAHN-*yah seh-*DEE-*kit* SAHD-*yah.*

I am from New York.
Saja berasal dari kota New York.
SAH-*yah* beh-RAH-*sahl* DAH-*ree* KOH-*tah New York.*

Where are you from?
Saudara berasal darimana?
Sah'oo-DAH-*rah* beh-RAH-*sahl dah-ree*-MAH-*nah?*

I like your country.
Saja suka sekali negeri saudara.
SAH-*yah* SOO-*kah* seh-KAH-*lee* NEH-*geh-ree sah'oo-*
DAH-*rah.*

I like your city.
Saja suka sekali kota saudara.
SAH-*yah* SOO-*kah* seh-KAH-*lee* KOH-*tah sah'oo-*DAH-
rah.

Have you been in America?
Apakah saudara sudah pernah di Amerika?
*Ah-*PAH-*kah sah'oo-*DAH-*rah* SOO-DAH *per-*NAH *dee*
*Ah-*MEH-*ree-kah?*

This is my first visit here.
Ini baru pertama kali saja mengundjungi disini.
EE-*nee* BAH-*roo per-*TAH-*mah* KAH-*lee* SAH-*yah*
*men-goond-*JOON-*ghee dee-*SEE-*nee.*

May I sit here?
Bolehkah saja duduk disini?
*Boh-*LEH-*kah* SAH-*yah doo-*DOOK *dee-*SEE-*nee?*

May I take your picture?
Bolehkah saja memotret saudara?
*Boh-*LEH-*kah* SAH-*yah mem-oh-*TREHT *sah'oo-*DAH-
rah?

This is a picture ot . . .
Inilah potret dari . . .
*Ee-*NEE-*lah poh-*TREHT *dah-ree* . . .

my wife.   **my husband.**
    isteri saja.   suami saja.
    EES-*ter-ree* SAH-*yah.*   SWAH-*mee* SAH-*yah.*

my son.
    anak lelaki saja.
    AH-*nahk leh-lah-kee* SAH-*yah.*

my daughter.
    anak wanita saja.
    AH-*nahk wah*-NEE-*tah* SAH-*yah.*

my mother.   **my father.**
    ibu saja.   ajah saja.
    EE-*boo* SAH-*yah.*   AH-*yah* SAH-*yah.*

Have you children?
    Apakah saudara punja anak?
    *Ah-*PAH-*kah sah'oo-*DAH-*rah* POON-*yah* AH-*nahk?*

How beautiful!
    Alangkah tjantiknja!
    *Ah-*LAHNG-*kah t'yahn-*TEEK-*n'yah!*

Very interesting!
    Sangat menarik perhatian!
    SAHN-*gaht meh-*NAH-*reek pehr-hah-*T'YAHN!

Would you like a cigarette?
    Apakah saudara mau rokok?
    *Ah-*PAH-*kah sah'oo-*DAH-*rah mah'oo roh-kohk?*

Would you like to drink lime juice?
    Apakah saudara mau minum air-djeruk?
    *Ah-*PAH-*kah sah'oo-*DAH-*rah mah'oo meen-oom*
    *ah-yer-jeh-*ROOHK?

Would you like to eat ... ?
    Apakah saudara mau makan ... ?
    *Ah-*PAH-*kah sah'oo-*DAH-*rah mah'oo* MAH-*kan ... ?*

Sit down, please.
    Silahkan duduk:
    *See-*LAH-*kan doo-*DOOK.

Don't be shy.
  Djanganlah malu-malu.
  Jahng-AHN-lah mah-loo-mah-loo.

Make yourself at home.
  Bikinlah seperti rumah saudara sendiri.
  *Bee-KEEN-lah seh-PEHR-tee roo-mah sah'oo-DAH-rah
    sen-DEE-ree.*

Good luck!
  Selamat!
  Seh-LAH-maht!

Good drinking!
  Selamat minum!
  Seh-LAH-maht meen-oom!

Good eating!
  Selamat makan!
  Seh-LAH-maht mah-kahn!

Good sleeping!
  Selamat tidur!
  Seh-LAH-maht tee-doohr!

When can I see you again?
  Bila kita bisa berdjumpa lagi?
  *BEE-lah KEE-tah BEE-sah behr-D'YOOM-pah lah-
    ghee?*

Where shall we meet?
  Dimana kita akan bertemu?
  Dee-MAH-nah KEE-tah AH-kan behr-TAY-moo?

Here is my address.
  Inilah alamat saja.
  Ee-NEE-lah ah-LAH-mat SAH-yah.

What is your address?
  Apakah alamat saudara?
  Ah-PAH-kah ah-LAH-mat sah'oo-DAH-rah?

What is your telephone number?
  Apakah nomor telepon saudara?
  *Ah-PAH-kah noh-mohr teh-leh-pohn sah'oo-DAH-
    rah?*

May I speak to ... ?
Bolehkah saja bitjara kepada ... ?
*Boh-*LEH*-kah* SAH*-yah bee-*CHAH*-rah keh-*PAH*-dah ... ?*

Would you like to have ...
Apakah saudara mau ...
*Ah-*PAH*-kah sah'oo-*DAH*-rah mah'oo ...*

lunch?	**dinner?**
makan-siang?	makan-malam?
MAH-*kahn-see-ahng?*	MAH-*kahn-*MAH-*lahm?*

Would you like ...
Apakah saudara suka ...
*Ah-*PAH*-kah sah'oo-*DAH*-rah sooh-kah ...*

to go to the movies?
pergi ke-bioskop?
*pehr-ghee k'*BEE*-oh-skohp?*

to the beach?	**take a walk?**
ke-pantai?	berdjalan-djalan?
k'-pahn-tah-ee?	*behr-*JAH*-lahn-*JAH*-lahn?*

With great pleasure!
Dengan senang hati!
DEHNG*-ahn seh-*NAHNG HAH*-tee!*

I am sorry.	**Another time.**
Maaf.	Lain kali sadja.
Mah-ahf.	*Lah-een kah-lee* SAH*-jah.*

I must go now.
Saja musti pergi sekarang.
SAH*-yah* MOOHS*-tee pher-ghee seh-*KAH*-rahng.*

This is for you.
Ini untuk saudara.
EE*-nee oohn-toohk sah'oo-*DAH*-rah.*

You are very kind.
Saudara baik sekali.
*Sah'oo-*DAH-*rah bah-eek seh-*KAH-*lee.*

With best regards.
Wasalam.
WAH-*sah-lahm.*

Congratulations!
Selamat!
*Seh-*LAH-*maht!*

7. EMERGENCIES

Help!
Tolong!
Toh-long!

Police!
Polisi!
*Poh-*LEE-*sih!*

Fire!
Kebakaran!
*Keh-bah-*KAH-*rahn!*

Stop that man!
Tangkap orang itu!
TAHNG-*kahp oh-rahng* EE-*tuh!*

Stop that woman!
Tangkap wanita itu!
TAHNG-*kahp wah-*NEE-*tah* EE-*tuh!*

My wallet has been stolen!
Dompet saja ditjuri!
DOHM-*peht sah-yah dee-*CHOOH-*ree!*

Look out!
Awas!
Ah-wahs!

Stop!
Berhenti!
*Behr-*HEHN-*tee!*

Wait a minute!
Tunggu satu menit!
TOOHNG-*goo* SAH-*tooh meh-neet!*

Get out!
Pergi keluar!
Pehr-ghee keh-looh-ahr!

Hurry up!
Lekas!
*Leh-*KAHS!

Don't bother me!
  Djangan ganggu saja!
  JAHNG-*ahn* GAHNG-*gooh* SAH-*yah!*

What's going on?
  Ada apa?
  AH-*dah* AH-*pah?*

Entrance	**Exit**
Masuk	Keluar
Mah-soohk	*Keh-looh-ahr*

Ladies	**Gentlemen**
Njonja	Tuan
Nyohn-yah	*Tooh-ahn*

Danger!
  Berbahaja!
  *Behr-bah-*HAH*-yah!*

Keep out!
  Dilarang masuk!
  *Dee-*LAH*-rahng mah-soohk!*

Do not enter!
  Djangan masuk!
  JAHNG-*ahn mah-soohk!*

No smoking
  Dilarang merokok
  *Dee-*LAH*-rahng meh-*ROH*-kohk*

No parking
  Dilarang berhenti disini
  *Dee-*LAH*-rahng behr-*HEHN*-tee dee-*SEE*-nee*

One way
  Hanja satu djalan
  HAHN-*yah* SAH-*tooh* JAH-*lahn*

I am ill.	**Call a doctor.**
Saja sakit.	Panggilkan doktor.
SAH-*yah* SAH-*keet.*	*Pahng-*GHEEL*-kahn dohk-tohr.*

It hurts here.
> Merasa sakit disini.
> *Meh-*RAH-*sah* SAH-*keet dee-*SEE-*nee.*

Take me to the hospital.
> Bawak saja kerumah sakit.
> BAH-*wahk* SAH-*yah keh-*ROOH-*mah* SAH-*keet.*

Where is there a dentist?
> Dimana ada doktor gigi?
> *Dee-*MAH-*nah ah-dah dohk-tohr ghee-ghee?*

I have lost my bag.
> Tas sajh hilang
> *Tahs* SAH-*yah* HEE-*lahng.*

I have lost my wallet.
> Dompet saja hilang.
> DOHM-*peht* SAH-*yah* HEE-*lahng.*

I have lost my camera.
> Kodak saja hilang.
> KOH-*dahk* SAH-*yah* HEE-*lahng.*

I have lost my passport.
> Paspor saja hilang.
> PAHS-*pohr* SAH-*yah* HEE-*lahng.*

I am an American.
> Saja orang warganergara Amerika Serikat.
> SAH-*yah oh-rahng wahr-gah-neh-*GAHR-*ah Ah-*MEH-*ree-kah Seh-*REE-*kaht.*

Where is the American Consulate?
> Dimana Kantor Konsol Amerika Serikat?
> *Dee-*MAH-*nah Kahn-tohr Kohn-sohl Ah-*MEH-*ree-kah Seh-*REE-*kaht?*

Don't worry!	**Everything is all right.**
Djangan kuatir!	Semuanja baik.
JAHNG-*ahn* KWAH-*teer!*	Seh-MWAHN-*yah bike.*

 # CHINESE

Facts About Chinese

Chinese is the native language of more people than any other in the world. The official Chinese, spoken in the north, is called Mandarin or *Kwo-Yü;* it is spoken by more than 450 million people. Many overseas Chinese, however, speak dialects that are written the same but pronounced differently. These include the dialect of central China (*Wu*), that of Fukien Province (*Min*), and Cantonese which is spoken by most Chinese in the United States. Although these dialects are used by many millions, the importance of Mandarin is constantly increasing throughout China and wherever else Chinese is studied. You will note in some of our English translations that Chinese politeness, developed through centuries of usage, is still present in modern Chinese. Chinese has strongly influenced other oriental languages such as Japanese, Korean, and Vietnamese.

It is interesting to note that the Chinese word for China is quite dissimilar from ours. China is called *Chung Hua*[2] *Min Kuo,* which means "The Middle Flowery People's Country." Even the Communists have retained this appellation but enlarged it to *Chung Hua Ren Ming Gung Ho Min Kuo;* the additional *Ren Ming Gung Ho* means "Belonging to People Together." The word "middle" indicated that the Chinese have always thought of themselves as being the center of civilization and have considered other people to be more or less on the outer fringes. The English word "China" comes from the Romans who traded with the Chinese when they were ruled by the *Chin* Dynasty.

Advice On Accent

Chinese is a tonal language, which means that the pitch of the voice determines the meaning of the word. This is extremely important for the correct meaning. For example, the words "buy" and "sell" are both pronounced like the English word "my," except that when you say it as if asking a question it means "buy," but if you say it as a sharp command it means "sell." As almost every Chinese word has four possible meanings according to the tone of voice, you must pay special attention to the key printed at the bottom of each page. This will give you the approximate tone as indicated by numbers printed at the upper right of each word.

Chinese has the reputation of being very difficult, but as a spoken language it is actually quite simple—even more so than English—once you master the tones. It is advisable to make a special effort to approximate these tones, even if you must speak very slowly, as the wrong tone can cause amusing and sometimes embarrassing consequences.

How Chinese Is Written

Here is an interesting example of a railroad warning in Chinese writing.

The four characters say "Small Heart Fire Wagon," meaning, by inference, "When the fire wagon passes, make your heart small." In other words, "Look out for the train."

Chinese is written in ideographs, that is, characters developed from pictures or ideas. For example, words like "sun," "moon," "mountain" still show the general shape of the object; the combination of a man standing means "honesty," the combination of "woman" and "child" means "good," while "woman" alone under "roof" means "peace," a sophisticated commentary on thousands of years of Chinese living experience.

There are more than 50,000 Chinese ideographs, but there exists a strong trend towards simplification and only a few thousand are used today in newspapers and magazines.

Although there are several systems for phoneticizing Chinese writing, we have used our own in this Chinese section to make it easier for you. Simply pronounce it as if you were reading English. (But remember to use the correct tone!)

1. FIRST CONTACT

Yes.
*Shih.***4**

No.
*Poo***2** *shih.***4**

Good.
*How.***3**

Thank you.
*Shee'yeh***4** *shee'yeh***4** *nee.***3**

You are welcome.
*Poo***2** *kah***4** *chee.***4**

Excuse me.
*Too'ee***4** *poo***4** *chee.***3**

It is all right.
*May***2** *yoo***3** *kwan***1** *shee.***4**

Please.
*Chin.***3**

I would like . . .
*Woh***3** *yow***4** . . .

What?
*Shem***2** *mah?***4**

This.
*Cheh***4** *koh.***4**

Where?
*Nah***2** *lee?***3**

Here.
*Cheh***4** *lee.***3**

When?
*Shem***2** *mah***4** *shee***2** *hoo?***4**

Now.
*Shee'yen***4** *ts'eye.***4**

Later.
*Yee***3** *hoo.***4**

Who?   **I**   **you**   **he**   **she**
*Shoo'ee?***2**   *Woh***3**   *nee***3**   *tah***1**   *tah***1**

Your name?
*Kweh***4** *shing?***4**

Good morning.
*Ts'ow.***3**

Good night.
*Wahn***3** *ahn.***1**

Good-by.
*Ts'eye***4** *chee'yen.***4**

NUMBERS INDICATE TONES

1. Normal tone (flat and short).
2. Said as if asking a question.
3. Said as if asking Wh-a-a-a-t?
4. Said as if giving a command.

How are you?
  Nee2 how3 poo4 how?3

Very well, thank you, and you?
  Hen2 how,3 shee'yeh4 shee'yeh,4 nee2 how3 mah?2

How much?
  Too-woh1 shah-oh3 chee'yen?2

I do not understand, please repeat.
  Woh3 poo4 toong,3 ching3 ts'eye4 shoo'oh.1

one	two	three	four	five	six
yee1	*er4*	*sahn1*	*ssoo4*	*woo3*	*lee-yoo4*

seven	eight	nine	ten
chee1	*pah1*	*chee'yoo3*	*shee2*

eleven	twelve
shee2 yee1	*shee2 erh4*

2. ACCOMMODATIONS

Where is a good hotel?
  How2 loo2 kwahn3 ts'eye4 na2 lee?3

I want a room ...   **for one person**
  Wo3 yow4 yee2 ko4 ...   *tan1 ren2 fahng2*

    for two persons
      shooahng1 ren2 fahng2

    with bath
      yoo2 shih2 ts'ow3 fahng2 teh4 fahng2 chee'yen1

    for two days   **for a week**
      leeahng3 t'yen1   *yee1 ko4 lee3 pie4*

    till Monday   **Tuesday**
      tow4 Lee3 pie4 yee1   *Lee3 pie4 er4*

Wednesday
  *Lee*3 *pie*4 *sahn*1

Thursday
  *Lee*3 *pie*4 *ssoo*4

Friday
  *Lee*3 *pie*4 *woo*3

Saturday
  *Lee*3 *pie*4 *l'yoo*4

Sunday
  *Lee*3 *pie*4 *t'yen*1

How much is it?
  *Two*1 *sha'oo*3 *chee'yen?*2

Here are my bags.
  *Chey*4 *lee*3 *shih*4 *wo*3 *teh*4 *shing*2 *lee.*4

Here is my passport.
  *Chey*4 *lee*3 *shih*4 *wo*3 *teh*4 *hoo*4 *ch'ow.*4

I like it.
  *Wo*2 *shee*3 *hwahn*4 *ta.*1

I do not like it.
  *Wo*3 *poo*4 *shee*3 *hwahn*4 *ta.*1

Show me another.
  *Guy*2 *wo*3 *kahn*4 *p'yeh*2 *teh.*4

Where is the toilet?
  *Tseh*4 *so*3 *ts'eye*4 *na*2 *lee?*3

Where is the men's room?
  *Nahn*2 *tseh*4 *so*3 *ts'eye*4 *na*2 *lee?*3

  the ladies' room?
    *noo*3 *tseh*4 *so*3 *ts'eye*4 *na*2 *lee?*3

hot water
  *reh*4 *shwee*3

a towel
  *mah'oo*2 *chin*1

soap
  *fey*2 *ts'ow*4

NUMBERS INDICATE TONES
1. Normal tone (flat and short).
2. Said as if asking a question.
3. Said as if asking Wh-a-a-a-t?
4. Said as if giving a command.

Come in!
  Ching³ chin!⁴

Please have this washed.
  Ching² pa³ cheh⁴ ko⁴ shee³ yee⁴ shee.³

pressed	cleaned
tahng⁴ yee⁴ tahng⁴	*kahn¹ shee³*

When will it be ready?
  Shem² ma⁴ shih² hoo⁴ ko² yee² how?³

I need it for tonight.
  Wo³ chin¹ t'yen¹ wahn³ shang⁴ yow.⁴

  for tomorrow
    ming² t'yen¹ yow⁴

My key, please.
  Ching² nee² guy² wo³ wo³ teh⁴ yow⁴ shih.⁴

Any mail for me?
  Wo² yoo³ may² yoo³ shin?⁴

Any packages?
  Yoo³ may² yoo³ pow¹ kuo?³

I want five airmail stamps for the U.S.
  *Wo³ yow⁴ woo³ ko⁴ tow⁴ may³ kwo² choo⁴ teh⁴
  hahng² koong¹ yoo² p'yow.⁴*

Have you postcards?
  Yoo³ may² yoo³ yoo² p'yen?⁴

I want to send a telegram.
  Wo³ yow⁴ ta³ t'yen⁴ pow.⁴

Call me at seven in the morning.
  *Ts'ow³ shahng⁴ chee¹ t'yen³ choong¹ ta³ t'yen⁴
  hwah⁴ chee'yow⁴ wo.³*

Where is the telephone?   **Hello!**
  T'yen⁴ hwa⁴ ts'eye⁴ na² lee?³   *Wy!⁴*

Send breakfast to room 702.
 *Sung4 tsao2 t'yen3 tao4 chee1 ling2 erh4 hao4
 fahng2 chee'yen1 lie.2*

orange juice
 choo2 tsoo4 shwee3

ham and eggs
 hwo2 twee3 tan4

rolls and coffee
 m'yen4 pow1 chee'ya1 feh'ee1

I am expecting a friend.
 Wo3 ts'eye4 teng3 yee2 ko4 peng2 yoo.4

Tell him (her) to wait.
 Chee'yow4 ta1 teng3 yee4 teng.3

Tell me, please, where is a restaurant?
 Chin3 kao4 ssu4 wo3 fan4 tien4 tsai4 na2 li?3

Tell me, please, where is a barbershop?
 Chin3 kao4 ssu4 wo3 li2 fa4 tien4 tsai4 na2 li?3

Tell me, please, where is a beauty parlor?
 Chin3 kao4 ssu4 wo3 mei3 yung2 yuan4 tsai4 na2 li?3

Tell me, please, where is a drug store?
 Chin3 kao4 ssu4 wo3 yao4 fang4 tsai4 na2 li?3

What is the telephone number?
 Tien4 hwa4 hao4 ma3 shih4 shem2-ma?4

What is the address?
 Tee4 chih3 shih4 shem2-ma?4

I want to change some money.
 Wo3 yao4 hwan4 yi4 tien3 chien.2

NUMBERS INDICATE TONES
1. Normal tone (flat and short).
2. Said as if asking a question.
3. Said as if asking Wh-a-a-a-t?
4. Said as if giving a command.

What is the rate for dollars?
Dou1 shao3 hwan4 yi2 kuai?4

ten	eleven	twelve
*shih*2	*shih*2-*yi*1	*shih*2-*erh*4

thirteen	fourteen	fifteen
*shih*2-*san*1	*shih*2-*ssu*4	*shih*2-*wu*3

sixteen	seventeen	eighteen
*shih*2-*liu*4	*shih*2-*chi*1	*shih*2-*pa*1

nineteen	twenty	thirty
*shih*2-*chiu*3	*erh*4-*shih*2	*san*1-*shih*2

forty	fifty	sixty
*ssu*4-*shih*2	*wu*3-*shih*2	*liu*4-*shih*2

seventy	eighty	ninety
*chi*1-*shih*2	*pa*1-*shih*2	*chiu*3-*shih*2

hundred	two hundred	three hundred
*yi*4-*pai*3	*erh*4 *pai*3	*san*1-*pai*3

four hundred	five hundred	six hundred
*ssu*4 *pai*3	*wu*2 *pai*3	*liu*4 *pai*3

seven hundred	eight hundred	nine hundred
*chi*1 *pai*3	*pa*1 *pai*3	*chiu*2 *pai*3

thousand	ten thousand
*chien*1	*wan*4

hundred thousand	My bill, please.
*shih*2 *wan*4	Chan4 tan.1

3. EATING

Where is a good restaurant?
Hoo3 fahn4 t'yen4 ts'eye4 na2 lee?3

A table for two, please.
Leeahng3 ko4 ren2 teh4 choo'oh1 tsuh.4

Waiter!
   *Ho*³ *chee!*⁴

The menu, please.
   *Ts'eye*⁴ *tahn.*¹

What's good today?
   *Chin*¹ *t'yen*¹ *shem*² *ma*⁴ *how?*³

How long will it take?
   *Yow*⁴ *doh*¹ *shah'oo*³ *shee*² *hoo?*⁴

This please ...   **and this.**
   *Yow*⁴ *cheh*⁴ *ko*⁴ ...   *toong*² *cheh*⁴ *ko.*⁴

Bring me ...   **water**
   *Guy*² *wo*³ ...   *shwee*³

milk   **a glass of beer**
   *new*² *nye*³   *yee*⁴ *pay*¹ *pee*² *chee'oo*³

a cocktail   **whisky soda**
   *chee*¹ *way*³ *chee'oo*³   *way*¹ *ssuh*⁴ *chee*¹ *soo*¹ *ta*³

A little more, please.   **That's enough.**
   *Ts'eye*⁴ *lie*² *yee*⁴ *t'yen.*³   *Koh*⁴ *leh.*⁴

soup   **fish**   **meat**
   *tahng*¹   *yoo*²   *roo*⁴

bread and butter   **a sandwich**
   *myen*⁴ *pow*¹ *hwahng*² *yoo*²   *san*¹ *min*² *chih*⁴

steak ...   **rare**
   *new*² *pie*² ...   *sheng*¹

    medium   **well done**
     *pan*⁴ *sheng*¹   *shoo*²

NUMBERS INDICATE TONES

1. Normal tone (flat and short).
2. Said as if asking a question.
3. Said as if asking Wh-a-a-a-t?
4. Said as if giving a command.

chicken
chee1

pork
choo1 roo4

lamb
yahng2 roo4

lamb chop
yahng2 pie2

fried rice
chow3 fan4

diced chicken with almonds
shing4 jen2 chee1 ting1

rice
fahn4

an omelet
foo2 yoong2 tahn4

And what vegetables?
Shem2 ma4 ts'eye?4

peas
too4

beans
ching1 too4

carrots
hoo2 lo2 po4

onions
yahng2 ts'oong1

a salad
pahn4 ching1 ts'eye4

lettuce
sheng1 ts'eye4

Please bring me another fork.
Ching2 nee3 ts'eye4 gay2 wo3 yee4 pa3 cha1 tsuh.4

chop sticks
kwy4 tsuh4

knife
t'ow1

spoon
t'yow2 keng1

glass
pay1

plate
pahn2 tsuh4

What is there for dessert?
Shem2 ma4 ts'yen3 shin?1

fruit
shoo'ee2 koo'oh3

pastry
t'yen3 shin1

cake
tahn4 k'ow1

ice cream
ping1 chee4 ling2

cheese
kahn1 l'ow4

Some coffee, please.
Ching2 gay2 wo3 chee'ah1 feh.1

sugar
tahng2

cream	tea	mineral water
noo2 nye3 ching1	*cha2*	*kwahng4 shwee3*

The check, please.
Chahn4 tahn1 gay2 wo.3

It was very good!
Hen3 how!3

Is the tip included?
Shee'ow3 chahng4 ts'eye4 nay4 ma?4

4. SHOPPING

I would like to buy this . . .   **that.**
Wo3 yow2 my3 cheh4 ko4 . . .   *na4 ko.4*

I am just looking around.
Wo3 chee'oo4 kahn4 yee2 kahn.4

Where is the section for . . .
. . . shee'yeh poo4 ts'y4 na2 lee3

men's clothing
nahn2 ren2 yee1 foo4

women's clothing
noo3 ren2 yee1 foo4

hats
m'ow4 ts'uh4

gloves
shoo3 t'ow4

underwear
chen4 yee1

shoes
shee'yeh2

stockings
wa4 ts'uh4

shirts
chen4 shahn1

The size in America is . . .
May3 ko2 teh4 how4 shoo4 . . .

toys
wahn2 choo4

perfumes
shee'ahng1 shwee3

NUMBERS INDICATE TONES

1. Normal tone (flat and short).
2. Said as if asking a question.
3. Said as if asking Wh-a-a-a-t?
4. Said as if giving a command.

jewelry
shoo3 shih4

watches
p'yow3

tooth paste
ya2 kow1

soap
fay2 ts'ou4

films
chee'ow1 chuahn3

souvenirs
chee4 n'yen4 pin3

jade
yoo4

ivory
shee'ahn4 ya2

embroideries
shoo4 hwah1

porcelain
tsoo2 chee4

earrings
erh3 hooahn2

Show me ...
Gay3 wo3 kahn4 ...

    something less expensive
    p'yen2 ee4 t'yen3 erh4 teh4

    another one
    p'yeh2 teh4

    a better quality
    how3 yee4 t'yen3 erh4 te4

    bigger
    da4 ee4 t'yen3 erh4 teh4

    smaller
    shee'yow3 ee4 t'yen3 erh4 teh4

I don't like the color.
Wo3 poo4 shee3 hwahn4 cheh4 yen2 seh.4

I want one ...
Wo3 yow4 yee2 ko4 ...

    in green
    lew4 teh4

    in yellow
    awahng2 teh4

    in blue
    lahn2 teh4

red	black	white
hoong2 teh4	*hay1 teh4*	*pie2 teh4*

grey	pink
hwee1 teh4	*foon3 hoong2 teh4*

brown
ts'oong1 teh4

I will take it with me.
Wo3 y'ow4 tie4 cheh4 ts'oo.3

The receipt, please.
Shoo1 t'yow.2

Please send it to this address.
Ching3 soong4 t'ow4 cheh4 ko4 tee4 t'yen.3

Where is there a flower shop?
Hwa1 d'yen4 ts'eye4 na2 lee?3

Where is there a food shop?
Fahn4 poo4 tsuh4 ts'eye4 na2 lee?3

5. TRANSPORTATION

Taxi!
Ch'oo1 tz'u1 ch'ee4 ch'eh!1

Take me to the airport.
Soong4 wo3 t'ow4 fay1 chee1 chahng3 choo.4

Turn right!
Shee'ahn4 yoo4 choo'ahn!3

NUMBERS INDICATE TONES
1. Normal tone (flat and short).
2. Said as if asking a question.
3. Said as if asking Wh-a-a-t?
4. Said as if giving a command.

Turn left!
  Shee'ahn4 t'soh3 choo-ahn!3

Not so fast!
  Poo2 y'ow4 tie4 k'why!4

Hurry up!
  K'why4 ee4 t'yen!3

Stop here!
  Ting2 ts'eye4 cheh4 lee!3

Wait for me!
  Teng3 cheh4 wo!3

How much is it?
  T'woh1 sh'ow3 chee'yen?2

How much is it to . . . ?
  T'woh1 sh'ow3 chee'yen2 t'ow4 . . . ?

    and back?
    h'way2 lie4 nee?4

How much by the hour?
  T'wow1 sh'ow3 chee'yen2 yee4 t'yen3 choong?1

    by the day?
    t'wow1 sh'ow3 chee'yen2 yee4 t'yen?1

Show me the sights.
  Ching3 tie4 wo3 kahn4 kahn.4

What is that building?
  Cheh4 k'ow1 loh2 shih4 shem2 ma?4

Can I go in?
  Wo2 ko2 ee3 chin4 choo4 ma?4

I want to see the Great Wall.
  Wo3 y'ow4 kahn4 wahn4 lee3 chahng2 cheng.2

To the railroad station!
  Hwoh3 cheh1 chahn!4

Porter!
  Chee'ow3 hang!2

I have two bags.
  Wo2 yoo2 lee'ahng3 ko4 shee'yang1 t'suh.4

A ticket to . . .
  T'ow4 . . . choo4 teh4 p'y'ow.4

one way
  tahn1 cheng2

round trip
  shoo'ahng1 cheng2

first class
  too2 teng3

second class
  erh4 teng3

When does it leave?
  Shem2 ma4 shih2 hoo4 lee2 kah'ee?4

Where is the train to Nanking?
  T'ow4 Nahn2 ching1 teh4 ho3 cheh1 ts'eye4 na2 lee?3

Is this the train for Suchow?
  Cheh4 shih4 t'ow4 Soo1-chow1 teh4 ho3 cheh1 ma?4

When do we get to Peking?
  Wo3 men4 shem2 ma4 shee2 how4 t'ow4 Peh3-ching?1

Open the window.
  Kie1 choo'ahng.1

Close the window.
  Kwahn1 choo'ahng.1

Where is the bus to Lanchow?
  T'ow4 Lahn2-chow1 teh4 koong1 koong4 chee4 cheh1 ts'eye4 na2 lee?3

I want to go to Foochow.
  Wo3 y'ow4 t'ow4 Foo2-chow1 choo.4

Please tell me where to get off.
  Ching3 k'ow4 soong4 wo3 na2 lee3 shee'yah4 cheh.1

Where is a gas station?
  Chee4 yoo2 chan4 ts'eye4 na2 lee?3

NUMBERS INDICATE TONES
1. Normal tone (flat and short).
2. Said as if asking a question.
3. Said as if asking Wh-a-a-a-t?
4. Said as if giving a command.

Fill it up.	**Check the oil . . .**
Chee'ah1 mahn.3	*Chah2 ee4 chah2 yoo2 . . .*

water	tires
shwee3	*cheh1 loo'en2*

Something is wrong with the car.
Cheh1 yoo3 ee4 t'yen3 erh2 mau2 ping.4

Can you fix it?
Nee3 ho'ee4 shee'yoo1 ma?4

How long will it take?
Y'ow4 t'wo1 shah'oo3 shih2 hoo?4

Is this the road to the town of Wu?
Chey4 shee4 t'ow4 woo2 shee'yen4 teh4 loo4 ma?4

Have you a map?
Nee3 yoo3 dee4 too2 mah?4

Where is the boat to Hong Kong?
*T'ow4 Shee'ahng1 Kang3 choo4 teh4 choo'ahn2
ts'eye4 na2 lee?3*

When does it leave?
Shem2 ma4 shih2 hoo4 lee2 kah'ee?4

6. MAKING FRIENDS

Good day!
Ts'ow!3

My name is . . .
Woh3 teh4 ming2 tsuh4 shih4 . . .

What is your name, Sir?
Ching3 wen4 ta4 ming?2

Please, may I ask your (honorable) name, Madam?
Ching3 wen4 tie4 tie4 ta4 ming?2

Please, may I ask your (honorable) name, Miss?
Ching³ wen⁴ shee'ow² chey³ ta⁴ ming?²

I am delighted to meet you.
Wo² shih³ h'wahn¹ chee'yen⁴ nee.³

Do you speak English?   **A little.**
Nee³ sho¹ ying¹ wen² ma?⁴   *Yee⁴ d'yah.³*

I speak only a little Chinese.
*Wo³ chee'yoo⁴ sho¹ ee⁴ t'yen³ erh⁴ Choong¹
K'woh² hwah.⁴*

Do you understand?
Nee³ ming² pie⁴ mah?⁴

Please speak slowly.
Ching³ mahn⁴ d'yen³ shoh.¹

I am from New York.
Wo³ tsoong² nee'yew³ yoo'eh⁴ lie² teh.⁴

Where are you from?
Nee³ tsoon² na² lee³ lie² teh?⁴

I like your (honorable) country.
Wo² shee³ hwahn¹ gweh⁴ kwo.²

I like your city.
Wo² shee³ hwan¹ nee³ teh⁴ cheng.²

Have you been in America?
Nee³ t'ow⁴ kwo⁴ may³ kwo² ma?⁴

This is my first visit here.
Chey⁴ shih⁴ wo³ dee⁴ yee¹ tsoo⁴ lie.²

NUMBERS INDICATE TONES

1. Normal tone (flat and short).
2. Said as if asking a question.
3. Said as if asking Wh-a-a-a-t?
4. Said as if giving a command.

May I sit here?
  Wo2 ko2 ee3 tso4 ts'eye4 chey4 lee3 ma?4

May I take your picture?
  Wo2 ko2 ee3 tee4 nee3 ch'ow4 shee'ahng4 ma?4

Come here.
  Lie2 jeh4 lee.3

This is a picture of my wife.
  Chey4 shih4 wo2 tie4 tie4 teh4 shee'ang.4

  my husband   **my son**
    wo3 shee'yen1 sheng4   *wo3 erh2 tsoo4*

  my daughter   **my mother**
    wo2 niew3 erh2   *wo2 moo3 chin4*

  my father   **my sister**
    wo3 foo4 chin4   *wo2 chee'yeh3 chee'yeh4*

  my brother
    wo3 shee'oong1 tee4

Have you children?
  Nee2 yoo3 high2 tsoo4 ma?4

How beautiful!   **Very interesting!**
  Cheng1 how3 kan!4   *Hen2 yoo3 yee4 ssoo!4*

Would you like a cigarette?
  Nee3 y'ow4 shee'ahng1 yen1 ma?4

Would you like something to drink?
  Nee3 y'ow4 heh1 shem2 ma?4

Would you like something to eat?
  Nee3 y'ow4 chih1 shem2 ma?4

Sit down, please.   **Make yourself at home.**
  Ching3 t'so.4   *Ching3 suey2 p'yen.4*

To your health!
  Kahn1-pay!1

When can I see you again?
Wo3 shem2 ma4 shih2 hoo4 ts'eye4 chee'yen4 t'ow4 nee?3

Where shall we meet?
Wo3 men4 ts'eye4 na2 lee3 chee'yen?4

What is your address?
Nee3 teh4 tee4 chih3 shih4 shem2 ma?4

Here is my address.
Cheh4 shih4 wo3 teh4 tee4 chih.3

What is your phone number?
Nee3 teh4 t'yen4 hwah4 shih4 shem2 ma?4

May I speak to ...
Wo2 kon2 ee3 ken1 ... shwoh1 hwah4 ma.4

Would you like to have lunch?
Nee3 y'ow4 chih1 choong1 fahn4 ma?4

    have dinner?
    wahn3 fahn4 ma?4

Would you like to go to the movies?
Ni3 y'ow4 choo4 kahn4 t'yen4 ying3 ma?4

    to go to the theatre?
    choo4 kahn4 shih4 ma?4

Would you like to go to the beach?
Choo4 high3 p'yen1 ma?4

    take a walk?
    choo4 sahn4 poo4 ma?4

NUMBERS INDICATE TONES
1. Normal tone (flat and short).
2. Said as if asking a question.
3. Said as if asking Wh-a-a-a-t?
4. Said as if giving a command.

With great pleasure! (Very happy!)
  Chen1 kao1 shing!4

I am sorry.
  Tuey4 poo4 chee.3

I cannot.
  Wo3 poo4 neng.2

Another time.
  Shee'yah4 yee4 tsoo.4

I must go now.
  Wo2 day2 t'soo3 leh.4

Thank you. I had a wonderful time.
  Shee'yeh4 shee'yeh4 nee3 wo3 war2 teh4 hen2 how.3

Thank you for such an excellent dinner.
  *Shee'yeh4 shee'yeh4 nee3 chuh4 ma4 how3 teh4
  wahn3 fahn.4*

This is for you.
  Cheh4 shih4 guy2 nee3 teh.4

You are very kind.
  Nee2 hen3 keh4 chee.4

It's nothing really.
  May2 shem2 ma.4

Congratulations!
  Koong1 shee!3

With best regards.
  Wen4 how.3

7. EMERGENCIES

Help!   **Police!**   **Fire!**
  Ch'yoo4 ming!4   *Chin3 cha!2*   *Ch'ow2 hwo!3*

Stop that man!
  Na2 choo4 na4 guh4 ren!2

Stop that woman!
  Na2 choo4 na4 guh4 n'yew3 ren!2

I have been robbed!
  Wo3 pay4 chee'ahng3 leh!4

Look out!
  Shee'ow3 shin!1

Wait a minute!
  Teng3 yee4 hwer!4

Stop!
 Ting2 choo!4

Get out!
 Ch'oo1 choo!4

Hurry up!
 K'why4 yee4 t'yen3 erh!4

Don't bother me!
 Poo2 y'ow4 chee'ow2 wo!3

What's going on?
 Shem2 ma4 shih?4

Entrance
 Roo4 koo3

Exit
 Choo1 koo3

Ladies
 N'yew3 shih4

Gentlemen
 Nahn2 shih4

Danger!
 Way1 shee'yen!3

Please don't enter.
 B'yeh2 chin4 lye.2

No smoking
 Poo4 shoo3 chow1 yen1

No parking
 Poo4 shoo3 ting2 cheh1

One way
 Yee4 p'yen1 t'soh3

I am ill.
 Wo3 ping4 leh.4

Call a doctor!
 Ching3 yee1 sheng!1

It hurts here.
 Cheh1 lee3 teng.2

Where is the drugstore?
 Y'ow4 fahng2 ts'eye4 na2 lee?3

NUMBERS INDICATE TONES
1. Normal tone (flat and short).
2. Said as if asking a question.
3. Said as if asking Wh-a-a-a-t?
4. Said as if giving a command.

Take me to the hospital.
Soong4 wo3 t'ow4 yee1 yoo'ahn.4

Where is there a dentist?
Ya2 yee1 ts'eye4 na2 lee?3

I have lost my bag.
Wo3 teh4 pee2 p'ow1 t'yoo1 leh.4

I have lost my camera.
Wo3 teh4 chow4 shee'ahng4 chee1 t'yoo1 leh.4

I have lost my wallet.
Wo3 teh4 chee'yen2 tie4 t'yoo1 leh.4

I have lost my passport.
Wo3 teh4 hoo4 ch'ow4 t'yoo1 leh.4

I am an American.
Wo3 shih4 may3 kwo2 ren.2

Where is the American Consulate?
May3 kwo2 ling3 shih4 kwan3 ts'eye4 na2 lee?3

Don't get excited!
Poo2 y'ow4 chow1 chee!2

Everything is all right.
Too1 h'ow.3

JAPANESE

Facts About Japanese

Almost 100 million people speak Japanese in the Japanese archipelago, Okinawa, and Korea. Japanese, originally thought to be a South Pacific language, has been strongly influenced by Chinese, especially in words pertaining to culture, art, literature, religion, science, etc.

Japanese conversation is extremely polite. In fact, instead of saying "your house," you say "the honorable house." The phrases used in this book have been developed with this in mind so that, in speaking exactly as the phrases are written, you will be speaking correct and polite Japanese.

In the Japanese system of counting, which is of Chinese origin, the word for 4 (*shi*) is seldom heard but is substituted for by *yon,* from an earlier Japanese system of counting. This is because *shi* means "death," and to use it in counting would possibly incur bad luck or at least be impolite.

The Japanese question mark is spoken as well as written—that is to say, the syllable *ka* is added at the end of the question.

Advice On Accent

As a general rule, no Japanese syllable is stressed more than any other. A useful hint for

the foreign speaker of Japanese is to accentuate the last syllable a little more than the other ones with the exception of the final *u*, which is hardly pronounced. Japanese is an extremely phonetic language and is pronounced almost exactly as it is written in Roman letters (except for the final *u*). *Attention:* when you see an apostrophe between letters (*sah'ee* for example), pronounce the whole combination as if it were one syllable.

How Japanese Is Written

Japanese is usually written with a combination of thousands of Japanese ideographs interspaced with a form of Japanese syllable writing called *katakana* in its simple form and *hiragana* in a more elaborate version. Japanese can also be written in Roman letters, called *Roma-ji* (Roman writing) to differentiate it from the usual *Kan-ji* (Chinese writing). In this section we have used not *Roma-ji* but an easier phonetic interpretation. Here is an example of some Japanese words written in Chinese ideographs. They mean "Entrance," "Exit," and "No Admittance," words especially useful to travelers.

入口, 出口,

立入禁止

You Already Know Some Japanese

Many American words have become part of the Japanese language. Some of them will be easily recognizable to you in spite of their Japanese pronunciation. They include *shigaretto, tobako, kissu, baseboru* (baseball), *icekreamu,* and others. In addition to these formations, numerous Japanese words have become a part of everyday English. Here are some with their literal Japanese meanings: *kimono* ("wearing thing"), *geisha* ("art person"), *nisei* ("second year" or "generation"), *harakiri* ("stomach cutting"), *kamikaze* ("divine wind"), *judo* (soft way), *banzai* ("ten thousand years"), *sukiyaki* ("assemble things to cook").

By an extremely curious coincidence the English word "so," as in "Is it not so?", is exactly the same in Japanese. The above expression is rendered in Japanese as *So desuka?*

1. FIRST CONTACT

Yes.
High.

No.
Ee-yeh.

Good.
Ee.

Thank you.
Ah-ree-gah-toh.

You are welcome.
Yoh-koh-soh.

Excuse me.
Soo-mee-mah-sen.

It's all right.
Ee dehss.

Please.
Doh-zoh.

I wish . . .
. . . gah hoh-shee dehss.

What?
Nan dehss-kah?

This.
Koh-reh.

Where?
Doh-koh dehss-kah?

Here.
Koh-koh.

Good evening.
Kohn-bahn-wah.

Good night.
Oh-yah-soo-mee.

Good-by.
Sah-yoh-nah-rah.

How are you?
Ee-kah-gah dehss-kah?

I do not understand, please repeat.
*Wah-kah-ree-mah-sen, moh-ee-chee-doh eet-teh
koo-dah-sah'ee.*

How much?
Ee-koo-rah dehss-kah?

Very well, thank you, and you?
Oh-kay-gheh-sah-mah deh, ah-nah-tah wah?

one
ee-chee

two
nee

three
sahn

379

four	**five**	**six**
shee (or) *yohn*	*goh*	*rohk*

seven	**eight**	**nine**
shee-chee	*hah-chee*	*koo* or *kie-yoo*

When?	**Now.**	**Later.**
Its dehss-kah?	*Ee-mah.*	*Ah-toh-deh.*

Who?	**I**
Dah-reh dehss-kah?	*Wah-tahk-shee*

you	**he (or) she**
ah-nah-tah	*ah-noh h'tòh*

Your name?
Ah-nah-tah-noh oh-nah-mah-ee wa?

Good morning.	**Good day.**
Oh-hah-yoh.	*Kohn-nee-chee-wah.*

2. ACCOMMODATIONS

Where is a good hotel?
Yoh'ee hoh-teh-roo wah doh-koh dehss-kah?

I want a room for one person.
Hee-toh-ree noh heh-yah gah hoh-shee-dehss.

I want a room for two persons.
F'tah-ree noh heh-yah gah hoh-shee dehss.

I want a room with bath.
Bah-soots-skee noh heh-yah gah hoh-shee dehss.

for two days	**for a week**
foot-sook-ah	*ees-shoo-kahn*

till Monday	**Tuesday**
get-soo-yoh mah-deh	*Kah-yoh*

| **Wednesday** | **Thursday** |
| *Soo'ee-yoh* | *Mohk-yoh* |

| **Friday** | **Saturday** | **Sunday** |
| *Kin-yoh* | *Doh-yoh* | *Nee-chee-yoh* |

How much is it?
Ee-koo-rah dehss-kah?

Here are my bags.
Wah-tahk-shee noh kah-bahn wah koh-koh dehss.

Here is my passport.
Wah-tahk-shee noh r'yoh-ken wah koh-reh dehss.

I like it.
Soh-reh gah ee dehss.

I do not like it.
Soh-reh wah ee-yah dehss.

Show me another.
Hoh-kah-noh oh mee-seh-teh koo-dah-sah'ee.

Where is the toilet?
Ben-joh wah doh-koh dehss-kah?

Where is the men's room?
Oh-toh-koh ben-joh wah doh-koh dehss-kah?

The ladies' room?
Ohn-nah ben-joh wah?

| **hot water** | **a towel** | **soap** |
| *you* | *tah'oh-roo* | *sek-ken* |

Come in! (literally, "Please").
Doh-zoh!

Please have this washed.
Koh-reh oh ah-raht-teh koo-dah-seh-ee.

Please have this pressed.
Koh-reh nee eye-rohn oh kah-keh-teh koo-dah-seh-ee.

Please have this cleaned.
Koh-reh oh koo-ree-nh-geh shee-teh koo-dah-sah'ee.

When will it be ready?
Its-soo deh-kee mahss-kah?

I need it for tonight.   for tomorrow.
Kohn-bahn e-ree-mahss.   ah-shee-tah.

Call me at seven in the morning.
Ah-sah shee-chee-jee nee oh-koh-shee-teh koo-dah-sah'ee.

Where is the telephone?
Den-wah wah doh-koh dehss-kah?

Hello.
Moh-shee moh-shee.

Send breakfast to room 12.
Ah-sah-goh-hahn oh joo-nee bahn noh heh-yah nee moht-teh-kee-teh koo-dah-sah'ee.

orange juice   ham and eggs   rolls and coffee
oh-ren-jee joos   hahm egg   pahn toh koh-hee

I am expecting a friend (friends).
Toh-moh-dah-chee gah-koo-roo hah-zoo-dehss.

Tell him (her, them) to wait.
Mahts-yoh eet-teh koo-dah sah'ee.

My key, please.
Wah-tahk-shee noh kah-ghee oh koo-dah-sah'ee.

Any mail for me?
Wah-tahk-shee noh yoo-bean wah ah-ree-mahss-kah?

Any packages?
Nee-moh-tsoo wah?

I want five airmail stamps for the U.S.
Ah-meh-ree-kah eh koh-koo-been noh keet-teh goh-mah'ee koo-dah-sah'ee.

Have you postcards?
Hah-gah-kee ah-ree-mahss-kah?

I want to send a telegram.
Den-poh oh oo-chee-tah'ee dehss.

If anyone calls,
Den-wah gah ah-ree-mah-stah-rah,

Please tell him I'll be back at six.
Roh-koo-jee nee kah-eh-roo t'soo-moh-ree-dehss toh ee-teh koo-dah-sah'ee.

Where is a restaurant?
Shoh-koo-doh wah doh-koh dehss-kah?

    a barber shop?   **a beauty parlor?**
    toh-koh-yah wah?   *bee-yoh-een wah?*

    a drugstore?
    k'soo-ree-yah wah?

What is the telephone number?
Den-wah wah nahn-bahn dehss-kah?

What is the address?
Joo-shoh wah doh-koh dehss-kah?

I want to change some money.
Kah-neh oh k'zoo-shee-tah'ee noh-deh-s'gah.

What is the rate for dollars?
Ee-chee doh-roo wah ee-koo-rah dehss-kah?

ten	**eleven**	**twelve**	**thirteen**
joo	*joo-ee-chee*	*joo-nee*	*joo-sahn*

fourteen	fifteen	sixteen
joo-shee	*joo-goh*	*joo-roh-koo*

seventeen	eighteen	nineteen
joo-shee-chee	*joo-hah-chee*	*joo-koo*

twenty	thirty	forty	fifty
nee-joo	*sahn-joo*	*shee-joo*	*goh-joo*

sixty	seventy	eighty
roh-koo-joo	*shee-chee-joo*	*hah-shee-joo*

ninety	hundred	two hundred
koo-joo	*h'yah-koo*	*nee h'yah-koo*

three hundred	four hundred	five hundred
sahn b'yah-koo	*shee-h'yah-koo*	*goh-h'yah-koo*

six hundred	seven hundred
roh-p'yah-koo	*she-chee-h'yah-koo*

eight hundred	nine hundred	thousand
hahp-p'yah-koo	*k'yoo-h'yah-koo*	*sen*

ten thousand	one hundred thousand
ee-chee-mahn	*joo-mahn*

one million
hyaku-man

My bill, please.
Say-k'yoo-skoh oh koo-dah-sah'ee.

3. EATING

Where is a good restaurant?
Ee shoh-koo-doh wah doh-koh dehss-kah?

A table for two, please.
F'tah-ree noh seh-kee oh neh-guy-mahss.

Waiter! (or waitress)
K'yoo-jee-sahn!

The menu, please.
Men-yoo oh koo-dah-sah'ee.

What is good today?
K'yoh wah nah-nee gah ee-dehss-kah?

Is it ready?
Yoy deh-kee-mahss-kah?

How long will it take?
Doh-reh-koo-rah'ee kah-kah-ree mahss-kah?

This please ...
Koh-reh oh koo-dah-sah'ee ...

    and this.
    soh-sheet-teh koh-reh.

Bring me ...
... oh moht-teh-kee-teh koo-dah-sah'ee

water	milk	beer
mee-zoo	*mee-roo-koo*	*bee-roo*

a cocktail	whisky and soda
kahk-teh-roo	*whisky toh soh-dah-swee*

soup	fish	meat
soo-poo	*sah-kah-nah*	*nee-koo*

bread and butter	a sandwich
pahn toh bah-tah	*sahn-doh-ee-chee*

steak ...
soo-tay-kee ...

    rare
    s'KOH-shee yah-koo

medium	well done
choo-koo-rah'ee	*yoh-koo yah-koo*

chicken	veal
toh-ree-nee-koo	*koh-oo-shee-nee-koo*

beef
 g'yoo-nee-koo

pork
 boo-tah-nee-koo

lamb chop
 hit-soo-jee-nee-koo

  with potatoes . . .
   jah-gah-ee-moh oh t'soo-keh-teh . . .

  fried shrimps
   tem-poo-rah

  raw fish (with sauce)
   sah-shee-mee

sukiyaki (*slices of meat and vegetables, usually cooked on table*)
 S'kee-yah-kee

rice
 koh-meh

an omelet
 oh-moo-rets

And what vegetables?
 DOH-*noh yah-sah'ee gah ah-ree-mahss-kah?*

peas
 en-doh-mah-meh

beans
 mah-meh

carrots
 neen-jeen

onions
 tah-mah-neh-ghee

a salad
 sah-rah-dah

lettuce
 ret-tah-soo

tomatoes
 toh-mah-toh

More, please.
 Moht-toh koo-dah-sah'ee.

That's enough.
 Joo-oo-boon dehss.

Please bring me another fork . . .
 Hoh-koo oh moh ip-poh koo-dah-sah'ee . . .

  knife
   nah'ee-foo

  spoon
   spoon

  glass
   koh-poo

  plate
   sah-rah

What is there for dessert?
 Deh-zah-toh wah nah-nee gah ah-ree-mahss-kah?

fruit	cake
koo-dah-moh-noh	*kay-kee*

ice cream
ice skree-moo

Some coffee, please.
Koh-hee oh koo-dah-sah'ee.

sugar	cream	tea
sah-toh	*kree-moo*	*koh-chah*

The check, please.
Kahn-joh neh-gay-mahss.

Is the tip included?
Cheep-poo wah high-teh ee-mahss-kah?

It was very good.
Toh-teh-moh oh'ee-shee deh-shee-tah.

4. SHOPPING

I would like to buy this.   I would like to buy that.
Koh-reh oh kigh-mahss.   Ah-reh oh kigh-mahss.

I am just looking around.
Eee-mah   mee-teh-mah-wah-teh   ee-roo   toh-koh-roh-dehss.

Where is . . . ?
. . . wah doh-koh dehss-kah?

men's clothing	women's clothing
shin-shee-foo-koo	*foo-jin-foo-koo*

hats	gloves	underwear
bohsh	*teh-boo-koo-roh*	*shee-tah-ghee*

shoes	stockings	shirts
koots	*koots-shee-tah*	*shahts*

The size in America is...
Ah-meh-ree-kah noh size deh-wah ...

toys	**perfumes**
oh-moh-chah	*koh-swee*
jewelry	**watches**
hoh-seh-kee	*toh-kay*
toilet articles	**sport articles**
keh-shoh-keen-r'wee	*oon-doh-goo*
films	**souvenirs**
hoo-ee-roo-moo	*mee-yah-gheh-moh-noh*
kimono	**silk**
kee-moh-noh	*kee-noo*
pearls	**Japanese paintings**
sheen-joo	*nee-hohn-gah*

Show me ...
... oh mee-seh-teh koo-dah-sah'ee.

something less expensive.
moht-toh yah-swee moh-noh mee-seh-teh koo-dah-sah'ee.

another one.
hoh-kah-noh moh-noh.

a better quality.
moht-toh ee-ee moh-noh.

bigger. **smaller.**
moht-toh oh-kee. *moht-toh chee-sah'ee.*

I don't like the color.
Koh-noh ee-roh wah kee-rah'ee dehss.

I want one in ...
... noh moh-noh gah hoh-shee dehss.

green **yellow**
mee-doh-ree *kee-ee-roh*

blue	red	black
ah-oh	*ah-kah*	*koo-roh*

white	grey
shee-roh	*hah'ee-ee-roh*

pink	brown
moh-moh-ee-roh	*chah-ee-roh*

I will take it with me.
Jee-boon deh moht-tek kah-eh-re-mahss.

The receipt, please.
Oo-keh-toh-ree oh koo-dah-seh'ee.

Please send it to this address.
*Soh-reh oh koh-noh joo-shoh nee oh-koot-teh
koo-dah-sah'ee.*

Where is the market?
Mah-keh-toh wah doh-koh dehss-kah?

Where is there a flower shop?
Hah-nah-yah wah doh-koh dehss-kah?

Where is there a bookstore?
Hohn-yah wah doh-koh dehss-kah?

Where can I buy food?
*Shoh-koo-r'yoh-heen wah doh-koh-deh kah'eh-
mahss-kah?*

5. TRANSPORTATION

Taxi!
Tahks-shi!

Take me to the airport.
Koo-koh nee eat-teh koo-dah-seh'ee.

To the right.	**To the left.**
Mee-ghee-nee.	*Hee-dah-ree nee.*

Straight ahead.
 Mahss-soo-goo.

Not so fast!   **Hurry up!**
 Mos-koshee yoo-koo-ree!   *Hah-yah-koo!*

Stop here!
 Koh-koh-deh stoh-poo!

Wait for me.
 Maht-teh ee-teh koo-day-seh'ee.

How much is it?
 EE-koo-rah dehss-kah?

How much is it to . . . ?
 . . . mah-deh EE-koo-rah dehss-kah?

   and back? (round trip)
    oh-hoo-koo deh-wah?

How much by the hour?
 *Jee-kahn-say dah-toh ee-chee-kahn EE-koo-rah
 dehss-kah?*

   by the day?
    ee-chee-nee-chee deh-wah?

Show me the sights.
 Ken-boots sah-seh-teh koo-dah-sah'ee.

car   **bicycle**
 jee-doh-shah   *jee-then-shah*

motorcycle   **horse**
 moh-tah-sigh-koo-roo   *oo-mah*

What is that building?
 Ah-noh tah-teh-moh-noh wah nan-dehss-kah?

May I go in?
 Hah'ee-reh mahss-kah?

I want to see the Imperial Palace.   **the temple.**
 K'yoo-joh gah mee-tah'ee-dehss.   *oh-teh-rah.*

To the railroad station!   **Porter!**
Teh'ee-shah-bah-eh!   *Ah-kah-boh-sahn!*

I have two bags.
Kah-bahn gah foo-tahts ah-ree-mahss.

A ticket to . . .
Yoo-kee noh ken . . .

one way   **round trip**
kah-tah-mee-chee   *oh-hoo-koo*

first class   **second class**
eat-toh   *nee-toh*

When does it leave?
EETS *shoo-pahts dehss-kah?*

Where is the train to Kyoto?
K'yoh-toh yoo-kee wah doh-koh-dehss-kah?

Is this the train for Nikko?
Koh-reh wah neek-koh yookeee dehss-kah?

When do we get to Nagoya?
Nah-goh-yah nee eats t'soo-kee-mahss-kah?

Open the window.
Mah-doh oh ah-keh-teh koo-dah-sah'ee.

Close the window.
Mah-doh oh shee-meh-teh koo-dah-sah'ee.

Where is the bus to Shibuya?
Shee-boo-yah oo-kee noh bahss wah soh-koh dehss-kah?

I want to go to Akasaka.
Wah-tahk-shee wah Ah-kah-sah-kah eh ee-kee-mahss.

Please tell me where to get off.
Oh-ree-roo toh-koh-roh oh oh-shee-yeh-tah koo-dah-sah'ee.

Where is there a gas station?
Gah-soh-reen soo-tahn-doh wah doh-koh dehss-kah?

Fill it up.
Ee-pah'ee ee-reh-teh.

Check the oil ...
Oh-ee-roo oh shee-rah-beh-teh ...

> water　　　　　　　tires
> *mee-zoo*　　　　　*tah'ee-yah*

Something is wrong with the car.
Koo-roo-mah noh doh-koh-kah gah wah-roo'ee-dehss.

Can you fix it?
Nah'oh-seh mahss-kah?

How long will it take?
Kee-kahn wah ee-koo-rah kah-kah-ree-mahss-kah?

Is this the road to Karuizawa?
Koh-reh wah Kah-roo'ee-zah-wah eh ee-koo mee-chee dehss-kah?

Have you a map?
Chee-zoo gah ah-ree-mahss-kah?

Where is the boat to ... ?
Yoo-kee noh foo-neh wah doh-koh dehss-kah ...?

When does it leave?
Eets shoop-pahts dehss-kah?

6. MAKING FRIENDS

How do you do.
Ee-kah-gah dehss-kah.

My name is ...
Wah-tahk-shee wah ... dehss.

What is your name, Sir, Madam, Miss?
Ah-nah-tah noh oh-nah-mah'ee wah?

I am delighted to see (meet) you.
Doh-zoh yoh-roh-shee-koo.

Do you speak English?
Eh-goh oh hah-nah-shee-mah-skah?

A little.   **Do you understand?**
Soo-kosh-ee.   *Wah-kah-ree-mah-skah.*

I speak only a little Japanese.
Nee-hon-go o choht-toh hah-nah-shee-mahss.

Please speak slowly.
Yoo-koo-ree hah-nah-shee-teh koo-dah-sah'ee.

I am from New York.
N'yoo-yohk kah-rah kee-mah-sh'tah.

Where are you from?
Doh-koh kah-rah kee-mah-sh'tah-kah?

I like your country.
Ah-nah-tah no koo-nee gah soo-kee dehss.

I like your city.
Ah-nah-tah no mah-chee-gah soo-kee dehss.

Have you been in America?
Ah-meh-ree-kah nee eet-tah koh-toh gah ah-ree-mahss-kah?

This is my first visit here.
Koh-koh wah hah-jee-meh-teh dehss.

May I sit here?
Koh-koh nee soo-waht-teh ee'ee-dehss-kah?

Come here please.
Koh-koh eh ee-rah-shah'ee.

May I take your picture?
Ah-nah-tah no shah-sheen o toht-teh ee'ee-dehss-kah?

This is a picture of my wife.
Koh-reh wah wah-tahk-shee no t'soo-mah no shah-sheen dehss.

   my husband
   wah-tahk-shee no oht-toh

   my son
   wah-tahk-shee no moo-soo-koh

   my daughter
   wah-tahk-shee no moo-soo-meh

   my mother
   wah-tahk-shee no hah-hah

   my father
   wah-tahk-shee no chee-chee

   my younger sister
   wah-tahk-shee no ee-moht-toh

   my elder sister
   wah-tahk-shee no ah-neh

   my younger brother
   wah-tahk-shee no o-toh-toh

   my elder brother
   wah-tahk-shee no ah-nee

Have you children?
Koh-doh-moh wah ee-mahss-kah?

How beautiful!	**Very interesting.**
Kee-ray dehss-neh!	*O-moh-shee-roy.*

Would you like a cigarette?
Tah-bah-koh wah ee-kah-gah dehss-kah?

Something to drink?
No-mee-moh-noh wah?

Something to eat?
Tah-beh-moh-noh wah?

Sit down, please.
O-kah-keh koo-dah-sah'ee.

Make yourself at home.
Doh-zoh yook-koo-ree shee-teh koo-dah-sah'ee.

Good luck.	**To your health! (literally "dry cup!")**
Go-koon o.	*Kahn-pah'ee!*

When can I see you again?
Ts'oo-ghee wah eets oh-ah'ee-deh-kee-mahss-kah?

Where shall we meet?
Doh-koh deh ah'ee-mah-shoh-kah?

Here is my address.
Koh-reh gah wah-tahk-shee no joo-shoh dehss.

What is your address?
Ah-nah-tah no joo-shoh wa?

What is your phone number?
Ah-nah-tah no den-wah wah?

May I speak to . . .
Toh hah-nah-she-tah'ee dehss-gah . . .

Would you like to have lunch?
Hee-roo-meh-shee wah ee-kah-gah dehss-kah?

    dinner?
     ban-meh-shee?

Would you like to go to the movies?
Eh-ga nee ee-kee-mah-sen-kah?

Would you like to go to the theater?
Shee-bah'ee nee ee-kee-mah-sen-kah?

Would you like to go to the beach?
Oo-mee eh ee-kee-mah-sen-kah?

Would you like to take a walk?
Sahm-poh nee ee-kee-mah-sen-kah?

With great pleasure.
Tah'ee-hen kek-ko dehss.

I am sorry.   **I cannot.**
Zahn-nen dehss.   *Deh-kee-mah-sen.*

Another time.
Mah-tah no toh-kee nee.

I must go now.
Sheet-soo-ray shee-nah-keh-reh-bah nah-ree-mah-sen.

Thank you for a wonderful time.
Tah'ee-hen o-jah-mah shee-mah-sh'tah.

Thank you for an excellent dinner.
Go-chee-so sah-mah deh-sh'tah.

This is for you.
Koh-reh o doh-zoh.

You are very kind.
Go-shin-sets nee ah-ree-gah-toh.

It's nothing really.
Do ee-tah-shee-mah-shee-teh.

With best regards.
Yoh-roh-shee-koo.

Congratulations!   **Have a good trip.**
O-meh-deh-toh!   *O-ghen-kee deh.*

7. EMERGENCIES

Help!   **Police!**   **Fire!**
  Tah-soo-keh-teh!   *Keh-sah-ts'oo!*   *Kah-jee!*

Stop that man!
  Soh-no o-toh-ko o ts'oo-kah-mah'ee-teh!

Stop that woman!
  Soh-noh ohn-nah o ts'oo-kah-mah'ee-teh!

I have been robbed!
  Noo-soo-mah-reh mah-sh'tah!

Look out!
  Mee-teh koo-dah-sah'ee!

Wait a minute!   **Stop!**
  Choh-toh maht-teh!   *Toh-maht-teh!*

Get out!   **Hurry up!**
  Deh-teh koo-dah-sah'ee!   *Hah-yah-koo!*

Don't bother me!
  Jah-mah shee-nah-ah'ee-deh koo-dah-sah'ee!

What is going on?
  Nahn dehss-kah?

Entrance   **Exit**
  Ee-ree-koo-chee   *Deh-goo-chee*

Ladies   **Gentlemen**
  Foo-jeen   *Dahn-shee*

Danger!   **Keep out!**
  Kee-ken!   *Tah-chee-ee-ree keen-shee!*

No smoking   **No parking**
  Keen-en   *Choo-shah keen-shee*

One way
  Eep-poh ts'oo-ko

I am ill.
Kah-rah-dah no goo-wye gah wah-r'yoo'ee-dehss.

Call a doctor!
Ee-sha o yohn-deh koo-dah-sah'ee!

It hurts here.
Koh-koh o keh-gah shee-mah-sh'tah.

Where is the drugstore?
Ks'oo-ree-yah wah doh-koh dehss-kah?

Take me to the hospital.
B'yoh-een eh ts'oo-reh-teh eet-teh koo-dah-sah'ee.

Where is there a dentist?
Hah'ee-shah wah doh-koh dehss-kah?

I have lost my bag.
Wah-tahk-shee noh kah-bahn o nah-koo-shee mah-sh'tah.

wallet	camera	passport
sah'ee-foo	*kah-meh-rah*	*r'yoh-ken*

I am an American.
Wah-tahk-shee wah ah-meh-ree-kah-gin dehss.

Where is the American Consulate?
Ah-meh-ree-kah r'yoh-jee-kahn wah doh-koh dehss-kah?

Don't get excited!
O-sheet-soo'ey-teh!

Everything is all right.
Sook-kah-ree dah'ee-joh-boo dehss.